One of Our Conquerors by George Meredith

George Meredith, OM, was born in Portsmouth, England on February 12th, 1828, a son and grandson of naval outfitters. His mother died when he was only five.

As a fourteen year old teenager he was sent to a Moravian School in Neuwied, Germany, staying there for two years.

After reading law he was articled as a solicitor, but quickly abandoned that career path for journalism and poetry. He collaborated with Edward Gryffydh Peacock, son of Thomas Love Peacock in publishing a privately circulated literary magazine, the Monthly Observer.

At age twenty-one he married Mary Ellen Nicolls, Edward Peacock's beautiful widowed sister, and mother of a child, on August 8th, 1849. Mary Ellen was twenty-eight. The marriage produced one child; Arthur (1853–1890).

Meredith collected his early writings, all previously published in periodicals, in an 1851 volume, Poems.

In 1856 he posed as the model for The Death of Chatterton, a well-known picture by the English Pre-Raphaelite painter Henry Wallis, which romantised the teenage Chatterton's demise.

Although Meredith received some publicity for this his wife received rather more attention from Wallis because of it. Mary Ellen ran off with Wallis in 1858, shortly before giving birth to a child that all assumed to be Wallis. Tragically she died three years later.

From that dreadful experience emerged a collection of sonnets entitled Modern Love in 1862 together with much of his first major novel; The Ordeal of Richard Feverel.

Meredith married Marie Vulliamy on September 20th, 1864 and they settled in Surrey. Together they had two children; William (born in 1865) and Mariette (born in 1874).

He continued writing novels and poetry, often inspired by nature. He had a keen understanding of comedy and his Essay on Comedy (1877) remains a reference work in the history of comic theory.

In The Egoist, published in 1879, he applies some of his theories of comedy in one of his most thoughtful and enduring novels.

During most of his career, he had difficulty crossing over from critical acclamation to popular success. It was only in 1885 that his first genuine commercial success appeared; Diana of the Crossways.

An artist's life throughout the ages, when not subsidised by a patron, is often difficult. Meredith found it no different. With an unreliable income stream he sought to bolster that with a job as a publisher's reader.

The company that gave him this lifeline was Chapman & Hall (an eminent publishing house who could include Charles Dickens, William Makepeace Thackeray, Elizabeth Barrett Browning and Anthony

Trollope on their roster). His advice to the company was very well received and made him influential in the world of letters.

To this influence he was able to add a circle of friends that included William and Dante Gabriel Rossetti, Algernon Charles Swinburne, Cotter Morison, Leslie Stephen, Robert Louis Stevenson, George Gissing and J. M. Barrie.

In 1868 Meredith was introduced to Thomas Hardy. Hardy had submitted his first novel, The Poor Man and the Lady. Meredith felt the book was too bitter a satire on the rich and told Hardy to put it aside as it was likely it would be savaged by reviewers and destroy his nascent career. Meredith had received the same reaction with The Ordeal of Richard Feverel. Although it had brought him success it was judged so shocking that Mudie's circulating library cancelled an order of 300 copies.

But these years, creatively, were very prolific and successful for Meredith. Novels and poems flowed from his pen including everything from The Adventures of Harry Richmond to Diana of the Crossways and many poetry volumes include The Lark Ascending (which later inspired the Vaughan Williams music)

In 1886, tragedy struck the Meredith household when his second wife, Marie Vulliamy, died of cancer.

Whilst his personal life was producing horrendous scars he was receiving many accolades. Oscar Wilde was a fan. In The Decay of Lying, (originally published in the January 1889 issue of The Nineteenth Century) he says of Meredith "Ah, Meredith! Who can define him? His style is chaos illumined by flashes of lightning".

In 1891 Meredith was even the subject of homage when Sir Arthur Conan Doyle in his Sherlock Holmes short story The Boscombe Valley Mystery, (published in the popular Strand magazine) when Sherlock Holmes turns to Watson during case discussions and says "And now let us talk about George Meredith, if you please, and we shall leave all minor matters until tomorrow."

Before his death, Meredith was honoured from many quarters: he succeeded Lord Tennyson as president of the Society of Authors; in 1905 he was appointed to the Order of Merit by King Edward VII.

George Meredith, aged 81, died at his home in Box Hill, Surrey on May 18th, 1909. He is buried in the cemetery at Dorking, Surrey.

Index of Contents

BOOK I

CHAPTER I

ACROSS LONDON BRIDGE

A gentleman, noteworthy for a lively countenance and a waistcoat to match it, crossing London Bridge at noon on a gusty April day, was almost magically detached from his conflict with the gale by some sly strip of slipperiness, abounding in that conduit of the markets, which had more or less adroitly performed the trick upon preceding passengers, and now laid this one flat amid the shuffle of feet, peaceful for the moment as the uncomplaining who have gone to Sabrina beneath the tides. He was unhurt, quite sound, merely astonished, he remarked, in reply to the inquiries of the first kind helper at his elbow; and it appeared an acceptable statement of his condition. He laughed, shook his coat-tails, smoothed the back of his head rather thoughtfully, thankfully received his runaway hat, nodded bright beams to right and left, and making light of the muddy stigmas imprinted by the pavement, he scattered another shower of his nods and smiles around, to signify, that as his good friends would wish, he thoroughly felt his legs and could walk unaided. And he was in the act of doing it, questioning his familiar behind the waistcoat amazedly, to tell him how such a misadventure could have occurred to him of all men, when a glance below his chin discomposed his outward face. 'Oh, confound the fellow!' he said, with simple frankness, and was humorously ruffled, having seen absurd blots of smutty knuckles distributed over the maiden waistcoat.

His outcry was no more than the confidential communication of a genial spirit with that distinctive article of his attire. At the same time, for these friendly people about him to share the fun of the annoyance, he looked hastily brightly back, seeming with the contraction of his brows to frown, on the little band of observant Samaritans; in the centre of whom a man who knew himself honourably unclean, perhaps consequently a bit of a political jewel, hearing one of their number confounded for his pains, and by the wearer of a superfine dashing-white waistcoat, was moved to take notice of the total deficiency of gratitude in this kind of gentleman's look and pocket. If we ask for nothing for helping gentlemen to stand upright on their legs, and get it, we expect civility into the bargain. Moreover, there are reasons in nature why we choose to give sign of a particular surliness when our wealthy superiors would have us think their condescending grins are cordials.

The gentleman's eyes were followed on a second hurried downward grimace, the necessitated wrinkles of which could be stretched by malevolence to a semblance of haughty disgust; reminding us, through our readings in journals, of the wicked overblown Prince Regent and his Court, together with the view taken of honest labour in the mind of supercilious luxury, even if indebted to it freshly for a trifle; and the hoar-headed nineteenth-century billow of democratic ire craved the word to be set swelling.

'Am I the fellow you mean, sir?' the man said.

He was answered, not ungraciously: 'All right, my man.'

But the balance of our public equanimity is prone to violent antic bobbings on occasions when, for example, an ostentatious garment shall appear disdainful our class and ourself, and coin of the realm has not usurped command of one of the scales: thus a fairly pleasant answer, cast in persuasive features, provoked the retort:

'There you're wrong; nor wouldn't be.'

'What's that?' was the gentleman's musical inquiry.

'That's flat, as you was half a minute ago,' the man rejoined.

'Ah, well, don't be impudent,' the gentleman said, by way of amiable remonstrance before a parting.

'And none of your dam punctilio,' said the man.

Their exchange rattled smartly, without a direct hostility, and the gentleman stepped forward.

It was observed in the crowd, that after a few paces he put two fingers on the back of his head.

They might suppose him to be condoling with his recent mishap. But, in fact, a thing had occurred to vex him more than a descent upon the pavement or damage to his waistcoat's whiteness: he abominated the thought of an altercation with a member of the mob; he found that enormous beat comprehensible only when it applauded him; and besides he wished it warmly well; all that was good for it; plentiful dinners, country excursions, stout menagerie bars, music, a dance, and to bed: he was for patting, stroking, petting the mob, for tossing it sops, never for irritating it to show an eye-tooth, much less for causing it to exhibit the grinders: and in endeavouring to get at the grounds of his dissension with that dirty-fisted fellow, the recollection of the word punctilio shot a throb of pain to the spot where his mishap had rendered him susceptible. Headache threatened—and to him of all men! But was there ever such a word for drumming on a cranium? Puzzles are presented to us now and then in the course of our days; and the smaller they are the better for the purpose, it would seem; and they come in rattle-boxes, they are actually children's toys, for what they contain, but not the less do they buzz at our understandings and insist that they break or we, and, in either case, to show a mere foolish idle rattle in hollowness. Or does this happen to us only after a fall?

He tried a suspension of his mental efforts, and the word was like the clapper of a disorderly bell, striking through him, with reverberations, in the form of interrogations, as to how he, of all men living, could by any chance have got into a wrangle, in a thoroughfare, on London Bridge, of all places in the world!—he, so popular, renowned for his affability, his amiability; having no dislike to common dirty dogs, entirely the reverse, liking them and doing his best for them; and accustomed to receive their applause. And in what way had he offered a hint to bring on him the charge of punctilio?

'But I am treating it seriously!' he said, and jerked a dead laugh while fixing a button of his coat.

That he should have treated it seriously, furnished next the subject of cogitation; and here it was plainly suggested, that a degradation of his physical system, owing to the shock of the fall, must be seen and acknowledged; for it had become a perverted engine, to pull him down among the puerilities, and very soon he was worrying at punctilio anew, attempting to read the riddle of the application of it to himself, angry that he had allowed it to be the final word, and admitting it a famous word for the closing of a controversy:—it banged the door and rolled drum-notes; it deafened reason. And was it a London cockney crow-word of the day, or a word that had stuck in the fellow's head from the perusal of his pothouse newspaper columns?

Furthermore, the plea of a fall, and the plea of a shock from a fall, required to account for the triviality of the mind, were humiliating to him who had never hitherto missed a step, or owed to the shortest of collapses. This confession of deficiency in explosive repartee—using a friend's term for the ready gift— was an old and a rueful one with Victor Radnor. His godmother Fortune denied him that. She bestowed it on his friend Fenellan, and little else. Simeon Fenellan could clap the halter on a coltish mob; he had positively caught the roar of cries and stilled it, by capping the cries in turn, until the people cheered him; and the effect of the scene upon Victor Radnor disposed him to rank the gift of repartee higher than a certain rosily oratorical that he was permitted to tell himself he possessed, in bottle if not on draught. Let it only be explosive repartee: the well-fused bomb, the bubble to the stone, echo round the horn. Fenellan, would have discharged an extinguisher on punctilio in emission. Victor Radnor was unable to cope with it reflectively.

No, but one doesn't like being beaten by anything! he replied to an admonishment of his better mind, as he touched his two fingers, more significantly dubious than the whole hand, at the back of his head, and checked or stemmed the current of a fear. For he was utterly unlike himself; he was dwelling on a trifle, on a matter discernibly the smallest, an incident of the streets; and although he refused to feel a bump or any responsive notification of a bruise, he made a sacrifice of his native pride to his intellectual, in granting that he must have been shaken, so childishly did he continue thinking.

Yes, well, and if a tumble distorts our ideas of life, and an odd word engrosses our speculations, we are poor creatures, he addressed another friend, from whom he stood constitutionally in dissent naming him Colney; and under pressure of the name, reviving old wrangles between them upon man's present achievements and his probable destinies: especially upon England's grandeur, vitality, stability, her intelligent appreciation of her place in the universe; not to speak of the historic dignity of London City. Colney had to be overcome afresh, and he fled, but managed, with two or three of his bitter phrases, to make a cuttle-fish fight of it, that oppressively shadowed his vanquisher:

The Daniel Lambert of Cities: the Female Annuitant of Nations:—and such like, wretched stuff, proper to Colney Durance, easily dispersed and out-laughed when we have our vigour. We have as much as we need of it in summoning a contemptuous Pooh to our lips, with a shrug at venomous dyspepsia.

Nevertheless, a malignant sketch of Colney's, in the which Hengist and Horsa, our fishy Saxon originals, in modern garb of liveryman and gaitered squire, flat-headed, paunchy, assiduously servile, are shown blacking Ben-Israel's boots and grooming the princely stud of the Jew, had come so near to Victor Radnor's apprehensions of a possible, if not an impending, consummation, that the ghastly vision of the Jew Dominant in London City, over England, over Europe, America, the world (a picture drawn in literary sepia by Colney: with our poor hang neck population uncertain about making a bell-rope of the forelock to the Satyr-snouty master; and the Norman Lord de Warenne handing him for a lump sum son and daughter, both to be Hebraized in their different ways), fastened on the most mercurial of patriotic men, and gave him a whole-length plunge into despondency.

It lasted nearly a minute. His recovery was not in this instance due to the calling on himself for the rescue of an ancient and glorious country; nor altogether to the spectacle of the shipping, over the parapet, to his right: the hundreds of masts rising out of the merchant river; London's unrivalled mezzotint and the City' rhetorician's inexhaustible argument: he gained it rather from the imperious demand of an animated and thirsty frame for novel impressions. Commonly he was too hot with his business, and airy fancies above it when crossing the bridge, to reflect in freshness on its wonders; though a phrase could spring him alive to them; a suggestion of the Foreigner, jealous, condemned to admire in despair of outstripping, like Satan worsted; or when a Premier's fine inflation magnified the scene at City banquets—exciting while audible, if a waggery in memory; or when England's cherished Bard, the Leading Article, blew bellows, and wind primed the lieges.

That a phrase on any other subject was of much the same effect, in relation to it, may be owned; he was lightly kindled. The scene, however, had a sharp sparkle of attractiveness at the instant. Down went the twirling horizontal pillars of a strong tide from the arches of the bridge, breaking to wild water at a remove; and a reddish Northern cheek of curdling pipeing East, at shrilly puffs between the Tower and the Custom House, encountered it to whip and ridge the flood against descending tug and long tail of stern-ajerk empty barges; with a steamer slowly noseing round off the wharf-cranes, preparing to swirl the screw; and half-bottom-upward boats dancing harpooner beside their whale; along an avenue, not fabulously golden, of the deputy masts of all nations, a wintry woodland, every rag aloft curling to volume; and here the spouts and the mounds of steam, and rolls of brown smoke there, variously undulated, curved to vanish; cold blue sky ashift with the whirl and dash of a very Tartar cavalry of cloud overhead.

Surely a scene pretending to sublimity?

Gazeing along that grand highway of the voyageing forest, your London citizen of good estate has reproached his country's poets for not pouring out, succinctly and melodiously, his multitudinous larvae of notions begotten by the scene. For there are times when he would, pay to have them sung; and he feels them big; he thinks them human in their bulk; they are Londinensian; they want but form and fire to get them scored on the tablets of the quotable at festive boards. This he can promise to his poets. As for otherwhere than at the festive, Commerce invoked is a Goddess that will have the reek of those boards to fill her nostrils, and poet and alderman alike may be dedicate to the sublime, she leads them, after two sniffs of an idea concerning her, for the dive into the turtle-tureen. Heels up they go, poet first—a plummet he!

And besides it is barely possible for our rounded citizen, in the mood of meditation, to direct his gaze off the bridge along the waterway North-eastward without beholding as an eye the glow of whitebait's bow-window by the riverside, to the front of the summer sunset, a league or so down stream; where he sees, in memory savours, the Elysian end of Commerce: frontispiece of a tale to fetch us up the out-wearied spectre of old Apicius; yea, and urge Crispinus to wheel his purse into the market for the purchase of a costlier mullet!

But is the Jew of the usury gold becoming our despot-king of Commerce?

In that case, we do not ask our country's poets to compose a single stanza of eulogy's rhymes—far from it. Far to the contrary, we bid ourselves remember the sons of whom we are; instead of revelling in the fruits of Commerce, we shoot scornfully past those blazing bellied windows of the aromatic dinners, and beyond Thames, away to the fishermen's deeps, Old England's native element, where the strenuous ancestry of a race yet and ever manful at the stress of trial are heard around and aloft whistling us back to the splendid strain of muscle, and spray fringes cloud, and strong heart rides the briny scoops and hillocks, and Death and Man are at grip for the haul.

There we find our nationality, our poetry, no Hebrew competing.

We do: or there at least we left it. Whether to recover it when wanted, is not so certain. Humpy Hengist and dumpy Horsa, quitting ledger and coronet, might recur to their sea bowlegs and red-stubble chins, might take to their tarpaulins again; they might renew their manhood on the capture of cod; headed by Harald and Hardiknut, they might roll surges to whelm a Dominant Jew clean gone to the fleshpots and effeminacy. Aldermen of our ancient conception, they may teach him that he has been backsliding once more, and must repent in ashes, as those who are for jewels, titles, essences, banquets, for wallowing in slimy spawn of lucre, have ever to do. They dispossess him of his greedy gettings.

And how of the Law?

But the Law is always, and must ever be, the Law of the stronger. —Ay, but brain beats muscle, and what if the Jew should prove to have superior power of brain? A dreaded hypothesis! Why, then you see the insurgent Saxon seamen (of the names in two syllables with accent on the first), and their Danish captains, and it may be but a remnant of high-nosed old Norman Lord de Warenne beside them, in the criminal box: and presently the Jew smoking a giant regalia cigar on a balcony giving view of a gallows-tree. But we will try that: on our side, to back a native pugnacity, is morality, humanity, fraternity—nature's rights, aha! and who withstands them? on his, a troop of mercenaries!

And that lands me in Red Republicanism, a hop and a skip from Socialism! said Mr. Radnor, and chuckled ironically at the natural declivity he had come to. Still, there was an idea in it....

A short run or attempt at running after the idea, ended in pain to his head near the spot where the haunting word punctilio caught at any excuse for clamouring.

Yet we cannot relinquish an idea that was ours; we are vowed to the pursuit of it. Mr. Radnor lighted on the tracks, by dint of a thought flung at his partner Mr. Inchling's dread of the Jews. Inchling dreaded Scotchmen as well, and Americans, and Armenians, and Greeks: latterly Germans hardly less; but his dread of absorption in Jewry, signifying subjection, had often precipitated a deplorable shrug, in which Victor Radnor now perceived the skirts of his idea, even to a fancy that something of the idea must have struck Inchling when he shrugged: the idea being... he had lost it again. Definition seemed to be an extirpation enemy of this idea, or she was by nature shy. She was very feminine; coming when she willed and flying when wanted. Not until nigh upon the close of his history did she return, full-statured and embraceable, to Victor Radnor.

CHAPTER II

THROUGH THE VAGUE TO THE INFINITELY LITTLE

The fair dealing with readers demands of us, that a narrative shall not proceed at slower pace than legs of a man in motion; and we are still but little more than midway across London Bridge. But if a man's mind is to be taken as a part of him, the likening of it, at an introduction, to an army on the opening march of a great campaign, should plead excuses for tardy forward movements, in consideration of the large amount of matter you have to review before you can at all imagine yourselves to have made his acquaintance. This it is not necessary to do when you are set astride the enchanted horse of the Tale, which leaves the man's mind at home while he performs the deeds befitting him: he can indeed be rapid. Whether more active, is a question asking for your notions of the governing element in the composition of man, and of hid present business here. The Tale inspirits one's earlier ardours, when we sped without baggage, when the Impossible was wings to imagination, and heroic sculpture the simplest act of the chisel. It does not advance, 'tis true; it drives the whirligig circle round and round the single existing central point; but it is enriched with applause of the boys and girls of both ages in this land; and all the English critics heap their honours on its brave old Simplicity: our national literary flag, which signalizes us while we float, subsequently to flap above the shallows. One may sigh for it. An ill-fortuned minstrel who has by fateful direction been brought to see with distinctness, that man is not as much comprised in external features as the monkey, will be devoted to the task of the fuller portraiture.

After his ineffectual catching at the volatile idea, Mr. Radnor found repose in thoughts of his daughter and her dear mother. They had begged him to put on an overcoat this day of bitter wind, or a silken kerchief for the throat. Faithful to the Spring, it had been his habit since boyhood to show upon his person something of the hue of the vernal month, the white of the daisied meadow, and although he owned a light overcoat to dangle from shoulders at the Opera crush, he declined to wear it for protection. His gesture of shaking and expanding whenever the tender request was urged on him, signified a physical opposition to the control of garments. Mechanically now, while doating in fancy over the couple beseeching him, he loosened the button across his defaced waistcoat, exposed a large measure of chest to flaws of a wind barbed on Norwegian peaks by the brewers of cough and catarrh— horrid women of the whistling clouts, in the pay of our doctors. He braved them; he starved the profession. He was that man in fifty thousand who despises hostile elements and goes unpunished, calmly erect among a sneezing and tumbled host, as a lighthouse overhead of breezy fleets. The coursing of his blood was by comparison electrical; he had not the sensation of cold, other than that of an effort of the elements to arouse him; and so quick was he, through this fine animation, to feel, think, act, that the three successive tributaries of conduct appeared as an irreflective flash and a gamester's daring in the vein to men who had no deep knowledge of him and his lightning arithmetic for measuring, sounding, and deciding.

Naturally he was among the happiest of human creatures; he willed it so, with consent of circumstances; a boisterous consent, as when votes are reckoned for a favourite candidate: excepting on the part of a small band of black dissentients in a corner, a minute opaque body, devilish in their irreconcilability, who maintain their struggle to provoke discord, with a cry disclosing the one error of his youth, the sole bad step chargeable upon his antecedents. But do we listen to them? Shall we not have them turned out? He gives the sign for it; and he leaves his buoying constituents to outroar them: and he tells a friend that it was not, as one may say, an error, although an erratic step: but let us explain to our bosom friend; it was a step quite unregretted, gloried in; a step deliberately marked, to be done again, were the time renewed: it was a step necessitated (emphatically) by a false preceding step; and having youth to plead for it, in the first instance, youth and ignorance; and secondly, and O how deeply truly! Love. Deep true love, proved by years, is the advocate.

He tells himself at the same time, after lending ear to the advocate's exordium and a favourite sentence, that, judged by the Powers (to them only can he expose the whole skeleton-cupboard of the case), judged by those clear-sighted Powers, he is exonerated.

To be exonerated by those awful Powers, is to be approved.

As to that, there is no doubt: whom they, all-seeing, discerning as they do, acquit they justify.

Whom they justify, they compliment.

They, seeing all the facts, are not unintelligent of distinctions, as the world is.

What, to them, is the spot of the error?—admitting it as an error. They know it for a thing of convention, not of Nature. We stand forth to plead it in proof of an adherence to Nature's laws: we affirm, that far from a defilement, it is an illumination and stamp of nobility. On the beloved who shares it with us, it is a stamp of the highest nobility. Our world has many ways for signifying its displeasure, but it cannot brand an angel.

This was another favourite sentence of Love's grand oration for the defence. So seductive was it to the Powers who sat in judgement on the case, that they all, when the sentence came, turned eyes upon the angel, and they smiled.

They do not smile on the condemnable.

She, then, were he rebuked, would have strength to uplift him. And who, calling her his own, could be placed in second rank among the blissful!

Mr. Radnor could rationally say that he was made for happiness; he flew to it, he breathed, dispensed it. How conceive the clear-sighted celestial Powers as opposing his claim to that estate? Not they. He knew, for he had them safe in the locked chamber of his breast, to yield him subservient responses. The world, or Puritanic members of it, had pushed him to the trial once or twice—or had put on an air of doing so; creating a temporary disturbance, ending in a merry duet with his daughter Nesta Victoria: a glorious trio when her mother Natalia, sweet lily that she was, shook the rainwater from her cup and followed the good example to shine in the sun.

He had a secret for them.

Nesta's promising soprano, and her mother's contralto, and his baritone—a true baritone, not so well trained as their accurate notes—should be rising in spirited union with the curtain of that secret: there was matter for song and concert, triumph and gratulation in it. And during the whole passage of the bridge, he had not once cast thought on a secret so palpitating, the cause of the morning's expedition and a long year's prospect of the present day! It seemed to have been knocked clean out of it—punctilioed out, Fenellan might say. Nor had any combinations upon the theme of business displaced it. Just before the fall, the whole drama of the unfolding of that secret was brilliant to his eyes as a scene on a stage.

He refused to feel any sensible bruise on his head, with the admission that he perhaps might think he felt one which was virtually no more than the feeling of a thought;—what his friend Dr. Peter Yatt would define as feeling a rotifer astir in the curative compartment of a homoeopathic globule: and a playful fancy may do that or anything. Only, Sanity does not allow the infinitely little to disturb us.

Mr. Radnor had a quaint experience of the effects of the infinitely little while threading his way to a haberdasher's shop for new white waistcoats. Under the shadow of the representative statue of City Corporations and London's majesty, the figure of Royalty, worshipful in its marbled redundancy, fronting the bridge, on the slope where the seas of fish and fruit below throw up a thin line of their drift, he stood contemplating the not unamiable, reposefully-jolly, Guelphic countenance, from the loose jowl to the bent knee, as if it were a novelty to him; unwilling to trust himself to the roadway he had often traversed, equally careful that his hesitation should not be seen. A trifle more impressible, he might have imagined the smoky figure and magnum of pursiness barring the City against him. He could have laughed aloud at the hypocrisy behind his quiet look of provincial wonderment at London's sculptor's art; and he was partly tickled as well by the singular fit of timidity enchaining him. Cart, omnibus, cab, van, barrow, donkey-tray, went by in strings, broken here and there, and he could not induce his legs to take advantage of the gaps; he listened to a warning that he would be down again if he tried it, among those wheels; and his nerves clutched him, like a troop of household women, to keep him from the hazard of an exposure to the horrid crunch, pitiless as tiger's teeth; and we may say truly, that once down, or once out of the rutted line, you are food for lion and jackal—the forces of the world will have you in their mandibles.

An idea was there too; but it would not accept pursuit.

'A pretty scud overheard?' said a voice at his ear.

'For fine!—to-day at least,' Mr. Radnor affably replied to a stranger; and gazing on the face of his friend Fenellan, knew the voice, and laughed: 'You?' He straightened his back immediately to cross the road, dismissing nervousness as a vapour, asking, between a cab and a van: 'Anything doing in the City?' For Mr. Fenellan's proper station faced Westward.

The reply was deferred until they had reached the pavement, when Mr. Fenellan said: 'I'll tell you,' and looked a dubious preface, to his friend's thinking.

But it was merely the mental inquiry following a glance at mud-spots on the coat.

'We'll lunch; lunch with me, I must eat, tell me then,' said Mr. Radnor, adding within himself: 'Emptiness! want of food!' to account for recent ejaculations and qualms. He had not eaten for a good four hours.

Fenellan's tone signified to his feverish sensibility of the moment, that the matter was personal; and the intimation of a touch on domestic affairs caused sinkings in his vacuity, much as though his heart were having a fall.

He mentioned the slip on the bridge, to explain his: need to visit a haberdasher's shop, and pointed at the waistcoat.

Mr. Fenellan was compassionate over the 'Poor virgin of the smoky city!'

'They have their ready-made at these shops—last year's: perhaps, never mind, do for the day,' said Mr. Radnor, impatient for eating, now that he had spoken of it. 'A basin of turtle; I can't wait. A brush of the coat; mud must be dry by this time. Clear turtle, I think, with a bottle of the Old Veuve. Not bad news to tell? You like that Old Veuve?'

'Too well to tell bad news of her,' said Mr. Fenellan in a manner to reassure his friend, as he intended. 'You wouldn't credit it for the Spring of the year, without the spotless waistcoat?'

'Something of that, I suppose.' And so saying, Mr. Radnor entered the shop of his quest, to be complimented by the shopkeeper, while the attendants climbed the ladder to upper stages for white-waistcoat boxes, on his being; the first bird of the season; which it pleased him to hear; for the smallest of our gratifications in life could give a happy tone to this brightly-constituted gentleman.

CHAPTER III

OLD VEUVE

They were known at the house of the turtle and the attractive Old Veuve: a champagne of a sobered sweetness, of a great year, a great age, counting up to the extremer maturity attained by wines of stilly depths; and their worthy comrade, despite the wanton sparkles, for the promoting of the state of reverential wonderment in rapture, which an ancient wine will lead to, well you wot. The silly girly sugary crudity his given way to womanly suavity, matronly composure, with yet the sparkles; they ascend; but hue and flavour tell of a soul that has come to a lodgement there. It conducts the youthful man to temples of dusky thought: philosophers partaking of it are drawn by the arms of garlanded nymphs about their necks into the fathomless of inquiries. It presents us with a sphere, for the pursuit of the thing we covet most. It bubbles over mellowness; it has, in the marriage with Time, extracted a spice of individuality from the saccharine: by miracle, one would say, were it not for our knowledge of the right noble issue of Time when he and good things unite. There should be somewhere legends of him and the wine-flask. There must be meanings to that effect in the Mythology, awaiting unravelment. For the subject opens to deeper than cellars, and is a tree with vast ramifications of the roots and the spreading growth, whereon half if not all the mythic Gods, Inferior and Superior, Infernal and Celestial, might be shown sitting in concord, performing in concert, harmoniously receiving sacrificial offerings of the black or the white; and the black not extinguishing the fairer fellow. Tell us of a certainty that Time has embraced the wine-flask, then may it be asserted (assuming the great year for the wine, i.e. combinations above) that a speck of the white within us who drink will conquer, to rise in main ascension over volumes of the black. It may, at a greater venture, but confidently, be said in plain speech, that the Bacchus of auspicious birth induces ever to the worship of the loftier Deities.

Think as you will; forbear to come hauling up examples of malarious men, in whom these pourings of the golden rays of life breed fogs; and be moved, since you are scarcely under an obligation to hunt the meaning, in tolerance of some dithyrambic inebriety of narration (quiverings of the reverent pen) when we find ourselves entering the circle of a most magnetic polarity. Take it for not worse than accompanying choric flourishes, in accord with Mr. Victor Radnor and Mr. Simeon Fenellan at their sipping of the venerable wine.

Seated in a cosy corner, near the grey City window edged with a sooty maze, they praised the wine, in the neuter and in the feminine; that for the glass, this for the widow-branded bottle: not as poets hymning; it was done in the City manner, briefly, part pensively, like men travelling to the utmost bourne of flying flavour (a dell in infinite nether), and still masters of themselves and at home.

Such a wine, in its capturing permeation of us, insists on being for a time a theme.

'I wonder!' said Mr. Radnor, completely restored, eyeing his half-emptied second glass and his boon-fellow.

'Low!' Mr. Fenellan shook his head.

'Half a dozen dozen left?'

'Nearer the half of that. And who's the culprit?'

'Old days! They won't let me have another dozen out of the house now.'

'They'll never hit on such another discovery in their cellar, unless they unearth a fifth corner.'

'I don't blame them for making the price prohibitive. And sound as ever!'

Mr. Radnor watched the deliberate constant ascent of bubbles through their rose-topaz transparency. He drank. That notion of the dish of turtle was an inspiration of the right: he ought always to know it for the want of replenishment when such a man as he went quaking. His latest experiences of himself were incredible; but they passed, as the dimples of the stream. He finished his third glass. The bottle, like the cellar-wine, was at ebb: unlike the cellar-wine, it could be set flowing again: He prattled, in the happy ignorance of compulsion:

'Fenellan, remember, I had a sort of right to the wine—to the best I could get; and this Old Veuve, more than any other, is a bridal wine! We heard of Giulia Sanfredini's marriage to come off with the Spanish Duke, and drank it to the toast of our little Nesta's godmother. I 've told you. We took the girl to the Opera, when quite a little one—that high:—and I declare to you, it was marvellous! Next morning after breakfast, she plants herself in the middle of the room, and strikes her attitude for song, and positively, almost with the Sanfredini's voice—illusion of it, you know,—trills us out more than I could have believed credible to be recollected by a child. But I've told you the story. We called her Fredi from that day. I sent the diva, with excuses and compliments, a nuptial present-necklace, Roman goldwork, locket-pendant, containing sunny curl, and below a fine pearl; really pretty; telling her our grounds for the liberty. She replied, accepting the responsible office; touching letter—we found it so; framed in Fredi's room, under her godmother's photograph. Fredi has another heroine now, though she worships her old one still; she never abandons her old ones. You've heard the story over and over!'

Mr. Fenellan nodded; he had a tenderness for the garrulity of Old Veuve, and for the damsel. Chatter on that subject ran pleasantly with their entertainment.

Mr. Radnor meanwhile scribbled, and despatched a strip of his Note-book, bearing a scrawl of orders, to his office. He was now fully himself, benevolent, combative, gay, alert for amusement or the probeing of schemes to the quick, weighing the good and the bad in them with his fine touch on proportion.

'City dead flat? A monotonous key; but it's about the same as fetching a breath after a run; only, true, it lasts too long—not healthy! Skepsey will bring me my letters. I was down in the country early this morning, looking over the house, with Taplow, my architect; and he speaks fairly well of the contractors. Yes, down at Lakelands; and saw my first lemon butterfly in a dell of sunshine, out of the wind, and had half a mind to catch it for Fredi,—and should have caught it myself, if I had! The truth is, we three are country born and bred; we pine in London. Good for a season; you know my old feeling. They are to learn the secret of Lakelands to-morrow. It 's great fun; they think I don't see they've had their suspicion for some time. You said—somebody said—"the eye of a needle for what they let slip of their secrets, and the point of it for penetrating yours":—women. But no; my dear souls didn't prick and bother. And they dealt with a man in armour. I carry them down to Lakelands to-morrow, if the City's flat.'

'Keeping a secret's the lid on a boiling pot with you,' Mr. Fenellan said; and he mused on the profoundness of the flavour at his lips.

'I do it.'

'You do: up to bursting at the breast.'

'I keep it from Colney!'

'As Vesuvius keeps it from Palmieri when shaking him.'

'Has old Colney an idea of it?'

'He has been foretelling an eruption of an edifice.'

The laugh between them subsided to pensiveness.

Mr. Fenellan's delay in the delivery of his news was eloquent to reveal the one hateful topic; and this being seen, it waxed to such increase of size with the passing seconds, that prudence called for it.

'Come!' said Mr. Radnor.

The appeal was understood.

'Nothing very particular. I came into the City to look at a warehouse they want to mount double guard on. Your idea of the fireman's night-patrol and wires has done wonders for the office.'

'I guarantee the City if all my directions are followed.'

Mr. Fenellan's remark, that he had nothing very particular to tell, reduced it to the mere touch upon a vexatious matter, which one has to endure in the ears at times; but it may be postponed. So Mr. Radnor encouraged him to talk of an Insurance Office Investment. Where it is all bog and mist, as in the City to-day, the maxim is, not to take a step, they agreed. Whether it was attributable to an unconsumed glut of the markets, or apprehension of a panic, had to be considered. Both gentlemen were angry with the Birds on the flags of foreign nations, which would not imitate a sawdust Lion to couch reposefully. Incessantly they scream and sharpen talons.

'They crack the City bubbles and bladders, at all events,' Mr. Fenellan said. 'But if we let our journals go on making use of them, in the shape of sham hawks overhead, we shall pay for their one good day of the game with our loss of the covey. An unstable London's no world's market-place.'

'No, no; it's a niggardly national purse, not the journals,' Mr. Radnor said. 'The journals are trading engines. Panics are grist to them; so are wars; but they do their duty in warning the taxpayer and rousing Parliament. Dr. Schlesien's right: we go on believing that our God Neptune will do everything for us, and won't see that Steam has paralyzed his Trident: good! You and Colney are hard on Schlesien—or at him, I should say. He's right: if we won't learn that we have become Continentals, we shall be marched over. Laziness, cowardice, he says.'

'Oh, be hanged!' interrupted Fenellan. 'As much of the former as you like. He 's right about our "individualismus" being another name for selfishness, and showing the usual deficiency in external features; it's an individualism of all of a pattern, as when a mob cuts its lucky, each fellow his own way. Well, then, conscript them, and they'll be all of a better pattern. The only thing to do, and the cheapest. By heaven! it's the only honourable thing to do.'

Mr. Radnor disapproved. 'No conscription here.'

'Not till you've got the drop of poison in your blood, in the form of an army landed. That will teach you to catch at the drug.'

'No, Fenellan! Besides they've got to land. I guarantee a trusty army and navy under a contract, at two-thirds of the present cost. We'll start a National Defence Insurance Company after the next panic.'

'During,' said Mr. Fenellan, and there was a flutter of laughter at the unobtrusive hint for seizing Dame England in the mood.

Both dropped a sigh.

'But you must try and run down with us to Lakelands to-morrow,' Mr. Radnor resumed on a cheerfuller theme. 'You have not yet seen all I 've done there. And it 's a castle with a drawbridge: no exchangeing of visits, as we did at Craye Farm and at Creckholt; we are there for country air; we don't court neighbours at all—perhaps the elect; it will depend on Nataly's wishes. We can accommodate our Concert-set, and about thirty or forty more, for as long as they like. You see, that was my intention—to be independent of neighbouring society. Madame Callet guarantees dinners or hot suppers for eighty— and Armandine is the last person to be recklessly boasting.—When was it I was thinking last of Armandine?' He asked himself that, as he rubbed at the back of his head.

Mr. Fenellan was reading his friend's character by the light of his remarks and in opposition to them, after the critical fashion of intimates who know as well as hear: but it was amiably and trippingly, on the dance of the wine in his veins.

His look, however, was one that reminded; and Mr. Radnor cried: 'Now! whatever it is!'

'I had an interview: I assure you,' Mr. Fenellan interposed to pacify: 'the smallest of trifles, and to be expected: I thought you ought to know it:—an interview with her lawyer; office business, increase of Insurance on one of her City warehouses.'

'Speak her name, speak the woman's name; we're talking like a pair of conspirators,' exclaimed Mr. Radnor.

'He informed me that Mrs. Burman has heard of the new mansion.'

'My place at Lakelands?'

Mr. Radnor's clear-water eyes hardened to stony as their vision ran along the consequences of her having heard it.

'Earlier this time!' he added, thrummed on the table, and thumped with knuckles. 'I make my stand at Lakelands for good! Nothing mortal moves me!'

'That butler of hers—'

'Jarniman, you mean: he's her butler, yes, the scoundrel—h'm-pah! Heaven forgive me! she's an honest woman at least; I wouldn't rob her of her little: fifty-nine or sixty next September, fifteenth of the month! with the constitution of a broken drug-bottle, poor soul! She hears everything from Jarniman: he catches wind of everything. All foreseen, Fenellan, foreseen. I have made my stand at Lakelands, and there's my flag till it's hauled down over Victor Radnor. London kills Nataly as well as Fredi—and me: that is—I can use the words to you—I get back to primal innocence in the country. We all three have the feeling. You're a man to understand. My beasts, and the wild flowers, hedge-banks, and stars. Fredi's poetess will tell you. Quiet waters reflecting. I should feel it in Paris as well, though they have nightingales in their Bois. It's the rustic I want to bathe me; and I had the feeling at school, biting at Horace. Well, this is my Sabine Farm, rather on a larger scale, for the sake of friends. Come, and pure air, water from the springs, walks and rides in lanes, high sand-lanes; Nataly loves them; Fredi worships the old roots of trees: she calls them the faces of those weedy sandy lanes. And the two dear souls on their own estate, Fenellan! And their poultry, cows, cream. And a certain influence one has in the country socially. I make my stand on a home—not empty punctilio.'

Mr. Fenellan repeated, in a pause, 'Punctilio,' and not emphatically.

'Don't bawl the word,' said Mr. Radnor, at the drum of whose ears it rang and sang. 'Here in the City the woman's harmless; and here,' he struck his breast. 'But she can shoot and hit another through me. Ah, the witch!—poor wretch! poor soul! Only, she's malignant. I could swear! But Colney 's right for once in something he says about oaths—"dropping empty buckets," or something.'

'"Empty buckets to haul up impotent demons, whom we have to pay as heavily as the ready devil himself,"' Mr. Fenellan supplied the phrase. 'Only, the moment old Colney moralizes, he's what the critics call sententious. We've all a parlous lot too much pulpit in us.'

'Come, Fenellan, I don't think...'

'Oh, yes, but it's true of me too.'

'You reserve it for your enemies.'

'I 'd like to distract it a bit from the biggest of 'em.' He pointed finger at the region of the heart.

'Here we have Skepsey,' said Mr. Radnor, observing the rapid approach of a lean small figure, that in about the time of a straight-aimed javelin's cast, shot from the doorway to the table.

CHAPTER IV

THE SECOND BOTTLE

This little dart of a man came to a stop at a respectful distance from his master, having the look of an arrested needle in mechanism. His lean slip of face was an illumination of vivacious grey from the quickest of prominent large eyes. He placed his master's letters legibly on the table, and fell to his posture of attention, alert on stiff legs, the hands like sucking-cubs at play with one another.

Skepsey waited for Mr. Fenellan to notice him.

'How about the Schools for Boxing?' that gentleman said.

Deploring in motion the announcement he had to make, Skepsey replied: 'I have a difficulty in getting the plan treated seriously: a person of no station:—it does not appear of national importance. Ladies are against. They decline their signatures; and ladies have great influence; because of the blood; which we know is very slight, rather healthy than not; and it could be proved for the advantage of the frailer sex. They seem to be unaware of their own interests—ladies. The contention all around us is with ignorance. My plan is written; I have shown it, and signatures of gentlemen, to many of our City notables favourable in most cases: gentlemen of the Stock Exchange highly. The clergy and the medical profession are quite with me.'

'The surgical, perhaps you mean?'

'Also, sir. The clergy strongly.'

'On the grounds of—what, Skepsey?'

'Morality. I have fully explained to them:—after his work at the desk all day, the young City clerk wants refreshment. He needs it, must have it. I propose to catch him on his way to his music-halls and other places, and take him to one of our establishments. A short term of instruction, and he would find a pleasure in the gloves; it would delight him more than excesses-beer and tobacco. The female in her right place, certainly.' Skepsey supplicated honest interpretation of his hearer, and pursued,

'It would improve his physical strength, at the same time add to his sense of personal dignity.'

'Would you teach females as well—to divert them from their frivolities?'

'That would have to be thought over, sir. It would be better for them than using their nails.'

'I don't know, Skepsey: I'm rather a Conservative there.'

'Yes; with regard to the female, sir: I confess, my scheme does not include them. They dance; that is a healthy exercise. One has only to say, that it does not add to the national force, in case of emergency. I look to that. And I am particular in proposing an exercise independent of—I have to say—sex. Not that there is harm in sex. But we are for training. I hope my meaning is clear?'

'Quite. You would have boxing with the gloves to be a kind of monastic recreation.'

'Recreation is the word, sir; I have often admired it,' said Skepsey, blinking, unsure of the signification of monastic.

'I was a bit of a boxer once,' Mr. Fenellan said, conscious of height and breadth in measuring the wisp of a figure before him.

'Something might be done with you still, sir.'

Skepsey paid him the encomium after a respectful summary of his gifts in a glimpse. Mr. Fenellan bowed to him.

Mr. Radnor raised head from the notes he was pencilling upon letters perused.

'Skepsey's craze: regeneration of the English race by boxing—nucleus of a national army?'

'To face an enemy at close quarters—it teaches that, sir. I have always been of opinion, that courage may be taught. I do not say heroism. And setting aside for a moment thoughts of an army, we create more valuable citizens. Protection to the weak in streets and by-places—shocking examples of ruffians maltreating women, in view of a crowd.'

'One strong man is an overmatch for your mob,' said Mr. Fenellan.

Skepsey toned his assent to the diminishing thinness where a suspicion of the negative begins to wind upon a distant horn.

'Knowing his own intentions; and before an ignorant mob:—strong, you say, sir? I venture my word that a decent lad, with science, would beat him. It is a question of the study and practice of first principles.'

'If you were to see a rascal giant mishandling a woman?' Skepsey conjured the scene by bending his head and peering abstractedly, as if over spectacles.

'I would beg him to abstain, for his own sake.'

Mr. Fenellan knew that the little fellow was not boasting.

'My brother Dartrey had a lesson or two from you in the first principles, I think?'

'Captain Dartrey is an athlete, sir: exceedingly quick and clever; a hard boxer to beat.'

'You will not call him captain when you see him; he has dismissed the army.'

'I much regret it, sir, much, that we have lost him. Captain Dartrey Fenellan was a beautiful fencer. He gave me some instruction; unhappily, I have to acknowledge, too late. It is a beautiful art. Captain Dartrey says, the French excel at it. But it asks for a weapon, which nature has not given: whereas the fists...'

'So,' Mr. Radnor handed notes and papers to Skepsey: 'No sign of life?'

'It is not yet seen in the City, sir.'

'The first principles of commercial activity have retreated to earth's maziest penetralia, where no tides are! is it not so, Skepsey?' said Mr. Fenellan, whose initiative and exuberance in loquency had been restrained by a slight oppression, known to guests; especially to the guest in the earlier process of his magnification and illumination by virtue of a grand old wine; and also when the news he has to communicate may be a stir to unpleasant heaps. The shining lips and eyes of his florid face now proclaimed speech, with his Puckish fancy jack-o'-lanterning over it. 'Business hangs to swing at every City door, like a ragshop Doll, on the gallows of overproduction. Stocks and Shares are hollow nuts not a squirrel of the lot would stop to crack for sight of the milky kernel mouldered to beard.

Percentage, like a cabman without a fare, has gone to sleep inside his vehicle. Dividend may just be seen by tiptoe: stockholders, twinkling heels over the far horizon. Too true!—and our merchants, brokers, bankers, projectors of Companies, parade our City to remind us of the poor steamed fellows trooping out of the burst-boiler-room of the big ship Leviathan, in old years; a shade or two paler than the crowd o' the passengers, apparently alive and conversible, but corpses, all of them to lie their length in fifteen minutes.'

'And you, Fenellan?' cried his host, inspired for a second bottle by the lovely nonsense of a voluble friend wound up to the mark.

'Doctor of the ship! with this prescription!' Mr. Fenellan held up his glass.

'Empty?'

Mr. Fenellan made it completely so. 'Confident!' he affirmed.

An order was tossed to the waiter, and both gentlemen screwed their lips in relish of his heavy consent to score off another bottle from the narrow list.

'At the office in forty minutes,' Skepsey's master nodded to him and shot him forth, calling him back: 'By the way, in case a man named Jarniman should ask to see me, you turn him to the rightabout.'

Skepsey repeated: 'Jarniman!' and flew.

'A good servant,' Mr. Radnor said. 'Few of us think of our country so much, whatever may be said of the specific he offers. Colney has impressed him somehow immensely: he studies to write too; pushes to improve himself; altogether a worthy creature.'

The second bottle appeared. The waiter, in sincerity a reluctant executioner, heightened his part for the edification of the admiring couple.

'Take heart, Benjamin,' said Mr. Fenellan; 'it's only the bottle dies; and we are the angels above to receive the spirit.'

'I'm thinking of the house,' Benjamin replied. He told them that again.

'It 's the loss of the fame of having the wine, that he mourns. But, Benjamin,' said Mr. Fenellan, 'the fame enters into the partakers of it, and we spread it, and perpetuate it for you.'

'That don't keep a house upright,' returned Benjamin.

Mr. Fenellan murmured to himself: 'True enough, it 's elegy—though we perform it through a trumpet; and there's not a doubt of our being down or having knocked the world down, if we're loudly praised.'

Benjamin waited to hear approval sounded on the lips uncertain as a woman is a wine of ticklish age. The gentlemen nodded, and he retired.

A second bottle, just as good as the first, should, one thoughtlessly supposes, procure us a similar reposeful and excursive enjoyment, as of men lying on their backs and flying imagination like a kite. The effect was quite other. Mr. Radnor drank hastily and spoke with heat: 'You told me All? tell me that!'

Mr. Fenellan gathered himself together; he sipped, and relaxed his bracing. But there really was a bit more to tell: not much, was it? Not likely to puff a gale on the voluptuous indolence of a man drawn along by Nereids over sunny sea-waves to behold the birth of the Foam-Goddess? 'According to Carling, her lawyer; that is, he hints she meditates a blow.'

'Mrs. Burman means to strike a blow?'

'The lady.'

'Does he think I fear any—does he mean a blow with a weapon? Is it a legal...? At last? Fenellan!'

'So I fancied I understood.'

'But can the good woman dream of that as a blow to strike and hurt, for a punishment?—that's her one aim.'

'She may have her hallucinations.'

'But a blow—what a word for it! But it's life to us life! It's the blow we've prayed for. Why, you know it! Let her strike, we bless her. We've never had an ill feeling to the woman; utterly the contrary—pity, pity, pity! Let her do that, we're at her feet, my Nataly and I. If you knew what my poor girl suffers! She 's a saint at the stake. Chiefly on behalf of her family. Fenellan, you may have a sort of guess at my fortune: I'll own to luck; I put in a claim to courage and calculation.'

'You've been a bulwark to your friends.'

'All, Fenellan, all-stocks, shares, mines, companies, industries at home and—abroad—all, at a sweep, to have the woman strike that blow! Cheerfully would I begin to build a fortune over again—singing! Ha! the woman has threatened it before. It's probably feline play with us.'

His chin took support, he frowned.

'You may have touched her.'

'She won't be touched, and she won't be driven. What 's the secret of her? I can't guess, I never could. She's a riddle.'

'Riddles with wigs and false teeth have to be taken and shaken for the ardently sought secret to reveal itself,' said Mr. Fenellan.

His picture, with the skeleton issue of any shaking, smote Mr. Radnor's eyes, they turned over. 'Oh!—her charms! She had a desperate belief in her beauty. The woman 's undoubtedly charitable; she's not without a mind—sort of mind: well, it shows no crack till it's put to use. Heart! yes, against me she has plenty of it. They say she used to be courted; she talked of it: "my courtiers, Mr. Victor!" There, heaven forgive me, I wouldn't mock at her to another.'

'It looks as if she were only inexorably human,' said Mr. Fenellan, crushing a delicious gulp of the wine, that foamed along the channel to flavour. 'We read of the tester of a bandit-bed; and it flattened unwary recumbents to pancakes. An escape from the like of that seems pleadable, should be: none but the drowsy would fail to jump out and run, or the insane.'

Mr. Radnor was taken with the illustration of his case. 'For the sake of my sanity, it was! to preserve my.... but any word makes nonsense of it. Could—I must ask you—could any sane man—you were abroad in those days, horrible days! and never met her: I say, could you consent to be tied—I admit the vow, ceremony, so forth-tied to—I was barely twenty-one: I put it to you, Fenellan, was it in reason an engagement—which is, I take it, a mutual plight of faith, in good faith; that is, with capacity on both sides to keep the engagement: between the man you know I was in youth and a more than middle-aged woman crazy up to the edge of the cliff—as Colney says half the world is, and she positively is when her spite is roused. No, Fenellan, I have nothing on my conscience with regard to the woman. She had wealth: I left her not one penny the worse for—but she was not one to reckon it, I own. She could be generous, was, with her money. If she had struck this blow—I know she thought of it: or if she would strike it now, I could not only forgive her, I could beg forgiveness.'

A sight of that extremity fetched prickles to his forehead.

'You've borne your part bravely, my friend.'

'I!' Mr. Radnor shrugged at mention of his personal burdens. 'Praise my Nataly if you like! Made for one another, if ever two in this world! You know us both, and do you doubt it? The sin would have been for us two to meet and—but enough when I say, that I am she, she me, till death and beyond it: that's my firm faith. Nataly teaches me the religion of life, and you may learn what that is when you fall in love with a woman. Eighteen-nineteen-twenty years!'

Tears fell from him, two drops. He blinked, bugled in his throat, eyed his watch, and smiled: 'The finishing glass! We should have had to put Colney to bed. Few men stand their wine. You and I are not lamed by it; we can drink and do business: my first experience in the City was, that the power to drink—keeping a sound head—conduces to the doing of business.'

'It's a pleasant way of instructing men to submit to their conqueror.'

'If it doubles the energies, mind.'

'Not if it fiddles inside. I confess to that effect upon me. I've a waltz going on, like the snake with the tail in his mouth, eternal; and it won't allow of a thought upon Investments.'

'Consult me to-morrow,' said Mr. Radnor, somewhat pained for having inconsiderately misled the man he had hitherto helpfully guided. 'You've looked at the warehouse?'

'That's performed.'

'Make a practice of getting over as much of your business in the early morning as you well can.'

Mr. Radnor added hints of advice to a frail humanity he was indulgent, the giant spoke in good fellowship. It would have been to have strained his meaning, for purposes of sarcasm upon him, if one had taken him to boast of a personal exemption from our common weakness.

He stopped, and laughed: 'Now I 'm pumping my pulpit-eh? You come with us to Lakelands. I drive the ladies down to my office, ten A.M.: if it's fine; train half-past. We take a basket. By the way, I had no letter from Dartrey last mail.'

'He has buried his wife. It happens to some men.'

Mr. Radnor stood gazing. He asked for the name of the place of the burial. He heard without seizing it. A simulacrum spectre-spark of hopefulness shot up in his imagination, glowed and quivered, darkening at the utterance of the Dutch syllables, leaving a tinge of witless envy. Dartrey—Fenellan had buried the wife whose behaviour vexed and dishonoured him: and it was in Africa! One would have to go to Africa to be free of the galling. But Dartrey had gone, and he was free!—The strange faint freaks of our sensations when struck to leap and throw off their load after a long affliction, play these disorderly pranks on the brain; and they are faint, but they come in numbers, they are recurring, always in ambush. We do not speak of them: we have not words to stamp the indefinite things; generally we should leave them unspoken if we had the words; we know them as out of reason: they haunt us, pluck at us, fret us, nevertheless.

Dartrey free, he was relieved of the murderous drama incessantly in the mind of shackled men.

It seemed like one of the miracles of a divine intervention, that Dartrey should be free, suddenly free; and free while still a youngish man. He was in himself a wonderful fellow, the pick of his country for vigour, gallantry, trustiness, high-mindedness; his heavenly good fortune decked him as a prodigy.

'No harm to the head from that fall of yours?' Mr. Fenellan said.

'None.' Mr. Radnor withdrew his hand from head to hat, clapped it on and cried cheerily: 'Now to business'; as men may, who have confidence in their ability to concentrate an instant attention upon the substantial. 'You dine with us. The usual Quartet: Peridon, Pempton, Colney, Yatt, or Catkin: Priscilla Graves and Nataly—the Rev. Septimus; Cormyn and his wife: Young Dudley Sowerby and I—flutes: he has precision, as naughty Fredi said, when some one spoke of expression. In the course of the evening, Lady Grace, perhaps: you like her.'

'Human nature in the upper circle is particularly likeable.'

'Fenellan,' said Mr. Radnor, emboldened to judge hopefully of his fortunes by mere pressure of the thought of Dartrey's, 'I put it to you: would you say, that there is anything this time behind your friend Carling's report?'

Although it had not been phrased as a report, Mr. Fenellan's answering look and gesture, and a run of indiscriminate words, enrolled it in that form, greatly to the inspiriting of Mr. Radnor.

Old Veuve in one, to the soul of Old Veuve in the other, they recalled a past day or two, touched the skies; and merriment or happiness in the times behind them held a mirror to the present: or the hour of the reverse of happiness worked the same effect by contrast: so that notions of the singular election of us by Dame Fortune, sprang like vinous bubbles. For it is written, that however powerful you be, you shall not take the Winegod on board to entertain him as a simple passenger; and you may captain your vessel, you may pilot it, and keep to your reckonings, and steer for all the ports you have a mind to, even to doing profitable exchange with Armenian and Jew, and still you shall do the something more, which proves that the Winegod is on board: he is the pilot of your blood if not the captain of your thoughts.

Mr. Fenellan was unused to the copious outpouring of Victor Radnor's confidences upon his domestic affairs; and the unwonted excitement of Victor's manner of speech would have perplexed him, had there not been such a fiddling of the waltz inside him.

Payment for the turtle and the bottles of Old Veuve was performed apart with Benjamin, while Simeon Fenellan strolled out of the house, questioning a tumbled mind as to what description of suitable entertainment, which would be dancing and flirting and fal-lallery in the season of youth, London City could provide near meridian hours for a man of middle age carrying his bottle of champagne, like a guest of an old-fashioned wedding-breakfast. For although he could stand his wine as well as his friend, his friend's potent capacity martially after the feast to buckle to business at a sign of the clock, was beyond him. It pointed to one of the embodied elements, hot from Nature's workshop. It told of the endurance of powers, that partly explained the successful, astonishing career of his friend among a people making urgent, if unequal, demands perpetually upon stomach and head.

CHAPTER V

In that nationally interesting Poem, or Dramatic Satire, once famous, THE RAJAH IN LONDON (London, Limbo and Sons, 1889), now obliterated under the long wash of Press-matter, the reflection—not unknown to philosophical observers, and natural perhaps in the mind of an Oriental Prince—produced by his observation of the march of London citizens Eastward at morn, Westward at eve, attributes their practice to a survival of the Zoroastrian form of worship. His Minister, favourable to the people or for the sake of fostering an idea in his Master's head, remarks, that they show more than the fidelity of the sunflower to her God. The Rajah, it would appear, frowns interrogatively, in the princely fashion, accusing him of obscureness of speech:—princes and the louder members of the grey public are fraternally instant to spurn at the whip of that which they do not immediately comprehend. It is explained by the Minister: not even the flower, he says, would hold constant, as they, to the constantly unseen—a trebly cataphractic Invisible. The Rajah professes curiosity to know how it is that the singular people nourish their loyalty, since they cannot attest to the continued being of the object in which they put their faith. He is informed by his prostrate servant of a settled habit they have of diligently seeking their Divinity, hidden above, below; and of copiously taking inside them doses of what is denied to their external vision: thus they fortify credence chemically on an abundance of meats and liquors; fire they eat, and they drink fire; they become consequently instinct with fire. Necessarily therefore they believe in fire. Believing, they worship. Worshipping, they march Eastward at morn, Westward at eve. For that way lies the key, this way the cupboard, of the supplies, their fuel.

According to Stage directions, THE RAJAH AND HIS MINISTER Enter a Gin-Palace.—It is to witness a service that they have learnt to appreciate as Anglicanly religious.

On the step of the return to their Indian clime, they speak of the hatted sect, which is most, or most commercially, succoured and fattened by our rule there: they wave adieu to the conquering Islanders, as to 'Parsees beneath a cloud.'

The two are seen last on the deck of the vessel, in perusal of a medical pamphlet composed of statistics and sketches, traceries, horrid blots, diagrams with numbers referring to notes, of the various maladies caused by the prolonged prosecution of that form of worship.

'But can they suffer so and live?' exclaims the Rajah, vexed by the physical sympathetic twinges which set him wincing.

'Science,' his Minister answers, 'took them up where Nature, in pity of their martyrdom, dropped them. They do not live; they are engines, insensible things of repairs and patches; insteamed to pursue their infuriate course, to the one end of exhausting supplies for the renewing of them, on peril of an instant suspension if they deviate a step or stop: nor do they.'

The Rajah is of opinion, that he sails home with the key of the riddle of their power to vanquish. In some apparent allusion to an Indian story of a married couple who successfully made their way, he accounts for their solid and resistless advance, resembling that of—

The doubly-wedded man and wife,
Pledged to each other and against the world
With mutual union.

One would like to think of the lengthened tide-flux of pedestrian citizens facing South-westward, as being drawn by devout attraction to our nourishing luminary: at the hour, mark, when the Norland cloud-king, after a day of wild invasion, sits him on his restful bank of bluefish smack-o'-cheek red above Whitechapel, to spy where his last puff of icy javelins pierces and dismembers the vapoury masses in cluster about the circle of flame descending upon the greatest and most elevated of Admirals at the head of the Strand, with illumination of smoke-plumed chimneys, house-roofs, window-panes, weather-vanes, monument and pedimental monsters, and omnibus umbrella. One would fair believe that they advance admireing; they are assuredly made handsome by the beams. No longer mere concurrent atoms of the furnace of business (from coal-dust to sparks, rushing, as it were, on respiratory blasts of an enormous engine's centripetal and centrifugal energy), their step is leisurely to meet the rosy Dinner, which is ever a see-saw with the God of Light in his fall; the mask of the noble human visage upon them is not roughened, as at midday, by those knotted hard ridges of the scrambler's hand seen from forehead down to jaw; when indeed they have all the appearance of sour scientific productions. And unhappily for the national portrait, in the Poem quoted, the Rajah's Minister chose an hour between morning and meridian, or at least before an astonished luncheon had come to composure inside their persons, for drawing his Master's attention to the quaint similarity of feature in the units of the busy antish congregates they had travelled so far to visit and to study:

These Britons wear
The driven and perplexed look of men
Begotten hastily 'twixt business hours

It could not have been late afternoon.

These Orientals should have seen them, with Victor Radnor among them, fronting the smoky splendours of the sunset. In April, the month of piled and hurried cloud, it is a Rape of the Sabines overhead from all quarters, either one of the winds brawnily larcenous; and London, smoking royally to the open skies, builds images of a dusty epic fray for possession of the portly dames. There is immensity, swinging motion, collision, dusky richness of colouring, to the sight; and to the mind idea. London presents it. If we can allow ourselves a moment for not inquireing scrupulously (you will do it by inhaling the aroma of the ripe kitchen hour), here is a noble harmony of heaven and the earth of the works of man, speaking a grander tongue than barren sea or wood or wilderness. Just a moment; it goes; as, when a well-attuned barrel-organ in a street has drawn us to recollections of the Opera or Italy, another harshly crashes, and the postman knocks at doors, and perchance a costermonger cries his mash of fruit, a beggar woman wails her hymn. For the pinched are here, the dinnerless, the weedy, the gutter-growths, the forces repressing them. That grand tongue of the giant City inspires none human to Bardic eulogy while we let those discords be. An embittered Muse of Reason prompts her victims to the composition of the adulatory Essay and of the Leading Article, that she may satiate an angry irony 'upon those who pay fee for their filling with the stuff. Song of praise she does not permit. A moment of satisfaction in a striking picture is accorded, and no more. For this London, this England, Europe, world, but especially this London, is rather a thing for hospital operations than for poetic rhapsody; in aspect, too, streaked scarlet and pock-pitted under the most cumbrous of jewelled tiaras; a Titanic work of long-tolerated pygmies; of whom the leaders, until sorely discomforted in body and doubtful in soul, will give gold and labour, will impose restrictions upon activity, to maintain a conservatism of diseases. Mind is absent, or somewhere so low down beneath material accumulations that it is inexpressive, powerless to drive the ponderous bulk to such excisings, purgeings, purifyings as might—as may, we will suppose, render it acceptable, for a theme of panegyric, to the Muse of Reason; ultimately, with her consent, to the Spirit of Song.

But first there must be the cleansing. When Night has fallen upon London, the Rajah remarks:

Monogamic Societies present
A decent visage and a hideous rear.

His Minister (satirically, or in sympathetic Conservatism) would have them not to move on, that they may preserve among beholders the impression of their handsome frontage. Night, however, will come; and they, adoreing the decent face, are moved on, made to expose what the Rajah sees. Behind his courteousness, he is an antagonistic observer of his conquerors; he pushes his questions farther than the need for them; his Minister the same; apparently to retain the discountenanced people in their state of exposure. Up to the time of the explanation of the puzzle on board the departing vessel (on the road to Windsor, at the Premier's reception, in the cell of the Police, in the presence of the Magistrate-whose crack of a totally inverse decision upon their case, when he becomes acquainted with the titles and station of these imputedly peccant, refreshes them), they hold debates over the mysterious contrarieties of a people professing in one street what they confound in the next, and practising by day a demureness that yells with the cat of the tiles at night.

Granting all that, it being a transient novelist's business to please the light-winged hosts which live for the hour, and give him his only chance of half of it, let him identify himself with them, in keeping to the quadrille on the surface and shirking the disagreeable.

Clouds of high colour above London City are as the light of the Goddess to lift the angry heroic head over human. They gloriously transfigure. A Murillo beggar is not more precious than sight of London in any of the streets admitting coloured cloud-scenes; the cunning of the sun's hand so speaks to us. And if haply down an alley some olive mechanic of street-organs has quickened little children's legs to rhythmic footing, they strike on thoughts braver than pastoral. Victor Radnor, lover of the country though he was, would have been the first to say it. He would indeed have said it too emphatically. Open London as a theme, to a citizen of London ardent for the clear air out of it, you have roused an orator; you have certainly fired a magazine, and must listen to his reminiscences of one of its paragraphs or pages.

The figures of the hurtled fair ones in sky were wreathing Nelson's cocked hat when Victor, distinguishably bright-faced amid a crowd of the irradiated, emerged from the tideway to cross the square, having thoughts upon Art, which were due rather to the suggestive proximity of the National Gallery than to the Flemish mouldings of cloud-forms under Venetian brushes. His purchases of pictures had been his unhappiest ventures. He had relied and reposed on the dicta of newspaper critics; who are sometimes unanimous, and are then taken for guides, and are fatal. He was led to the conclusion that our modern-lauded pictures do not ripen. They have a chance of it, if abused. But who thinks of buying the abused? Exalted by the critics, they have, during the days of Exhibition, a glow, a significance or a fun, abandoning them where examination is close and constant, and the critic's trumpet-note dispersed to the thinness of the fee for his blowing. As to foreign pictures, classic pictures, Victor had known his purse to leap for a Raphael with a history in stages of descent from the Master, and critics to swarm: a Raphael of the dealers, exposed to be condemned by the critics, universally derided. A real Raphael in your house is aristocracy to the roof-tree. But the wealthy trader will reach to title before he may hope to get the real Raphael or a Titian. Yet he is the one who would, it may be, after enjoyment of his prize, bequeath it to the nation—PRESENTED TO THE NATION BY VICTOR MONTGOMERY RADNOR. There stood the letters in gilt; and he had a thrill of his generosity; for few were the generous acts he could not perform; and if an object haunted the deed, it came of his trader's habit of mind.

He revelled in benevolent projects of gifts to the nation, which would coat a sensitive name. Say, an ornamental City Square, flowers, fountains, afternoon bands of music—comfortable seats in it, and a shelter, and a ready supply of good cheap coffee or tea. Tobacco? why not rolls of honest tobacco! nothing so much soothes the labourer. A volume of plans for the benefit of London smoked out of each ascending pile in his brain. London is at night a moaning outcast round the policeman's legs. What of an all-night-long, cosy, brightly lighted, odoriferous coffee-saloon for rich or poor, on the model of the hospitable Paduan? Owner of a penny, no soul among us shall be rightly an outcast....

Dreams of this kind are taken at times by wealthy people as a cordial at the bar of benevolent intentions. But Victor was not the man to steal his refreshments in that known style. He meant to make deeds of them, as far as he could, considering their immense extension; and except for the sensitive social name, he was of single-minded purpose.

Turning to the steps of a chemist's shop to get a prescription made up for his Nataly's doctoring of her domestics, he was arrested by a rap on his elbow; and no one was near; and there could not be a doubt of the blow—a sharp hard stroke, sparing the funny-bone, but ringing. His head, at the punctilio bump, throbbed responsively—owing to which or indifference to the prescription, as of no instant requirement, he pursued his course, resembling mentally the wanderer along a misty beach, who hears cannon across the waters.

He certainly had felt it. He remembered the shock: he could not remember much of pain. How about intimations? His asking caused a smile.

Very soon the riddle answered itself. He had come into view of the diminutive marble cavalier of the infantile cerebellum; recollecting a couplet from the pen of the disrespectful Satirist Peter, he thought of a fall: his head and his elbow responded simultaneously to the thought.

All was explained save his consequent rightabout from the chemist's shop: and that belongs to the minor involutions of circumstances and the will. It passed like a giver's wrinkle. He read the placards of the Opera; reminding himself of the day when it was the single Opera-house; and now we have two-or three. We have also a distracting couple of Clowns and Pantaloons in our Pantomimes: though Colney says that the multiplication of the pantaloon is a distinct advance to representative truth—and bother Colney! Two Columbines also. We forbear to speak of men, but where is the boy who can set his young heart upon two Columbines at once! Victor felt the boy within him cold to both: and in his youth he had doated on the solitary twirling spangled lovely Fairy. The tale of a delicate lady dancer leaping as the kernel out of a nut from the arms of Harlequin to the legalized embrace of a wealthy brewer, and thenceforth living, by repute, with unagitated legs, as holy a matron, despite her starry past, as any to be shown in a country breeding the like abundantly, had always delighted him. It seemed a reconcilement of opposing stations, a defeat of Puritanism. Ay, and poor women!—women in the worser plight under the Puritan's eye. They may be erring and good: yes, finding the man to lift them the one step up! Read the history of the error. But presently we shall teach the Puritan to act by the standards of his religion. All is coming right—must come right. Colney shall be confounded.

Hereupon Victor hopped on to Fenellan's hint regarding the designs of Mrs. Burman.

His Nataly might have to go through a short sharp term of scorching—Godiva to the gossips.

She would come out of it glorified. She would be reconciled with her family. With her story of her devotion to the man loving her, the world would know her for the heroine she was: a born lady, in appearance and manner an empress among women. It was a story to be pleaded in any court, before the sternest public. Mrs. Burman had thrown her into temptation's way. It was a story to touch the heart, as none other ever written of over all the earth was there a woman equalling his Nataly!

And their Nesta would have a dowry to make princesses envious:—she would inherit... he ran up an arithmetical column, down to a line of figures in addition, during three paces of his feet. Dartrey Fenellan had said of little Nesta once, that she had a nature pure and sparkling as mid-sea foam. Happy he who wins her! But she was one of the young women who are easily pleased and hardly enthralled. Her father strained his mind for the shape of the man to accomplish the feat. Whether she had an ideal of a youth in her feminine head, was beyond his guessing. She was not the damsel to weave a fairy waistcoat for the identical prince, and try it upon all comers to discover him: as is done by some; excuseably, if we would be just. Nesta was of the elect, for whom excuses have not to be made. She would probably like a flute-player best; because her father played the flute, and she loved him—laughably a little maiden's reason! Her father laughed at her.

Along the street of Clubs, where a bruised fancy may see black balls raining, the narrow way between ducal mansions offers prospect of the sweep of greensward, all but touching up to the sunset to draw it to the dance.

Formerly, in his very early youth, he clasped a dream of gaining way to an alliance with one of these great surrounding houses; and he had a passion for the acquisition of money as a means. And it has to be confessed, he had sacrificed in youth a slice of his youth, to gain it without labour—usually a costly purchase. It had ended disastrously: or say, a running of the engine off the rails, and a speedy re-establishment of traffic. Could it be a loss, that had led to the winning of his Nataly? Can we really loathe the first of the steps when the one in due sequence, cousin to it, is a blessedness? If we have been righted to health by a medical draught, we are bound to be respectful to our drug. And so we are, in spite of Nature's wry face and shiver at a mention of what we went through during those days, those horrible days:—hide them!

The smothering of them from sight set them sounding he had to listen. Colney Durance accused him of entering into bonds with somebody's grandmother for the simple sake of browsing on her thousands: a picture of himself too abhorrent to Victor to permit of any sort of acceptance. Consequently he struck away to the other extreme of those who have a choice in mixed motives: he protested that compassion had been the cause of it. Looking at the circumstance now, he could see, allowing for human frailty-perhaps a wish to join the ranks of the wealthy compassion for the woman as the principal motive. How often had she not in those old days praised his generosity for allying his golden youth to her withered age—Mrs. Burman's very words! And she was a generous woman or had been: she was generous in saying that. Well, and she was generous in having a well-born, well-bred beautiful young creature like Nataly for her companion, when it was a case of need for the dear girl; and compassionately insisting, against remonstrances: they were spoken by him, though they were but partial. How, then, had she become—at least, how was it that she could continue to behave as the vindictive Fury who persecuted remorselessly, would give no peace, poisoned the wells round every place where he and his dear one pitched their tent!

But at last she had come to charity, as he could well believe. Not too late! Victor's feeling of gratitude to Mrs. Burman assured him it was genuine because of his genuine conviction, that she had determined to end her incomprehensibly lengthened days in reconcilement with him: and he had always been ready to 'forget and forgive.' A truly beautiful old phrase! It thrilled off the most susceptible of men.

His well-kept secret of the spacious country-house danced him behind a sober demeanour from one park to another; and along beside the drive to view of his townhouse—unbeloved of the inhabitants, although by acknowledgement it had, as Fredi funnily drawled, to express her sense of justice in depreciation, 'good accommodation.' Nataly was at home, he was sure. Time to be dressing: sun sets at six-forty, he said, and glanced at the stained West, with an accompanying vision of outspread primroses flooding banks of shadowy fields near Lakelands.

He crossed the road and rang.

Upon the opening of the door, there was a cascade of muslin downstairs. His darling Fredi stood out of it, a dramatic Undine.

CHAPTER VI

NATALY

'Il segreto!' the girl cried commandingly, with a forefinger at his breast.

He crossed arms, toning in similar recitative, with anguish, 'Dove volare!'

They joined in half a dozen bars of operatic duet.

She flew to him, embraced and kissed.

'I must have it, my papa! unlock. I've been spying the bird on its hedgerow nest so long! And this morning, my own dear cunning papa, weren't you as bare as winter twigs? "Tomorrow perhaps we will have a day in the country." To go and see the nest? Only, please, not a big one. A real nest; where mama and I can wear dairymaid's hat and apron all day—the style you like; and strike roots. We've been torn away two or three times: twice, I know.'

'Fixed, this time; nothing shall tear us up,' said her father, moving on to the stairs, with an arm about her.

'So, it is...?'

'She's amazed at her cleverness!'

'A nest for three?'

'We must have a friend or two.'

'And pretty country?'

'Trust her papa for that.'

'Nice for walking and running over fields? No rich people?'

'How escape that rabble in England! as Colney says. It's a place for being quite independent of neighbours, free as air.'

'Oh! bravo!'

'And Fredi will have her horse, and mama her pony-carriage; and Fredi can have a swim every Summer morning.'

'A swim?' Her note was dubious. 'A river?'

'A good long stretch—fairish, fairish. Bit of a lake; bathing-shed; the Naiad's bower: pretty water to see.'

'Ah. And has the house a name?'

'Lakelands. I like the name.'

'Papa gave it the name!'

'There's nothing he can conceal from his girl. Only now and then a little surprise.'

'And his girl is off her head with astonishment. But tell me, who has been sharing the secret with you?'

'Fredi strikes home! And it is true, you dear; I must have a confidant: Simeon Fenellan.'

'Not Mr. Durance?'

He shook out a positive negative. 'I leave Col to his guesses. He'd have been prophesying fire the works before the completion.'

'Then it is not a dear old house, like Craye and Creckholt?'

'Wait and see to-morrow.'

He spoke of the customary guests for concert practice; the music, instrumental and vocal; quartet, duet, solo; and advising the girl to be quick, as she had but twenty-five minutes, he went humming and trilling into his dressing-room.

Nesta signalled at her mother's door for permission to enter. She slipped in, saw that the maid was absent, and said: 'Yes, mama; and prepare, I feared it; I was sure.'

Her mother breathed a little moan: 'Not a cottage?'

'He has not mentioned it to Mr. Durance.'

'Why not?'

'Mr. Fenellan has been his confidant.'

'My darling, we did wrong to let it go on, without speaking. You don't know for certain yet?'

'It's a large estate, mama, and a big new house.'

Nataly's bosom sank. 'Ah me! here's misery! I ought to have known. And too late now it has gone so far! But I never imagined he would be building.'

She caught herself languishing at her toilette-glass, as, if her beauty were at stake; and shut her eyelids angrily. To be looking in that manner, for a mere suspicion, was too foolish. But Nesta's divinations were target-arrows; they flew to the mark. Could it have been expected that Victor would ever do anything on a small scale? O the dear little lost lost cottage! She thought of it with a strain of the arms of womanhood's longing in the unblessed wife for a babe. For the secluded modest cottage would not rack her with the old anxieties, beset her with suspicions....

'My child, you won't possibly have time before the dinner-hour,' she said to Nesta, dismissing her and taking her kiss of comfort with a short and straining look out of the depths.

Those bitter doubts of the sentiments of neighbours are an incipient dislike, when one's own feelings to the neighbours are kind, could be affectionate. We are distracted, perverted, made strangers to ourselves by a false position.

She heard his voice on a carol. Men do not feel this doubtful position as women must. They have not the same to endure; the world gives them land to tread, where women are on breaking seas. Her Nesta knew no more than the pain of being torn from a home she loved. But now the girl was older, and if once she had her imagination awakened, her fearful directness would touch the spot, question, bring on the scene to-come, necessarily to come, dreaded much more than death by her mother. But if it might be postponed till the girl was nearer to an age of grave understanding, with some knowledge of our world, some comprehension of a case that could be pleaded!

He sang: he never acknowledged a trouble, he dispersed it; and in her present wrestle with the scheme of a large country estate involving new intimacies, anxieties, the courtship of rival magnates, followed by the wretched old cloud, and the imposition upon them to bear it in silence though they knew they could plead a case, at least before charitable and discerning creatures or before heaven, the despondent lady could have asked whether he was perfectly sane.

Who half so brilliantly!—Depreciation of him, fetched up at a stroke the glittering armies of her enthusiasm. He had proved it; he proved it daily in conflicts and in victories that dwarfed emotional troubles like hers: yet they were something to bear, hard to bear, at times unbearable.

But those were times of weakness. Let anything be doubted rather than the good guidance of the man who was her breath of life! Whither he led, let her go, not only submissively, exultingly.

Thus she thought, under pressure of the knowledge, that unless rushing into conflicts bigger than conceivable, she had to do it, and should therefore think it.

This was the prudent woman's clear deduction from the state wherein she found herself, created by the one first great step of the mad woman. Her surrender then might be likened to the detachment of a flower on the river's bank by swell of flood: she had no longer root of her own; away she sailed, through beautiful scenery, with occasionally a crashing fall, a turmoil, emergence from a vortex, and once more the sunny whirling surface. Strange to think, she had not since then power to grasp in her abstract mind a notion of stedfastness without or within.

But, say not the mad, say the enamoured woman. Love is a madness, having heaven's wisdom in it—a spark. But even when it is driving us on the breakers, call it love: and be not unworthy of it, hold to it. She and Victor had drunk of a cup. The philtre was in her veins, whatever the directions of the rational mind.

Exulting or regretting, she had to do it, as one in the car with a racing charioteer. Or up beside a more than Titanically audacious balloonist. For the charioteer is bent on a goal; and Victor's course was an ascension from heights to heights. He had ideas, he mastered Fortune. He conquered Nataly and held her subject, in being above his ambition; which was now but an occupation for his powers, while the aim of his life was at the giving and taking of simple enjoyment. In spite of his fits of unreasonableness in the means—and the woman loving him could trace them to a breath of nature—his gentle good friendly innocent aim in life was of this very simplest; so wonderful, by contrast with his powers, that she, assured of it as she was by experience of him, was touched, in a transfusion of her feelings through lucent globes of admiration and of tenderness, to reverence. There had been occasions when her wish for the whole world to have proof and exhibition of his greatness, goodness, and simplicity amid his gifts, prompted her incitement of him to stand forth eminently: ['lead a kingdom,' was the phrase behind the curtain within her shy bosom;) and it revealed her to herself, upon reflection, as being still the Nataly who drank the cup with him, to join her fate with his.

And why not? Was that regretted? Far from it. In her maturity, the woman was unable to send forth any dwelling thought or more than a flight of twilight fancy, that cancelled the deed of her youth, and therewith seemed to expunge near upon the half—of her term of years. If it came to consideration of her family and the family's opinion of her conduct, her judgement did not side with them or with herself, it whirled, swam to a giddiness and subsided.

Of course, if she and Victor were to inhabit a large country-house, they might as well have remained at Craye Farm or at Creckholt; both places dear to them in turn. Such was the plain sense of the surface question. And how strange it was to her, that he, of the most quivering sensitiveness on her behalf; could not see, that he threw her into situations where hard words of men and women threatened about her head; where one or two might on a day, some day, be heard; and where, in the recollection of two years back, the word 'Impostor' had smacked her on both cheeks from her own mouth.

Now once more they were to run the same round of alarms, undergo the love of the place, with perpetual apprehensions of having to leave it: alarms, throbbing suspicions, like those of old travellers through the haunted forest, where whispers have intensity of meaning, and unseeing we are seen, and unaware awaited.

Nataly shook the rolls of her thick brown hair from her forehead; she took strength from a handsome look of resolution in the glass. She could always honestly say, that her courage would not fail him.

Victor tapped at the door; he stepped into the room, wearing his evening white flower over a more open white waistcoat; and she was composed and uninquiring. Their Nesta was heard on the descent of the stairs, with a rattle of Donizetti's Il segreto to the skylights.

He performed his never-omitted lover's homage.

Nataly enfolded him in a homely smile. 'A country-house? We go and see it to-morrow?'

'And you've been pining for a country home, my dear soul.'

'After the summer six weeks, the house in London does not seem a home to return to.'

'And next day, Nataly draws five thousand pounds for the first sketch of the furniture.'

'There is the Creckholt...' she had a difficulty in saying.

'Part of it may do. Lakelands requires—but you will see to-morrow.'

After a close shutting of her eyes, she rejoined: 'It is not a cottage?'

'Well, dear, no: when the Slave of the Lamp takes to building, he does not run up cottages. And we did it without magic, all in a year; which is quite as good as a magical trick in a night.' He drew her close to him. 'When was it my dear girl guessed me at work?'

'It was the other dear girl. Nesta is the guesser.'

'You were two best of souls to keep from bothering me; and I might have had to fib; and we neither of us like that.' He noticed a sidling of her look. 'More than the circumstances oblige:—to be frank. But now we can speak of them. Wait—and the change comes; and opportunely, I have found. It's true we have waited long; my darling has had her worries. However, it 's here at last. Prepare yourself. I speak positively. You have to brace up for one sharp twitch—the woman's portion! as Natata says—and it's over.' He looked into her eyes for comprehension; and not finding inquiry, resumed: 'Just in time for the entry into Lakelands. With the pronouncement of the decree, we present the licence... at an altar we've stood before, in spirit... one of the ladies of your family to support you:—why not? Not even then?'

'No, Victor; they have cast me off.'

'Count on my cousins, the Duvidney ladies. Then we can say, that those two good old spinsters are less narrow than the Dreightons. I have to confess I rather think I was to blame for leaving Creckholt. Only, if I see my girl wounded, I hate the place that did the mischief. You and Fredi will clap hands for the country about Lakelands.'

'Have you heard from her... of her... is it anything, Victor?' Nataly asked him shyly; with not much of hope, but some readiness to be inflated. The prospect of an entry into the big new house, among a new society, begirt by the old nightmares and fretting devils, drew her into staring daylight or furnace-light.

He answered: 'Mrs. Burman has definitely decided. In pity of us?—to be free herself?—who can say! She 's a woman with a conscience—of a kind: slow, but it brings her to the point at last. You know her, know her well. Fenellan has it from her lawyer—her lawyer! a Mr. Carting; a thoroughly trustworthy man—'

'Fenellan, as a reporter?'

'Thoroughly to be trusted on serious matters. I understand that Mrs. Burman:—her health is awful: yes, yes; poor woman! poor woman! we feel for her:—she has come to perceive her duty to those she leaves behind. Consider: she HAS used the rod. She must be tired out—if human. And she is. One remembers traits.'

Victor sketched one or two of the traits allusively to the hearer acquainted with them. They received strong colouring from midday's Old Veuve in his blood. His voice and words had a swing of conviction: they imparted vinousness to a heart athirst.

The histrionic self-deceiver may be a persuasive deceiver of another, who is again, though not ignorant of his character, tempted to swallow the nostrums which have made so gallant a man of him: his imperceptible sensible playing of the part, on a substratum of sincereness, induces fascinatingly to the like performance on our side, that we may be armed as he is for enjoying the coveted reality through the partial simulation of possessing it. And this is not a task to us when we have looked our actor in the face, and seen him bear the look, knowing that he is not intentionally untruthful; and when we incline to be captivated by his rare theatrical air of confidence; when it seems as an outside thought striking us, that he may not be altogether deceived in the present instance; when suddenly an expectation of the thing desired is born and swims in a credible featureless vagueness on a misty scene: and when we are being kissed and the blood is warmed. In fine, here as everywhere along our history, when the sensations are spirited up to drown the mind, we become drift-matter of tides, metal to magnets. And if we are women, who commonly allow the lead to men, getting it for themselves only by snaky cunning or desperate adventure, credulity—the continued trust in the man—is the alternative of despair.

'But, Victor, I must ask,' Nataly said: 'you have it through Simeon Fenellan; you have not yourself received the letter from her lawyer?'

'My knowledge of what she would do near the grave—poor soul, yes! I shall soon be hearing.'

'You do not, propose to enter this place until—until it is over?'

'We enter this place, my love, without any sort of ceremony. We live there independently, and we can we have quarters there for our friends. Our one neighbour is London—there! And at Lakelands we are able to entertain London and wife;—our friends, in short; with some, what we have to call, satellites. You inspect the house and grounds to-morrow—sure to be fair. Put aside all but the pleasant recollections of Craye and Creckholt. We start on a different footing. Really nothing can be simpler. Keeping your town-house, you are now and then in residence at Lakelands, where you entertain your set, teach them to feel the charm of country life: we have everything about us; could have had our own milk and cream up to London the last two months. Was it very naughty?—I should have exploded my surprise! You will see, you will see to-morrow.'

Nataly nodded, as required. 'Good news from the mines?' she said.

He answered: 'Dartrey is—yes, poor fellow! Dartrey is confident, from the yield of stones, that the value of our claim counts in a number of millions. The same with the gold. But gold-mines are lodgeings, not homes.'

'Oh, Victor! if money...! But why did you say "poor fellow" of Dartrey Fenellan?'

'You know how he's...'

'Yes, yes,' she said hastily. 'But has that woman been causing fresh anxiety?'

'And Natata's chief hero on earth is not to be named a poor fellow,' said he, after a negative of the head on a subject they neither of them liked to touch.

Then he remembered that Dartrey Fenellan was actually a lucky fellow; and he would have mentioned the circumstance confided to him by Simeon, but for a downright dread of renewing his painful fit of envy. He had also another, more distant, very faint idea, that it had better not be mentioned just yet, for a reason entirely undefined.

He consulted his watch. The maid had come in for the robeing of her mistress. Nataly's mind had turned to the little country cottage which would have given her such great happiness. She raised her eyes to him; she could not check their filling; they were like a river carrying moonlight on the smooth roll of a fall.

He loved the eyes, disliked the water in them. With an impatient, 'There, there!' and a smart affectionate look, he retired, thinking in our old satirical vein of the hopeless endeavour to satisfy a woman's mind without the intrusion of hard material statements, facts. Even the best of women, even the most beautiful, and in their moments of supremest beauty, have this gross ravenousness for facts. You must not expect to appease them unless you administer solids. It would almost appear that man is exclusively imaginative and poetical; and that his mate, the fair, the graceful, the bewitching, with the sweetest and purest of natures, cannot help being something of a groveller.

Nataly had likewise her thoughts.

CHAPTER VII

BETWEEN A GENERAL MAN OF THIN WORLD AND A PROFESSIONAL

Rather earlier in the afternoon of that day, Simeon Fenellan, thinking of the many things which are nothing, and so melancholy for lack of amusements properly to follow Old Veuve, that he could ask himself whether he had not done a deed of night, to be blinking at his fellow-men like an owl all mad for the reveller's hoots and flights and mice and moony roundels behind his hypocritical judex air of moping composure, chanced on Mr. Carling, the solicitor, where Lincoln's Inn pumps lawyers into Fleet Street through the drain-pipe of Chancery Lane. He was in the state of the wine when a shake will rouse the sluggish sparkles to foam. Sight of Mrs. Burman's legal adviser had instantly this effect upon him: his bubbling friendliness for Victor Radnor, and the desire of the voice in his bosom for ears to hear, combined like the rush of two waves together, upon which he may be figured as the boat: he caught at Mr. Carling's hand more heartily than their acquaintanceship quite sanctioned; but his grasp and his look of overflowing were immediately privileged; Mr. Carling, enjoying this anecdotal gentleman's conversation as he did, liked the warmth, and was flattered during the squeeze with a prospect of his wife and friends partaking of the fun from time to time.

'I was telling my wife yesterday your story of the lady contrabandist: I don't think she has done laughing since,' Mr. Calling said.

Fenellan fluted: 'Ah?' He had scent, in the eulogy of a story grown flat as Election hats, of a good sort of man in the way of men, a step or two behind the man of the world. He expressed profound regret at not having heard the silvery ring of the lady's laughter.

Carling genially conceived a real gratification to be conferred on his wife. 'Perhaps you will some day honour us?'

'You spread gold-leaf over the days to come, sir.'

'Now, if I might name the day?'

'You lump the gold and make it current coin;—says the blushing bride, who ought not to have delivered herself so boldly, but she had forgotten her bashful part and spoilt the scene, though, luckily for the damsel, her swain was a lover of nature, and finding her at full charge, named the very next day of the year, and held her to it, like the complimentary tyrant he was.'

'To-morrow, then!' said Carling intrepidly, on a dash of enthusiasm, through a haggard thought of his wife and the cook and the netting of friends at short notice. He urged his eagerness to ask whether he might indeed have the satisfaction of naming to-morrow.

'With happiness,' Fenellan responded.

Mrs. Carling was therefore in for it.

'To-morrow, half-past seven: as for company to meet you, we will do what we can. You go Westward?'

'To bed with the sun,' said the reveller.

'Perhaps by Covent Garden? I must give orders there.'

'Orders given in Covent Garden, paint a picture for bachelors of the domestic Paradise an angel must help them to enter! Ah, dear me! Is there anything on earth to compare with the pride of a virtuous life?'

'I was married at four and twenty,' said Carling, as one taking up the expository second verse of a poem; plain facts, but weighty and necessary: 'my wife was in her twentieth year: we have five children; two sons, three daughters, one married, with a baby. So we are grandfather and mother, and have never regretted the first step, I may say for both of us.'

'Think of it! Good luck and sagacity joined hands overhead on the day you proposed to the lady: and I'd say, that all the credit is with her, but that it would seem to be at the expense of her sex.'

'She would be the last to wish it, I assure you.'

'True of all good women! You encourage me, touching a matter of deep interest, not unknown to you. The lady's warm heart will be with us. Probably she sees Mrs. Burman?'

'Mrs. Burman Radnor receives no one.'

A comic severity in the tone of the correction was deferentially accepted by Fenellan.

'Pardon. She flies her flag, with her captain wanting; and she has, queerly, the right. So, then, the worthy dame who receives no one, might be treated, it struck us, conversationally, as a respectable harbour-hulk, with more history than top-honours. But she has the indubitable legal right to fly them—to proclaim it; for it means little else.'

'You would have her, if I follow you, divest herself of the name?'

'Pin me to no significations, if you please, O shrewdest of the legal sort! I have wit enough to escape you there. She is no doubt an estimable person.'

'Well, she is; she is in her way a very good woman.'

'Ah. You see, Mr. Carling, I cannot bring myself to rank her beside another lady, who has already claimed the title of me; and you will forgive me if I say, that your word "good" has a look of being stuck upon the features we know of her, like a coquette's naughty patch; or it's a jewel of an eye in an ebony idol: though I've heard tell she performs her charities.'

'I believe she gives away three parts of her income and that is large.'

'Leaving the good lady a fine fat fourth.'

'Compare her with other wealthy people.'

'And does she outshine the majority still with her personal attractions.

Carling was instigated by the praise he had bestowed on his wife to separate himself from a female pretender so ludicrous; he sought Fenellan's nearest ear, emitting the sound of 'hum.'

'In other respects, unimpeachable!'

'Oh! quite!'

'There was a fishfag of classic Billingsgate, who had broken her husband's nose with a sledgehammer fist, and swore before the magistrate, that the man hadn't a crease to complain of in her character. We are condemned, Mr. Carling, sometimes to suffer in the flesh for the assurance we receive of the inviolability of those moral fortifications.'

'Character, yes, valuable—I do wish you had named to-night for doing me the honour of dining with me!' said the lawyer impulsively, in a rapture of the appetite for anecdotes. 'I have a ripe Pichon Longueville, '65.'

'A fine wine. Seductive to hear of. I dine with my friend Victor Radnor. And he knows wine.—There are good women in the world, Mr. Carling, whose characters...'

'Of course, of course there are; and I could name you some. We lawyers...!'

'You encounter all sorts.'

'Between ourselves,' Carling sank his tones to the indiscriminate, where it mingled with the roar of London.

'You do?' Fenellan hazarded a guess at having heard enlightened liberal opinions regarding the sex. 'Right!'

'Many!'

'I back you, Mr. Carling.'

The lawyer pushed to yet more confidential communication, up to the verge of the clearly audible: he spoke of examples, experiences. Fenellan backed him further.

'Acting on behalf of clients, you understand, Mr. Fenellan.'

'Professional, but charitable; I am with you.'

'Poor things! we—if we have to condemn—we owe them something.'

'A kind word for poor Polly Venus, with all the world against her! She doesn't hear it often.'

'A real service,' Carling's voice deepened to the legal 'without prejudice,'—'I am bound to say it—a service to Society.'

'Ah, poor wench! And the kind of reward she gets?'

'We can hardly examine... mysterious dispensations... here we are to make the best we can of it.'

'For the creature Society's indebted to? True. And am I to think there's a body of legal gentlemen to join with you, my friend, in founding an Institution to distribute funds to preach charity over the country, and win compassion for her, as one of the principal persons of her time, that Society's indebted to for whatever it's indebted for?'

'Scarcely that,' said Carling, contracting.

'But you 're for great Reforms?'

'Gradual.'

'Then it's for Reformatories, mayhap.'

'They would hardly be a cure.'

'You 're in search of a cure?'

'It would be a blessed discovery.'

'But what's to become of Society?'

'It's a puzzle to the cleverest.'

'All through History, my dear Mr. Carling, we see that.

'Establishments must have their sacrifices. Beware of interfering: eh?'

'By degrees, we may hope....'

'Society prudently shuns the topic; and so 'll we. For we might tell of one another, in a fit of distraction, that t' other one talked of it, and we should be banished for an offence against propriety. You should read my friend Durance's Essay on Society. Lawyers are a buttress of Society. But, come: I wager they don't know what they support until they read that Essay.'

Carling had a pleasant sense of escape, in not being personally asked to read the Essay, and not hearing that a copy of it should be forwarded to him.

He said: 'Mr. Radnor is a very old friend?'

'Our fathers were friends; they served in the same regiment for years. I was in India when Victor Radnor took the fatal!'

'Followed by a second, not less...?'

'In the interpretation of a rigid morality arming you legal gentlemen to make it so!'

'The Law must be vindicated.'

'The law is a clumsy bludgeon.'

'We think it the highest effort of human reason—the practical instrument.'

'You may compare it to a rustic's finger on a fiddlestring, for the murdered notes you get out of the practical instrument.

'I am bound to defend it, clumsy bludgeon or not.'

'You are one of the giants to wield it, and feel humanly, when, by chance, down it comes on the foot an inch off the line.—Here's a peep of Old London; if the habit of old was not to wash windows. I like these old streets!'

'Hum,' Carling hesitated. 'I can remember when the dirt at the windows was appalling.'

'Appealing to the same kind of stuff in the passing youngster's green-scum eye: it was. And there your Law did good work.—You're for Bordeaux. What is your word on Burgundy?'

'Our Falernian!'

'Victor Radnor has the oldest in the kingdom. But he will have the best of everything. A Romanee! A Musigny! Sip, my friend, you embrace the Goddess of your choice above. You are up beside her at a sniff of that wine.—And lo, venerable Drury! we duck through the court, reminded a bit by our feelings of our first love, who hadn't the cleanest of faces or nicest of manners, but she takes her station in memory because we were boys then, and the golden halo of youth is upon her.'

Carling, as a man of the world, acquiesced in souvenirs he did not share. He said urgently: 'Understand me; you speak of Mr. Radnor; pray, believe I have the greatest respect for Mr. Radnor's abilities. He is one of our foremost men... proud of him. Mr. Radnor has genius; I have watched him; it is genius; he shows it in all he does; one of the memorable men of our times. I can admire him, independent of— well, misfortune of that kind... a mistaken early step. Misfortune, it is to be named. Between ourselves— we are men of the world—if one could see the way! She occasionally... as I have told you. I have ventured suggestions. As I have mentioned, I have received an impression...'

'But still, Mr. Carling, if the lady doesn't release him and will keep his name, she might stop her cowardly persecutions.'

'Can you trace them?'

'Undisguised!'

'Mrs. Burman Radnor is devout. I should not exactly say revengeful. We have to discriminate. I gather, that her animus is, in all honesty, directed at the—I quote—state of sin. We are mixed, you know.'

The Winegod in the blood of Fenellan gave a leap. 'But, fifty thousand times more mixed, she might any moment stop the state of sin, as she calls it, if it pleased her.'

'She might try. Our Judges look suspiciously on long delayed actions. And there are, too, women who regard the marriage-tie as indissoluble. She has had to combat that scruple.'

'Believer in the renewing of the engagement overhead!—well. But put a by-word to Mother Nature about the state of sin. Where, do you imagine, she would lay it? You'll say, that Nature and Law never agreed. They ought.'

'The latter deferring to the former?'

'Moulding itself on her swelling proportions. My dear dear sir, the state of sin was the continuing to live in defiance of, in contempt of, in violation of, in the total degradation of, Nature.'

'He was under no enforcement to take the oath at the altar.'

'He was a small boy tempted by a varnished widow, with pounds of barley sugar in her pockets;—and she already serving as a test-vessel or mortar for awful combinations in druggery! Gilt widows are equal to decrees of Fate to us young ones. Upon my word, the cleric who unites, and the Law that sanctions, they're the criminals. Victor Radnor is the noblest of fellows, the very best friend a man can have. I will tell you: he saved me, after I left the army, from living on the produce of my pen—which means, if there is to be any produce, the prostrating of yourself to the level of the round middle of the public: saved me from that! Yes, Mr. Carling, I have trotted our thoroughfares a poor Polly of the pen; and it is owing to Victor Radnor that I can order my thoughts as an individual man again before I blacken paper. Owing to him, I have a tenderness for mercenaries; having been one of them and knowing how little we can help it. He is an Olympian—who thinks of them below. The lady also is an admirable woman at all points. The pair are a mated couple, such as you won't find in ten households over Christendom. Are you aware of the story?'

Carling replied: 'A story under shadow of the Law, has generally two very distinct versions.'

'Hear mine.—And, by Jove! a runaway cab. No, all right. But a crazy cab it is, and fit to do mischief in narrow Drury. Except that it's sheer riff-raff here to knock over.'

'Hulloa?—come!' quoth the wary lawyer.

'There's the heart I wanted to rouse to hear me! One may be sure that the man for old Burgundy has it big and sound, in spite of his legal practices; a dear good spherical fellow! Some day, we'll hope, you will be sitting with us over a magnum of Victor Radnor's Romance Conti aged thirty-one: a wine, you'll say at the second glass, High Priest for the celebration of the uncommon nuptials between the body and the soul of man.'

'You hit me rightly,' said Carting, tickled and touched; sensually excited by the bouquet of Victor Radnor's hospitality and companionship, which added flavour to Fenellan's compliments. These came home to him through his desire to be the 'good spherical fellow'; for he, like modern diplomatists in the track of their eminent Berlinese New Type of the time, put on frankness as an armour over wariness, holding craft in reserve: his aim was at the refreshment of honest fellowship: by no means to discover that the coupling of his native bias with his professional duty was unprofitable nowadays. Wariness, however, was not somnolent, even when he said: 'You know, I am never the lawyer out of my office. Man of the world to men of the world; and I have not lost by it. I am Mrs. Barman Radnor's legal adviser: you are Mr. Victor Radnor's friend. They are, as we see them, not on the best of terms. I would rather—at its lowest, as a matter of business—be known for having helped them to some kind of footing than send in a round bill to my client—or another. I gain more in the end. Frankly, I mean to prove, that it's a lawyer's interest to be human.'

'Because, now, see!' said Fenellan, 'here's the case. Miss Natalia Dreighton, of a good Yorkshire family—a large one, reads an advertisement for the post of companion to a lady, and answers it, and engages herself, previous to the appearance of the young husband. Miss Dreighton is one of the finest young women alive. She has a glorious contralto voice. Victor and she are encouraged by Mrs. Barman to sing duets together. Well?

Why, Euclid would have theorem'd it out for you at a glance at the trio. You have only to look on them, you chatter out your three Acts of a Drama without a stop. If Mrs. Barman cares to practise charity, she has only to hold in her Fury-forked tongue, or her Jarniman I think 's the name.'

Carting shrugged.

'Let her keep from striking, if she's Christian,' pursued Fenetlan, 'and if kind let her resume the name of her first lord, who did a better thing for himself than for her, when he shook off his bars of bullion, to rise the lighter, and left a wretched female soul below, with the devil's own testimony to her attractions—thousands in the Funds, houses in the City. She threw the young couple together. And my friend Victor Radnor is of a particularly inflammable nature. Imagine one of us in such a situation, Mr. Carting!'

'Trying!' said the lawyer.

'The dear fellow was as nigh death as a man can be and know the sweetness of a woman's call to him to live. And here's London's garden of pines, bananas, oranges; all the droppings of the Hesperides here! We don't reflect on it, Mr. Carling.'

'Not enough, not enough.'

'I feel such a spout of platitudes that I could out With a Leading Article on a sheet of paper on your back while you're bending over the baskets. I seem to have got circularly round again to Eden when I enter a garden. Only, here we have to pay for the fruits we pluck. Well, and just the same there; and no end to the payment either. We're always paying! By the way, Mrs. Victor Radnor's dinner-table's a spectacle. Her taste in flowers equals her lord's in wine. But age improves the wine and spoils the flowers, you'll say. Maybe you're for arguing that lovely women show us more of the flower than the grape, in relation to the course of time. I pray you not to forget the terrible intoxicant she is. We reconcile it, Mr. Carling, with the notion that the grape's her spirit, the flower her body. Or is it the reverse? Perhaps an intertwining. But look upon bouquets and clusters, and the idea of woman springs up at once, proving she's composed of them. I was about to remark, that with deference to the influence of Mrs. Burman's legal adviser, an impenitent or penitent sinner's pastor, the Reverend gentleman ministering to her spiritual needs, would presumptively exercise it, in this instance, in a superior degree.'

Carling murmured: 'The Rev. Groseman Buttermore'; and did so for something of a cover, to continue a run of internal reflections: as, that he was assuredly listening to vinous talk in the streets by day; which impression placed him on a decorous platform above the amusing gentleman; to whom, however, he grew cordial, in recognizing consequently, that his exuberant flow could hardly be a mask; and that an indication here and there of a trap in his talk, must have been due rather to excess of wariness, habitual in the mind of a long-headed man, whose incorrigibly impulsive fits had necessarily to be rectified by a vigilant dexterity.

'Buttermore!' ejaculated Fenellan: 'Groseman Buttermore! Mrs. Victor's Father Confessor is the Rev. Septimus Barmby. Groseman Buttermore—Septimus Barmby. Is there anything in names? Truly, unless these clerical gentlemen take them up at the crossing of the roads long after birth, the names would appear the active parts of them, and themselves mere marching supports, like the bearers of street placard-advertisements. Now, I know a Septimus Barmby, and you a Groseman Buttermore, and beyond the fact that Reverend starts up before their names without mention, I wager it's about all we do know of them. They're Society's trusty rock-limpets, no doubt.'

'My respect for the cloth is extreme.' Carling's short cough prepared the way for deductions. 'Between ourselves, they are men of the world.'

Fenellan eyed benevolently the worthy attorney, whose innermost imp burst out periodically, like a Dutch clocksentry, to trot on his own small grounds for thinking himself of the community of the man of the world. 'You lawyers dress in another closet,' he said. 'The Rev. Groseman has the ear of the lady?'

'He has:—one ear.'

'Ah? She has the other open for a man of the world, perhaps.'

'Listens to him, listens to me, listens to Jarniman; and we neither of us guide her. She's very curious—a study. You think you know her—next day she has eluded you. She's emotional, she's hard; she's a woman, she's a stone. Anything you like; but don't count on her. And another thing—I'm bound to say it of myself,' Carling claimed close hearing of Fenellan over a shelf of saladstuff, 'no one who comes near her has any real weight with her in this matter.'

'Probably you mix cream in your salad of the vinegar and oil,' said Fenellan. 'Try jelly of mutton.'—'You give me a new idea. Latterly, fond as I am of salads, I've had rueful qualms. We'll try it.'

'You should dine with Victor Radnor.'

'French cook, of course!'

'Cordon bleu.'

'I like to be sure of my cutlet.'

'I like to be sure of a tastiness in my vegetables.'

'And good sauces!'

'And pretty pastry. I said, Cordon bleu. The miracle is, it 's a woman that Victor Radnor has trained: French, but a woman; devoted to him, as all who serve him are. Do I say "but" a woman? There's not a Frenchman alive to match her. Vatel awaits her in Paradise with his arms extended; and may he wait long!'

Carling indulged his passion for the genuine by letting a flutter of real envy be seen. 'My wife would like to meet such a Frenchwoman. It must be a privilege to dine with him—to know him. I know what he has done for English Commerce, and to build a colossal fortune: genius, as I said: and his donations to Institutions. Odd, to read his name and Mrs. Burman Radnor's at separate places in the lists! Well, we'll hope. It's a case for a compromise of sentiments and claims.'

'A friend of mine, spiced with cynic, declares that there's always an amicable way out of a dissension, if we get rid of Lupus and Vulpus.'

Carling spied for a trap in the citation of Lupus and Vulpus; he saw none, and named the square of his residence on the great Russell property, and the number of the house, the hour of dinner next day. He then hung silent, breaking the pause with his hand out and a sharp 'Well?' that rattled a whirligig sound in his head upward. His leave of people was taken in this laughing falsetto, as of one affected by the curious end things come to.

Fenellan thought of him for a moment or two, that he was a better than the common kind of lawyer; who doubtless knew as much of the wrong side of the world as lawyers do, and held his knowledge for the being a man of the world:—as all do, that have not Alpine heights in the mind to mount for a look out over their own and the world's pedestrian tracks. I could spot the lawyer in your composition, my friend, to the exclusion of the man he mused. But you're right in what you mean to say of yourself: you're a good fellow, for a lawyer, and together we may manage somehow to score a point of service to Victor Radnor.

CHAPTER VIII

SOME FAMILIAR GUESTS

Nesta read her mother's face when Mrs. Victor entered the drawing-room to receive the guests. She saw a smooth fair surface, of the kind as much required by her father's eyes as innocuous air by his nostrils: and it was honest skin, not the deceptive feminine veiling, to make a dear man happy over his volcano. Mrs. Victor was to meet the friends with whom her feelings were at home, among whom her musical gifts gave her station: they liked her for herself; they helped her to feel at home with herself and be herself: a rarer condition with us all than is generally supposed. So she could determine to be cheerful in the anticipation of an evening that would at least be restful to the outworn sentinel nerve of her heart, which was perpetually alert and signalling to the great organ; often colouring the shows and seems of adverse things for an apeing of reality with too cruel a resemblance. One of the scraps of practical wisdom gained by hardened sufferers is, to keep from spying at horizons when they drop into a pleasant dingle. Such is the comfort of it, that we can dream, and lull our fears, and half think what we wish: and it is a heavenly truce with the fretful mind divided from our wishes.

Nesta wondered at her mother's complacent questions concerning this Lakelands: the house, the county, the kind of people about, the features of the country. Physically unable herself to be regretful under a burden three parts enrapturing her, the girl expected her mother to display a shadowy vexation, with a proud word or two, that would summon her thrilling sympathy in regard to the fourth part: namely, the aristocratic iciness of country magnates, who took them up and cast them off; as they had done, she thought, at Craye Farm and at Creckholt: she remembered it, of the latter place, wincingly, insurgently, having loved the dear home she had been expelled from by her pride of the frosty surrounding people—or no, not all, but some of them. And what had roused their pride?

Striking for a reason, her inexperience of our modern England, supplemented by readings in the England of a preceding generation, had hit on her father's profession of merchant. It accounted to her for the behaviour of the haughty territorial and titled families. But certain of the minor titles headed City Firms, she had heard; certain of the families were avowedly commercial. 'They follow suit,' her father said at Creckholt, after he had found her mother weeping, and decided instantly to quit and fly once more. But if they followed suit in such a way, then Mr. Durance must be right when he called the social English the most sheepy of sheep:—and Nesta could not consent to the cruel verdict, she adored her compatriots. Incongruities were pacified for her by the suggestion of her quick wits, that her father, besides being a merchant, was a successful speculator; and perhaps the speculator is not liked by merchants; or they were jealous of him; or they did not like his being both.

She pardoned them with some tenderness, on a suspicion that a quaint old high-frilled bleached and puckered Puritanical rectitude (her thoughts rose in pictures) possibly condemned the speculator as a description of gambler. An erratic severity in ethics is easily overlooked by the enthusiast for things old English. She was consciously ahead of them in the knowledge that her father had been, without the taint of gambling, a beneficent speculator. The Montgomery colony in South Africa, and his dealings with the natives in India, and his Railways in South America, his establishment of Insurance Offices, which were Savings Banks, and the Stores for the dispensing of sound goods to the poor, attested it. O and he was hospitable, the kindest, helpfullest of friends, the dearest, the very brightest of parents: he was his girl's playmate. She could be critic of him, for an induction to the loving of him more justly: yet if he had an excessive desire to win the esteem of people, as these keen young optics perceived in him, he strove to deserve it; and no one could accuse him of laying stress on the benefits he conferred. Designedly, frigidly to wound a man so benevolent, appeared to her as an incomprehensible baseness. The dropping of acquaintanceship with him, after the taste of its privileges, she ascribed, in the void of any better elucidation, to a mania of aristocratic conceit. It drove her, despite her youthful contempt of politics, into a Radicalism that could find food in the epigrams of Mr. Colney Durance, even when they passed her understanding; or when he was not too distinctly seen by her to be shooting at all the parties of her beloved England, beneath the wicked semblance of shielding each by turns.

The young gentleman introduced to the Radnor Concert-parties by Lady Grace Halley as the Hon. Dudley Sowerby, had to bear the sins of his class. Though he was tall, straight-featured, correct in costume, appearance, deportment, second son of a religious earl and no scandal to the parentage, he was less noticed by Nesta than the elderly and the commoners. Her father accused her of snubbing him. She reproduced her famous copy of the sugared acid of Mr. Dudley Sowerby's closed mouth: a sort of sneer in meekness, as of humility under legitimate compulsion; deploring Christianly a pride of race that stamped it for this cowled exhibition: the wonderful mimicry was a flash thrown out by a born mistress of the art, and her mother was constrained to laugh, and so was her father; but he wilfully denied the likeness. He charged her with encouraging Colney Durance to drag forth the sprig of nobility, in the nakedness of evicted shell-fish, on themes of the peril to England, possibly ruin, through the loss of that ruling initiative formerly possessed, in the days of our glory, by the titular nobles of the land. Colney spoke it effectively, and the Hon. Dudley's expressive lineaments showed print of the heaving word Alas, as when a target is penetrated, centrally. And he was not a particularly dull fellow 'for his class and country,' Colney admitted; adding: 'I hit his thought and out he came.' One has, reluctantly with Victor Radnor, to grant, that when a man's topmost unspoken thought is hit, he must be sharp on his guard to keep from coming out:—we have won a right to him.

'Only, it's too bad; it's a breach of hospitality,' Victor said, both to Nesta and to Nataly, alluding to several instances of Colney's ironic handling of their guests, especially of this one, whom Nesta would attack, and Nataly would not defend.

They were alive at a signal to protect the others. Miss Priscilla Graves, an eater of meat, was ridiculous in her ant'alcoholic exclusiveness and scorn: Mr. Pempton, a drinker of wine, would laud extravagantly the more transparent purity of vegetarianism. Dr. Peter Yatt jeered at globules: Dr. John Cormyn mourned over human creatures treated as cattle by big doses. The Rev. Septimus Barmby satisfactorily smoked: Mr. Peridon traced mortal evil to that act. Dr. Schlesien had his German views, Colney Durance his ironic, Fenellan his fanciful and free-lance. And here was an optimist, there a pessimist; and the rank Radical, the rigid Conservative, were not wanting. All of them were pointedly opposed, extraordinarily for so small an assembly: absurdly, it might be thought: but these provoked a kind warm smile, with the exclamation: 'They are dears!' They were the dearer for their fads and foibles.

Music harmonized them. Music, strangely, put the spell on Colney Durance, the sayer of bitter things, manufacturer of prickly balls, in the form of Discord's apples of whom Fenellan remarked, that he took to his music like an angry little boy to his barley-sugar, with a growl and a grunt. All these diverse friends could meet and mix in Victor's Concert-room with an easy homely recognition of one another's musical qualities, at times enthusiastic; and their natural divergencies and occasional clashes added a salient tastiness to the group of whom Nesta could say: 'Mama, was there ever such a collection of dear good souls with such contrary minds?' Her mother had the deepest of reasons for loving them, so as not to wish to see the slightest change in their minds, that the accustomed features making her nest of homeliness and real peace might be retained, with the humour of their funny silly antagonisms and the subsequent march in concord; excepting solely as regarded the perverseness of Priscilla Graves in her open contempt of Mr. Pempton's innocent two or three wine-glasses. The vegetarian gentleman's politeness forbore to direct attention to the gobbets of meat Priscilla consumed, though he could express disapproval in general terms; but he entertained sentiments as warlike to the lady's habit of 'drinking the blood of animals.' The mockery of it was, that Priscilla liked Mr. Pempton and admired his violoncello-playing, and he was unreserved in eulogy of her person and her pure soprano tones. Nataly was a poetic match-maker. Mr. Peridon was intended for Mademoiselle de Seilles, Nesta's young French governess; a lady of a courtly bearing, with placid speculation in the eyes she cast on a foreign people, and a voluble muteness shadowing at intervals along the line of her closed lips.

The one person among them a little out of tune with most, was Lady Grace Halley. Nataly's provincial gentlewoman's traditions of the manners indicating conduct, reproved unwonted licences assumed by Lady Grace; who, in allusion to Hymen's weaving of a cousinship between the earldom of Southweare and that of Cantor, of which Mr. Sowerby sprang, set her mouth and fan at work to delineate total distinctions, as it were from the egg to the empyrean. Her stature was rather short, all of it conversational, at the eyebrows, the shoulders, the finger-tips, the twisting shape; a ballerina's expressiveness; and her tongue dashed half sentences through and among these hieroglyphs, loosely and funnily candid. Anybody might hear that she had gone gambling into the City, and that she had got herself into a mess, and that by great good luck she had come across Victor Radnor, who, with two turns of the wrist, had plucked her out of the mire, the miraculous man! And she had vowed to him, never again to run doing the like without his approval.

The cause of her having done it, was related with the accompaniments; brows twitching, flitting smiles, shrugs, pouts, shifts of posture: she was married to a centaur; out of the saddle a man of wood, 'an excellent man.' For the not colloquial do not commit themselves. But one wants a little animation in a husband. She called on bell-motion of the head to toll forth the utter nightcap negative. He had not any: out of the saddle, he was asleep:—'next door to the Last Trump,' Colney Durance assisted her to describe the soundest of sleep in a husband, after wooing her to unbosom herself. She was awake to his guileful arts, and sailed along with him, hailing his phrases, if he shot a good one; prankishly exposing a flexible nature, that took its holiday thus in a grinding world, among maskers, to the horrification of the prim. So to refresh ourselves, by having publicly a hip-bath in the truth while we shock our hearers enough to be discredited for what we reveal, was a dexterous merry twist, amusing to her; but it was less a cynical malice than her nature that she indulged, 'A woman must have some excitement.' The most innocent appeared to her the Stock Exchange. The opinions of husbands who are not summoned to pay are hardly important; they vary.

Colney helped her now and then to step the trifle beyond her stride, but if he was humorous, she forgave; and if together they appalled the decorous, it was great gain. Her supple person, pretty lips, the style she had, gave a pass to the wondrous confidings, which were for masculine ears, whatever the sex. Nataly might share in them, but women did not lead her to expansiveness; or not the women of the contracted class: Miss Graves, Mrs. Cormyn, and others at the Radnor Concerts. She had a special consideration for Mademoiselle de Seilles, owing to her exquisite French, as she said; and she may have liked it, but it was the young Frenchwoman's air of high breeding that won her esteem. Girls were spring frosts to her. Fronting Nesta, she put on her noted smile, or wood-cut of a smile, with its label of indulgence; except when the girl sang. Music she loved. She said it was the saving of poor Dudley. It distinguished him in the group of the noble Evangelical Cantor Family; and it gave him a subject of assured discourse in company; and oddly, it contributed to his comelier air. Flute [This would be the German Blockeflute or our Recorder. D.W.] in hand, his mouth at the blow-stop was relieved of its pained updraw by the form for puffing; he preserved a gentlemanly high figure in his exercises on the instrument, out of ken of all likeness to the urgent insistency of Victor Radnor's punctuating trunk of the puffing frame at almost every bar—an Apollo brilliancy in energetic pursuit of the nymph of sweet sound. Too methodical one, too fiery the other.

In duets of Hauptmann's, with Nesta at the piano, the contrast of dull smoothness and overstressed significance was very noticeable beside the fervent accuracy of her balanced fingering; and as she could also flute, she could criticize; though latterly, the flute was boxed away from lips that had devoted themselves wholly to song: song being one of the damsel's present pressing ambitions. She found nothing to correct in Mr. Sowerby, and her father was open to all the censures; but her father could plead vitality, passion. He held his performances cheap after the vehement display; he was a happy listener, whether to the babble of his 'dear old Corelli,' or to the majesty of the rattling heavens and swaying forests of Beethoven.

His air of listening was a thing to see; it had a look of disembodiment; the sparkle conjured up from deeps, and the life in the sparkle, as of a soul at holiday. Eyes had been given this man to spy the pleasures and reveal the joy of his pasture on them: gateways to the sunny within, issues to all the outer Edens. Few of us possess that double significance of the pure sparkle. It captivated Lady Grace. She said a word of it to Fenellan: 'There is a man who can feel rapture!' He had not to follow the line of her sight: she said so on a previous evening, in a similar tone; and for a woman to repeat herself, using the very emphasis, was quaint. She could feel rapture; but her features and limbs were in motion to designate it, between simply and wilfully; she had the instinct to be dimpling, and would not for a moment control it, and delighted in its effectiveness: only when observing that winged sparkle of eyes did an idea of envy, hardly a consciousness, inform her of being surpassed; and it might be in the capacity to feel besides the gift to express. Such a reflection relating to a man, will make women mortally sensible that they are the feminine of him.

'His girl has the look,' Fenellan said in answer.

She cast a glance at Nesta, then at Nataly.

And it was true, that the figure of a mother, not pretending to the father's vividness, eclipsed it somewhat in their child. The mother gave richness of tones, hues and voice, and stature likewise, and the thick brown locks, which in her own were threads of gold along the brush from the temples: she gave the girl a certain degree of the composure of manner which Victor could not have bestowed; she gave nothing to clash with his genial temper; she might be supposed to have given various qualities, moral if you like. But vividness was Lady Grace's admirable meteor of the hour: she was unable to perceive, so as to compute, the value of obscurer lights. Under the charm of Nataly's rich contralto during a duet with Priscilla Graves, she gesticulated ecstasies, and uttered them, and genuinely; and still, when reduced to meditations, they would have had no weight, they would hardly have seemed an apology for language, beside Victor's gaze of pleasure in the noble forthroll of the notes.

Nataly heard the invitation of the guests of the evening to Lakelands next day.

Her anxieties were at once running about to gather provisions for the baskets. She spoke of them at night. But Victor had already put the matter in the hands of Madame Callet; and all that could be done, would be done by Armandine, he knew. 'If she can't muster enough at home, she'll be off to her Piccadilly shop by seven A.M. Count on plenty for twice the number.'

Nataly was reposing on the thought that they were her friends, when Victor mentioned his having in the afternoon despatched a note to his relatives, the Duvidney ladies, inviting them to join him at the station to-morrow, for a visit of inspection to the house of his building on his new estate. He startled her. The Duvidney ladies were, to his knowledge, of the order of the fragile minds which hold together by the cement of a common trepidation for the support of things established, and have it not in them to be able to recognize the unsanctioned. Good women, unworldly of the world, they were perforce harder than the world, from being narrower and more timorous.

'But, Victor, you were sure they would refuse!'

He answered: 'They may have gone back to Tunbridge Wells. By the way, they have a society down there I want for Fredi. Sure, do you say, my dear? Perfectly sure. But the accumulation of invitations and refusals in the end softens them, you will see. We shall and must have them for Fredi.'

She was used to the long reaches of his forecasts, his burning activity on a project; she found it idle to speak her thought, that his ingenuity would have been needless in a position dictated by plain prudence, and so much happier for them.

They talked of Mrs. Burman until she had to lift a prayer to be saved from darker thoughts, dreadfully prolific, not to be faced. Part of her prayer was on behalf of Mrs. Burman, for life to be extended to her, if the poor lady clung to life—if it was really humane to wish it for her: and heaven would know: heaven had mercy on the afflicted.

Nataly heard the snuffle of hypocrisy in her prayer. She had to cease to pray.

CHAPTER IX

AN INSPECTION OF LAKELANDS

One may not have an intention to flourish, and may be pardoned for a semblance of it, in exclaiming, somewhat royally, as creator and owner of the place: 'There you see Lakelands.'

The conveyances from the railway station drew up on a rise of road fronting an undulation, where our modern English architect's fantasia in crimson brick swept from central gables to flying wings, over pents, crooks, curves, peaks, cowled porches, balconies, recesses, projections, away to a red village of stables and dependent cottages; harmonious in irregularity; and coloured homely with the greensward about it, the pines beside it, the clouds above it. Not many palaces would be reckoned as larger. The folds and swells and stream of the building along the roll of ground, had an appearance of an enormous banner on the wind. Nataly looked. Her next look was at Colney Durance. She sent the expected nods to Victor's carriage. She would have given the whole prospect for the covering solitariness of her chamber. A multitude of clashing sensations, and a throat-thickening hateful to her, compelled her to summon so as to force herself to feel a groundless anger, directed against none, against nothing, perfectly crazy, but her only resource for keeping down the great wave surgent at her eyes.

Victor was like a swimmer in morning sea amid the exclamations encircling him. He led through the straight passage of the galleried hall, offering two fair landscapes at front door and at back, down to the lake, Fredi's lake; a good oblong of water, notable in a district not abounding in the commodity. He would have it a feature of the district; and it had been deepened and extended; up rose the springs, many ran the ducts. Fredi's pretty little bathshed or bower had a space of marble on the three-feet shallow it overhung with a shade of carved woodwork; it had a diving-board for an eight-feet plunge; a punt and small row-boat of elegant build hard by. Green ran the banks about, and a beechwood fringed with birches curtained the Northward length: morning sun and evening had a fair face of water to paint. Saw man ever the like for pleasing a poetical damsel? So was Miss Fredi, the coldest of the party hitherto, and dreaming a preference of 'old places' like Creckholt and Craye Farm, 'captured to be enraptured,' quite according to man's ideal of his beneficence to the sex. She pressed the hand of her young French governess, Louise de Seilles. As in everything he did for his girl, Victor pointed boastfully to his forethought of her convenience and her tastes: the pine-panels of the interior, the shelves for her books, pegs to hang her favourite drawings, and the couch-bunk under a window to conceal the summerly recliner while throwing full light on her book; and the hearth-square for logs, when she wanted fire: because Fredi bathed in any weather: the oaken towel-coffer; the wood-carvings of doves, tits, fishes; the rod for the flowered silken hangings she was to choose, and have shy odalisque peeps of sunny water from her couch.

'Fredi's Naiad retreat, when she wishes to escape Herr Strauscher or Signor Ruderi,' said Victor, having his grateful girl warm in an arm; 'and if they head after her into the water, I back her to leave them puffing; she's a dolphin. That water has three springs and gets all the drainage of the upland round us. I chose the place chiefly on account of it and the pines. I do love pines!'

'But, excellent man! what do you not love?' said Lady Grace, with the timely hit upon the obvious, which rings.

'It saves him from accumulation of tissue,' said Colney.

'What does?' was eagerly asked by the wife of the homoeopathic Dr. John Cormyn, a sentimental lady beset with fears of stoutness.

Victor cried: 'Tush; don't listen to Colney, pray.'

But she heard Colney speak of a positive remedy; more immediately effective than an abjuration of potatoes and sugar. She was obliged by her malady to listen, although detesting the irreverent ruthless man, who could direct expanding frames, in a serious tone, to love; love everybody, everything; violently and universally love; and so without intermission pay out the fat created by a rapid assimilation of nutriment. Obeseness is the most sensitive of our ailments: probably as being aware, that its legitimate appeal to pathos is ever smothered in its pudding-bed of the grotesque. She was pained, and showed it, and was ashamed of herself for showing it; and that very nearly fetched the tear.

'Our host is an instance in proof,' Colney said. He waved hand at the house. His meaning was hidden; evidently he wanted victims. Sight of Lakelands had gripped him with the fell satiric itch; and it is a passion to sting and tear, on rational grounds. His face meanwhile, which had points of the handsome, signified a smile asleep, as if beneath a cloth. Only those who knew him well were aware of the claw-like alertness under the droop of eyelids.

Admiration was the common note, in the various keys. The station selected for the South-eastward aspect of the dark-red gabled pile on its white shell-terrace, backed by a plantation of tall pines, a mounded and full-plumed company, above the left wing, was admired, in files and in volleys. Marvellous, effectively miraculous, was the tale of the vow to have the great edifice finished within one year: and the strike of workmen, and the friendly colloquy with them, the good reasoning, the unanimous return to duty; and the doubling, the trebling of the number of them; and the most glorious of sights—O the grand old English working with a will! as Englishmen do when they come at last to heat; and they conquer, there is then nothing that they cannot conquer. So the conqueror said.—And admirable were the conservatories running three long lines, one from the drawing-room, to a central dome for tropical growths. And the parterres were admired; also the newly-planted Irish junipers bounding the West-walk; and the three tiers of stately descent from the three green terrace banks to the grassy slopes over the lake. Again the lake was admired, the house admired. Admiration was evoked for great orchid-houses 'over yonder,' soon to be set up.

Off we go to the kitchen-garden. There the admiration is genial, practical. We admire the extent of the beds marked out for asparagus, and the French disposition of the planting at wide intervals; and the French system of training peach, pear, and plum trees on the walls to win length and catch sun, we much admire. We admire the gardener. We are induced temporarily to admire the French people. They are sagacious in fruit-gardens. They have not the English Constitution, you think rightly; but in fruit-gardens they grow for fruit, and not, as Victor quotes a friend, for wood, which the valiant English achieve. We hear and we see examples of sagacity; and we are further brought round to the old confession, that we cannot cook; Colney Durance has us there; we have not studied herbs and savours; and so we are shocked backward step by step until we retreat precipitately into the nooks where waxen tapers, carefully tended by writers on the Press, light-up mysterious images of our national selves for admiration. Something surely we do, or we should not be where we are. But what is it we do (excepting cricket, of course) which others cannot do? Colney asks; and he excludes cricket and football.

An acutely satiric man in an English circle, that does not resort to the fist for a reply to him, may almost satiate the excessive fury roused in his mind by an illogical people of a provocative prosperity, mainly tongueless or of leaden tongue above the pressure of their necessities, as he takes them to be. They give him so many opportunities. They are angry and helpless as the log hissing to the saw. Their instinct to make use of the downright in retort, restrained as it is by a buttoned coat of civilization, is amusing, inviting. Colney Durance allured them to the quag's edge and plunged them in it, to writhe patriotically; and although it may be said, that they felt their situation less than did he the venom they sprang in his blood, he was cruel; he caused discomfort. But these good friends about him stood for the country, an illogical country; and as he could not well attack his host Victor Radnor, an irrational man, he selected the abstract entity for the discharge of his honest spite.

The irrational friend was deeper at the source of his irritation than the illogical old motherland. This house of Lakelands, the senselessness of his friend in building it and designing to live in it, after experiences of an incapacity to stand in a serene contention with the world he challenged, excited Colney's wasp. He was punished, half way to frenzy behind his placable demeanour, by having Dr. Schlesien for chorus. And here again, it was the unbefitting, not the person, which stirred his wrath. A German on English soil should remember the dues of a guest. At the same time, Colney said things to snare the acclamation of an observant gentleman of that race, who is no longer in his first enthusiasm for English beef and the complexion of the women. 'Ah, ya, it is true, what you say: "The English grow as fast as odders, but they grow to corns instead of brains." They are Bull. Quaat true.' He bellowed on a laugh the last half of the quotation.

Colney marked him. His encounters with Fenellan were enlivening engagements and left no malice; only a regret, when the fencing passed his guard, that Fenellan should prefer to flash for the minute. He would have met a pert defender of England, in the person of Miss Priscilla Graves, if she had not been occupied with observation of the bearing of Lady Grace Halley toward Mr. Victor Radnor; which displeased her on behalf of Mrs. Victor; she was besides hostile by race and class to an aristocratic assumption of licence. Sparing Colney, she with some scorn condemned Mr. Pempton for allowing his country to be ridiculed without a word. Mr. Pempton believed that the Vegetarian movement was more progressive in England than in other lands, but he was at the disadvantage with the fair Priscilla, that eulogy of his compatriots on this account would win her coldest approval. 'Satire was never an argument,' he said, too evasively.

The Rev. Septimus Barmby received the meed of her smile, for saying in his many-fathom bass, with an eye on Victor: 'At least we may boast of breeding men, who are leaders of men.'

The announcement of luncheon, by Victor's butler Arlington, opportunely followed and freighted the remark with a happy recognition of that which comes to us from the hands of conquerors. Dr. Schlesien himself, no antagonist to England, but like Colney Durance, a critic, speculated in view of the spread of pic-nic provision beneath the great glass dome, as to whether it might be, that these English were on another start out of the dust in vigorous commercial enterprise, under leadership of one of their chance masterly minds-merchant, in this instance: and be debated within, whether Genius, occasionally developed in a surprising superior manner by these haphazard English, may not sometimes wrest the prize from Method; albeit we count for the long run, that Method has assurance of success, however late in the race to set forth.

Luncheon was a merry meal, with Victor and Nataly for host and hostess; Fenellan, Colney Durance, and Lady Grace Halley for the talkers. A gusty bosom of sleet overhung the dome, rattled on it, and rolling Westward, became a radiant mountain-land, partly worthy of Victor's phrase: 'A range of Swiss Alps in air.'

'With periwigs Louis Quatorze for peaks,' Colney added.

And Fenellan improved on him: 'Or a magnified Bench of Judges at the trial of your caerulean Phryne.'

The strip of white cloud flew on a whirl from the blue, to confirm it.

But Victor and Lady Grace rejected any play of conceits upon nature. Violent and horrid interventions of the counterfeit, such mad similes appeared to them, when pure coin was offered. They loathed the Rev. Septimus Barmby for proclaiming, that he had seen 'Chapters of Hebrew History in the grouping of clouds.'

His gaze was any one of the Chapters upon Nesta. The clerical gentleman's voice was of a depth to claim for it the profoundest which can be thought or uttered; and Nesta's tender youth had taken so strong an impression of sacredness from what Fenellan called 'his chafer tones,' that her looks were often given him in gratitude, for the mere sound. Nataly also had her sense of safety in acquiescing to such a voice coming from such a garb. Consequently, whenever Fenellan and Colney were at him, drawing him this way and that for utterances cathedral in sentiment and sonorousness, these ladies shed protecting beams; insomuch that he was inspired to the agreeable conceptions whereof frequently rash projects are an issue.

Touching the neighbours of Lakelands, they were principally enriched merchants, it appeared; a snippet or two of the fringe of aristocracy lay here and there among them; and one racy-of-the-soil old son of Thames, having the manners proper to last century's yeoman. Mr. Pempton knew something of this quaint Squire of Hefferstone, Beaves Urmsing by name; a ruddy man, right heartily Saxon; a still glowing brand amid the ashes of the Heptarchy hearthstone; who had a song, The Marigolds, which he would troll out for you anywhere, on any occasion. To have so near to the metropolis one from the centre of the venerable rotundity of the country, was rare. Victor exclaimed 'Come!' in ravishment over the picturesqueness of a neighbour carrying imagination away to the founts of England; and his look at Nataly proposed. Her countenance was inapprehensive. He perceived resistance, and said: 'I have met two or three of them in the train: agreeable men: Gladding, the banker; a General Fanning; that man Blathenoy, great billbroker. But the fact is, close on London, we're independent of neighbours; we mean to be. Lakelands and London practically join.'

'The mother city becoming the suburb,' murmured Colney, in report of the union.

'You must expect to be invaded, sir,' said Mr. Sowerby; and Victor shrugged: 'We are pretty safe.'

'The lock of a door seems a potent security until some one outside is heard fingering the handle nigh midnight,' Fenellan threw out his airy nothing of a remark.

It struck on Nataly's heart. 'So you will not let us be lonely here,' she said to her guests.

The Rev. Septimus Barmby was mouthpiece for congregations. Sound of a subterranean roar, with a blast at the orifice, informed her of their 'very deep happiness in the privilege.'

He comforted her. Nesta smiled on him thankfully.

'Don't imagine, Mrs. Victor, that you can be shut off from neighbours, in a house like this; and they have a claim,' said Lady Grace, quitting the table.

Fenellan and Colney thought so:

'Like mice at a cupboard.'

'Beetles in a kitchen.'

'No, no-no, no!' Victor shook head, pitiful over the good people likened to things unclean, and royally upraising them: in doing which, he scattered to vapour the leaden incubi they had been upon his flatter moods of late. 'No, but it's a rapture to breathe the air here!' His lifted chest and nostrils were for the encouragement of Nataly to soar beside him.

She summoned her smile and nodded.

He spoke aside to Lady Grace: 'The dear soul wants time to compose herself after a grand surprise.'

She replied: 'I think I could soon be reconciled. How much land?'

'In treaty for some hundred and eighty or ninety acres... in all at present three hundred and seventy, including plantations, lake, outhouses.'

'Large enough; land paying as it does—that is, not paying. We shall be having to gamble in the City systematically for subsistence.'

'You will not so much as jest on the subject.'

Coming from such a man, that was clear sky thunder. The lady played it off in a shadowy pout and shrug while taking a stamp of his masterfulness, not so volatile.

She said to Nataly: 'Our place in Worcestershire is about half the size, if as much. Large enough when we're not crowded out with gout and can open to no one. Some day you will visit us, I hope.'

'You we count on here, Lady Grace.'

It was an over-accentuated response; unusual with this well-bred woman; and a bit of speech that does not flow, causes us to speculate. The lady resumed: 'I value the favour. We're in a horsey-doggy-foxy circle down there. We want enlivening. If we had your set of musicians and talkers!'

Nataly smiled in vacuous kindness, at a loss for the retort of a compliment to a person she measured. Lady Grace also was an amiable hostile reviewer. Each could see, to have cited in the other, defects common to the lower species of the race, admitting a superior personal quality or two; which might be pleaded in extenuation; and if the apology proved too effective, could be dispersed by insistence upon it, under an implied appeal to benevolence. When we have not a liking for the creature whom we have no plain cause to dislike, we are minutely just.

During the admiratory stroll along the ground-floor rooms, Colney Durance found himself beside Dr. Schlesien; the latter smoking, striding, emphasizing, but bearable, as the one of the party who was not perpetually at the gape in laudation. Colney was heard to say: 'No doubt: the German is the race the least mixed in Europe: it might challenge aboriginals for that. Oddly, it has invented the Cyclopaedia for knowledge, the sausage for nutrition! How would you explain it?'

Dr. Schlesien replied with an Atlas shrug under fleabite to the insensately infantile interrogation.

He in turn was presently heard.

'But, my good sir! you quote me your English Latin. I must beg of you you write it down. It is orally incomprehensible to Continentals.'

'We are Islanders!' Colney shrugged in languishment.

'Oh, you do great things...' Dr. Schlesien rejoined in kindness, making his voice a musical intimation of the smallness of the things.

'We build great houses, to employ our bricks'

'No, Colney, to live in,' said Victor.

'Scarcely long enough to warm them.'

'What do you... fiddle!'

'They are not Hohenzollerns!'

'It is true,' Dr. Schlesien called. 'No, but you learn discipline; you build. I say wid you, not Hohenzollerns you build! But you shall look above: Eyes up. Ire necesse est. Good, but mount; you come to something. Have ideas.'

'Good, but when do we reach your level?'

'Sir, I do not say more than that we do not want instruction from foreigners.'

'Pupil to paedagogue indeed. You have the wreath in Music, in Jurisprudence, Chemistry, Scholarship, Beer, Arms, Manners.'

Dr. Schlesien puffed a tempest of tobacco and strode.

'He is chiselling for wit in the Teutonic block,' Colney said, falling back to Fenellan.

Fenellan observed: 'You might have credited him with the finished sculpture.'

'They're ahead of us in sticking at the charge of wit.'

'They've a widening of their swallow since Versailles.'

'Manners?'

'Well, that's a tight cravat for the Teutonic thrapple! But he's off by himself to loosen it.'

Victor came on the couple testily. 'What are you two concocting! I say, do keep the peace, please. An excellent good fellow; better up in politics than any man I know; understands music; means well, you can see. You two hate a man at all serious. And he doesn't bore with his knowledge. A scholar too.'

'If he'll bring us the atmosphere of the groves of Academe, he may swing his ferule pickled in himself, and welcome,' said Fenellan.

'Yes!' Victor nodded at a recognized antagonism in Fenellan; 'but Colney's always lifting the Germans high above us.'

'It's to exercise his muscles.'

Victor headed to the other apartments, thinking that the Rev. Septimus and young Sowerby, Old England herself, were spared by the diversion of these light skirmishing shots from their accustomed victims to the 'masculine people of our time. His friends would want a drilling to be of aid to him in his campaign to come. For it was one, and a great one. He remembered his complete perception of the plan, all the elements of it, the forward whirling of it, just before the fall on London Bridge. The greatness of his enterprise laid such hold of him that the smallest of obstacles had a villanous aspect; and when, as anticipated, Colney and Fenellan were sultry flies for whomsoever they could fret, he was blind to the reading of absurdities which caused Fredi's eyes to stream and Lady Grace beside him to stand awhile and laugh out her fit. Young Sowerby appeared forgiving enough—he was a perfect gentleman: but Fredi's appalling sense of fun must try him hard. And those young fellows are often more wounded by a girl's thoughtless laughter than by a man's contempt. Nataly should have protected him. Her face had the air of a smiling general satisfaction; sign of a pleasure below the mark required; sign too of a sleepy partner for a battle. Even in the wonderful kitchen, arched and pillared (where the explanation came to Nesta of Madame Callet's frequent leave of absence of late, when an inferior dinner troubled her father in no degree), even there his Nataly listened to the transports of the guests with benign indulgence.

'Mama!' said Nesta, ready to be entranced by kitchens in her bubbling animation: she meant the recalling of instances of the conspirator her father had been.

'You none of you guessed Armandine's business!' Victor cried, in a glee that pushed to make the utmost of this matter and count against chagrin. 'She was off to Paris; went to test the last inventions:—French brains are always alert:—and in fact, those kitchen-ranges, gas and coal, and the apparatus for warming plates and dishes, the whole of the battery is on the model of the Duc d'Ariane's—finest in Europe. Well,' he agreed with Colney, 'to say France is enough.'

Mr. Pempton spoke to Miss Graves of the task for a woman to conduct a command so extensive. And, as when an inoffensive wayfarer has chanced to set foot near a wasp's nest, out on him came woman and her champions, the worthy and the sham, like a blast of powder.

Victor ejaculated: 'Armandine!' Whoever doubted her capacity, knew not Armandine; or not knowing Armandine, knew not the capacity in women.

With that utterance of her name, he saw the orangey spot on London Bridge, and the sinking Tower and masts and funnels, and the rising of them, on his return to his legs; he recollected, that at the very edge of the fall he had Armandine strongly in his mind. She was to do her part: Fenellan and Colney on the surface, she below: and hospitality was to do its part, and music was impressed—the innocent Concerts; his wealth, all his inventiveness were to serve;—and merely to attract and win the tastes of people, for a social support to Lakelands! Merely that? Much more:—if Nataly's coldness to the place would but allow him to form an estimate of how much. At the same time, being in the grasp of his present disappointment, he perceived a meanness in the result, that was astonishing and afflicting. He had not ever previously felt imagination starving at the vision of success. Victor had yet to learn, that the man with a material object in aim, is the man of his object; and the nearer to his mark, often the farther is he from a sober self; he is more the arrow of his bow than bow to his arrow. This we pay for scheming: and success is costly; we find we have pledged the better half of ourselves to clutch it; not to be redeemed with the whole handful of our prize! He was, however, learning after his leaping fashion. Nataly's defective sympathy made him look at things through the feelings she depressed. A shadow of his missed

Idea on London Bridge seemed to cross him from the close flapping of a wing within reach. He could say only, that it would, if caught, have been an answer to the thought disturbing him.

Nataly drew Colney Durance with her eyes to step beside her, on the descent to the terrace. Little Skepsey hove in sight, coming swift as the point of an outrigger over the flood.

CHAPTER X

SKEPSEY IN MOTION

The bearer of his master's midday letters from London shot beyond Nataly as soon as seen, with an apparent snap of his body in passing. He steamed to the end of the terrace and delivered the packet, returning at the same rate of speed, to do proper homage to the lady he so much respected. He had left the railway-station on foot instead of taking a fly, because of a calculation that he would save three minutes; which he had not lost for having to come through the raincloud. 'Perhaps the contrary,' Skepsey said: it might be judged to have accelerated his course: and his hat dripped, and his coat shone, and he soaped his hands, cheerful as an ouzel-cock when the sun is out again.

'Many cracked crowns lately, in the Manly Art?' Colney inquired of him. And Skepsey answered with precision of statement: 'Crowns, no, sir; the nose, it may happen; but it cannot be said to be the rule.'

'You are of opinion, that the practice of Scientific Pugilism offers us compensation for the broken bridge of a nose?'

'In an increase of manly self-esteem: I do, sir, yes.'

Skepsey was shy of this gentleman's bite; and he fancied his defence had been correct. Perceiving a crumple of the lips of Mr. Durance, he took the attitude of a watchful dubiety.

'But, my goodness, you are wet through!' cried Nataly, reproaching herself for the tardy compassion; and Nesta ran up to them and heaped a thousand pities on her 'poor dear Skip,' and drove him in beneath the glass-dome to the fragments of pic-nic, and poured champagne for him, 'lest his wife should have to doctor him for a cold,' and poured afresh, when he had obeyed her: 'for the toasting of Lakelands, dear Skepsey!' impossible to resist: so he drank, and blinked; and was then told, that before using his knife and fork he must betake himself to some fire of shavings and chips, where coffee was being made, for the purpose of drying his clothes. But this he would not hear of: he was pledged to business, to convey his master's letters, and he might have to catch a train by the last quarter-minute, unless it was behind the time-tables; he must hold himself ready to start. Entreated, adjured, commanded, Skepsey commiseratingly observed to Colney Durance, 'The ladies do not understand, sir!' For Turk of Constantinople had never a more haremed opinion of the unfitness of women in the brave world of action. The persistence of these ladies endeavouring to obstruct him in the course of his duty, must have succeeded save that for one word of theirs he had two, and twice the promptitude of motion. He explained to them, as to good children, that the loss of five minutes might be the loss of a Post, the loss of thousands of pounds, the loss of the character of a Firm; and he was away to the terrace. Nesta headed him and waved him back. She and her mother rebuked him: they called him unreasonable; wherein they resembled the chief example of the sex to him, in a wife he had at home, who levelled that charge against her husband when most she needed discipline: the woman laid hand on the very word legitimately his own for the justification of his process with her.

'But, Skips! if you are ill and we have to nurse you!' said Nesta.

She forgot the hospital, he told her cordially, and laughed at the notion of a ducking producing a cold or a cold a fever, or anything consumption, with him. So the ladies had to keep down their anxious minds and allow him to stand in wet clothing to eat his cold pie and salad.

Miss Priscilla Graves entering to them, became a witness that they were seductresses for inducing him to drink wine—and a sparkling wine.

'It is to warm him,' they pleaded; and she said: 'He must be warm from his walk'; and they said: 'But he is wet'; and said she, without a show of feeling: 'Warm water, then'; and Skepsey writhed, as if in the grasp of anatomists, at being the subject of female contention or humane consideration. Miss Graves caught signs of the possible proselyte in him; she remarked encouragingly:

'I am sure he does not like it; he still has a natural taste.'

She distressed his native politeness, for the glass was in his hand, and he was fully aware of her high-principled aversion; and he profoundly bowed to principles, believing his England to be pillared on them; and the lady looked like one who bore the standard of a principle; and if we slap and pinch and starve our appetites, the idea of a principle seems entering us to support. Subscribing to a principle, our energies are refreshed; we have a faith in the country that was not with us before the act; and of a real well-founded faith come the glowing thoughts which we have at times: thoughts of England heading the nations; when the smell of an English lane under showers challenges Eden, and the threading of a London crowd tunes discords to the swell of a cathedral organ. It may be, that by the renunciation of any description of alcohol, a man will stand clearer-headed to serve his country. He may expect to have a clearer memory, for certain: he will not be asking himself, unable to decide, whether his master named a Mr. Journeyman or a Mr. Jarniman, as the person he declined to receive. Either of the two is repulsed upon his application, owing to the guilty similarity of sounds but what we are to think of is, our own sad state of inefficiency in failing to remember; which accuses our physical condition, therefore our habits.—Thus the little man debated, scarcely requiring more than to hear the right word, to be a convert and make him a garland of the proselyte's fetters.

Destructively for the cause she advocated, Miss Priscilla gestured the putting forth of an abjuring hand, with the recommendation to him, so to put aside temptation that instant; and she signified in a very ugly jerk of her features, the vilely filthy stuff Morality thought it, however pleasing it might be to a palate corrupted by indulgence of the sensual appetites.

But the glass had been handed to him by the lady he respected, who looked angelical in offering it, divinely other than ugly; and to her he could not be discourteous; not even to pay his homage to the representative of a principle. He bowed to Miss Graves, and drank, and rushed forth; hearing shouts behind him.

His master had a packet of papers ready, easy for the pocket.

'By the way, Skepsey,' he said, 'if a man named Jarniman should call at the office, I will see him.'

Skepsey's grey eyes came out.

Or was it Journeyman, that his master would not see; and Jarniman that he would?

His habit of obedience, pride of apprehension, and the time to catch the train, forbade inquiry. Besides he knew of himself of old, that his puzzles were best unriddled running.

The quick of pace are soon in the quick of thoughts.

Jarniman, then, was a man whom his master, not wanting to see, one day, and wanting to see, on another day, might wish to conciliate: a case of policy. Let Jarniman go. Journeyman, on the other hand, was nobody at all, a ghost of the fancy. Yet this Journeyman was as important an individual, he was a dread reality; more important to Skepsey in the light of patriot: and only in that light was he permitted of a scrupulous conscience and modest mind to think upon himself when the immediate subject was his master's interests. For this Journeyman had not an excuse for existence in Mr. Radnor's pronunciation: he was born of the buzz of a troubled ear, coming of a disordered brain, consequent necessarily upon a disorderly stomach, that might protest a degree of comparative innocence, but would be shamed utterly under inspection of the eye of a lady of principle.

What, then, was the value to his country of a servant who could not accurately recollect his master's words! Miss Graves within him asked the rapid little man, whether indeed his ideas were his own after draughts of champagne.

The ideas, excited to an urgent animation by his racing trot, were a quiverful in flight over an England terrible to the foe and dancing on the green. Right so: but would we keep up the dance, we must be red iron to touch: and the fighter for conquering is the one who can last and has the open brain;—and there you have a point against alcohol. Yes, and Miss Graves, if she would press it, with her natural face, could be pleasant and persuasive: and she ought to be told she ought to marry, for the good of the country. Women taking liquor: Skepsey had a vision of his wife with rheumy peepers and miauly mouth, as he had once beheld the creature:—Oh! they need discipline not such would we have for the mothers of our English young. Decidedly the women of principle are bound to enter wedlock; they should be bound by law. Whereas, in the opposing case—the binding of the unprincipled to a celibate state—such a law would have saved Skepsey from the necessitated commission of deeds of discipline with one of the female sex, and have rescued his progeny from a likeness to the corn-stalk reverting to weed. He had but a son for England's defence; and the frame of his boy might be set quaking by a thump on the wind of a drum; the courage of William Barlow Skepsey would not stand against a sheep; it would wind-up hares to have a run at him out in the field. Offspring of a woman of principle!... but there is no rubbing out in life: why dream of it? Only that one would not have one's country the loser!

Dwell a moment on the reverse—and first remember the lesson of the Captivity of the Jews and the outcry of their backsliding and repentance:—see a nation of the honourably begotten; muscular men disdaining the luxuries they will occasionally condescend to taste, like some tribe in Greece; boxers, rowers, runners, climbers; braced, indomitable; magnanimous, as only the strong can be; an army at word, winning at a stroke the double battle of the hand and the heart: men who can walk the paths through the garden of the pleasures. They receive fitting mates, of a build to promise or aid in ensuring depth of chest and long reach of arm for their progeny.

Down goes the world before them.

And we see how much would be due for this to a corps of ladies like Miss Graves, not allowed to remain too long on the stalk of spinsterhood. Her age might count twenty-eight: too long! She should be taught that men can, though truly ordinary women cannot, walk these orderly paths through the garden. An admission to women, hinting restrictions, on a ticket marked 'in moderation' (meaning, that they may pluck a flower or fruit along the pathway border to which they are confined), speedily, alas, exhibits them at a mad scramble across the pleasure-beds. They know not moderation. Neither for their own sakes nor for the sakes of Posterity will they hold from excess, when they are not pledged to shun it.

The reason is, that their minds cannot conceive the abstract, as men do.

But there are grounds for supposing that the example before them of a sex exercising self-control in freedom, would induce women to pledge themselves to a similar abnegation, until they gain some sense of touch upon the impalpable duty to the generations coming after us thanks to the voluntary example we set them.

The stupendous task, which had hitherto baffled Skepsey in the course of conversational remonstrances with his wife;—that of getting the Idea of Posterity into the understanding of its principal agent, might then be mastered.

Therefore clearly men have to begin the salutary movement: it manifestly devolves upon them. Let them at once take to rigorous physical training. Women under compulsion, as vessels: men in their magnanimity, patriotically, voluntarily.

Miss Graves must have had an intimation for him; he guessed it; and it plunged him into a conflict with her, that did not suffer him to escape without ruefully feeling the feebleness of his vocabulary: and consequently he made a reluctant appeal to figures, and it hung upon the bolder exhibition of lists and tables as to whether he was beaten; and if beaten, he was morally her captive; and this being the case, nothing could be more repulsive to Skepsey; seeing that he, unable of his nature passively or partially to undertake a line of conduct, beheld himself wearing a detestable 'ribbon,' for sign of an oath quite needlessly sworn (simply to satisfy the lady overcoming him with nimbler tongue), and blocking the streets, marching in bands beneath banners, howling hymns.

Statistics, upon which his master and friends, after exchanging opinions in argument, always fell back, frightened him. As long as they had no opponents of their own kind, they swept the field, they were intelligible, as the word 'principle' had become. But the appearance of one body of Statistics invariably brought up another; and the strokes and counterstrokes were like a play of quarter-staff on the sconce, to knock all comprehension out of Skepsey. Otherwise he would not unwillingly have inquired to-morrow into the Statistics of the controversy between the waters of the wells and of the casks, prepared to walk over to the victorious, however objectionable that proceeding. He hoped to question his master some day except that his master would very naturally have a tendency to sum-up in favour of wine—good wine, in moderation; just as Miss Graves for the cup of tea—not so thoughtfully stipulating that it should be good and not too copious. Statistics are according to their conjurors; they are not independent bodies, with native colours; they needs must be painted by the different hands they pass through, and they may be multiplied; a nought or so counts for nothing with the teller. Skepsey saw that. Yet they can overcome: even as fictitious battalions, they can overcome. He shrank from the results of a ciphering match having him for object, and was ashamed of feeling to Statistics as women to giants; nevertheless he acknowledged that the badge was upon him, if Miss Graves should beat her master in her array of figures, to insist on his wearing it, as she would, she certainly would. And against his internal conviction perhaps; with the knowledge that the figures were an unfortified display, and his oath of bondage an unmanly servility, the silliest of ceremonies! He was shockingly feminine to Statistics.

Mr. Durance despised them: he called them, arguing against Mr. Radnor, 'those emotional things,' not comprehensibly to Skepsey. But Mr. Durance, a very clever gentleman, could not be right in everything. He made strange remarks upon his country. Dr. Yatt attributed them to the state of 'his digestion.

And Mr. Fenellan had said of Mr. Durance that, as 'a barrister wanting briefs, the speech in him had been bottled too long and was an overripe wine dripping sour drops through the rotten cork.' Mr. Fenellan said it laughing, he meant no harm. Skepsey was sure he had the words. He heard no more than other people hear; he remembered whole sentences, and many: on one of his runs, this active little machine, quickened by motion to fire, revived the audible of years back; whatever suited his turn of mind at the moment rushed to the rapid wheels within him. His master's business and friends, his country's welfare and advancement, these, with records, items, anticipations, of the manlier sports to decorate, were his current themes; all being chopped and tossed and mixed in salad accordance by his fervour of velocity. And if you would like a further definition of Genius, think of it as a form of swiftness. It is the lively young great-grandson, in the brain, of the travelling force which mathematicians put to paper, in a row of astounding ciphers, for the motion of earth through space; to the generating of heat, whereof is multiplication, whereof deposited matter, and so your chaos, your half-lighted labyrinth, your, ceaseless pressure to evolvement; and then Light, and so Creation, order, the work of Genius. What do you say?

Without having a great brain, the measure of it possessed by Skepsey was alive under strong illumination. In his heart, while doing penance for his presumptuousness, he believed that he could lead regiments of men. He was not the army's General, he was the General's Lieutenant, now and then venturing to suggest a piece of counsel to his Chief. On his own particular drilled regiments, his Chief may rely; and on his knowledge of the country of the campaign, roads, morasses, masking hills, dividing rivers. He had mapped for himself mentally the battles of conquerors in his favourite historic reading; and he understood the value of a plan, and the danger of sticking to it, and the advantage of a big army for flanking; and he manoeuvred a small one cunningly to make it a bolt at the telling instant. Dartrey Fenellan had explained to him Frederick's oblique attack, Napoleon's employment of the artillery arm preparatory to the hurling of the cataract on the spot of weakness, Wellington's parallel march with Marmont up to the hour of the decisive cut through the latter at Salamanca; and Skepsey treated his enemy to the like, deferentially reporting the engagement to a Chief whom his modesty kept in eminence, for the receiving of the principal honours. As to his men, of all classes and sorts, they are so supple with training that they sustain a defeat like the sturdy pugilist a knock off his legs, and up smiling a minute after—one of the truly beautiful sights on this earth! They go at the double half a day, never sounding a single pair of bellows among them. They have their appetites in full control, to eat when they can, or cheerfully fast. They have healthy frames, you see; and as the healthy frame is not artificially heated, it ensues that, under any title you like, they profess the principles—into the bog we go, we have got round to it!—the principles of those horrible marching and chanting people!

Then, must our England, to be redoubtable to the enemy, be a detestable country for habitation?

Here was a knot.

Skepsey's head dropped lower, he went as a ram. The sayings of Mr. Durance about his dear England: that 'her remainder of life is in the activity of her diseases'—that 'she has so fed upon Pap of Compromise as to be unable any longer to conceive a muscular resolution': that 'she is animated only as the carcase to the blow-fly'; and so forth:—charged on him during his wrestle with his problem. And the gentlemen had said, had permitted himself to say, that our England's recent history was a provincial apothecary's exhibition of the battle of bane and antidote. Mr. Durance could hardly mean it. But how could one answer him when he spoke of the torpor of the people, and of the succeeding Governments as a change of lacqueys—or the purse-string's lacqueys? He said, that Old England has taken to the arm-chair for good, and thinks it her whole business to pronounce opinions and listen to herself; and that, in the face of an armed Europe, this great nation is living on sufferance. Oh!

Skepsey had uttered the repudiating exclamation.

'Feel quite up to it?' he was asked by his neighbour.

The mover of armed hosts for the defence of the country sat in a third-class carriage of the train, approaching the first of the stations on the way to town. He was instantly up to the level of an external world, and fell into give and take with a burly broad communicative man; located in London, but born in the North, in view of Durham cathedral, as he thanked his Lord; who was of the order of pork-butcher; which succulent calling had carried him down to near upon the borders of Surrey and Sussex, some miles beyond the new big house of a Mister whose name he had forgotten, though he had heard it mentioned by an acquaintance interested in the gentleman's doings. But his object was to have a look at a rare breed of swine, worth the journey; that didn't run to fat so much as to flavour, had longer legs, sharp snouts to plump their hams; over from Spain, it seemed; and the gentleman owning them was for selling them, finding them wild past correction. But the acquaintance mentioned, who was down to visit t' other gentleman's big new edifice in workmen's hands, had a mother, who had been cook to a family, and was now widow of a cook's shop; ham, beef, and sausages, prime pies to order; and a good specimen herself; and if ever her son saw her spirit at his bedside, there wouldn't be room for much else in that chamber—supposing us to keep our shapes. But he was the right sort of son, anxious to push his mother's shop where he saw a chance, and do it cheap; and those foreign pigs, after a disappointment to their importer, might be had pretty cheap, and were accounted tasty.

Skepsey's main thought was upon war: the man had discoursed of pigs.

He informed the man of his having heard from a scholar, that pigs had been the cause of more bloody battles than any other animal.

How so? the pork-butcher asked, and said he was not much of a scholar, and pigs might be provoking, but he had not heard they were a cause of strife between man and man. For possession of them, Skepsey explained. Oh! possession! Why, we've heard of bloody battles for the possession of women! Men will fight for almost anything they care to get or call their own, the pork-butcher said; and he praised Old England for avoiding war. Skepsey nodded. How if war is forced on us? Then we fight. Suppose we are not prepared?—We soon get that up. Skepsey requested him to state the degree of resistance he might think he could bring against a pair of skilful fists, in a place out of hearing of the police.

'Say, you!' said the pork-butcher, and sharply smiled, for he was a man of size.

'I would give you two minutes,' rejoined Skepsey, eyeing him intently and kindly: insomuch that it could be seen he was not in the conundrum vein.

'Rather short allowance, eh, master?' said the bigger man. 'Feel here'; he straightened out his arm and doubled it, raising a proud bridge of muscle.

Skepsey performed the national homage to muscle.

'Twice that, would not help without the science,' he remarked, and let his arm be gripped in turn.

The pork-butcher's throat sounded, as it were, commas and colons, punctuations in his reflections, while he tightened fingers along the iron lump. 'Stringy. You're a wiry one, no mistake.' It was encomium. With the ingrained contempt of size for a smallness that has not yet taught it the prostrating lesson, he said: 'Weight tells.'

'In a wrestle,' Skepsey admitted. 'Allow me to say, you would not touch me.'

'And how do you know I'm not a trifle handy with the maulers myself?'

'You will pardon me for saying, it would be worse for you if you were.'

The pork-butcher was flung backward. 'Are you a Professor, may I inquire?'

Skepsey rejected the title. 'I can engage to teach young men, upon a proper observance of first principles.'

'They be hanged!' cried the ruffled pork-butcher. 'Our best men never got it out of books. Now, you tell me—you've got a spiflicating style of talk about you—no brag, you tell me—course, the best man wins, if you mean that: now, if I was one of 'em, and I fetches you a bit of a flick, how then? Would you be ready to step out with a real Professor?'

'I should claim a fair field,' was the answer, made in modesty.

'And you'd expect to whop me with they there principles of yours?'

'I should expect to.'

'Bang me!' was roared. After a stare at the mild little figure with the fitfully dead-levelled large grey eyes in front of him, the pork-butcher resumed: 'Take you for the man you say you be, you're just the man for my friend Jam and me. He dearly loves to see a set-to, self the same. What prettier? And if you would be so obliging some day as to favour us with a display, we'd head a cap conformably, whether you'd the best of it, according to your expectations, or t' other way:—For there never was shame in a jolly good licking as the song says: that is, if you take it and make it appear jolly good. And find you an opponent meet and fit, never doubt. Ever had the worse of an encounter, sir?'

'Often, Sir.'

'Well, that's good. And it didn't destroy your confidence?'

'Added to it, I hope.'

At this point, it became a crying necessity for Skepsey to escape from an area of boastfulness, into which he had fallen inadvertently; and he hastened to apologize 'for his personal reference,' that was intended for an illustration of our country caught unawares by a highly trained picked soldiery, inferior in numbers to the patriotic levies, but sharp at the edge and knowing how to strike. Measure the axe, measure the tree; and which goes down first?

'Invasion, is it?—and you mean, we're not to hit back?' the pork-butcher bellowed, and presently secured a murmured approbation from an audience of three, that had begun to comprehend the dialogue, and strengthened him in a manner to teach Skepsey the foolishness of ever urging analogies of too extended a circle to close sharply on the mark. He had no longer a chance, he was overborne, identified with the fated invader, rolled away into the chops of the Channel, to be swallowed up entire, and not a rag left of him, but John Bull tucking up his shirtsleeves on the shingle beach, ready for a second or a third; crying to them to come on.

Warmed by his Bullish victory, and friendly to the vanquished, the pork-butcher told Skepsey he should like to see more of him, and introduced himself on a card Benjamin Shaplow, not far from the Bank.

They parted at the Terminus, where three shrieks of an engine, sounding like merry messages of the damned to their congeners in the anticipatory stench of the cab-droppings above, disconnected sane hearing; perverted it, no doubt. Or else it was the stamp of a particular name on his mind, which impressed Skepsey, as he bored down the street and across the bridge, to fancy in recollection, that Mr. Shaplow, when reiterating the wish for self and friend to witness a display of his cunning with the fists, had spoken the name of Jarniman. An unusual name yet more than one Jarniman might well exist. And unlikely that a friend of the pork-butcher would be the person whom Mr. Radnor first prohibited and then desired to receive. It hardly mattered:—considering that the Dutch Navy did really, incredible as it seems now, come sailing a good way up the River Thames, into the very main artery of Old England. And what thought the Tower of it? Skepsey looked at the Tower in sympathy, wondering whether the Tower had seen those impudent Dutch a nice people at home, he had heard. Mr. Shaplow's Jarniman might actually be Mr. Radnor's, he inclined to think. At any rate he was now sure of the name.

CHAPTER XI

WHEREIN WE BEHOLD THE COUPLE JUSTIFIED OF LOVE HAVING SIGHT OF THEIR SCOURGE

Fenellan, in a musing exclamation, that was quite spontaneous, had put a picture on the departing Skepsey, as observed from an end of the Lakelands upper terrace-walk.

'Queer little water-wagtail it is!' And Lady Grace Halley and Miss Graves and Mrs. Cormyn, snugly silken dry ones, were so taken with the pretty likeness after hearing Victor call the tripping dripping creature the happiest man in England, that they nursed it in their minds for a Bewick tailpiece to the chapter of a pleasant rural day. It imbedded the day in an idea that it had been rural.

We are indebted almost for construction to those who will define us briefly: we are but scattered leaves to the general comprehension of us until such a work of binding and labelling is done. And should the definition be not so correct as brevity pretends to make it at one stroke, we are at least rendered portable; thus we pass into the conceptions of our fellows, into the records, down to posterity. Anecdotes of England's happiest man were related, outlines of his personal history requested. His nomination in chief among the traditionally very merry Islanders was hardly borne out by the tale of his enchainment with a drunken yokefellow—unless upon the Durance version of the felicity of his countrymen; still, the water-wagtail carried it, Skepsey trotted into memories. Heroes conducted up Fame's temple-steps by ceremonious historians, who are studious, when the platform is reached, of the art of setting them beneath the flambeau of a final image, before thrusting them inside to be rivetted on their pedestals, have an excellent chance of doing the same, let but the provident narrators direct that image to paint the thing a moth-like humanity desires, in the thing it shrinks from. Miss Priscilla Graves now fastened her meditations upon Skepsey; and it was important to him.

Tobacco withdrew the haunting shadow of the Rev. Septimus Barmby from Nesta. She strolled beside Louise de Seilles, to breathe sweet-sweet in the dear friend's ear and tell her she loved her. The presence of the German had, without rousing animosity, damped the young Frenchwoman, even to a revulsion when her feelings had been touched by hearing praise of her France, and wounded by the subjects of the praise. She bore the national scar, which is barely skin-clothing of a gash that will not heal since her country was overthrown and dismembered. Colney Durance could excuse the unreasonableness in her, for it had a dignity, and she controlled it, and quietly suffered, trusting to the steady, tireless, concentrated aim of her France. In the Gallic mind of our time, France appears as a prematurely buried Glory, that heaves the mound oppressing breath and cannot cease; and calls hourly, at times keenly, to be remembered, rescued from the pain and the mould-spots of that foul sepulture. Mademoiselle and Colney were friends, partly divided by her speaking once of revanche; whereupon he assumed the chair of the Moralist, with its right to lecture, and went over to the enemy; his talk savoured of a German. Our holding of the balance, taking two sides, is incomprehensible to a people quivering with the double wound to body and soul. She was of Breton blood. Cymric enough was in Nesta to catch any thrill from her and join to her mood, if it hung out a colour sad or gay, and was noble, as any mood of this dear Louise would surely be.

Nataly was not so sympathetic. Only the Welsh and pure Irish are quick at the feelings of the Celtic French. Nataly came of a Yorkshire stock; she had the bravery, humaneness and generous temper of our civilized North, and a taste for mademoiselle's fine breeding, with a distaste for the singular air of superiority in composure which it was granted to mademoiselle to wear with an unassailable reserve when the roughness of the commercial boor was obtrusive. She said of her to Colney, as they watched the couple strolling by the lake below: 'Nesta brings her out of her frosts. I suppose it's the presence of Dr. Schlesien. I have known it the same after an evening of Wagner's music.'

'Richard Wagner Germanized ridicule of the French when they were down,' said Colney. 'She comes of a blood that never forgives.'

'"Never forgives" is horrible to think of! I fancied you liked your "Kelts," as you call them.'

Colney seized on a topic that shelved a less agreeable one that he saw coming. 'You English won't descend to understand what does not resemble you. The French are in a state of feverish patriotism. You refuse to treat them for a case of fever. They are lopped of a limb: you tell them to be at rest!'

'You know I am fond of them.'

'And the Kelts, as they are called, can't and won't forgive injuries; look at Ireland, look at Wales, and the Keltic Scot. Have you heard them talk? It happened in the year 1400: it's alive to them as if it were yesterday. Old History is as dead to the English as their first father. They beg for the privilege of pulling the forelock to the bearers of the titles of the men who took their lands from them and turn them to the uses of cattle. The Saxon English had, no doubt, a heavier thrashing than any people allowed to subsist ever received: you see it to this day; the crick of the neck at the name of a lord is now concealed and denied, but they have it and betray the effects; and it's patent in their Journals, all over their literature. Where it's not seen, another blood's at work. The Kelt won't accept the form of slavery. Let him be servile, supple, cunning, treacherous, and to appearance time-serving, he will always remember his day of manly independence and who robbed him: he is the poetic animal of the races of modern men.'

'You give him Pagan colours.'

'Natural colours. He does not offer the other cheek or turn his back to be kicked after a knock to the ground. Instead of asking him to forgive, which he cannot do, you must teach him to admire. A mercantile community guided by Political Economy from the ledger to the banquet presided over by its Dagon Capital, finds that difficult. However, there 's the secret of him; that I respect in him. His admiration of an enemy or oppressor doing great deeds, wins him entirely. He is an active spirit, not your negative passive letter-of-Scripture Insensible. And his faults, short of ferocity, are amusing.'

'But the fits of ferocity!'

'They are inconscient, real fits. They come of a hot nerve. He is manageable, sober too, when his mind is charged. As to the French people, they are the most mixed of any European nation; so they are packed with contrasts: they are full of sentiment, they are sharply logical; free-thinkers, devotees; affectionate, ferocious; frivolous, tenacious; the passion of the season operating like sun or moon on these qualities; and they can reach to ideality out of sensualism. Below your level, they're above it: a paradox is at home with them!'

'My friend, you speak seriously—an unusual compliment,' Nataly said, and ungratefully continued: 'You know what is occupying me. I want your opinion. I guess it. I want to hear—a mean thirst perhaps, and you would pay me any number of compliments to avoid the subject; but let me hear:—this house!'

Colney shrugged in resignation. 'Victor works himself out,' he replied.

'We are to go through it all again?'

'If you have not the force to contain him.'

'How contain him?'

Up went Colney's shoulders.

'You may see it all before you,' he said, 'straight as the Seine chaussee from the hill of La Roche Guyon.'

He looked for her recollection of the scene.

'Ah, the happy ramble that year!' she cried. 'And my Nesta just seven. We had been six months at Craye. Every day of our life together looks happy to me, looking back, though I know that every day had the same troubles. I don't think I'm deficient in courage; I think I could meet.... But the false position so cruelly weakens me. I am no woman's equal when I have to receive or visit. It seems easier to meet the worst in life-danger, death, anything. Pardon me for talking so. Perhaps we need not have left Craye or Creckholt...?' she hinted an interrogation. 'Though I am not sorry; it is not good to be where one tastes poison. Here it may be as deadly, worse. Dear friend, I am so glad you remember La Roche Guyon. He was popular with the dear French people.'

'In spite of his accent.'

'It is not so bad?'

'And that you'll defend!'

'Consider: these neighbours we come among; they may have heard...'

'Act on the assumption.'

'You forget the principal character. Victor promises; he may have learnt a lesson at Creckholt. But look at this house he has built. How can I—any woman—contain him! He must have society.'

'Paraitre!'

'He must be in the front. He has talked of Parliament.'

Colney's liver took the thrust of a skewer through it. He spoke as in meditative encomium: 'His entry into Parliament would promote himself and family to a station of eminence naked over the Clock Tower of the House.'

She moaned. 'At the vilest, I cannot regret my conduct—bear what I may. I can bear real pain: what kills me is, the suspicion. And I feel it like a guilty wretch! And I do not feel the guilt! I should do the same again, on reflection. I do believe it saved him. I do; oh! I do, I do. I cannot expect my family to see with my eyes. You know them—my brother and sisters think I have disgraced them; they put no value on my saving him. It sounds childish; it is true. He had fallen into a terrible black mood.'

'He had an hour of gloom.'

'An hour!'

'But an hour, with him! It means a good deal.'

'Ah, friend, I take your words. He sinks terribly when he sinks at all.—Spare us a little while.—We have to judge of what is good in the circumstances: I hear your reply! But the principal for me to study is Victor. You have accused me of being the voice of the enamoured woman. I follow him, I know; I try to advise; I find it is wisdom to submit. My people regard my behaviour as a wickedness or a madness. I did save him. I joined my fate with his. I am his mate, to help, and I cannot oppose him, to distract him. I do my utmost for privacy. He must entertain. Believe me, I feel for them—sisters and brother. And now that my sisters are married... My brother has a man's hardness.'

'Colonel Dreighton did not speak harshly, at our last meeting.'

'He spoke of me?'

'He spoke in the tone of a brother.'

'Victor promises—I won't repeat it. Yes, I see the house! There appears to be a prospect, a hope—I cannot allude to it. Craye and Creckholt may have been some lesson to him. Selwyn spoke of me kindly? Ah, yes, it is the way with my people to pretend that Victor has been the ruin of me, that they may come round to family sentiments. In the same way, his relatives, the Duvidney ladies, have their picture of the woman misleading him. Imagine me the naughty adventuress!'—Nataly falsified the thought insurgent at her heart, in adding: 'I do not say I am blameless.' It was a concession to the circumambient enemy, of whom even a good friend was apart, and not better than a respectful emissary. The dearest of her friends belonged to that hostile world. Only Victor, no other, stood with her against the world. Her child, yes; the love of her child she had; but the child's destiny was an alien phantom, looking at her with harder eyes than she had vision of in her family. She did not say she was blameless, did not affect the thought. She would have wished to say, for small encouragement she would have said, that her case could be pleaded.

Colney's features were not inviting, though the expression was not repellent. She sighed deeply; and to count on something helpful by mentioning it, reverted to the 'prospect' which there appeared to be. 'Victor speaks of the certainty of his release.'

His release! Her language pricked a satirist's gallbladder. Colney refrained from speaking to wound, and enjoyed a silence that did it.

'Do you see any possibility?—you knew her,' she said coldly.

'Counting the number of times he has been expecting the release, he is bound to believe it near at hand.'

'You don't?' she asked: her bosom was up in a crisis of expectation for the answer: and on a pause of half-a-minute, she could have uttered the answer herself.

He perceived the insane eagerness through her mask, and despised it, pitying the woman. 'And you don't,' he said. 'You catch at delusions, to excuse the steps you consent to take. Or you want me to wear the blinkers, the better to hoodwink your own eyes. You see it as well as I: If you enter that house, you have to go through the same as at Creckholt:—and he'll be the first to take fright.'

'He finds you in tears: he is immensely devoted; he flings up all to protect "his Nataly."'

'No: you are unjust to him. He would fling up all:'—

'But his Nataly prefers to be dragged through fire? As you please!'

She bowed to her chastisement. One motive in her consultation with him came of the knowledge of his capacity to inflict it and his honesty in the act, and a thirst she had to hear the truth loud-tongued from him; together with a feeling that he was excessive and satiric, not to be read by the letter of his words: and in consequence, she could bear the lash from him, and tell her soul that he overdid it, and have an unjustly-treated self to cherish.—But in very truth she was a woman who loved to hear the truth; she was formed to love the truth her position reduced her to violate; she esteemed the hearing it as medical to her; she selected for counsellor him who would apply it: so far she went on the straight way; and the desire for a sustaining deception from the mouth of a trustworthy man set her hanging on his utterances with an anxious hope of the reverse of what was to come and what she herself apprehended, such as checked her pulses and iced her feet and fingers. The reason being, not that she was craven or absurd or paradoxical, but that, living at an intenser strain upon her nature than she or any around her knew, her strength snapped, she broke down by chance there where Colney was rendered spiteful in beholding the display of her inconsequent if not puling sex.

She might have sought his counsel on another subject, if a paralyzing chill of her frame in the foreview of it had allowed her to speak: she felt grave alarms in one direction, where Nesta stood in the eye of her father; besides an unformed dread that the simplicity in generosity of Victor's nature was doomed to show signs of dross ultimately, under the necessity he imposed upon himself to run out his forecasts, and scheme, and defensively compel the world to serve his ends, for the protection of those dear to him.

At night he was particularly urgent with her for the harmonious duet in praise of Lakelands; and plied her with questions all round and about it, to bring out the dulcet accord. He dwelt on his choice of costly marbles, his fireplace and mantelpiece designs, the great hall, and suggestions for imposing and beautiful furniture; concordantly enough, for the large, the lofty and rich of colour won her enthusiasm; but overwhelmingly to any mood of resistance; and strangely in a man who had of late been adopting, as if his own, a modern tone, or the social and literary hints of it, relating to the right uses of wealth, and the duty as well as the delight of living simply.

'Fredi was pleased.'

'Yes, she was, dear.'

'She is our girl, my love. "I could live and die here!" Live, she may. There's room enough.'

Nataly saw the door of a covert communication pointed at in that remark. She gathered herself for an effort to do battle.

'She's quite a child, Victor.'

'The time begins to run. We have to look forward now:—I declare, it's I who seem the provident mother for Fredi!'

'Let our girl wait; don't hurry her mind to... She is happy with her father and mother. She is in the happiest time of her life, before those feelings distract.'

'If we see good fortune for her, we can't let it pass her.'

A pang of the resolution now to debate the case with Victor, which would be of necessity to do the avoided thing and roll up the forbidden curtain opening on their whole history past and prospective, was met in Nataly's bosom by the more bitter immediate confession that she was not his match. To speak would be to succumb; and shamefully after the effort; and hopelessly after being overborne by him. There was not the anticipation of a set contest to animate the woman's naturally valiant heart; he was too strong: and his vividness in urgency overcame her in advance, fascinated her sensibility through recollection; he fanned an inclination, lighted it to make it a passion, a frenzied resolve—she remembered how and when. She had quivering cause to remember the fateful day of her step, in a letter received that morning from a married sister, containing no word of endearment or proposal for a meeting. An unregretted day, if Victor would think of the dues to others; that is, would take station with the world to see his reflected position, instead of seeing it through their self-justifying knowledge of the honourable truth of their love, and pressing to claim and snatch at whatsoever the world bestows on its orderly subjects.

They had done evil to no one as yet. Nataly thought that; not-withstanding the outcry of the ancient and withered woman who bore Victor Radnor's name: for whom, in consequence of the rod the woman had used, this tenderest of hearts could summon no emotion. If she had it, the thing was not to be hauled up to consciousness. Her feeling was, that she forgave the wrinkled Malignity: pity and contrition dissolving in the effort to produce the placable forgiveness. She was frigid because she knew rightly of herself, that she in the place of power would never have struck so meanly. But the mainspring of the feeling in an almost remorseless bosom drew from certain chance expressions of retrospective physical distaste on Victor's part;—hard to keep from a short utterance between the nuptial two, of whom the unshamed exuberant male has found the sweet reverse in his mate, a haven of heavenliness, to delight in:—these conjoined with a woman's unspoken pleading ideas of her own, on her own behalf, had armed her jealously in vindication of Nature.

Now, as long as they did no palpable wrong about them, Nataly could argue her case in her conscience—deep down and out of hearing, where women under scourge of the laws they have not helped decree may and do deliver their minds. She stood in that subterranean recess for Nature against the Institutions of Man: a woman little adapted for the post of revel; but to this, by the agency of circumstances, it had come; she who was designed by nature to be an ornament of those Institutions opposed them and when thinking of the rights and the conduct of the decrepit Legitimate—virulent in a heathen vindictiveness declaring itself holy—she had Nature's logic, Nature's voice, for self-defence. It was eloquent with her, to the deafening of other voices in herself, even to the convincing of herself, when she was wrought by the fires within to feel elementally. The other voices within her issued of the acknowledged dues to her family and to the world—the civilization protecting women: sentences thereanent in modern books and Journals. But the remembrance of moods of fiery exaltation, when the Nature she called by name of Love raised the chorus within to stop all outer buzzing, was, in a perpetual struggle with a whirlpool, a constant support while she and Victor were one at heart. The sense of her standing alone made her sway; and a thought of differences with him caused frightful apprehensions of the abyss.

Luxuriously she applied to his public life for witness that he had governed wisely as well as affectionately so long; and he might therefore, with the chorussing of the world of public men, expect a woman blindfold to follow his lead. But no; we may be rebels against our time and its Laws: if we are really for Nature, we are not lawless. Nataly's untutored scruples, which came side by side with her ability to plead for her acts, restrained her from complicity in the ensnaring of a young man of social rank to espouse the daughter of a couple socially insurgent-stained, to common thinking, should denunciation come. The Nature upholding her fled at a vision of a stranger entangled. Pitiable to reflect, that he was not one of the adventurer-lords of prey who hunt and run down shadowed heiresses and are congratulated on their luck in a tolerating country! How was the young man to be warned? How, under the happiest of suppositions, propitiate his family! And such a family, if consenting with knowledge, would consent only for the love of money. It was angling with as vile a bait as the rascal lord's. Humiliation hung on the scheme; it struck to scorching in the contemplation of it. And it darkened her reading of Victor's character.

She did not ask for the specification of a 'good fortune that might pass'; wishing to save him from his wonted twists of elusiveness, and herself with him from the dread discussion it involved upon one point.

'The day was pleasant to all, except perhaps poor mademoiselle,' she said.

'Peridon should have come?'

'Present or absent, his chances are not brilliant, I fear.'

'And Pempton and Priscy!'

'They are growing cooler!'

'With their grotesque objections to one another's habits at table!'

'Can we ever hope to get them over it?'

'When Priscy drinks Port and Pempton munches beef, Colney says.'

'I should say, when they feel warmly enough to think little of their differences.'

'Fire smoothes the creases, yes; and fire is what they're both wanting in. Though Priscy has Concert-pathos in her voice:—couldn't act a bit! And Pempton's 'cello tones now and then have gone through me—simply from his fiddle-bow, I believe. Don't talk to me of feeling in a couple, within reach of one another and sniffing objections.—Good, then, for a successful day to-day so far?'

He neared her, wooing her; and she assented, with a franker smile than she had worn through the day.

The common burden on their hearts—the simple discussion to come of the task of communicating dire actualities to their innocent Nesta—was laid aside.

BOOK II

CHAPTER XII

TREATS OF THE DUMBNESS POSSIBLE WITH MEMBERS OF A HOUSEHOLD HAVING ONE HEART

Two that live together in union are supposed to be intimate on every leaf. Particularly when they love one another and the cause they have at heart is common to them in equal measure, the uses of a cordial familiarity forbid reserves upon important matters between them, as we think; not thinking of an imposed secretiveness, beneath the false external of submissiveness, which comes of an experience of repeated inefficiency to maintain a case in opposition, on the part of the loquently weaker of the pair. In Constitutional Kingdoms a powerful Government needs not to be tyrannical to lean oppressively; it is more serviceable to party than agreeable to country; and where the alliance of men and women binds a loving couple, of whom one is a torrent of persuasion, their differings are likely to make the other resemble a log of the torrent. It is borne along; it dreams of a distant corner of the way for a determined stand; it consents to its whirling in anticipation of an undated hour when it will no longer be neutral.

There may be, moreover, while each has the key of the fellow breast, a mutually sensitive nerve to protest against intrusion of light or sound. The cloud over the name of their girl could now strike Nataly and Victor dumb in their taking of counsel. She divined that his hint had encouraged him to bring the crisis nearer, and he that her comprehension had become tremblingly awake. They shrank, each of them, the more from an end drawing closely into view. All subjects glooming off or darkening up to it were shunned by them verbally, and if they found themselves entering beneath that shadow, conversation passed to an involuntary gesture, more explicit with him, significant of the prohibited, though not acknowledging it.

All the stronger was it Victor's purpose, leaping in his fashion to the cover of action as an escape from perplexity, to burn and scheme for the wedding of their girl—the safe wedding of that dearest, to have her protected, secure, with the world warm about her. And he well knew why his Nataly had her look of a closed vault (threatening, if opened, to thunder upon Life) when he dropped his further hints. He chose to call it feminine inconsistency, in a woman who walked abroad with a basket of marriage-ties for the market on her arm. He knew that she would soon have to speak the dark words to their girl; and the idea of any doing of it, caught at his throat. Reasonably she dreaded the mother's task; pardonably indeed. But it is for the mother to do, with a girl. He deputed it lightly to the mother because he could see himself stating the facts to a son. 'And, my dear boy, you will from this day draw your five thousand a year, and we double it on the day of your marriage, living at Lakelands or where you will.'

His desire for his girl's protection by the name of one of our great Families, urged him to bind Nataly to the fact, with the argument, that it was preferable for the girl to hear their story during her green early youth, while she reposed her beautiful blind faith in the discretion of her parents, and as an immediate step to the placing of her hand in a husband's. He feared that her mother required schooling to tell the story vindicatingly and proudly, in a manner to distinguish instead of degrading or temporarily seeming to accept degradation.

The world would weigh on her confession of the weight of the world on her child; she would want inciting and strengthening, if one judged of her capacity to meet the trial by her recent bearing; and how was he to do it! He could not imagine himself encountering the startled, tremulous, nascent intelligence in those pure brown darklashed eyes of Nesta; he pitied the poor mother. Fancifully directing her to say this and that to the girl, his tongue ran till it was cut from his heart and left to wag dead colourless words.

The prospect of a similar business of exposition, certainly devolving upon the father in treaty with the fortunate youth, gripped at his vitals a minute, so intense was his pride in appearing woundless and scarless, a shining surface, like pure health's, in the sight of men. Nevertheless he skimmed the story, much as a lecturer strikes his wand on the prominent places of a map, that is to show us how he arrived at the principal point, which we are all agreed to find chiefly interesting. This with Victor was the naming of Nesta's bridal endowment. He rushed to it. 'My girl will have ten thousand a year settled on her the day of her marriage.' Choice of living at Lakelands was offered.

It helped him over the unpleasant part of that interview. At the same time, it moved him to a curious contempt of the youth. He had to conjure-up an image of the young man in person, to correct the sentiment:—and it remained as a kind of bruise only half cured.

Mr. Dudley Sowerby was not one of the youths whose presence would rectify such an abstract estimate of the genus pursuer. He now came frequently of an evening, to practise a duet for flutes with Victor;—a Mercadante, honeyed and flowing; too honeyed to suit a style that, as Fenellan characterized it to Nataly, went through the music somewhat like an inquisitive tourist in a foreign town, conscientious to get to the end of the work of pleasure; until the notes had become familiar, when it rather resembled a constable's walk along the midnight streets into collision with a garlanded roysterer; and the man of order and the man of passion, true to the measure though they were, seeming to dissent, almost to wrangle, in their different ways of winding out the melody, on to the last movement; which was plainly a question between home to the strayed reveller's quarters or off to the lockup. Victor was altogether the younger of the two. But his vehement accompaniment was a tutorship; Mr. Sowerby improved; it was admitted by Nesta and mademoiselle that he gained a show of feeling; he had learnt that feeling was wanted. Passion, he had not a notion of: otherwise he would not be delaying; the interview, dramatized by the father of the young bud of womanhood, would be taking place, and the entry into Lakelands calculable, for Nataly's comfort, as under the aegis of the Cantor earldom. Gossip flies to a wider circle round the members of a great titled family, is inaudible; or no longer the diptherian whisper the commonalty hear of the commonalty: and so we see the social uses of our aristocracy survive. We do not want the shield of any family; it is the situation that wants it; Nataly ought to be awake to the fact. One blow and we have silenced our enemy: Nesta's wedding-day has relieved her parents.

Victor's thoughts upon the instrument for striking that, blow, led him to suppose Mr. Sowerby might be meditating on the extent of the young lady's fortune. He talked randomly of money, in a way to shatter Nataly's conception of him. He talked of City affairs at table, as it had been his practice to shun the doing; and hit the resounding note on mines, which have risen in the market like the crest of a serpent, casting a certain spell upon the mercantile understanding. 'Fredi's diamonds from her own mine, or what once was—and she still reserves a share,' were to be shown to Mr. Sowerby.

Nataly respected the young fellow for not displaying avidity at the flourish of the bait, however it might be affecting him; and she fancied that he did laboriously, in his way earnestly, study her girl, to sound for harmony between them, previous to a wooing. She was a closer reader of social character than Victor; from refraining to run on the broad lines which are but faintly illustrative of the individual one in being common to all—unless we have hit by chance on an example of the downright in roguery or folly or simple goodness. Mr. Sowerby'g bearing to Nesta was hardly warmed by the glitter of diamonds. His next visit showed him livelier in courtliness, brighter, fresher; but that was always his way at the commencement of every visit, as if his reflections on the foregone had come to a satisfactory conclusion; and the labours of the new study of the maiden ensued again in due course to deaden him.

Gentleman he was. In the recognition of his quality as a man of principle and breeding, Nataly was condemned by thoughts of Nesta's future to question whether word or act of hers should, if inclination on both sides existed, stand between her girl and a true gentleman. She counselled herself, as if the counsel were in requisition, to be passive; and so doing, she more acutely than Victor—save in his chance flashes—discerned the twist of her very nature caused by their false position. And her panacea for ills, the lost little cottage, would not have averted it: she would there have had the same coveting desire to name a man of breeding, honour, station, for Nesta's husband. Perhaps in the cottage, choosing at leisure, her consent to see the brilliant young creature tied to the best of dull men would have been unready, without the girl to push it. For the Hon. Dudley was lamentably her pupil in liveliness; he took the second part, as it is painful for a woman with the old-fashioned ideas upon the leading of the sexes to behold; resembling in his look the deaf, who constantly require to have an observation repeated; resembling the most intelligent of animals, which we do not name, and we reprove ourselves for seeing likeness.

Yet the likeness or apparent likeness would suggest that we have not so much to fear upon the day of the explanation to him. Some gain is there. Shameful thought! Nataly hastened her mind to gather many instances or indications testifying to the sterling substance in young Mr. Sowerby, such as a mother would pray for her son-in-law to possess. She discovered herself feeling as the burdened mother, not providently for her girl, in the choice of a mate. The perception was clear, and not the less did she continue working at the embroidery of Mr. Sowerby on the basis of his excellent moral foundations, all the while hoping, praying, that he might not be lured on to the proposal for Nesta. But her subservience to the power of the persuasive will in Victor—which was like the rush of a conflagration—compelled her to think realizingly of any scheme he allowed her darkly to read.

Opposition to him, was comparable to the stand of blocks of timber before flame. Colney Durance had done her the mischief we take from the pessimist when we are overweighted: in darkening the vision of external aid from man or circumstance to one who felt herself mastered. Victor could make her treacherous to her wishes, in revolt against them, though the heart protested. His first conquest of her was in her blood, to weaken a spirit of resistance. For the precedent of submission is a charm upon the faint-hearted through love: it unwinds, unwills them. Nataly resolved fixedly, that there must be a day for speaking; and she had her moral sustainment in the resolve; she had also a tormenting consciousness of material support in the thought, that the day was not present, was possibly distant, might never arrive. Would Victor's release come sooner? And that was a prospect bearing resemblance to hopes of the cure of a malady through a sharp operation.

These were matters going on behind the curtain; as wholly vital to her, and with him at times almost as dominant, as the spiritual in memory, when flesh has left but its shining track in dust of a soul outwritten; and all their talk related to the purchase of furniture, the expeditions to Lakelands, music, public affairs, the pardonable foibles of friends created to amuse their fellows, operatic heroes and heroines, exhibitions of pictures, the sorrows of Crowned Heads, so serviceable ever to mankind as an admonition to the ambitious, a salve to the envious!—in fine, whatsoever can entertain or affect the most social of couples, domestically without a care to appearance. And so far they partially—dramatically—deceived themselves by imposing on the world while they talked and duetted; for the purchase of furniture from a flowing purse is a cheerful occupation; also a City issuing out of hospital, like this poor City of London, inspires good citizens to healthy activity. But the silence upon what they were most bent on, had the sinister effect upon Victor, of obscuring his mental hold of the beloved woman, drifting her away from him. In communicating Fenellan's news through the lawyer Carling of Mrs. Burman's intentions, he was aware that there was an obstacle to his being huggingly genial, even candidly genial with her, until he could deal out further news, corroborative and consecutive, to show the action of things as progressive. Fenellan had sunk into his usual apathy:—and might plead the impossibility of his moving faster than the woman professing to transform herself into, beneficence out of malignity;—one could hear him saying the words! Victor had not seen him since last Concert evening, and he deemed it as well to hear the words Fenellan's mouth had to say. He called at an early hour of the Westward tidal flow at the Insurance Office looking over the stormy square of the first of Seamen.

CHAPTER XIII

THE LATEST OF MRS. BURMAN

After cursory remarks about the business of the Office and his friend's contributions to periodical literature, in which he was interested for as long as he had assurance that the safe income depending upon official duties was not endangered by them, Victor kicked his heels to and fro. Fenellan waited for him to lead.

'Have you seen that man, her lawyer, again?'

'I have dined with Mr. Carling:—capital claret.'

Emptiness was in the reply.

Victor curbed himself and said: 'By the way, you're not likely to have dealings with Blathenoy. The fellow has a screw to the back of a shifty eye; I see it at work to fix the look for business. I shall sit on the Board of my Bank. One hears things. He lives in style at Wrensham. By the way, Fredi has little Mab Mountney from Creckholt staying with her. You said of little Mabsy—"Here she comes into the room all pink and white, like a daisy." She's the daisy still; reminds us of our girl at that age.—So, then, we come to another dead block!'

'Well, no; it's a chemist's shop, if that helps us on,' said Fenellan, settling to a new posture in his chair. 'She's there of an afternoon for hours.'

'You mean it's she?'

'The lady. I 'll tell you. I have it from Carling, worthy man; and lawyers can be brought to untruss a point over a cup of claret. He's a bit of a "Mackenzie Man," as old aunts of mine used to say at home—a Man of Feeling. Thinks he knows the world, from having sifted and sorted a lot of our dustbins; as the modern Realists imagine it's an exposition of positive human nature when they've pulled down our noses to the worst parts—if there's a worse where all are useful: but the Realism of the dogs is to have us by the nose:—excite it and befoul it, and you're fearfully credible! You don't read that olfactory literature. However, friend Carling is a conciliatory carle. Three or four days of the week the lady, he says, drives to her chemist's, and there she sits in the shop; round the corner, as you enter; and sees all Charing in the shop looking-glass at the back; herself a stranger spectacle, poor lady, if Carling's picture of her is not overdone; with her fashionable no-bonnet striding the contribution chignon on the crown, and a huge square green shade over her forehead. Sits hours long, and cocks her ears at orders of applicants for drugs across the counter, and sometimes catches wind of a prescription, and consults her chemist, and thinks she 'll try it herself. It's a basket of medicine bottles driven to Regent's Park pretty well every day.'

'Ha! Regent's Park!' exclaimed Victor, and shook at recollections of the district and the number of the house, dismal to him. London buried the woman deep until a mention of her sent her flaring over London. 'A chemist's shop! She sits there?'

'Mrs. Burman. We pass by the shop.'

'She had always a turn for drugs.—Not far from here, did you say? And every day! under a green shade?'

'Dear fellow, don't be suggesting ballads; we'll go now,' said Fenellan. 'It 's true it's like sitting on the banks of the Stygian waters.'

He spied at an obsequious watch, that told him it was time to quit the office.

'You've done nothing?' Victor asked in a tone of no expectation.

'Only to hear that her latest medical man is Themison.'

'Where did you hear?'

'Across the counter of Boyle and Luckwort, the lady's chemists. I called the day before yesterday, after you were here at our last Board Meeting.'

'The Themison?'

'The great Dr. Themison; who kills you kindlier than most, and is much in request for it.'

'There's one of your echoes of Colney!' Victor cried. 'One gets dead sick of that worn-out old jibeing at doctors. They don't kill, you know very well. It 's not to their interest to kill. They may take the relish out of life; and upon my word, I believe that helps to keep the patient living!'

Fenellan sent an eye of discreet comic penetration travelling through his friend.

'The City's mending; it's not the weary widow woman of the day when we capsized the diurnal with your royal Old Veuve,' he said, as they trod the pavement. 'Funny people, the English! They give you all the primeing possible for amusement and jollity, and devil a sentry-box for the exercise of it; and if you shake a leg publicly, partner or not, you're marched off to penitence. I complain, that they have no philosophical appreciation of human nature.'

'We pass the shop?' Victor interrupted him.

'You're in view of it in a minute. And what a square, for recreative dancing! And what a people, to be turning it into a place of political agitation! And what a country, where from morning to night it's an endless wrangle about the first conditions of existence! Old Colney seems right now and then: they 're the offspring of pirates, and they 've got the manners and tastes of their progenitors, and the trick of quarrelling everlastingly over the booty. I 'd have band-music here for a couple of hours, three days of the week at the least; and down in the East; and that forsaken North quarter of London; and the Baptist South too. But just as those omnibus-wheels are the miserable music of this London of ours, it 's only too sadly true that the people are in the first rumble of the notion of the proper way to spend their lives. Now you see the shop: Boyle and Luckwort: there.'

Victor looked. He threw his coat open, and pulled the waistcoat, and swelled it, ahemming. 'That shop?' said he. And presently: 'Fenellan, I'm not superstitious, I think. Now listen; I declare to you, on the day of our drinking Old Veuve together last—you remember it,—I walked home up this way across the square, and I was about to step into that identical shop, for some household prescription in my pocket, having forgotten Nataly's favourite City chemists Fenbird and Jay, when—I'm stating a fact—I distinctly—I 'm sure of the shop—felt myself plucked back by the elbow; pulled back the kind of pull when you have to put a foot backward to keep your equilibrium.'

So does memory inspired by the sensations contribute an additional item for the colouring of history.

He touched the elbow, showed a flitting face of crazed amazement in amusement, and shrugged and half-laughed, dismissing the incident, as being perhaps, if his hearer chose to have it so, a gem of the rubbish tumbled into the dustcart out of a rather exceptional householder's experience.

Fenellan smiled indulgently. 'Queer things happen. I recollect reading in my green youth of a clergyman, who mounted a pulpit of the port where he was landed after his almost solitary rescue from a burning ship at midnight in mid-sea, to inform his congregation, that he had overnight of the catastrophe a personal Warning right in his ear from a Voice, when at his bed or bunk-side, about to perform the beautiful ceremony of undressing: and the Rev. gentleman was to lie down in his full uniform, not so much as to relieve himself of his boots, the Voice insisted twice; and he obeyed it, despite the discomfort to his poor feet; and he jumped up in his boots to the cry of Fire, and he got them providentially over the scuffling deck straight at the first rush into the boat awaiting them, and had them safe on and polished the day he preached the sermon of gratitude for the special deliverance. There was a Warning! and it might well be called, as he called it, from within. We're cared for, never doubt. Aide-toi. Be ready dressed to help yourself in a calamity, or you'll not stand in boots at your next Sermon, contrasting with the burnt. That sounds like the moral.'

'She could have seen me,' Victor threw out an irritable suggestion. The idea of the recent propinquity set hatred in motion.

'Scarcely likely. I'm told she sits looking on her lap, under the beetling shade, until she hears an order for tinctures or powders, or a mixture that strikes her fancy. It's possible to do more suicidal things than sit the afternoons in a chemist's shop and see poor creatures get their different passports to Orcus.'

Victor stepped mutely beneath the windows of the bellied glass-urns of chemical wash. The woman might be inside there now! She might have seen his figure in the shop-mirror! And she there! The wonder of it all seemed to be, that his private history was not walking the streets. The thinness of the partition concealing it, hardly guaranteed a day's immunity: because this woman would live in London, in order to have her choice of a central chemist's shop, where she could feed a ghastly imagination on the various recipes... and while it would have been so much healthier for her to be living in a recess of the country!

He muttered: 'Diseases—drugs!'

Those were the corresponding two strokes of the pendulum which kept the woman going.

'And deadly spite.' That was the emanation of the monotonous horrible conflict, for which, and by which, the woman lived.

In the neighbourhood of the shop, he could not but think of her through the feelings of a man scorched by a furnace.

A little further on, he said: 'Poor soul!' He confessed to himself, that latterly he had, he knew not why, been impatient with her, rancorous in thought, as never before. He had hitherto aimed at a picturesque tolerance of her vindictiveness; under suffering, both at Craye and Creckholt; and he had been really forgiving. He accused her of dragging him down to humanity's lowest.

But if she did that, it argued the possession of a power of a sort.

Her station in the chemist's shop he passed almost daily, appeared to him as a sudden and a terrific rush to the front; though it was only a short drive from the house in Regent's Park; but having shaken-off that house, he had pushed it back into mists, obliterated it. The woman certainly had a power.

He shot away to the power he knew of in himself; his capacity for winning men in bodies, the host of them, when it came to an effort of his energies: men and, individually, women. Individually, the women were to be counted on as well; warm supporters.

It was the admission of a doubt that he might expect to enroll them collectively. Eyeing the men, he felt his command of them. Glancing at congregated women, he had a chill. The Wives and Spinsters in ghostly judicial assembly: that is, the phantom of the offended collective woman: that is, the regnant Queen Idea issuing from our concourse of civilized life to govern Society, and pronounce on the orderly, the tolerable, the legal, and banish the rebellious: these maintained an aspect of the stand against him.

Did Nataly read the case: namely, that the crowned collective woman is not to be subdued? And what are we to say of the indefinite but forcible Authority, when we see it upholding Mrs. Burman to crush a woman like Nataly!

Victor's novel exercises in reflection were bringing him by hard degrees to conceive it to be the impalpable which has prevailing weight. Not many of our conquerors have scored their victories on the road of that index: nor has duration been granted them to behold the minute measure of value left even tangible after the dust of the conquest subsides. The passing by a shop where a broken old woman might be supposed to sit beneath her green forehead-shade—Venetian-blind of a henbane-visage!—had precipitated him into his first real grasp of the abstract verity: and it opens on to new realms, which are a new world to the practical mind. But he made no advance. He stopped in a fever of sensibility, to contemplate the powerful formless vapour rolling from a source that was nothing other than yonder weak lonely woman.

In other words, the human nature of the man was dragged to the school of its truancy by circumstances, for him to learn the commonest of sums done on a slate, in regard to payment of debts and the unrelaxing grip of the creditor on the defaulter. Debtors are always paying like those who are guilty of the easiest thing in life, the violation of Truth, they have made themselves bondmen to pay, if not in substance, then in soul; and the nipping of the soul goes on for as long as the concrete burden is undischarged. You know the Liar; you must have seen him diminishing, until he has become a face without features, withdrawn to humanity's preliminary sketch (some half-dozen frayed threads of woeful outline on our original tapestry-web); and he who did the easiest of things, he must from such time sweat in being the prodigy of inventive nimbleness, up to the day when he propitiates Truth by telling it again. There is a repentance that does reconstitute! It may help to the traceing to springs of a fable whereby men have been guided thus far out of the wood.

Victor would have said truly that he loved Truth; that he paid every debt with a scrupulous exactitude: money, of course; and prompt apologies for a short brush of his temper. Nay, he had such a conscience for the smallest eruptions of a transient irritability, that the wish to say a friendly mending word to the Punctilio donkey of London Bridge, softened his retrospective view of the fall there, more than once. Although this man was a presentation to mankind of the force in Nature which drives to unresting speed, which is the vitality of the heart seen at its beating after a plucking of it from the body, he knew himself for the reverse of lawless; he inclined altogether to good citizenship. So social a man could not otherwise incline. But when it came to the examination of accounts between Mrs. Burman and himself, spasms of physical revulsion, loathings, his excessive human nature, put her out of Court. To men, it was impossible for him to speak the torments of those days of the monstrous alliance. The heavens were cognizant. He pleaded his case in their accustomed hearing:—a youngster tempted by wealth, attracted, besought, snared, revolted, etc. And Mrs. Burman, when roused to jealousy, had shown it by teazing him for a confession of his admiration of splendid points in the beautiful Nataly, the priceless fair woman living under their roof, a contrast of very life, with the corpse and shroud; and she seen by him daily, singing with him, her breath about him, her voice incessantly upon every chord of his being!

He pleaded successfully. But the silence following the verdict was heavy; the silence contained an unheard thunder. It was the sound, as when out of Court the public is dissatisfied with a verdict. Are we expected to commit a social outrage in exposing our whole case to the public?—Imagine it for a moment as done. Men are ours at a word—or at least a word of invitation. Women we woo; fluent smooth versions of our tortures, mixed with permissible courtship, win the individual woman. And that unreasoning collective woman, icy, deadly, condemns the poor racked wretch who so much as remembers them! She is the enemy of Nature.—Tell us how? She is the slave of existing conventions.—And from what cause? She is the artificial production of a state that exalts her so long as she sacrifices daily and hourly to the artificial.

Therefore she sides with Mrs. Burman—the foe of Nature: who, with her arts and gold lures, has now possession of the Law (the brass idol worshipped by the collective) to drive Nature into desolation.

He placed himself to the right of Mrs. Burman, for the world to behold the couple: and he lent the world a sigh of disgust.

What he could not do, as in other matters he did, was to rise above the situation, in a splendid survey and rapid view of the means of reversing it. He was too social to be a captain of the socially insurgent; imagination expired.

But having a courageous Nataly to second him!—how then? It was the succour needed. Then he would have been ready to teach the world that Nature—honest Nature—is more to be prized than Convention: a new Era might begin.

The thought was tonic for an instant and illuminated him springingly. It sank, excused for the flaccidity by Nataly's want of common adventurous daring. She had not taken to Lakelands; she was purchasing furniture from a flowing purse with a heavy heart—unfeminine, one might say; she preferred to live obscurely; she did not, one had to think—but it was unjust: and yet the accusation, that she did not cheerfully make a strain and spurt on behalf of her child, pressed to be repeated.

These short glimpses at reflection in Victor were like the verberant twang of a musical instrument that has had a smart blow, and wails away independent of the player's cunning hand. He would have said, that he was more his natural self when the cunning hand played on him, to make him praise and uplift his beloved: mightily would it have astonished him to contemplate with assured perception in his own person the Nature he invoked. But men invoking Nature, do not find in her the Holy Mother she in such case becomes to her daughters, whom she so persecutes. Men call on her for their defence, as a favourable witness: she is a note of their rhetoric. They are not bettered by her sustainment; they have not, as women may have, her enaemic aid at a trying hour. It is not an effort at epigram to say, that whom she scourges most she most supports.

An Opera-placard drew his next remark to Fenellan.

'How Wagner seems to have stricken the Italians! Well, now, the Germans have their Emperor to head their armies, and I say that the German emperor has done less for their lasting fame and influence than Wagner has done. He has affected the French too; I trace him in Gounod's Romeo et Juliette—and we don't gain by it; we have a poor remuneration for the melody gone; think of the little shepherd's pipeing in Mireille; and there's another in Sapho-delicious. I held out against Wagner as long as I could. The Italians don't much more than Wagnerize in exchange for the loss of melody. They would be wiser in going back to Pergolese, Campagnole. The Mefistofole was good—of the school of the foreign master. Aida and Otello, no. I confess to a weakness for the old barleysugar of Bellini or a Donizetti-Serenade. Aren't you seduced by cadences? Never mind Wagner's tap of his paedagogue's baton—a cadence catches me still. Early taste for barley-sugar, perhaps! There's a march in Verdi's Attila and I Lombardi, I declare I'm in military step when I hear them, as in the old days, after leaving the Opera. Fredi takes little Mab Mountney to her first Opera to-night. Enough to make us old ones envious! You remember your first Opera, Fenellan? Sonnambula, with me. I tell you, it would task the highest poetry—say, require, if you like—showing all that's noblest, splendidest, in a young man, to describe its effect on me. I was dreaming of my box at the Opera for a year after. The Huguenots to-night. Not the best suited for little Mabsy; but she'll catch at the Rataplan. Capital Opera; we used to think it the best, before we had Tannhauser and Lohengrin and the Meistersinger.'

Victor hinted notes of the Conspiration Scene closing the Third Act of the Huguenots. That sombre Chorus brought Mrs. Burman before him. He drummed the Rataplan, which sent her flying. The return of a lively disposition for dinner and music completed his emancipation from the yoke of the baleful creature sitting half her days in the chemist's shop; save that a thought of drugs brought the smell, and the smell the picture; she threatened to be an apparition at any moment pervading him through his nostrils. He spoke to Fenellan of hunger for dinner, a need for it; singular in one whose appetite ran to the stroke of the hour abreast with Armandine's kitchen-clock. Fenellan proposed a glass of sherry and bitters at his Club over the way. He had forgotten a shower of black-balls (attributable to the conjurations of old Ate) on a certain past day. Without word of refusal, Victor entered a wine-merchant's office, where he was unknown, and stating his wish for bitters and dry sherry, presently received the glass, drank, nodded to the administering clerk, named the person whom he had obliged and refreshed, and passed out, remarking to Fenellan: 'Colney on Clubs! he's right; they're the mediaeval in modern times, our Baron's castles, minus the Baron; dead against public life and social duties. Business excuses my City Clubs; but I shall take my name off my Club up West.'

'More like monasteries, with a Committee for Abbot, and Whist for the services,' Fenellan said. 'Or tabernacles for the Chosen, and Grangousier playing Divinity behind the veil. Well, they're social.'

'Sectionally social, means anything but social, my friend. However—and the monastery had a bell for the wanderer! Say, I'm penniless or poundless, up and down this walled desert of a street, I feel, I must feel, these palaces—if we're Christian, not Jews: not that the Jews are uncharitable; they set an: example, in fact....'

He rambled, amusingly to the complacent hearing of Fenellan, who thought of his pursuit of wealth and grand expenditure.

Victor talked as a man having his mind at leaps beyond the subject. He was nearing to the Idea he had seized and lost on London Bridge.

The desire for some good news wherewith to inspirit Nataly, withdrew him from his ineffectual chase. He had nought to deliver; on the contrary, a meditation concerning her comfort pledged him to concealment which was the no step, or passive state, most abhorrent to him.

He snatched at the name of Themison.

With Dr. Themison fast in his grasp, there was a report of progress to be made to Nataly; and not at all an empty report.

Themison, then: he leaned on Themison. The woman's doctor should have an influence approaching to authority with her.

Land-values in the developing Colonies, formed his theme of discourse to Fenellan: let Banks beware.

Fenellan saw him shudder and rub the back of his head. 'Feel the wind?' he said.

Victor answered him with that humane thrill of the deep tones, which at times he had: 'No: don't be alarmed; I feel the devil. If one has wealth and a desperate wish, he will speak. All he does, is to make me more charitable to those who give way to him. I believe in a devil.'

'Horns and tail?'

'Bait and hook.'

'I haven't wealth, and I wish only for dinner,' Fenellan said.

'You know that Armandine is never two minutes late. By the way, you haven't wealth—you have me.'

'And I thank God for you!' said Fenellan, acutely reminiscent of his having marked the spiritual adviser of Mrs. Burman, the Rev. Groseman Buttermore, as a man who might be useful to his friend.

CHAPTER XIV

A fortnight later, an extremely disconcerting circumstance occurred: Armandine was ten minutes behind the hour with her dinner. But the surprise and stupefaction expressed by Victor, after glances at his watch, were not so profound as Fenellan's, on finding himself exchangeing the bow with a gentleman bearing the name of Dr. Themison. His friend's rapidity in pushing the combinations he conceived, was known: Fenellan's wonder was not so much that Victor had astonished him again, as that he should be called upon again to wonder at his astonishment. He did; and he observed the doctor and Victor and Nataly: aided by dropping remarks. Before the evening was over, he gathered enough of the facts, and had to speculate only on the designs. Dr. Themison had received a visit from the husband of Mrs. Victor Radnor concerning her state of health. At an interview with the lady, laughter greeted him; he was confused by her denial of the imputation of a single ailment: but she, to recompose him, let it be understood, that she was anxious about her husband's condition, he being certainly overworked; and the husband's visit passed for a device on the part of the wife. She admitted a willingness to try a change of air, if it was deemed good for her husband. Change of air was prescribed to each for both. 'Why not drive to Paris?' the doctor said, and Victor was taken with the phrase.

He told Fenellan at night that Mrs. Burman, he had heard, was by the sea, on the South coast. Which of her maladies might be in the ascendant, he did not know. He knew little. He fancied that Dr. Themison was unsuspicious of the existence of a relationship between him and Mrs. Burman: and Fenellan opined, that there had been no communication upon private affairs. What, then, was the object in going to Dr. Themison? He treated her body merely; whereas the Rev. Groseman Buttermore could be expected to impose upon her conduct. Fenellan appreciated his own discernment of the superior uses to which a spiritual adviser may be put, and he too agreeably flattered himself for the corrective reflection to ensue, that he had not done anything. It disposed him to think a happy passivity more sagacious than a restless activity. We should let Fortune perform her part at the wheel in working out her ends, should we not?—for, ten to one, nine times out of ten we are thwarting her if we stretch out a hand. And with the range of enjoyments possessed by Victor, why this unceasing restlessness? Why, when we are not near drowning, catch at apparent straws, which may be instruments having sharp edges? Themison, as Mrs. Burman's medical man, might tell the lady tales that would irritate her bag of venom.

Rarely though Fenellan was the critic on his friend, the shadow cast over his negligent hedonism by Victor's boiling pressure, drove him into the seat of judgement. As a consequence, he was rather a dull table-guest in the presence of Dr. Themison, whom their host had pricked to anticipate high entertainment from him. He did nothing to bridge the crevasse and warm the glacier air at table when the doctor, anecdotal intentionally to draw him out, related a decorous but pungent story of one fair member of a sweet new sisterhood in agitation against the fixed establishment of our chain-mail marriage-tie. An anecdote of immediate diversion was wanted, expected: and Fenellan sat stupidly speculating upon whether the doctor knew of a cupboard locked. So that Dr. Themison was carried on by Lady Grace Halley's humourous enthusiasm for the subject to dilate and discuss and specify, all in the irony of a judicial leaning to the side of the single-minded social adventurers, under an assumed accord with his audience; concluding: 'So there's an end of Divorce.'

'By the trick of multiplication,' Fenellan, now reassured, was content to say. And that did not extinguish the cracker of a theme; handled very carefully, as a thing of fire, it need scarce be remarked, three young women being present.

Nataly had eyes on her girl, and was pleased at an alertness shown by Mr. Sowerby to second her by crossing the dialogue. As regarded her personal feelings, she was hardened, so long as the curtains were about her to keep the world from bending black brows of inquisition upon one of its culprits. But her anxiety was vigilant to guard her girl from an infusion of any of the dread facts of life not coming through the mother's lips: and she was a woman having the feminine mind's pudency in that direction, which does not consent to the revealing of much. Here was the mother's dilemma: her girl—Victor's girl, as she had to think in this instance,—the most cloudless of the young women of earth, seemed, and might be figured as really, at the falling of a crumb off the table of knowledge, taken by the brain to shoot up to terrific heights of surveyal; and there she rocked; and only her youthful healthiness brought her down to grass and flowers. She had once or twice received the electrical stimulus, to feel and be as lightning, from a seizure of facts in infinitesimal doses, guesses caught off maternal evasions or the circuitous explanation of matters touching sex in here and there a newspaper, harder to repress completely than sewer-gas in great cities: and her mother had seen, with an apprehensive pang of anguish, how witheringly the scared young intelligence of the innocent creature shocked her sensibility. She foresaw the need to such a flameful soul, as bride, wife, woman across the world, of the very princeliest of men in gifts of strength, for her sustainer and guide. And the provident mother knew this peerless gentleman: but he had his wife.

Delusions and the pain of the disillusioning were to be feared for the imaginative Nesta; though not so much as that on some future day of a perchance miserable yokemating—a subjection or an entanglement—the nobler passions might be summoned to rise for freedom, and strike a line to make their logically estimable sequence from a source not honourable before the public. Constantly it had to be thought, that the girl was her father's child.

At present she had no passions; and her bent to the happiness she could so richly give, had drawn her sailing smoothly over the harbour-bar of maidenhood; where many of her sisters are disconcerted to the loss of simplicity. If Nataly with her sleepless watchfulness and forecasts partook of the French mother, Nesta's Arcadian independence likened her somewhat in manner to the Transatlantic version of the English girl. Her high physical animation and the burden of themes it plucked for delivery carried her flowing over impediments of virginal self-consciousness, to set her at her ease in the talk with men; she had not gone through the various Nursery exercises in dissimulation; she had no appearance of praying forgiveness of men for the original sin of being woman; and no tricks of lips or lids, or traitor scarlet on the cheeks, or assumptions of the frigid mask, or indicated reserve-cajoleries. Neither ignorantly nor advisedly did she play on these or other bewitching strings of her sex, after the fashion of the stamped innocents, who are the boast of Englishmen and matrons, and thrill societies with their winsome ingenuousness; and who sometimes when unguarded meet an artful serenader, that is a cloaked bandit, and is provoked by their performances, and knows anthropologically the nature behind the devious show; a sciential rascal; as little to be excluded from our modern circles as Eve's own old deuce from Eden's garden whereupon, opportunity inviting, both the fool and the cunning, the pure donkey princess of insular eulogy, and the sham one, are in a perilous pass.

Damsels of the swiftness of mind of Nesta cannot be ignorant utterly amid a world where the hints are hourly scattering seed of the inklings; when vileness is not at work up and down our thoroughfares, proclaiming its existence with tableau and trumpet. Nataly encountered her girl's questions, much as one seeks to quiet an enemy. The questions had soon ceased. Excepting repulsive and rejected details, there is little to be learnt when a little is known: in populous communities, density only will keep the little out. Only stupidity will suppose that it can be done for the livelier young. English mothers forethoughtful for their girls, have to take choice of how to do battle with a rough-and-tumble Old England, that lumbers bumping along, craving the precious things, which can be had but in semblance under the conditions allowed by laziness to subsist, and so curst of its shifty inconsequence as to worship in the concrete an hypocrisy it abhors in the abstract. Nataly could smuggle or confiscate here and there a newspaper; she could not interdict or withhold every one of them, from a girl ardent to be in the race on all topics of popular interest: and the newspapers are occasionally naked savages; the streets are imperfectly garmented even by day; and we have our stumbling social anecdotist, our spot-mouthed young man, our eminently silly woman; our slippery one; our slimy one, the Rahab of Society; not to speak of Mary the maid and the footman William. A vigilant mother has to contend with these and the like in an increasing degree. How best?

There is a method: one that Colney Durance advocated. The girl's intelligence and sweet blood invited a trial of it. Since, as he argued, we cannot keep the poisonous matter out, mothers should prepare and strengthen young women for the encounter with it, by lifting the veil, baring the world, giving them knowledge to arm them for the fight they have to sustain; and thereby preserve them further from the spiritual collapse which follows the nursing of a false ideal of our life in youth:—this being, Colney said, the prominent feminine disease of the time, common to all our women; that is, all having leisure to shine in the sun or wave in the wind as flowers of the garden.

Whatever there was of wisdom in his view, he spoilt it for English hearing, by making use of his dry compressed sentences. Besides he was a bachelor; therefore but a theorist. And his illustrations of his theory were grotesque; meditation on them extracted a corrosive acid to consume, in horrid derision, the sex, the nation, the race of man. The satirist too devotedly loves his lash to be a persuasive teacher. Nataly had excuses to cover her reasons for not listening to him.

One reason was, as she discerned through her confusion at the thought, that the day drew near for her speaking fully to Nesta; when, between what she then said and what she said now, a cruel contrast might strike the girl and in toneing revelations now, to be more consonant with them then;—in softening and shading the edges of social misconduct, it seemed painfully possible to be sowing in the girl's mind something like the reverse of moral precepts, even to smoothing the way to a rebelliousness partly or wholly similar to her own. But Nataly's chief and her appeasing reason for pursuing the conventional system with this exceptional young creature, referred to the sentiments on that subject of the kind of young man whom a mother elects from among those present and eligible, as perhaps next to worthy to wed the girl, by virtue of good promise in the moral department. She had Mr. Dudley Sowerby under view; far from the man of her choice and still the practice of decorum, discretion, a pardonable fastidiousness, appears, if women may make any forecast of the behaviour of young men or may trust the faces they see, to, promise a future stability in the husband. Assuredly a Dudley Sowerby would be immensely startled to find in his bride a young woman more than babily aware of the existence of one particular form of naughtiness on earth.

Victor was of no help: he had not an idea upon the right education of the young of the sex. Repression and mystery, he considered wholesome for girls; and he considered the enlightening of them—to some extent—a prudential measure for their defence; and premature instruction is a fire-water to their wild-in-woods understanding; and histrionic innocence is no doubt the bloom on corruption; also the facts of current human life, in the crude of the reports or the cooked of the sermon in the newspapers, are a noxious diet for our daughters; whom nevertheless we cannot hope to be feeding always on milk: and there is a time when their adorable pretty ignorance, if credibly it exists out of noodledom, is harmful:—but how beautiful the shining simplicity of our dear young English girls! He was one of the many men to whose minds women come in pictures and are accepted much as they paint themselves. Like his numerous fellows, too, he required a conflict with them, and a worsting at it, to be taught, that they are not the mere live stock we scheme to dispose of for their good: unless Love should interpose, he would have exclaimed. He broke from his fellows in his holy horror of a father's running counter to love. Nesta had only to say, that she loved another, for Dudley Sowerby to be withdrawn into the background of aspirants. But love was unknown to the girl.

Outwardly, the plan of the Drive to Paris had the look of Victor's traditional hospitality. Nataly smiled at her incorrigibly lagging intelligence of him, on hearing that he had invited a company: 'Lady Grace, for gaiety; Peridon and Catkin, fiddles; Dudley Sowerby and myself, flutes; Barmby, intonation; in all, nine of us; and by the dear old Normandy route, for the sake of the voyage, as in old times; towers of Dieppe in the morning-light; and the lovely road to the capital! Just three days in Paris, and home by any of the other routes. It's the drive we want. Boredom in wet weather, we defy; we have our Concert—an hour at night and we're sure of sleep.' It had a sweet simple air, befitting him; as when in bygone days they travelled with the joy of children. For travelling shook Nataly out of her troubles and gave her something of the child's inheritance of the wisdom of life—the living ever so little ahead of ourselves; about as far as the fox in view of the hunt. That is the soul of us out for novelty, devouring as it runs, an endless feast; and the body is eagerly after it, recording the pleasures, a daily chase. Remembrance of them is almost a renewal, anticipation a revival. She enraptured Victor with glimpses of the domestic fun she had ceased to show sign of since the revelation of Lakelands. Her only regret was on account of the exclusion of Colney Durance from the party, because of happy memories associating him with the Seine-land, and also that his bilious criticism of his countrymen was moderated by a trip to the Continent. Fenellan reported Colney to be 'busy in the act of distilling one of his Prussic acid essays.' Fenellan would have jumped to go. He informed Victor, as a probe, that the business of the Life Insurance was at periods 'fearfully necrological! Inexplicably, he was not invited. Did it mean, that he was growing dull? He looked inside instead of out, and lost the clue.

His behaviour on the evening of the departure showed plainly what would have befallen Mr. Sowerby on the expedition, had not he as well as Colney been excluded. Two carriages and a cab conveyed the excursionists, as they merrily called themselves, to the terminus. They were Victor's guests; they had no trouble, no expense, none of the nipper reckonings which dog our pleasures; the state of pure bliss. Fenellan's enviousness drove him at the Rev. Mr. Barmby until the latter jumped to the seat beside Nesta in her carriage, Mademoiselle de Seilles and Mr. Sowerby facing them. Lady Grace Halley, in the carriage behind, heard Nesta's laugh; which Mr. Barmby had thought vacuous, beseeming little girls, that laugh at nothings. She questioned Fenellan.

'Oh,' said he, 'I merely mentioned that the Rev. gentleman carries his musical instrument at the bottom of his trunk.'

She smiled: 'And who are in the cab?'

'Your fiddles are in the cab, in charge of Peridon and Catkin. Those two would have writhed like head and tail of a worm, at a division on the way to the station. Point a finger at Peridon, you run Catkin through the body. They're a fabulous couple.'

Victor cut him short. 'I deny that those two are absurd.'

'And Catkin's toothache is a galvanic battery upon Peridon.'

Nataly strongly denied it. Peridon and Catkin pertained to their genial picture of the dear sweet nest in life; a dale never traversed by the withering breath they dreaded.

Fenellan then, to prove that he could be as bad in his way as Colney, fell to work on the absent Miss Priscilla Graves and Mr. Pempton, with a pitchfork's exaltation of the sacred attachment of the divergently meritorious couple, and a melancholy reference to implacable obstacles in the principles of each. The pair were offending the amatory corner in the generous good sense of Nataly and Victor; they were not to be hotly protected, though they were well enough liked for their qualities, except by Lady Grace, who revelled in the horrifying and scandalizing of Miss Graves. Such a specimen of the Puritan middle English as Priscilla Graves, was eastwind on her skin, nausea to her gorge. She wondered at having drifted into the neighbourhood of a person resembling in her repellent formal chill virtuousness a windy belfry tower, down among those districts of suburban London or appalling provincial towns passed now and then with a shudder, where the funereal square bricks-up the Church, that Arctic hen-mother sits on the square, and the moving dead are summoned to their round of penitential exercise by a monosyllabic tribulation-bell. Fenellan's graphic sketch of the teetotaller woman seeing her admirer pursued by Eumenides flagons—abominations of emptiness—to the banks of the black river of suicides, where the one most wretched light is Inebriation's nose; and of the vegetarian violoncello's horror at his vision of the long procession of the flocks and herds into his lady's melodious Ark of a mouth, excited and delighted her antipathy. She was amused to transports at the station, on hearing Mr. Barmby, in a voice all ophicleide, remark: 'No, I carry no instrument.' The habitation of it at the bottom of his trunk, was not forgotten when it sounded.

Reclining in warmth on the deck of the vessel at night, she said, just under Victor's ear: 'Where are those two?'

'Bid me select the couple,' said he.

She rejoined: 'Silly man'; and sleepily gave him her hand for good night, and so paralyzed his arm, that he had to cover the continued junction by saying more than he intended: 'If they come to an understanding!'

'Plain enough on one side.'

'You think it suitable?'

'Perfection; and well-planned to let them discover it.' 'This is really my favourite route; I love the saltwater and the night on deck.'

'Go on.'

'How?'

'Number your loves. It would tax your arithmetic.'

'I can hate.'

'Not me?'

Positively the contrary, an impulsive squeeze of fingers declared it; and they broke the link, neither of them sensibly hurt; though a leaf or two of the ingenuities, which were her thoughts, turned over in the phantasies of the lady; and the gentleman was taught to feel that a never so slightly lengthened compression of the hand female shoots within us both straight and far and round the corners. There you have Nature, if you want her naked in her elements, for a text. He loved his Nataly truly, even fervently, after the twenty years of union; he looked about at no other woman; it happened only that the touch of one, the chance warm touch, put to motion the blind forces of our mother so remarkably surcharging him. But it was without kindling. The lady, the much cooler person, did nurse a bit of flame. She had a whimsical liking for the man who enjoyed simple things when commanding the luxuries; and it became a fascination, by extreme contrast, at the reminder of his adventurous enterprises in progress while he could so childishly enjoy. Women who dance with the warrior-winner of battles, and hear him talk his ball-room trifles to amuse, have similarly a smell of gunpowder to intoxicate them.

For him, a turn on the deck brought him into new skies. Nataly lay in the cabin. She used to be where Lady Grace was lying. A sort of pleadable, transparent, harmless hallucination of the renewal of old service induced him to refresh and settle the fair semi-slumberer's pillow, and fix the tarpaulin over her silks and wraps; and bend his head to the soft mouth murmuring thanks. The women who can dare the nuit blanche, and under stars; and have a taste for holiday larks after their thirtieth, are rare; they are precious. Nataly nevertheless was approved for guarding her throat from the nightwind. And a softer southerly breath never crossed Channel! The very breeze he had wished for! Luck was with him.

Nesta sat by the rails of the vessel beside her Louise. Mr. Sowerby in passing, exchanged a description of printed agreement with her, upon the beauty of the night—a good neutral topic for the encounter of the sexes not that he wanted it neutral; it furnished him with a vocabulary. Once he perceptibly washed his hands of dutiful politeness, in addressing Mademoiselle de Seilles, likewise upon the beauty of the night; and the French lady, thinking—too conclusively from the breath on the glass at the moment, as it is the Gallic habit—that if her dear Nesta must espouse one of the uninteresting creatures called men in her native land, it might as well be this as another, agreed that the night was very beautiful.

'He speaks grammatical French,' Nesta commented on his achievement. 'He contrives in his walking not to wet his boots,' mademoiselle rejoined.

Mr. Peridon was a more welcome sample of the islanders, despite an inferior pretension to accent. He burned to be near these ladies, and he passed them but once. His enthusiasm for Mademoiselle de Seilles was notorious. Gratefully the compliment was acknowledged by her, in her demure fashion; with a reserve of comic intellectual contempt for the man who could not see that women, or Frenchwomen, or eminently she among them, must have their enthusiasm set springing in the breast before they can be swayed by the most violent of outer gales. And say, that she is uprooted;—he does but roll a log. Mr. Peridon's efforts to perfect himself in the French tongue touched her.

A night of May leaning on June, is little more than a deliberate wink of the eye of light. Mr. Barmby, an exile from the ladies by reason of an addiction to tobacco, quitted the forepart of the vessel at the first greying. Now was the cloak of night worn threadbare, and grey astir for the heralding of gold, day visibly ready to show its warmer throbs. The gentle waves were just a stronger grey than the sky, perforce of an interfusion that shifted gradations; they were silken, in places oily grey; cold to drive the sight across their playful monotonousness for refuge on any far fisher-sail.

Miss Radnor was asleep, eyelids benignly down, lips mildly closed. The girl's cheeks held colour to match a dawn yet unawakened though born. They were in a nest shading amid silks of pale blue, and there was a languid flutter beneath her chin to the catch of the morn-breeze. Bacchanal threads astray from a disorderly front-lock of rich brown hair were alive over an eyebrow showing like a seal upon the lightest and securest of slumbers.

Mr. Barmby gazed, and devoutly. Both the ladies were in their oblivion; the younger quite saintly; but the couple inseparably framed, elevating to behold; a reproach to the reminiscence of pipes. He was near; and quietly the eyelids of mademoiselle lifted on him. Her look was grave, straight, uninquiring, soon accurately perusing; an arrow of Artemis for penetration. He went by, with the sound in the throat of a startled bush-bird taking to wing; he limped off some nail of the deck, as if that young Frenchwoman had turned the foot to a hoof. Man could not be more guiltless, yet her look had perturbed him; nails conspired; in his vexation, he execrated tobacco. And ask not why, where reason never was.

Nesta woke babbling on the subject she had relinquished for sleep. Mademoiselle touched a feathery finger at her hair and hood during their silvery French chimes.

Mr. Sowerby presented the risen morning to them, with encomiums, after they had been observing every variation in it. He spoke happily of the pleasant passage, and of the agreeable night; particularly of the excellent idea of the expedition by this long route at night; the prospect of which had disfigured him with his grimace of speculation—apparently a sourness that did not exist. Nesta had a singular notion, coming of a girl's mingled observation and intuition, that the impressions upon this gentleman were in arrear, did not strike him till late. Mademoiselle confirmed it when it was mentioned; she remembered to have noticed the same in many small things. And it was a pointed perception.

Victor sent his girl down to Nataly, with a summons to hurry up and see sunlight over the waters. Nataly came; she looked, and the outer wakened the inner, she let the light look in on her, her old feelings danced to her eyes like a string of bubbles in ascent. 'Victor, Victor, it seems only yesterday that we crossed, twelve years back—was it?—and in May, and saw the shoal of porpoises, and five minutes after, Dieppe in view. Dear French people! I share your love for France.'

'Home of our holidays!—the "drives"; and they may be the happiest. And fifty minutes later we were off the harbour; and Natata landed, a stranger; and at night she was the heroine of the town.'

Victor turned to a stately gentleman and passed his name to Nataly: 'Sir Rodwell Balchington, a neighbour of Lakelands! She understood that Lady Grace Halley was acquainted with Sir Rodwell:— hence this dash of brine to her lips while she was drinking of happy memories, and Victor evidently was pluming himself upon his usual luck in the fortuitous encounter with an influential neighbour of Lakelands. He told Sir Rodwell the story of how they had met in the salle a manger of the hotel the impresario of a Concert in the town, who had in his hand the doctor's certificate of the incapacity of the chief cantatrice to appear, and waved it, within a step of suicide. 'Well, to be brief, my wife—"noble dame Anglaise," as the man announced her on the Concert platform, undertook one of the songs, and sang another of her own-pure contralto voice, as you will say; with the result that there was a perfect tumult of enthusiasm. Next day, the waiters of the hotel presented her with a bouquet of Spring flowers, white, and central violets. It was in the Paris papers, under the heading: Une amie d'outre Manche—I think that was it?' he asked Nataly.

'I forget,' said she.

He glanced at her: a cloud had risen. He rallied her, spoke of the old Norman silver cross which the manager of the Concert had sent, humbly imploring her to accept the small memento of his gratitude. She nodded an excellent artificial brightness.

And there was the coast of France under young sunlight over the waters. Once more her oft-petitioning wish through the years, that she had entered the ranks of professional singers, upon whom the moral scrutiny is not so microscopic, invaded her, resembling a tide-swell into rock-caves, which have been filled before and left to emptiness, and will be left to emptiness again. Nataly had the intimation visiting us when, in a decline of physical power, the mind's ready vivacity to conjure illusions forsakes us; and it was, of a wall ahead, and a force impelling her against it, and no hope of deviation. And this is the featureless thing, Destiny; not without eyes, if we have a conscience to throw them into it to look at us.

Counsel to her to live in the hour, came, as upon others on the vessel, from an active breath of the salt prompting to healthy hunger; and hardly less from the splendour of the low full sunlight on the waters, the skimming and dancing of the thousands of golden shells away from under the globe of fire.

CHAPTER XV

A PATRIOT ABROAD

Nine days after his master's departure, Daniel Skepsey, a man of some renown of late, as a subject of reports and comments in the newspapers, obtained a passport, for the identification, if need were, of his missing or misapprehended person in a foreign country, of the language of which three unpronounceable words were knocking about his head to render the thought of the passport a staff of safety; and on the morning that followed he was at speed through Normandy, to meet his master rounding homeward from Paris, at a town not to be spoken as it is written, by reason of the custom of the good people of the country, with whom we would fain live on neighbourly terms:—yes, and they had proof of it, not so very many years back, when they were enduring the worst which can befall us— though Mr. Durance, to whom he was indebted for the writing of the place of his destination large on a card, and the wording of the French sound beside it, besides the jotting down of trains and the station for the change of railways, Mr. Durance could say, that the active form of our sympathy consisted in the pouring of cheeses upon them when they were prostrate and unable to resist!

A kind gentleman, Mr. Durance, as Daniel Skepsey had recent cause to know, but often exceedingly dark; not so patriotic as desireable, it was to be feared; and yet, strangely indeed, Mr. Durance had said cogent things on the art of boxing and on manly exercises, and he hoped—he was emphatic in saying he hoped—we should be regenerated. He must have meant, that boxing—on a grand scale would contribute to it. He said, that a blow now and then was wholesome for us all. He recommended a monthly private whipping for old gentlemen who decline the use of the gloves, to disperse their humours; not excluding Judges and Magistrates: he could hardly be in earnest. He spoke in a clergyman's voice, and said it would be payment of good assurance money, beneficial to their souls: he seemed to mean it. He said, that old gentlemen were bottled vapours, and it was good for them to uncork them periodically. He said, they should be excused half the strokes if they danced nightly—they resented motion. He seemed sadly wanting in veneration.

But he might not positively intend what he said. Skepsey could overlook everything he said, except the girding at England. For where is a braver people, notwithstanding appearances! Skepsey knew of dozens of gallant bruisers, ready for the cry to strip to the belt; worthy, with a little public encouragement, to rank beside their grandfathers of the Ring, in the brilliant times when royalty and nobility countenanced the manly art, our nursery of heroes, and there was not the existing unhappy division of classes. He still trusted to convince Mr. Durance, by means of argument and happy instances, historical and immediate, that the English may justly consider themselves the elect of nations, for reasons better than their accumulation of the piles of gold-better than 'usurers' reasons,' as Mr. Durance called them. Much that Mr. Durance had said at intervals was, although remembered almost to the letter of the phrase, beyond his comprehension, and he put it aside, with penitent blinking at his deficiency.

All the while, he was hearing a rattle of voluble tongues around him, and a shout of stations, intelligible as a wash of pebbles, and blocks in a torrent. Generally the men slouched when they were not running. At Dieppe he had noticed muscular fellows; he admitted them to be nimbler on the legs than ours; and that may count both ways, he consoled a patriotic vanity by thinking; instantly rebuking the thought; for he had read chapters of Military History. He sat eyeing the front row of figures in his third-class carriage, musing on the kind of soldiers we might, heaven designing it, have to face, and how to beat them; until he gazed on Rouen, knowing by the size of it and by what Mr. Durance had informed him of the city on the river, that it must be the very city of Rouen, not so many years back a violated place, at the mercy of a foreign foe. Strong pity laid hold of Skepsey. He fortified the heights for defence, but saw at a glance that it was the city for modern artillery to command, crush and enter. He lost idea of these afflicted people as foes, merely complaining of their attacks on England, and their menaces in their Journals and pamphlets; and he renounced certain views of the country to be marched over on the road by this route to Paris, for the dictation of terms of peace at the gates of the French capital, sparing them the shameful entry; and this after the rout of their attempt at an invasion of the Island!

A man opposite him was looking amicably on his lively grey eyes. Skepsey handed a card from his pocket. The man perused it, and crying: 'Dreux?' waved out of the carriage-window at a westerly distance, naming Rouen as not the place, not at all, totally other. Thus we are taught, that a foreign General, ignorant of the language, must confine himself to defensive operations at home; he would be a child in the hands of the commonest man he meets. Brilliant with thanks in signs, Skepsey drew from his friend a course of instruction in French names, for our necessities on a line of march. The roads to Great Britain's metropolis, and the supplies of forage and provision at every stage of a march on London, are marked in the military offices of these people; and that, with their barking Journals, is a piece of knowledge to justify a belligerent return for it. Only we pray to be let live peacefully.

Fervently we pray it when this good man, a total stranger to us, conducts an ignorant foreigner from one station to another through the streets of Rouen, after a short stoppage at the buffet and assistance in the identification of coins; then, lifting his cap to us, retires.

And why be dealing wounds and death? It is a more blessed thing to keep the Commandments. But how is it possible to keep the Commandments if you have a vexatious wife?

Martha Skepsey had given him a son to show the hereditary energy in his crying and coughing; and it was owing, he could plead, to her habits and her tongue, that he sometimes, that he might avoid the doing of worse—for she wanted correction and was improved by it—courted the excitement of a short exhibition of skill, man to man, on publicans' first floors. He could have told the magistrates so, in part apology for the circumstances dragging him the other day, so recently, before his Worship; and he might have told it, if he had not remembered Captain Dartrey Fenellan's words about treating women chivalrously which was interpreted by Skepsey as correcting them, when called upon to do it, but never exposing them only, if allowed to account for the circumstances pushing us into the newspapers, we should not present so guilty a look before the public.

Furthermore, as to how far it is the duty of a man to serve his master, there is likewise question: whether is he, while receiving reproof and punishment for excess of zeal in the service of his master, not to mention the welfare of the country, morally—without establishing it as a principle—exonerated? Miss Graves might be asked save that one would not voluntarily trouble a lady on such subjects. But supposing, says the opposing counsel, now at work in Skepsey's conscience, supposing this act, for which, contraveneing the law of the land, you are reproved and punished, to be agreeable to you, how then? We answer, supposing it—and we take uncomplainingly the magistrate's reproof and punishment—morally justified can it be expected of us to have the sense of guilt, although we wear and know we wear a guilty look before the public?

His master and the dear ladies would hear of it; perhaps they knew of it now; with them would rest the settlement of the distressing inquiry. The ladies would be shocked ladies cannot bear any semblance of roughness, not even with the gloves:—and knowing, as they must, that our practise of the manly art is for their protection.

Skepsey's grievous prospect of the hour to come under judgement of a sex that was ever a riddle unread, clouded him on the approach to Dreux. He studied the country and the people eagerly; he forbore to conduct great military operations. Mr. Durance had spoken of big battles round about the town of Dreux; also of a wonderful Mausoleum there, not equally interesting. The little man was in deeper gloom than a day sobering on crimson dusk when the train stopped and his quick ear caught the sound of the station, as pronounced by his friend at Rouen.

He handed his card to the station-master. A glance, and the latter signalled to a porter, saying: 'Paradis'; and the porter laid hold of Skepsey's bag. Skepsey's grasp was firm; he pulled, the porter pulled. Skepsey heard explanatory speech accompanying a wrench. He wrenched back with vigour, and in his own tongue exclaimed, that he held to the bag because his master's letters were in the bag, all the way from England. For a minute, there was a downright trial of muscle and will: the porter appeared furiously excited, Skepsey had a look of cooled steel. Then the Frenchman, requiring to shrug, gave way to the Englishman's eccentric obstinacy, and signified that he was his guide. Quite so, and Skepsey showed alacrity and confidence in following; he carried his bag. But with the remembrance of the kindly serviceable man at Rouen, he sought to convey to the porter, that the terms of their association were cordial. A waving of the right hand to the heavens ratified the treaty on the French side. Nods and smiles and gesticulations, with across-Channel vocables, as it were Dover cliffs to Calais sands and back, pleasantly beguiled the way down to the Hotel du Paradis, under the Mausoleum heights, where Skepsey fumbled at his pocket for coin current; but the Frenchman, all shaken by a tornado of negation, clapped him on the shoulder, and sang him a quatrain. Skepsey had in politeness to stand listening, and blinking, plunged in the contrition of ignorance, eclipsed. He took it to signify something to the effect, that money should not pass between friends. It was the amatory farewell address of Henri IV. to his Charmante Gabrielle; and with

'Perce de mille lords,
L'honneur m'appelle

Au champ de Mars,'

the Frenchman, in a backing of measured steps, apologized for his enforced withdrawal from the stranger who had captured his heart.

Skepsey's card was taken in the passage of the hotel. A clean-capped maid, brave on the legs, like all he had seen of these people, preceded him at quick march to an upper chamber. When he descended, bag in hand, she flung open the salon-door of a table d'hote, where a goodly number were dining and chattering; waiters drew him along to the section occupied by his master's party. A chair had been kept vacant for him; his master waved a hand, his dear ladies graciously smiled; he struck the bag in front of a guardian foot, growing happy. He could fancy they had not seen the English newspapers. And his next observation of the table showed him wrecked and lost: Miss Nesta's face was the oval of a woeful O at his wild behaviour in England during their absence. She smiled. Skepsey had nevertheless to consume his food—excellent, very tasty soup-with the sour sauce of the thought that he must be tongue-tied in his defence for the time of the dinner.

'No, dear Skips, please! you are to enjoy yourself,' said Nesta.

He answered confusedly, trying to assure her that he was doing so, and he choked.

His master had fixed his arrival for twenty minutes earlier. Skepsey spoke through a cough of long delays at stations. The Rev. Septimus Barmby, officially peacemaker, sounded the consequent excuse for a belated comer. It was final; such is the power of sound. Looks were cast from the French section of the table at the owner of the prodigious organ. Some of the younger men, intent on the charms of Albion's daughters, expressed in a sign and a word or two alarm at what might be beneath the flooring: and 'Pas encore Lui!' and 'Son avant-courrier!' and other flies of speech passed on a whiff, under politest of cover, not to give offence. But prodigies, claim attention.

Our English, at the close of the dinner, consented to say it was good, without specifying a dish, because a selection of this or that would have seemed to italicize, and commit, them, in the presence of ladies, to a notice of the matter of-course, beneath us, or the confession of a low sensual enjoyment; until Lady Grace Halley named the particular dressing of a tete de veau approvingly to Victor; and he stating, that he had offered a suggestion for the menu of the day, Nataly exclaimed, that she had suspected it: upon which Mr. Sowerby praised the menu, Mr. Barmby, Peridon and Catkin named other dishes, there was the right after-dinner ring in Victor's ears, thanks to the woman of the world who had travelled round to nature and led the shackled men to deliver themselves heartily. One tap, and they are free. That is, in the moments after dinner, when nature is at the gates with them. Only, it must be a lady and a prevailing lady to give the tap. They need (our English) and will for the ages of the process of their transformation need a queen.

Skepsey, bag in hand, obeyed the motion of his master's head and followed him.

He was presently back, to remain with the ladies during his master's perusal of letters. Nataly had decreed that he was not to be troubled; so Nesta and mademoiselle besought him for a recital of his French adventures; and strange to say, he had nothing to tell. The journey, pregnant at the start, exciting in the course of it, was absolutely blank at the termination. French people had been very kind; he could not say more. But there was more; there was a remarkable fulness, if only he could subordinate it to narrative. The little man did not know, that time was wanted for imagination to make the roadway or riverway of a true story, unless we press to invent; his mind had been too busy on the way for him to clothe in speech his impressions of the passage of incidents at the call for them. Things had happened, numbers of interesting minor things, but they all slipped as water through the fingers; and he being of the band of honest creatures who will not accept a lift from fiction, drearily he sat before the ladies, confessing to an emptiness he was far from feeling.

Nesta professed excessive disappointment. 'Now, if it had been in England, Skips!' she said, under her mother's gentle gloom of brows.

He made show of melancholy submission.

'There, Skepsey, you have a good excuse, we are sure,' Nataly said.

And women, when they are such ladies as these, are sent to prove to us that they can be a blessing; instead of the dreadful cry to Providence for the reason of the spread of the race of man by their means! He declared his readiness, rejecting excuses, to state his case to them, but for his fear of having it interpreted as an appeal for their kind aid in obtaining his master's forgiveness. Mr. Durance had very considerately promised to intercede. Skepsey dropped a hint or two of his naughty proceedings drily aware that their untutored antipathy to the manly art would not permit of warmth.

Nesta said: 'Do you know, Skips, we saw a grand exhibition of fencing in Paris.'

He sighed. 'Ladies can look on at fencing! foils and masks! Captain Dartrey Fenellan has shown me, and says, the French are our masters at it.' He bowed constrainedly to mademoiselle.

'You box, M. Skepsey!' she said.

His melancholy increased: 'Much discouragement from Government, Society! If ladies... but I do not venture. They are not against Games. But these are not a protection... to them, when needed; to the country. The country seems asleep to its position. Mr. Durance has remarked on it:—though I would not always quote Mr. Durance... indeed, he says, that England has invested an Old Maid's All in the Millennium, and is ruined if it delays to come. "Old Maid," I do not see. I do not—if I may presume to speak of myself in the same breath with so clever a gentleman, agree with Mr. Durance in everything. But the chest-measurement of recruits, the stature of the men enlisted, prove that we are losing the nursery of our soldiers.'

'We are taking them out of the nursery, Skips, if you 're for quoting Captain Dartrey,' said Nesta. 'We'll never haul down our flag, though, while we have him!'

'Ah! Captain Dartrey!' Skepsey was refreshed by the invocation of the name.

A summons to his master's presence cut short something he was beginning to say about Captain Dartrey.

CHAPTER XVI

His master opened on the bristling business.

'What's this, of your name in the papers, your appearing before a magistrate, and a fine? Tell the tale shortly.'

Skepsey fell upon his attitude for dialectical defence the modest form of the two hands at rolling play and the head deferentially sidecast. But knowing that he had gratified his personal tastes in the act of serving his master's interests, an interfusion of sentiments plunged him into self-consciousness; an unwonted state with him, clogging to a simple story.

'First, sir, I would beg you to pardon the printing of your name beside mine...'

'Tush: on with you.'

'Only to say, necessitated by the circumstances of the case. I read, that there was laughter in the court at my exculpation of my conduct—as I have to call it; and there may have been. I may have expressed myself .... I have a strong feeling for the welfare of the country.'

'So, it seems, you said to the magistrate. Do you tell me, that the cause of your gross breach of the law, was a consideration for the welfare of the country? Run on the facts.'

'The facts—I must have begun badly, sir.' Skepsey rattled the dry facts in his head to right them. From his not having begun well, they had become dry as things underfoot. It was an error to have led off with the sentiments. 'Two very, two very respectable persons—respectable—were desirous to witness a short display of my, my system, I would say; of my science, they call it.'

'Don't be nervous. To the point; you went into a field five miles out of London, in broad day, and stood in a ring, the usual Tiff-raff about you!'

'With the gloves: and not for money, Sir: for the trial of skill; not very many people. I cannot quite see the breach of the law.'

'So you told the magistrate. You were fined for your inability to quite see. And you had to give security.'

'Mr. Durance was kindly responsible for me, sir: an acquaintance of the magistrate.'

'This boxing of yours is a positive mania, Skepsey. You must try to get the better of it—must! And my name too! I'm to be proclaimed, as having in my service an inveterate pugilist—who breaks the law from patriotism! Male or female, these very respectable persons—the people your show was meant for?'

'Male, sir. Females!... that is, not the respectable ones.'

'Take the opinion of the respectable ones for your standard of behaviour in future.'

'It was a mere trial of skill, sir, to prove to one of the spectators, that I could be as good as my word. I wished I may say, to conciliate him, partly. He would not—he judged by size—credit me with... he backed my adversary Jerry Scroom—a sturdy boxer, without the knowledge of the first principles.'

'You beat him?'

'I think I taught the man that I could instruct, sir; he was complimentary before we parted. He thought I could not have lasted. After the second round, the police appeared.'

'And you ran!'

'No, sir; I had nothing on my conscience.'

'Why not have had your pugilistic display in a publican's room in town, where you could have hammer-nailed and ding-donged to your heart's content for as long as you liked!'

'That would have been preferable, from the point of view of safety from intrusion, I can admit-speaking humbly. But one of the parties—I had a wish to gratify him—is a lover of old English times and habits and our country scenes. He wanted it to take place on green grass. We drove over Hampstead in three carts and a gig, as a company of pleasure—as it was. A very beautiful morning. There was a rest at a public-house. Mr. Shaplow traces the misfortune to that. Mr. Jarniman, I hear, thinks it what he calls a traitor in the camp. I saw no sign; we were all merry and friendly.'

'Jarniman?' said Victor sharply. 'Who is the Jarniman?'

'Mr. Jarniman is, I am to understand from the acquaintance introducing us—a Mr. Shaplow I met in the train from Lakelands one day, and again at the corner of a street near Drury Lane, a ham and beef shop kept by a Mrs. Jarniman, a very stout lady, who does the chief carving in the shop, and is the mother of Mr. Jarniman: he is in a confidential place, highly trusted.' Skepsey looked up from the hands he soaped: 'He is a curious mixture; he has true enthusiasm for boxing, he believes in ghosts. He mourns for the lost days of prize-fighting, he thinks that spectres are on the increase. He has a very large appetite, depressed spirits. Mr. Shaplow informs me he is a man of substance, in the service of a wealthy lady in poor health, expecting a legacy and her appearance to him. He has the look—Mr. Shaplow assures me he does not drink to excess: he is a slow drinker.'

Victor straightened: 'Bad way of health, you said?'

'Mr. Jarniman spoke of his expectations, as being immediate: he put it, that he expected her spirit to be out for him to meet it any day—or night. He desires it. He says, she has promised it—on oath, he says, and must feel that she must do her duty to him before she goes, if she is to appear to him with any countenance after. But he is anxious for her in any case to show herself, and says, he should not have the heart to reproach her. He has principles, a tear for suffering; he likes to be made to cry. Mrs. Jarniman, his mother, he is not married, is much the same so far, except ghosts; she will not have them; except after strong tea, they come, she says, come to her bed. She is foolish enough to sleep in a close-curtained bed. But the poor lady is so exceedingly stout that a puff of cold would carry her off, she fears.'

Victor stamped his foot. 'This man Jarniman serves a lady now in a—serious, does he say? Was he precise?'

'Mr. Jarniman spoke of a remarkable number of diseases; very complicated, he says. He has no opinion of doctors. He says, that the lady's doctor and the chemist—she sits in a chemist's shop and swallows other people's prescriptions that take her fancy. He says, her continuing to live is wonderful. He has no reason to hurry her, only for the satisfaction of a natural curiosity.'

'He mentioned her name?'

'No name, sir.'

Skepsey's limpid grey eyes confirmed the negative to Victor, who was assured that the little man stood clean of any falsity.

'You are not on equal terms. You and the magistrate have helped him to know who it is you serve, Skepsey.'

'Would you please to direct me, sir.'

'Another time. Now go and ease your feet with a run over the town. We have music in half an hour. That you like, I know. See chiefly to amusing yourself.'

Skepsey turned to go; he murmured, that he had enjoyed his trip.

Victor checked him: it was to ask whether this Jarniman had specified one, any one of the numerous diseases afflicting his aged mistress.

Now Jarniman had shocked Skepsey with his blunt titles for a couple of the foremost maladies assailing the poor lady's decayed constitution: not to be mentioned, Skepsey's thought, in relation to ladies; whose organs and functions we, who pay them a proper homage by restricting them to the sphere so worthily occupied by their mothers up to the very oldest date, respectfully curtain; their accepted masters are chivalrous to them, deploring their need at times for the doctors and drugs. He stood looking most unhappy. 'She was to appear, sir, in a few—perhaps a week, a month.'

A nod dismissed him.

The fun of the expedition (and Dudley Sowerby had wound himself up to relish it) was at night in the towns, when the sound of instrumental and vocal music attracted crowds beneath the windows of the hotel, and they heard zon, zon, violon, fete et basse; not bad fluting, excellent fiddling, such singing as a maestro, conducting his own Opera, would have approved. So Victor said of his darlings' voices. Nesta's and her mother's were a perfect combination; Mr. Barmby's trompe in union, sufficiently confirmed the popular impression, that they were artistes. They had been ceremoniously ushered to their carriages, with expressions of gratitude, at the departure from Rouen; and the Boniface at Gisors had entreated them to stay another night, to give an entertainment. Victor took his pleasure in letting it be known, that they were a quiet English family, simply keeping-up the habits they practiced in Old England: all were welcome to hear them while they were doing it; but they did not give entertainments.

The pride of the pleasure of reversing the general idea of English dulness among our neighbours, was perceived to have laid fast hold of Dudley Sowerby at Dreux. He was at the window from time to time, counting heads below. For this reason or a better, he begged Nesta to supplant the flute duet with the soprano and contralto of the Helena section of the Mefistofele, called the Serenade: La Luna immobile. She consulted her mother, and they sang it. The crowds below, swollen to a block of the street, were dead still, showing the instinctive good manners of the people. Then mademoiselle astonished them with a Provencal or Cevennes air, Huguenot, though she was Catholic; but it suited her mezzo-soprano tones; and it rang massively of the martial-religious. To what heights of spiritual grandeur might not a Huguenot France have marched! Dudley Sowerby, heedlessly, under an emotion that could be stirred in him with force, by the soul of religion issuing through music, addressed his ejaculation to Lady Grace Halley. She did nor shrug or snub him, but rejoined: 'I could go to battle with that song in the ears.' She liked seeing him so happily transformed; and liked the effect of it on Nesta when his face shone in talking. He was at home with the girl's eyes, as he had never been. A song expressing in one of the combative and devotional, went to the springs of his blood; for he was of an old warrior race, beneath the thick crust of imposed peaceful maxims and commercial pursuits and habitual stiff correctness. As much as wine, will music bring out the native bent of the civilized man: endow him with language too. He was as if unlocked; he met Nesta's eyes and ran in a voluble interchange, that gave him flattering after-thoughts; and at the moment sensibly a new and assured, or to some extent assured, station beside a girl so vivid; by which the young lady would be helped to perceive his unvoiced solider gifts.

Nataly observed them, thinking of Victor's mastering subtlety. She had hoped (having clearly seen the sheep's eye in the shepherd) that Mr. Barmby would be watchful to act as a block between them; and therefore she had stipulated for his presence on the journey. She remembered Victor's rapid look of readiness to consent:—he reckoned how naturally Mr. Barmby would serve as a foil to any younger man. Mr. Barmby had tried all along to perform his part: he had always been thwarted; notably once at Gisors, where by some cunning management he and mademoiselle found themselves in the cell of the prisoner's Nail-wrought work while Nesta had to take Sowerby's hand for help at a passage here and there along the narrow outer castle-walls. And Mr. Barmby, upon occasions, had set that dimple in Nesta's cheek quivering, though Simeon Fenellan was not at hand, and there was no telling how it was done, beyond the evidence that Victor willed it so.

From the day of the announcement of Lakelands, she had been brought more into contact with his genius of dexterity and foresight than ever previously: she had bent to the burden of it more; had seen herself and everybody else outstripped—herself, of course; she did not count in a struggle with him. But since that red dawn of Lakelands, it was almost as if he had descended to earth from the skies. She now saw his mortality in the miraculous things he did. The reason of it was, that through the perceptible various arts and shifts on her level, an opposing spirit had plainer view of his aim, to judge it. She thought it a mean one.

The power it had to hurry her with the strength of a torrent to an end she dreaded, impressed her physically; so far subduing her mind, in consequence, as to keep the idea of absolute resistance obscure, though her bosom heaved with the breath; but what was her own of a mind hung hovering above him, criticizing; and involuntarily, discomfortingly. She could have prayed to be led blindly or blindly dashed on: she could trust him for success; and her critical mind seemed at times a treachery. Still she was compelled to judge.

When he said to her at night, pressing both her hands: 'This is the news of the day, my love! It's death at last. We shall soon be thanking heaven for freedom'; her fingers writhed upon his and gripped them in a torture of remorse on his behalf. A shattering throb of her heart gave her sight of herself as well. For so it is with the woman who loves in subjection, she may be a critic of the man, she is his accomplice.'

'You have a letter, Victor?'

'Confirmation all round: Fenellan, Themison, and now Skepsey.'

He told her the tale of Skepsey and Jarniman, colouring it, as any interested animated conduit necessarily will. Neither of them smiled.

The effort to think soberly exhausted and rolled her back on credulity.

It might not be to-day or next week or month: but so much testimony pointed to a day within the horizon, surely!

She bowed her head to heaven for forgiveness. The murderous hope stood up, stood out in forms and pictures. There was one of a woman at her ease at last in the reception of guests; contrasting with an ironic haunting figure of the woman of queenly air and stature under a finger of scorn for a bold-faced impostor. Nataly's lips twitched at the remembrance of quaint whimpers of complaint to the Fates, for directing that a large instead of a rather diminutive woman should be the social offender fearing exposure. Majesty in the criminal's dock, is a confounding spectacle. To the bosom of the majestic creature, all her glorious attributes have become the executioner's implements. She must for her soul's health believe that a day of release and exoneration approaches.

'Barmby!—if my dear girl would like him best,' Victor said, in tenderest undertones, observing the shadowing variations of her face; and pierced her cruelly, past explanation or understanding;—not that she would have objected to the Rev. Septimus as officiating clergyman.

She nodded. Down rolled the first big tear.

We cry to women; Land, ho!—a land of palms after storms at sea; and at once they inundate us with a deluge of eye-water.

'Half a minute, dear Victor, not longer,' Nataly said, weeping, near on laughing over his look of wanton abandonment to despair at sight of her tears. 'Don't mind me. I am rather like Fenellan's laundress, the tearful woman whose professional apparatus was her soft heart and a cake of soap. Skepsey has made his peace with you?'

Victor answered: 'Yes, yes; I see what he has been about. We're a mixed lot, all of us-the best! You've noticed, Skepsey has no laugh: however absurd the thing he tells you, not a smile!'

'But you trust his eyes; you look fathoms into them. Captain Dartrey thinks him one of the men most in earnest of any of his country.'

'So Nataly of course thinks the same. And he's a worthy little velocipede, as Fenellan calls him. One wishes Colney had been with us. Only Colney!—pity one can't cut his talons for the space before they grow again.'

Ay, and in the presence of Colney Durance, Victor would not have been so encouraging, half boyishly caressing, with Dudley Sowerby! It was the very manner to sow seed of imitativeness in the girl, devoted as she was to her father. Nataly sighed, foreseeing evil, owning it a superstition, feeling it a certainty. We are easily prophets, sure of being justified, when the cleverness of schemes devoted to material ends appears most delicately perfect. History, the tales of households, the tombstone, are with us to inspire. In Nataly's bosom, the reproof of her inefficiency for offering counsel where Victor for his soul's sake needed it, was beginning to thunder at whiles as a reproach of unfittingness in his mate, worse than a public denunciation of the sin against Society.

It might be decreed that she and Society were to come to reconcilement. A pain previously thought of, never previously so realized, seized her at her next sight of Nesta. She had not taken in her front mind the contrast of the innocent one condemned to endure the shadow from which the guilty was by a transient ceremony released. Nature could at a push be eloquent to defend the guilty. Not a word of vindicating eloquence rose up to clear the innocent. Nothing that she could do; no devotedness, not any sacrifice, and no treaty of peace, no possible joy to come, nothing could remove the shadow from her child. She dreamed of the succour in eloquence, to charm the ears of chosen juries while a fact spoke over the population, with a relentless rolling out of its one hard word. But eloquence, powerful on her behalf, was dumb when referred to Nesta. It seemed a cruel mystery. How was it permitted by the Merciful Disposer! .... Nataly's intellect and her reverence clashed. They clash to the end of time if we persist in regarding the Spirit of Life as a remote Externe, who plays the human figures, to bring about this or that issue, instead of being beside us, within us, our breath, if we will; marking on us where at each step we sink to the animal, mount to the divine, we and ours who follow, offspring of body or mind. She was in her error, from judgeing of the destiny of man by the fate of individuals. Chiefly her error was, to try to be thinking at all amid the fevered tangle of her sensations.

A darkness fell upon the troubled woman, and was thicker overhead when her warm blood had drawn her to some acceptance of the philosophy of existence, in a savour of gratification at the prospect of her equal footing with the world while yet she lived. She hated herself for taking pleasure in anything to be bestowed by a world so hap-hazard, ill-balanced, unjust; she took it bitterly, with such naturalness as not to be aware that it was irony and a poisonous irony moving her to welcome the restorative ceremony because her largeness of person had a greater than common need of the protection.

CHAPTER XVII

CHIEFLY UPON THE THEME OF A YOUNG MAID'S IMAGININGS

That Mausoleum at Dreux may touch to lift us. History, pleads for the pride of the great discrowned Family giving her illumination there. The pride is reverently postured, the princely mourning-cloak it wears becomingly braided at the hem with fair designs of our mortal humility in the presence of the vanquisher; against whom, acknowledgeing a visible conquest of the dust, it sustains a placid contention in coloured glass and marbles.

Mademoiselle de Seilles, a fervid Orleanist, was thanked for having advised the curvature of the route homeward to visit 'the spot of so impressive a monument': as it, was phrased by the Rev. Septimus Barmby; whose exposition to Nesta of the beautiful stained-glass pictures of incidents in the life of the crusading St. Louis, was toned to be likewise impressive:—Colney Durance not being at hand to bewail the pathos of his exhaustless 'whacking of the platitudes'; which still retain their tender parts, but cry unheard when there is no cynic near. Mr. Barmby laid-on solemnly.

Professional devoutness is deemed more righteous on such occasions than poetic fire. It robes us in the cloak of the place, as at a funeral. Generally, Mr. Barmby found, and justly, that it is in superior estimation among his countrymen of all classes. They are shown by example how to look, think, speak; what to do. Poets are disturbing; they cannot be comfortably imitated, they are unsafe, not certainly the metal, unless you have Laureates, entitled to speak by their pay and decorations; and these are but one at a time-and a quotation may remind us of a parody, to convulse the sacred dome! Established plain prose officials do better for our English. The audience moved round with heads of undertakers.

Victor called to recollection Fenellan's 'Rev. Glendoveer' while Mr. Barmby pursued his discourse, uninterrupted by tripping wags. And those who have schemes, as well as those who are startled by the criticism in laughter to discover that they have cause for shunning it, rejoice when wits are absent. Mr. Sowerby and Nesta interchanged a comment on Mr. Barmby's remarks: The Fate of Princes! The Paths of Glory! St. Louis was a very distant Roman Catholic monarch; and the young gentleman of Evangelical education could admire him as a Crusader. St. Louis was for Nesta a figure in the rich hues of royal Saintship softened to homeliness by tears. She doated on a royalty crowned with the Saint's halo, that swam down to us to lift us through holy human showers. She listened to Mr. Barmby, hearing few sentences, lending his eloquence all she felt: he rolled forth notes of a minster organ, accordant with the devotional service she was holding mutely. Mademoiselle upon St. Louis: 'Worthy to be named King of Kings!' swept her to a fount of thoughts, where the thoughts are not yet shaped, are yet in the breast of the mother emotions. Louise de Seilles had prepared her to be strangely and deeply moved. The girl had a heart of many strings, of high pitch, open to be musical to simplest wandering airs or to the gales. This crypt of the recumbent sculptured figures and the coloured series of acts in the passage of the crowned Saint thrilled her as with sight of flame on an altar-piece of History. But this King in the lines of the Crucifixion leading, gave her a lesson of life, not a message from death. With such a King, there would be union of the old order and the new, cessation to political turmoil: Radicalism, Socialism, all the monster names of things with heads agape in these our days to gobble-up the venerable, obliterate the beautiful, leave a stoniness of floods where field and garden were, would be appeased, transfigured. She hoped, she prayed for that glorious leader's advent.

On one subject, conceived by her only of late, and not intelligibly, not communicably: a subject thickly veiled; one which struck at her through her sex and must, she thought, ever be unnamed (the ardent young creature saw it as a very thing torn by the winds to show hideous gleams of a body rageing with fire behind the veil): on this one subject, her hopes and prayers were dumb in her bosom. It signified shame. She knew not the how, for she had no power to contemplate it: there was a torment of earth and a writhing of lurid dust-clouds about it at a glimpse. But if the new crusading Hero were to come attacking that—if some born prince nobly man would head the world to take away the withering scarlet from the face of women, she felt she could kiss the print of his feet upon the ground. Meanwhile she had enjoyment of her plunge into the inmost forest-well of mediaeval imaginativeness, where youthful minds of good aspiration through their obscurities find much akin to them.

She had an eye for little Skepsey too: unaware that these French Princes had hurried him off to Agincourt, for another encounter with them and the old result—poor dear gentlemen, with whom we do so wish to be friendly! What amused her was, his evident fatigue in undergoing the slow parade, and sheer deference to his betters, as to the signification of a holiday on arrested legs. Dudley Sowerby's attention to him, in elucidating the scenes with historical scraps, greatly pleased her. The Rev. Septimus of course occupied her chiefly.

Mademoiselle was always near, to receive his repeated expressions of gratitude for the route she had counselled. Without personal objections to a well-meaning orderly man, whose pardonable error it was to be aiming too considerably higher than his head, she did but show him the voluble muteness of a Frenchwoman's closed lips; not a smile at all, and certainly no sign of hostility; when bowing to his reiterated compliment in the sentence of French. Mr. Barmby had noticed (and a strong sentiment rendered him observant, unwontedly) a similar alert immobility of her lips, indicating foreign notions of this kind or that, in England: an all but imperceptible shortening or loss of corners at the mouth, upon mention of marriages of his clergy: particularly once, at his reading of a lengthy report in a newspaper of a Wedding Ceremony involving his favourite Bishop for bridegroom: a report to make one glow like Hymen rollicking the Torch after draining the bumper to the flying slipper. He remembered the look, and how it seemed to intensify on the slumbering features, at a statement, that his Bishop was a widower, entering into nuptials in his fifty-fourth year. Why not? But we ask it of Heaven and Man, why not? Mademoiselle was pleasant: she was young or youngish; her own clergy were celibates, and—no, he could not argue the matter with a young or youngish person of her sex. Could it be a reasonable woman—a woman!—who, disapproved the holy nuptials of the pastors of the flocks? But we are forbidden to imagine the conducting of an argument thereon with a lady.

Luther... but we are not in Luther's time:—Nature... no, nor can there possibly be allusions to Nature. Mr. Barmby wondered at Protestant parents taking a Papistical governess for their young flower of English womanhood. However, she venerated St. Louis; he cordially also; there they met; and he admitted, that she had, for a Frenchwoman, a handsome face, and besides an agreeably artificial ingenuousness in the looks which could be so politely dubious as to appear only dubiously adverse.

The spell upon Nesta was not blown away on English ground; and when her father and mother were comparing their impressions, she could not but keep guard over the deeper among her own. At the Chateau de Gisors, leftward off Vernon on Seine, it had been one of romance and wonderment, with inquisitive historic soundings of her knowledge and mademoiselle's, a reverence for the prisoner's patient holy work, and picturings of his watchful waiting daily, Nail in hand, for the heaven-sent sunlight on the circular dungeon-wall through the slits of the meurtrieres. But the Mausoleum at Dreux spake religiously; it enfolded Mr. Barmby, his voice re-edified it. The fact that he had discoursed there, though not a word of the discourse was remembered, allied him to the spirit of a day rather increasing in sacredness as it receded and left her less the possessor of it, more the worshipper.

Mademoiselle had to say to herself: 'Impossible!' after seeing the drift of her dear Nesta's eyes in the wake of the colossal English clergyman. She fed her incredulousness indignantly on the evidence confounding it. Nataly was aware of unusual intonations, treble-stressed, in the Bethesda and the Galilee of Mr. Barmby on Concert evenings: as it were, the towering wood-work of the cathedral organ in quake under emission of its multitudinous outroar. The 'Which?' of the Rev. Septimus, addressed to Nesta, when song was demanded of him; and her 'Either'; and his gentle hesitation, upon a gaze at her for the directing choice, could not be unnoticed by women.

Did he know a certain thing?—and dream of urging the suit, as an indulgent skipper of parental pages?

Such haunting interrogations were the conspirators' daggers out at any instant, or leaping in sheath, against Nataly's peace of mind. But she trusted her girl's laughing side to rectify any little sentimental overbalancing. She left the ground where maternal meditations are serious, at an image of Mr. Barmby knocking at Nesta's heart as a lover. Was it worth inquiry?

A feminine look was trailed across the eyes of mademoiselle, with mention of Mr. Barmby's name.

Mademoiselle rippled her shoulders. 'We are at present much enamoured of Bethesda.'

That watchfullest showing no alarm, the absurdity of the suspicion smothered it.

Nataly had moreover to receive startling new guests:

Lady Rodwell Blachington: Mrs. Fanning, wife of the General: young Mrs. Blathenoy, wife of the great bill-broker: ladies of Wrensham and about. And it was a tasking of her energies equal to the buffeting of recurrent waves on deep sea. The ladies were eager for her entry into Lakelands. She heard that Victor had appointed Lady Blachington's third son to the coveted post of clerk in the Indian house of Inchling and Radnor. These are the deluge days when even aristocracy will cry blessings on the man who procures a commercial appointment for one of its younger sons offended and rebutted by the barrier of Examinations for the Civil Service. 'To have our Adolphus under Mr. Victor Radnor's protection, is a step!' Lady Blachington said. Nataly was in an atmosphere of hints and revealings. There were City Dinners, to which one or other of the residents about Lakelands had been taken before he sat at Victor's London table. He was already winning his way, apparently without effort, to be the popular man of that neighbourhood. A subterranean tide or a slipping of earth itself seemed bearing her on. She had his promise indeed, that he would not ask of her to enter Lakelands until the day of his freedom had risen; but though she could trust to his word, the heart of the word went out of it when she heard herself thanked by Lady Blachington (who could so well excuse her at such a time of occupation for not returning her call, that she called in a friendly way a second time, warmly to thank her) for throwing open the Concert room at Lakelands in August, to an Entertainment in assistance of the funds for the purpose of erecting an East of London Clubhouse, where the children of the poor by day could play, and their parents pass a disengaged evening. Doubtless a worthy Charity. Nataly was alive to the duties of wealth. Had it been simply a demand for a donation, she would not have shown that momentary pucker of the brows, which Lady Blachington read as a contrast with the generous vivacity of the husband.

Nataly read a leaf of her fate in this announcement. Nay, she beheld herself as the outer world wexedly beholds a creature swung along to the doing of things against the better mind. An outer world is thoughtless of situations which prepare us to meet the objectionable with a will benumbed;—if we do not, as does that outer world, belong to the party of the readily heroical. She scourged her weakness: and the intimation of the truth stood over her, more than ever manifest, that the deficiency affecting her character lay in her want of language. A tongue to speak and contend, would have helped her to carve a clearer way. But then again, the tongue to speak must be one which could reproach, and strike at errors; fence, and continually summon resources to engage the electrical vitality of a man like Victor. It was an exultation of their life together, a mark of his holiness for them both, that they had never breathed a reproach upon one another.

She dropped away from ideas of remonstrance; faintly seeing, in her sigh of submission, that the deficiency affecting her character would have been supplied by a greater force of character, pressing either to speech or acts. The confession of a fated inevitable in the mind, is weakness prostrate. She knew it: but she could point to the manner of man she was matched with; and it was not a poor excuse.

Mr. Barmby, she thought, deserved her gratitude in some degree for stepping between Mr. Sowerby and Nesta. The girl not having inclinations, and the young gentleman being devoid of stratagem, they were easily kept from the dangerous count of two.

Mademoiselle would have said, that the shepherd also had rarely if ever a minute quite alone with her lamb. Incredulously she perceived signs of a shock. The secret following the signs was betrayed by Nesta in return for a tender grasp of hands and a droll flutter of eyelids. Out it came, on a nod first; then a dreary mention of a date, and an incident, to bring it nearer to comprehension. Mr. Barmby—and decide who will whether it is that Love was made to elude or that curates impelled by his fires are subtle as nether—had outwitted French watchfulness by stealing minutes enough on a day at Lakelands to declare himself. And no wonder the girl looked so forlorn: he had shivered her mediaeval forest-palace of illuminated glass, to leave her standing like a mountain hind, that sniffs the tainted gale off the crag of her first quick leap from hounds; her instincts alarmed, instead of rich imagination colouring and fostering.

She had no memory for his words; so, and truly, she told her Louise: meaning that she had only a spiceless memory; especially for the word love in her ears from the mouth of a man.

There had been a dream of it; with the life-awakening marvel it would be, the humbleness it would bring to her soul beneath the golden clothing of her body: one of those faint formless dreams, which are as the bend of grasses to the breath of a still twilight. She lived too spiritedly to hang on any dream; and had moreover a muffled dread-shadow-sister to the virginal desire—of this one, as of a fateful power that might drag her down, disorder, discolour. But now she had heard it: the word, the very word itself! in her own ears! addressed to her! in a man's voice! The first utterance had been heard, and it was over; the chapter of the book of bulky promise of the splendours and mysteries;—the shimmering woods and bushy glades, and the descent of the shape celestial, and the recognition—the mutual cry of affinity; and overhead the crimson outrolling of the flag of beneficent enterprises hand in hand, all was at an end. These, then, are the deceptions our elders tell of! That masculine voice should herald a new world to the maiden. The voice she had heard did but rock to ruin the world she had been living in.

Mademoiselle prudently forbore from satirical remarks on his person or on his conduct. Nesta had nothing to defend: she walked in a bald waste.

'Can I have been guilty of leading him to think...?' she said, in a tone that writhed, at a second discussion of this hapless affair.

'They choose to think,' mademoiselle replied. 'It is he or another. My dear and dearest, you have entered the field where shots fly thick, as they do to soldiers in battle; and it is neither your fault nor any one's, if you are hit.'

Nesta gazed at her, with a shy supplicating cry of 'Louise.'

Mademoiselle immediately answered the tone of entreaty. 'Has it happened to me? I am of the age of eight and twenty; passable, to look at: yes, my dear, I have gone through it. To spare you the questions tormenting you, I will tell you, that perhaps our experience of our feelings comes nigh on a kind of resemblance. The first gentleman who did me the honour to inform me of his passion, was a hunchback.'

Nesta cried 'Oh!' in a veritable pang of sympathy, and clapped hands to her ears, to shut out Mr. Barmby's boom of the terrific word attacking Louise from that deformed one.

Her disillusionment became of the sort which hears derision. A girl of quick blood and active though unregulated intellect, she caught at the comic of young women's hopes and experiences, in her fear of it.

'My own precious poor dear Louise! what injustice there is in the world for one like my Louise to have a hunchback to be the first...!'

'But, my dear, it did me no harm.'

'But if it had been known!'

'But it was known!'

Nesta controlled a shuddering: 'It is the knowledge of it in ourselves—that it has ever happened;—you dear Louise, who deserve so much better! And one asks—Oh, why are we not left in peace! And do look at the objects it makes of us!' Mademoiselle: could see, that the girl's desperation had got hold of her humour for a life-buoy. 'It is really worse to have it unknown—when you are compelled to be his partner in sharing the secret, and feel as if it were a dreadful doll you conceal for fear that everybody will laugh at its face.'

She resumed her seriousness: 'I find it so hard to be vexed with him and really really like him. For he is a good man; but he will not let one shake him off. He distresses: because we can't quite meet as we did. Last Wednesday Concert evening, he kept away; and I am annoyed that I was glad.'

'Moths have to pass through showers, and keep their pretty patterns from damage as best they can,' said mademoiselle.

Nesta transformed herself into a disciple of Philosophy on the spot. 'Yes, all these feelings of ours are moth-dust! One feels them. I suppose they pass. They must. But tell me, Louise, dear soul, was your poor dear good little afflicted suitor—was he kindly pitied?'

'Conformably with the regulations prescribed to young damsels who are in request to surrender the custody of their hands. It is easy to commit a dangerous excess in the dispensing of that article they call pity of them.'

'And he—did he?—vowed to you he could not take No for an answer?'

At this ingenuous question, woefully uttered, mademoiselle was pricked, to smile pointedly. Nesta had a tooth on her under-lip. Then, shaking vapours to the winds, she said: 'It is an honour, to be asked; and we cannot be expected to consent. So I shall wear through it.—Only I do wish that Mr. Fenellan would not call him The Inchcape Bell!' She murmured this to herself.

Mr. Barmby was absent for two weeks. 'Can anything have offended him?' Victor inquired, in some consternation, appreciating the man's worth, and the grand basso he was; together with the need for him at the Lakelands Concert in August.

Nataly wrote Mr. Barmby a direct invitation. She had no reply. Her speculations were cut short by Victor, who handed her a brief note addressed to him and signed by the Rev. Septimus, petitioning for a private interview.

The formality of the request incensed Victor. 'Now, dear love, you see Colney's meaning, when he says, there are people who have no intimacy in them. Here's a man who visits me regularly once a week or more, has been familiar for years—four, at least; and he wants to speak to me, and must obtain the "privilege" by special appointment! What can be the meaning of it?'

'You will hear to-morrow afternoon,' Nataly said, seeing one paved way to the meaning—a too likely meaning... 'He hasn't been... nothing about Fredi, surely!'

'I have had no information.'

'Impossible! Barmby has good sense; Bottesini can't intend to come scraping on that string. But we won't lose him; he's one of us. Barmby counts for more at a Charity Concert than all the catalogue, and particularly in the country. But he's an excellent fellow—eh?'

'That he is,' Nataly agreed.

Victor despatched a cheerful curt consent to see Mr. Barmby privately on the late afternoon of the day to follow.

Nesta, returning home from the park at that hour of the interview, ignorant of Mr. Barmby's purpose though she was, had her fires extinguished by the rolling roar of curfew along the hall-passage, out of the library.

CHAPTER XVIII

SUITORS FOR THE HAND OF NESTA VICTORIA

When, upon the well-known quest, the delightful singer Orpheus took that downward way, coming in sight of old Cerberus centiceps, he astutely feigned inattention to the hostile appearances of the multiple beast, and with a wave of his plectrum over the responsive lyre, he at the stroke raised voice. This much you know. It may be communicated to you, that there was then beheld the most singular spectacle ever exhibited on the dizzy line of division between the living and the dead. For those unaccustomed musical tones in the last thin whiff of our sustaining air were so smartingly persuasive as to pierce to the vitals of the faithful Old Dog before his offended sentiments had leisure to rouse their heads against a beggar of a mortal. The terrible sugariness which poured into him worked like venom to cause an encounter and a wrestling: his battery of jaws expressed it. They gaped. At the same time, his eyeballs gave up. All the Dog, that would have barked the breathing intruder an hundredfold back to earth, was one compulsory centurion yawn. Tears, issue of the frightful internal wedding of the dulcet and the sour (a ravishing rather of the latter by the former), rolled off his muzzles.

Now, if you are not for insisting that a magnificent simile shall be composed of exactly the like notes in another octave, you will catch the fine flavour of analogy and be wafted in a beat of wings across the scene of the application of the Rev. Septimus Barmby to Mr. Victor Radnor, that he might enter the house in the guise of suitor for the hand of Nesta Victoria. It is the excelling merit of similes and metaphors to spring us to vault over gaps and thickets and dreary places. But, as with the visits of Immortals, we must be ready to receive them. Beware, moreover, of examining them too scrupulously: they have a trick of wearing to vapour if closely scanned. Let it be gratefully for their aid.

So far the comparison is absolute, that Mr. Barmby passed: he was at liberty to pursue his quest.

Victor could not explain how he had been brought to grant it. He was at pains to conceal the bewilderment Mr. Barmby had cast on him, and make Nataly see the smallness of the grant:—both of them were unwilling to lose Barmby; there was not the slightest fear about Fredi, he said; and why should not poor Barmby have his chance with the others in the race!—and his Nataly knew that he hated to speak unkindly: he could cry the negative like a crack of thunder in the City. But such matters as these! and a man pleading merely for the right to see the girl!—and pleading in a tone... 'I assure you, my love, he touched chords.'

'Did he allude to advantages in the alliance with him?' Nataly asked smoothly.

'His passion—nothing else. Candid enough. And he had a tone—he has a tone, you know. It 's not what he said. Some allusion to belief in a favourable opinion of him... encouragement... on the part of the mama. She would have him travelling with us! I foresaw it.'

'You were astonished when it came.'

'We always are.'

Victor taunted her softly with having encouraged Mr. Barmby.

She had thought in her heart—not seriously; on a sigh of despondency—that Mr. Barmby espousing the girl would smooth a troubled prospect: and a present resentment at her weakness rendered her shrewd to detect Victor's cunning to cover his own: a thing imaginable of him previously in sentimental matters, yet never accurately and so legibly printed on her mind. It did not draw her to read him with a novel familiarity; it drew her to be more sensible of foregone intimations of the man he was—irresistible in attack, not impregnably defensive. Nor did he seem in this instance humanely considerate: if mademoiselle's estimate of the mind of the girl was not wrong, then Mr. Barmby's position would be both a ridiculous and a cruel one. She had some silly final idea that the poor man might now serve permanently to check the more dreaded applicant: a proof that her ordinary reflectiveness was blunted.

Nataly acknowledged, after rallying Victor for coming to have his weakness condoned, a justice in his counter-accusation, of a loss of her natural cheerfulness, and promised amendment, with a steely smile, that his lips mimicked fondly; and her smile softened. To strengthen the dear soul's hopes, he spoke, as one who had received the latest information, of Dr. Themison and surgeons; little conscious of the tragic depths he struck or of the burden he gave her heart to bear. Her look alarmed him. She seemed to be hugging herself up to the tingling scalp, and was in a moment marble to sight and touch. She looked like the old engravings of martyrs taking the bite of the jaws of flame at the stake.

He held her embraced, feeling her body as if it were in the awful grip of fingers from the outside of life.

The seizure was over before it could be called ominous. When it was once over, and she had smiled again and rebuked him for excessive anxiety, his apprehensions no longer troubled him, but subsided sensationally in wrath at the crippled woman who would not obey the dictate of her ailments instantly to perish and spare this dear one annoyance.

Subsequently, later than usual, he performed his usual mental penance for it. In consequence, the wrath, and the wish, and the penitence, haunted him, each swelling to possession of him in turn; until they united to head a plunge into retrospects; which led to his reviewing the army of charges against Mrs. Burman.

And of this he grew ashamed, attributing it to the morbid indulgence in reflection: a disease never afflicting him anterior to the stupid fall on London Bridge. He rubbed instinctively for the punctilio-bump, and could cheat his fancy to think a remainder of it there, just below, half an inch to the right of, the spot where a phrenologist, invited by Nataly in old days, had marked philo-progenitiveness on his capacious and enviable cerebrum. He knew well it was a fancy. But it was a fact also, that since the day of the fall (never, save in merest glimpses, before that day), he had taken to look behind him, as though an eye had been knocked in the back of his head.

Then, was that day of the announcement of Lakelands to Nataly, to be accounted a gloomy day? He would not have it so.

She was happily occupied with her purchases of furniture, Fredi with her singing lessons, and he with his business; a grasp of many ribands, reining-in or letting loose; always enjoyable in the act. Recently only had he known when at home, a relaxation, a positive pleasure in looking forward to the hours of the City office. This was odd, but so it was; and looking homeward from the City, he had a sense of disappointment when it was not Concert evening. The Cormyns, the Yatts, and Priscilla Graves, and Pempton, foolish fellow, and that bothering Barmby, and Peridon and Catkin, were the lineing of his nest. Well, and so they had been before Lakelands rose. What had induced!... he suddenly felt foreign to himself. The shrouded figure of his lost Idea on London Bridge went by.

A peep into the folds of the shroud was granted him:—Is it a truth, that if we are great owners of money, we are so swollen with a force not native to us, as to be precipitated into acts the downright contrary of our tastes?

He inquired it of his tastes, which have the bad habit of unmeasured phrasing when they are displeased, and so they yield no rational answer. Still he gave heed to violent extraneous harpings against money. Epigrams of Colney's; abuse of it and the owners of it by Socialist orators reported in some newspaper corner; had him by the ears.

They ceased in the presence of Lady Grace Halley, who entered his office to tell him she was leaving town for Whinfold, her husband's family-seat, where the dear man lay in evil case. She signified her resignation to the decrees from above, saying generously:

'You look troubled, my friend. Any bad City news?'

'I look troubled?' Victor said laughing, and bethought him of what the trouble might be. 'City news would not cause the look. Ah, yes;—I was talking in the street to a friend of mine on horseback the other day, and he kept noticing his horse's queer starts. We spied half a dozen children in the gutter, at the tail of the horse, one of them plucking at a hair. "Please, sir, may I have a hair out of your horse's tail?" said the mite. We patted the poor horse that grew a tail for urchins to pluck at. Men come to the fathers about their girls. It's my belief that mothers more easily say no. If they learn the word as maids, you'll say! However, there's no fear about my girl. Fredi's hard to snare. And what brings you Cityward?'

'I want to know whether I shall do right in selling out of the Tiddler mine.'

'You have multiplied your investment by ten.'

'If it had been thousands!'

'Clearly, you sell; always jump out of a mounted mine, unless you're at the bottom of it.'

'There are City-articles against the mine this morning—or I should have been on my way to Whinfold at this moment. The shares are lower.'

'The merry boys are at work to bring your balloon to the ground, that you may quit it for them to ascend. Tiddler has enemies, like the best of mines: or they may be named lovers, if you like. And mines that have gone up, go down for a while before they rise again; it's an affair of undulations; rocket mines are not so healthy. The stories are false, for the time. I had the latest from Dartrey Fenellan yesterday. He's here next month; some time in August.'

'He is married, is he not?'

'Was.'

Victor's brevity sounded oddly to Lady Grace.

'Is he not a soldier?' she said.

'Soldiers and parsons!' Victor interjected.

Now she saw. She understood the portent of Mr. Barmby's hovering offer of the choice of songs, and the recent tremulousness of the welling Bethesda.

But she had come about her own business; and after remarking, that when there is a prize there must be competition, or England will have to lower her flag, she declared her resolve to stick to Tiddler, exclaiming: 'It's only in mines that twenty times the stake is not a dream of the past!'

'The Riviera green field on the rock is always open to you,' said Victor.

She put out her hand to be taken. 'Not if you back me here. It really is not gambling when yours is the counsel I follow. And if I'm to be a widow, I shall have to lean on a friend, gifted like you. I love adventure, danger;—well, if we two are in it; just to see my captain in a storm. And if the worst happens, we go down together. It 's the detestation of our deadly humdrum of modern life; some inherited love of fighting.'

'Say, brandy.'

'Does not Mr. Durance accuse you of an addiction to the brandy novel?'

'Colney may call it what he pleases. If I read fiction, let it be fiction; airier than hard fact. If I see a ballet, my troop of short skirts must not go stepping like pavement policemen. I can't read dull analytical stuff or "stylists" when I want action—if I'm to give my mind to a story. I can supply the reflections. I'm English—if Colney 's right in saying we always come round to the story with the streak of supernaturalism.

I don't ask for bloodshed: that's what his "brandy" means.'

'But Mr. Durance is right, we require a shedding; I confess I expect it where there's love; it's part of the balance, and justifies one's excitement. How otherwise do you get any real crisis? I must read and live something unlike this flat life around us.'

'There's the Adam life and the Macadam life, Fenellan says. Pass it in books, but in life we can have quite enough excitement coming out of our thoughts. No brandy there! And no fine name for personal predilections or things done in domino!' Victor said, with his very pleasant face, pressing her hand, to keep the act of long holding it in countenance and bring it to a well-punctuated conclusion: thinking involuntarily of the other fair woman, whose hand was his, and who betrayed a beaten visage despite— or with that poor kind of—trust in her captain. But the thought was not guilty of drawing comparisons. 'This is one that I could trust, as captain or mate,' he pressed the hand again before dropping it.

'You judge entirely by the surface, if you take me for a shifty person at the trial,' said Lady Grace.

Skepsey entered the room with one of his packets, and she was reminded of trains and husbands.

She left Victor uncomfortably rufed: and how? for she had none of the physical charms appealing peculiarly to the man who was taken with grandeur of shape. She belonged rather to the description physically distasteful to him.

It is a critical comment on a civilization carelessly distilled from the jealous East, when visits of fair women to City offices can have this effect. If the sexes are separated for an hour, the place where one is excluded or not common to see, becomes inflammable to that appearing spark. He does outrage to a bona Dea: she to the monasticism of the Court of Law: and he and she awaken unhallowed emotions. Supposing, however, that western men were to de-orientalize their gleeful notions of her, and dis-Turk themselves by inviting the woman's voluble tongue to sisterly occupation there in the midst of the pleading Court, as in the domestic circle: very soon would her eyes be harmless: unless directed upon us with intent.

That is the burning core of the great Question, our Armageddon in Morality: Is she moral? Does she mean to be harmless? Is she not untamable Old Nature? And when once on an equal footing with her lordly half, would not the spangled beauty, in a turn, like the realistic transformation-trick of a pantomime, show herself to be that wanton old thing—the empress of disorderliness? You have to recollect, as the Conservative acutely suggests, that her timidities, at present urging her to support Establishments, pertain to her state of dependence. The party views of Conservatism are, must be, founded, we should remember, on an intimate acquaintance with her in the situations where she is almost unrestrictedly free and her laughter rings to confirm the sentences of classical authors and Eastern sages. Conservatives know what they are about when they refuse to fling the last lattice of an ancient harem open to air and sun-the brutal dispersers of mystery, which would despoil an ankle of its flying wink.

Victor's opinions were those of the entrenched majority; objecting to the occult power of women, as we have the women now, while legislating to maintain them so; and forbidding a step to a desperately wicked female world lest the step should be to wickeder. His opinions were in the background, rarely stirred; but the lady had brought them forward; and he fretted at his restlessness, vexed that it should be due to the intrusion of the sex instead of to the charms of the individual. No sting of the sort had bothered him, he called to mind, on board the Channel boat-nothing to speak of. 'Why does she come here! Why didn't she go to her husband! She gets into the City scramble blindfold, and catches at the nearest hand to help her out! Nice woman enough.' Yes, but he was annoyed with her for springing sensations that ran altogether heartless to the object, at the same time that they were disloyal to the dear woman their natural divinity. And between him and that dear woman, since the communication made by Skepsey in the town of Dreux, nightly the dividing spirit of Mrs. Burman lay cold as a corpse. They both felt her there. They kissed coldly, pressed a hand, said good night.

Next afternoon the announcement by Skepsey of the Hon. Dudley Sowerby, surprised Victor's eyebrows at least, and caused him genially to review the visit of Lady Grace.

Whether or not Colney Durance drew his description of a sunken nobility from the 'sick falcon' distinguishing the handsome features of Mr. Sowerby, that beaked invalid was particularly noticeable to Victor during the statement of his case, although the young gentleman was far from being one, in Colney's words, to enliven the condition of domestic fowl with an hereditary turn for 'preying'; eminently the reverse; he was of good moral repute, a worker, a commendable citizen. But there was the obligation upon him to speak—it is expected in such cases, if only as a formality—of his 'love': hard to do even in view and near to the damsel's reddening cheeks: it perplexed him. He dropped a veil on the bashful topic; his tone was the same as when he reverted to the material points; his present income, his position in the great Bank of Shotts and Co., his prospects, the health of the heir to the Cantor earldom. He considered that he spoke to a member of the City merchants, whose preference for the plain positive, upon the question of an alliance between families by marriage, lends them for once a resemblance to lords. When a person is not read by character, the position or profession is called on to supply raised print for the finger-ends to spell.

Hard on poor Fredi! was Victor's thought behind the smile he bent on this bald Cupid. She deserved a more poetical lover! His paternal sympathies for the girl besought in love, revived his past feelings as a wooer; nothing but a dread of the influence of Mr. Barmby's toned eloquence upon the girl, after her listening to Dudley Sowerby's addresses, checked his contempt for the latter. He could not despise the suitor he sided with against another and seemingly now a more dangerous. Unable quite to repress the sentiment, he proceeded immediately to put it to his uses. For we have no need to be scrupulously formal and precise in the exposition of circumstances to a fellow who may thank the stars if such a girl condescends to give him a hearing. He had this idea through the conception of his girl's generosity. And furthermore, the cognizant eye of a Lucretian Alma Mater having seat so strongly in Victor, demanded as a right an effusion of the promising amorous graces on the part of the acceptable applicant to the post of husband of that peerless. These being absent, evidently non-existent, it seemed sufficient for the present, after the fashion of the young gentleman, to capitulate the few material matters briefly.

They were dotted along with a fine disregard of the stateliness of the sum to be settled on Nesta Victoria, and with a distant but burning wish all the while, that the suitor had been one to touch his heart and open it, inspiriting it—as could have been done—to disclose for good and all the things utterable. Victor loved clear honesty, as he loved light: and though he hated to be accused of not showing a clean face in the light, he would have been moved and lifted to confess to a spot by the touch at his heart. Dudley Sowerby's deficiencies, however, were outweighed by the palpable advantages of his birth, his prospects, and his good repute for conduct; add thereto his gentlemanly manners. Victor sighed again over his poor Fredi; and in telling Mr. Sowerby that the choice must be left to her, he had the regrets of a man aware of his persuasive arts and how they would be used, to think that he was actually making the choice.

Observe how fatefully he who has a scheme is the engine of it; he is no longer the man of his tastes or of his principles; he is on a line of rails for a terminus; and he may cast languishing eyes across waysides to right and left, he has doomed himself to proceed, with a self-devouring hunger for the half desired; probably manhood gone at the embrace of it. This may be or not, but Nature has decreed to him the forfeit of pleasure. She bids us count the passage of a sober day for the service of the morrow; that is her system; and she would have us adopt it, to keep in us the keen edge for cutting, which is the guarantee of enjoyment: doing otherwise, we lose ourselves in one or other of the furious matrix instincts; we are blunt to all else.

Young Dudley fully agreed that the choice must be with Miss Radnor; he alluded to her virtues, her accomplishments. He was waxing to fervidness. He said he must expect competitors; adding, on a start, that he was to say, from his mother, she, in the case of an intention to present Miss Radnor at Court....

Victor waved hand for a finish, looking as though, his head had come out of hot water. He sacrificed Royalty to his necessities, under a kind of sneer at its functions: 'Court! my girl? But the arduous duties are over for the season. We are a democratic people retaining the seductions of monarchy, as a friend says; and of course a girl may like to count among the flowers of the kingdom for a day, in the list of Court presentations; no harm. Only there's plenty of time... very young girls have their heads turned—though I don't say, don't imagine, my girl would. By and by perhaps.'

Dudley was ushered into Mr. Inchling's room and introduced to the figure-head of the Firm of Inchling, Pennergate, and Radnor: a respectable City merchant indeed, whom Dudley could read-off in a glimpse of the downright contrast to his partner. He had heard casual remarks on the respectable City of London merchant from Colney Durance. A short analytical gaze at him, helped to an estimate of the powers of the man who kept him up. Mr. Inchling was a florid City-feaster, descendant of a line of City merchants, having features for a wife to identify; as drovers, they tell us, can single one from another of their round-bellied beasts. Formerly the leader of the Firm, he was now, after dreary fits of restiveness, kickings, false prophecies of ruin, Victor's obedient cart-horse. He sighed in set terms for the old days of the Firm, when, like trouts in the current, the Firm had only to gape for shoals of good things to fatten it: a tale of English prosperity in quiescence; narrated interjectorily among the by-ways of the City, and wanting only metre to make it our national Poem.

Mr. Inchling did not deny that grand mangers of golden oats were still somehow constantly allotted to him. His wife believed in Victor, and deemed the loss of the balancing Pennergate a gain. Since that lamentable loss, Mr. Inchling, under the irony of circumstances the Tory of Commerce, had trotted and galloped whither driven, racing like mad against his will and the rival nations now in the field to force the pace; a name for enterprise; the close commercial connection of a man who speculated—who, to put it plainly, lived on his wits; hurried onward and onward; always doubting, munching, grumbling at satisfaction, in perplexity of the gratitude which is apprehensive of black Nemesis at a turn of the road,—to confound so wild a whip as Victor Radnor. He had never forgiven the youth's venture in India of an enormous purchase of Cotton many years back, and which he had repudiated, though not his share of the hundreds of thousands realized before the refusal to ratify the bargain had come to Victor. Mr. Inchling dated his first indigestion from that disquieting period. He assented to the praise of Victor's genius, admitting benefits; his heart refused to pardon, and consequently his head wholly to trust, the man who robbed him of his quondam comfortable feeling of security. And if you will imagine the sprite of the aggregate English Taxpayer personifying Steam as the malignant who has despoiled him of the blessed Safety-Assurance he once had from his God Neptune against invaders, you will comprehend the state of Mr. Inchling's mind in regard to his terrific and bountiful, but very disturbing partner.

He thanked heaven to his wife often, that he had nothing to do with North American or South American mines and pastures or with South Africa and, gold and diamonds: and a wife must sometimes listen, mastering her inward comparisons. Dr. Schlesien had met and meditated on this example of the island energy. Mr. Inchling was not permitted by his wife to be much the guest of the Radnor household, because of the frequent meeting there with Colney Durance; Colney's humour for satire being instantly in bristle at sight of his representative of English City merchants: 'over whom,' as he wrote of the venerable body, 'the disciplined and instructed Germans not deviously march; whom acute and adventurous Americans, with half a cock of the eye in passing, compassionately outstrip.' He and Dr. Schlesien agreed upon Mr. Inchling. Meantime the latter gentleman did his part at the tables of the wealthier City Companies, and retained his appearance of health; he was beginning to think, upon a calculation of the increased treasures of those Companies and the country, that we, the Taxpayer, ought not to leave it altogether to Providence to defend them; notwithstanding the watchful care of us hitherto shown by our briny Providence, to save us from anxiety and expense. But there are, he said, 'difficulties'; and the very word could stop him, as commonly when our difficulty lies in the exercise of thinking.

Victor's African room, containing large wall-maps of auriferous regions, was inspected; and another, where clerks were busy over miscellaneous Continents. Dudley Sowerby hoped he might win the maiden.

He and Victor walked in company Westward. The shop of Boyle and Luckwort, chemists, was not passed on this occasion. Dudley grieved that he had to be absent from the next Concert for practise, owing to his engagement to his mother to go down to the family seat near Tunbridge Wells. Victor mentioned his relatives, the Duvidney maiden ladies, residing near the Wells. They measured the distance between Cronidge and Moorsedge, the two houses, as for half an hour on horseback.

Nesta told her father at home that the pair of them had been observed confidentially arm in arm, and conversing so profoundly.

'Who, do you think, was the topic?' Victor asked.

She would not chase the little blue butterfly of a guess.

BOOK III

CHAPTER XIX

TREATS OF NATURE AND CIRCUMSTANCE AND THE DISSENSION BETWEEN THEM AND OF A SATIRIST'S MALIGNITY IN THE DIRECTION OF HIS COUNTRY

There is at times in the hearts of all men of active life a vivid wild moment or two of dramatic dialogue between the veteran antagonists, Nature and Circumstance, when they, whose business it should be to be joyfully one, furiously split; and the Dame is up with her shrillest querulousness to inquire of her offspring, for the distinct original motive of his conduct. Why did he bring her to such a pass! And what is the gain? If he be not an alienated issue of the great Mother, he will strongly incline to her view, that he put himself into harness to join with a machine going the dead contrary way of her welfare; and thereby wrote himself donkey, for his present reading. Soldiers, heroes, even the braided, even the wearers of the gay cock's feathers, who get the honours and the pocket-pieces, know the moment of her electrical eloquence. They have no answer for her, save an index at the machine pushing them on yet farther under the enemy's line of fire, where they pluck the golden wreath or the livid, and in either case listen no more. They glorify her topping wisdom while on the march to confound it. She is wise in her way. But, it is asked by the disputant, If we had followed her exclusively, how far should we have travelled from our starting-point? We of the world and its prizes and duties must do her an injury to make her tongue musical to us, and her argument worthy of attention. So it seems. How to keep the proper balance between those two testy old wranglers, that rarely pull the right way together, is as much the task for men in the grip of the world, as for the wanton youthful fry under dominion of their instincts; and probably, when it is done, man will have attained the golden age of his retirement from service.

Why be scheming? Victor asked. Unlike the gallant soldiery, his question was raised in the blush of a success, from an examination of the quality of the thing won; although it had not changed since it was first coveted; it was demonstrably the same: and an astonishing dry stick he held, as a reward for perpetual agitations and perversions of his natural tastes. Here was a Dudley Sowerby, the direct issue of the conception of Lakelands; if indeed they were not conceived together in one; and the young gentleman had moral character, good citizen substance, and station, rank, prospect of a title; and the grasp of him was firm. Yet so far was it from hearty, that when hearing a professed satirist like Colney Durance remark on the decorous manner of Dudley's transparent courtship of the girl, under his look of an awakened approval of himself, that he appeared to be asking everybody:—Do you not think I bid fair for an excellent father of Philistines?—Victor had a nip of spite at the thought of Dudley's dragging him bodily to be the grandfather. Poor Fredi, too!—necessarily the mother: condemned by her hard fate to feel proud of Philistine babies! Though women soon get reconciled to it! Or do they? They did once. What if his Fredi turned out one of the modern young women, who have drunk of ideas? He caught himself speculating on that, as on a danger. The alliance with Dudley really seemed to set him facing backward.

Colney might not have been under prompting of Nataly when he derided Dudley; but Victor was at war with the picture of her, in her compression of a cruel laugh, while her eyelids were hard shut, as if to exclude the young patriarch of Philistines' ridiculous image.

He hearkened to the Nature interrogating him, why had he stepped on a path to put division between himself and his beloved?—the smallest of gaps; and still the very smallest between nuptial lovers is a division—and that may become a mortal wound to their one-life. Why had he roused a slumbering world? Glimpses of the world's nurse-like, old-fashioned, mother-nightcap benevolence to its kicking favourites; its long-suffering tolerance for the heroic breakers of its rough-cast laws, while the decent curtain continues dropped, or lifted only ankle-high; together with many scenes, lively suggestions, of the choice of ways he liked best, told of things, which were better things, incomprehensibly forfeited. So that the plain sense of value insisted on more than one weighing of the gain in hand: a dubious measure.

He was as little disposed to reject it as to stop his course at a goal of his aim. Nevertheless, a gain thus poorly estimated, could not command him to do a deed of humiliation on account of it. The speaking to this dry young Dudley was not imperative at present. A word would do in the day to come.

Nataly was busy with her purchases of furniture, and the practise for the great August Concert. He dealt her liberal encouragements, up to the verge of Dr. Themison's latest hummed words touching Mrs. Burman, from which he jumped in alarm lest he should paralyze her again: the dear soul's dreaded aspect of an earthy pallor was a spectre behind her cheeks, ready to rush forth. Fenellan brought Carling to dine with him; and Themison was confirmed by Carting, with incidents in proof; Caning by Jarniman, also with incidents; one very odd one—or so it seemed, in the fury of the first savour of it:—she informed Jarniman, Skepsey said his friend Jarniman said, that she had dreamed of making her appearance to him on the night of the 23rd August, and of setting the date on the calendar over his desk, when she entered his room: 'Sitting-room, not bedroom; she was always quite the lady,' Skepsey reported his Jarniman. Mrs. Burman, as a ghost, would respect herself; she would keep to her character. Jarniman quite expected the dream to be verified; she was a woman of her word: he believed she had received a revelation of the approaching fact: he was preparing for the scene.

Victor had to keep silent and discourse of general prosperity. His happy vivaciousness assisted him to feel it by day. Nataly heard him at night, on a moan: 'Poor soul!' and loudly once while performing an abrupt demi-vault from back to side: 'Perhaps now!' in a voice through doors. She schooled herself to breathe equably.

Not being allowed to impart the distressing dose of comfort he was charged with, he swallowed it himself; and these were the consequences. And an uneasy sleep was traditionally a matter for grave debate in the Radnor family. The Duvidney ladies, Dorothea and Virginia, would have cited ancestral names, showing it to be the worst of intimations. At night, lying on his back beneath a weight of darkness, one heavily craped figure, distinguishable through the gloom, as a blot on a black pad, accused the answering darkness within him, until his mind was dragged to go through the whole case by morning light; and the compassionate man appealed to common sense, to stamp and pass his delectable sophistries; as, that it was his intense humaneness, which exposed him to an accusation of inhumanity; his prayer for the truly best to happen, which anticipated Mrs. Burman's expiry. They were simple sophistries, fabricated to suit his needs, readily taking and bearing the imprimatur of common sense. They refreshed him, as a chemical scent a crowded room.

All because he could not open his breast to Nataly, by reason of her feebleness; or feel enthusiasm in the possession of young Dudley! A dry stick indeed beside him on the walk Westward. Good quality wood, no doubt, but dry, varnished for conventional uses. Poor dear Fredi would have to crown it like the May-day posy of the urchins of Craye Farm and Creckholt!

Dudley wished the great City-merchant to appreciate him as a diligent student of commercial matters: rivalries of Banks; Foreign and Municipal Loans, American Rails, and Argentine; new Companies of wholesome appearance or sinister; or starting with a dram in the stomach, or born to bleat prostrate, like sheep on their backs in a ditch; Trusts and Founders; Breweries bursting vats upon the markets, and England prone along the gutters, gobbling, drunk for shares, and sober in the possession of certain of them. But when, as Colney says, a grateful England has conferred the Lordship on her Brewer, he gratefully hands-over the establishment to his country; and both may disregard the howls of a Salvation Army of shareholders.—Beaten by the Germans in Brewery, too! Dr. Schlesien has his right to crow. We were ahead of them, and they came and studied us, and they studied Chemistry as well; while we went on down our happy-go-lucky old road; and then had to hire their young Professors, and then to import their beer.

Have the Germans more brains than we English? Victor's blood up to the dome of his cranium knocked the patriotic negative. But, as old Colney says (and bother him, for constantly intruding!), the comfortably successful have the habit of sitting, and that dulls the brain yet more than it eases the person: hence are we outpaced; we have now to know we are racing. Victor scored a mark for one of his projects. A well-conducted Journal of the sharpest pens in the land might, at a sacrifice of money grandly sunk, expose to his English how and to what degree their sports, and their fierce feastings, and their opposition to ideas, and their timidity in regard to change, and their execration of criticism applied to themselves, and their unanimous adoption of it for a weapon against others, are signs of a prolonged indulgence in the cushioned seat. Victor saw it. But would the people he loved? He agreed with Colney, forgetting the satirist's venom: to-wit; that the journalists should be close under their editor's rod to put it in sound bold English;—no metaphors, no similes, nor flowery insubstantiality: but honest Saxon manger stuff: and put it repeatedly, in contempt of the disgust of iteration; hammering so a soft place on the Anglican skull, which is rubbed in consequence, and taught at last through soreness to reflect.—A Journal?—with Colney Durance for Editor?—and called conformably THE WHIPPING-TOP? Why not, if it exactly hits the signification of the Journal and that which it would have the country do to itself, to keep it going and truly topping? For there is no vulgarity in a title strongly signifying the intent. Victor wrote it at night, naming Colney for Editor, with a sum of his money to be devoted to the publication, in a form of memorandum; and threw it among the papers in his desk.

Young Dudley had a funny inquisitiveness about Dartrey Fenellan; owing to Fredi's reproduction or imitation of her mother's romantic sentiment for Dartrey, doubtless: a bit of jealousy, indicating that the dry fellow had his feelings. Victor touched—off an outline of Dartrey's history and character:—the half-brother of Simeon, considerably younger, and totally different. 'Dartrey's mother was Lady Charlotte Kiltorne, one of the Clanconans; better mother than wife, perhaps; and no reproach on her, not a shadow; only she made the General's Bank-notes fly black paper. And—if you 're for heredity—the queer point is, that Simeon, whose mother was a sober-minded woman, has always been the spendthrift. Dartrey married one of the Hennen women, all an odd lot, all handsome. I met her once. Colney said, she came up here with a special commission from the Prince of Darkness. There are women who stir the unholy in men—whether they mean it or not, you know.'

Dudley pursed to remark, that he could not say he did know. And good for Fredi if he did not know, and had his objections to the knowledge! But he was like the men who escape colds by wrapping in comforters instead of trusting to the spin of the blood.

'She played poor Dartrey pranks before he buried—he, behaved well to her; and that says much for him; he has: a devil of a temper. I 've seen the blood in his veins, mount to cracking. But there's the man: because she was a woman, he never let it break out with her. And, by heaven, he had cause. She couldn't be left. She tricked him, and she loved him-passionately, I believe. You don't understand women loving the husband they drag through the mire?'

Dudley did not. He sharpened his mouth.

'Buried, you said, sir?—a widower?'

'I've no positive information; we shall hear when he: comes back,' Victor replied hurriedly. 'He got a drenching of all the damns in the British service from his. Generalissimo one day at a Review, for a trooper's negligence-button or stock missing, or something; and off goes Dartrey to his hut, and breaks his sword, and sends in his resignation. Good soldier lost. And I can't complain; he has been a right-hand man to me over in Africa. But a man ought to have some control of his temper, especially a soldier.'

Dudley put emphasis into his acquiescence.

'Worse than that temper of Dartrey's, he can't forgive an injury. He bears a grudge against his country. You've heard Colney Durance abuse old England. It's three parts factitious-literary exercise. It 's milk beside the contempt of Dartrey's shrug. He thinks we're a dead people, if a people; "subsisting on our fat," as Colney says.'

'I am not of opinion that we show it,' observed Dudley.

'We don't,' Victor agreed. He disrelished his companion's mincing tone of a monumental security, and yearned for Dartrey or Simeon or Colney to be at his elbow rather than this most commendable of orderly citizens, who little imagined the treacherous revolt from him in the bosom of the gentleman cordially signifying full agreement. But Dudley was not gifted to read behind words and looks.

They were in the Park of the dwindling press of carriages, and here was this young Dudley saying, quite commendably: 'It's a pity we seem to have no means of keeping our parks select.'

Victor flung Simeon Fenellan at him in thought. He remembered a fable of Fenellan's, about a Society of the Blest, and the salt it was to them to discover an intruder from below, and the consequent accelerated measure in their hymning.

'Have you seen anything offensive to you?' he asked.

'One sees notorious persons.'

Dudley spoke aloof from them—'out of his cold attics,' Fenellan would have said.

Victor approved: with the deadened feeling common to us when first in sad earnest we consent to take life as it is.

He perceived, too, the comicality of his having to resign himself to the fatherly embrace of goodness.

Lakelands had him fast, and this young Dudley was the kernel of Lakelands. If he had only been intellectually a little flexible in his morality! But no; he wore it cap a pie, like a mediaeval knight his armour. One had to approve. And there was no getting away from him. He was good enough to stay in town for the practise of the opening overture of the amateurs, and the flute-duet, when his family were looking for him at Tunbridge Wells; and almost every day Victor was waylaid by him at a corner of the Strand.

Occasionally, Victor appeared at the point of interception armed with Colney Durance, for whom he had called in the Temple, bent on self-defence, although Colney was often as bitter to his taste as to Dudley's. Latterly the bitter had become a tonic. We rejoice in the presence of goodness, let us hope; and still an impersonation of conventional, goodness perpetually about us depresses. Dudley drove him to Colney for relief. Besides it pleased Nataly that he should be bringing Colney home; it looked to her as if he were subjecting Dudley to critical inspection before he decided a certain question much, and foolishly, dreaded by the dear soul. That quieted her. And another thing, she liked him to be with Colney, for a clog on him; as it were, a tuning-fork for the wild airs he started. A little pessimism, also, she seemed to like; probably as an appeasement after hearing, and having to share, high flights. And she was, in her queer woman's way, always reassured by his endurance of Colney's company:—she read it to mean, that he could bear Colney's perusal of him, and satiric stings. Victor had seen these petty matters among the various which were made to serve his double and treble purposes; now, thanks to the operation of young Dudley within him, he felt them. Preferring Fenellan's easy humour to Colney's acid, he was nevertheless braced by the latter's antidote to Dudley, while reserving his entire opposition in the abstract.

For Victor Radnor and Colney Durance were the Optimist and Pessimist of their society. They might have headed those tribes in the country. At a period when the omnibus of the world appears to its quaint occupants to be going faster, men are shaken into the acceptation, if not performance, of one part or the other as it is dictated to them by their temperaments. Compose the parts, and you come nigh to the meaning of the Nineteenth Century: the mother of these gosling affirmatives and negatives divorced from harmony and awakened by the slight increase of incubating motion to vitality. Victor and Colney had been champion duellists for the rosy and the saturnine since the former cheerfully slaved for a small stipend in the City of his affection, and the latter entered on an inheritance counted in niggard hundreds, that withdrew a briefless barrister disposed for scholarship from the forlornest of seats in the Courts. They had foretold of one another each the unfulfilled; each claimed the actual as the child of his prediction. Victor was to have been ruined long back; Colney the prey of independent bachelors. Colney had escaped his harpy, and Victor could be called a millionaire and more. Prophesy was crowned by Colney's dyspepsia, by Victor's ticklish domestic position. Their pity for one another, their warm regard, was genuine; only, they were of different temperaments; and we have to distinguish, that in many estimable and some gifted human creatures, it is the quality of the blood which directs the current of opinion.

Victor played-off Colney upon Dudley, for his internal satisfaction, and to lull Nataly and make her laugh; but he could not, as she hoped he was doing, take Colney into his confidence; inasmuch as the Optimist, impelled by his exuberant anticipatory trustfulness, is an author, and does things; whereas the Pessimist is your chaired critic, with the delivery of a censor, generally an undoer of things. Our Optimy has his instinct to tell him of the cast of Pessimy's countenance at the confession of a dilemma-foreseen! He hands himself to Pessimy, as it were a sugar-cane, for the sour brute to suck the sugar and whack with the wood. But he cannot perform his part in return; he gets no compensation: Pessimy is invulnerable. You waste your time in hurling a common 'tu-quoque' at one who hugs the worst.

The three walking in the park, with their bright view, and black view, and neutral view of life, were a comical trio. They had come upon the days of the unfanned electric furnace, proper to London's early August when it is not pipeing March. Victor complacently bore heat as well as cold: but young Dudley was a drought, and Colney a drug to refresh it; and why was he stewing in London? It was for this young Dudley, who resembled a London of the sparrowy roadways and wearisome pavements and blocks of fortress mansions, by chance a water-cart spirting a stale water: or a London of the farewell dinner-parties, where London's professed anecdotist lays the dust with his ten times told: Why was not Nataly relieved of her dreary round of the purchases of furniture! They ought all now to be in Switzerland or Tyrol. Nesta had of late been turning over leaves of an Illustrated book of Tyrol, dear to her after a run through the Innthal to the Dolomites one splendid August; and she and Nataly had read there of Hofer, Speckbacker, Haspinger; and wrath had filled them at the meanness of the Corsican, who posed after it as victim on St. Helena's rock; the scene in grey dawn on Mantua's fortress-walls blasting him in the Courts of History, when he strikes for his pathetic sublime.

Victor remembered how he had been rhetorical, as the mouthpiece of his darlings. But he had in memory prominently now the many glorious pictures of that mountain-land beckoning to him, waving him to fly forth from the London oven:—lo, the Tyrolese limestone crags with livid peaks and snow lining shelves and veins of the crevices; and folds of pinewood undulations closed by a shoulder of snow large on the blue; and a dazzling pinnacle rising over green pasture-Alps, the head of it shooting aloft as the blown billow, high off a broken ridge, and wide-armed in its pure white shroud beneath; tranced, but all motion in immobility, to the heart in the eye; a splendid image of striving, up to crowned victory. And see the long valley-sweeps of the hanging meadows and maize, and lower vineyards and central tall green spires! Walking beside young Dudley, conversing, observing too, Victor followed the trips and twists of a rill, that was lured a little further down through scoops, ducts, and scaffolded channels to serve a wainwright.

He heard the mountain-song of the joyful water: a wren-robin-thrush on the dance down of a faun; till it was caught and muted, and the silver foot slid along the channel, swift as moonbeams through a cloud, with an air of 'Whither you will, so it be on'; happy for service as in freedom. Then the yard of the inn below, and the rillwater twirling rounded through the trout-trough, subdued, still lively for its beloved onward: dues to business, dues to pleasure; a wedding of the two, and the wisest on earth:-eh? like some one we know, and Nataly has made the comparison. Fresh forellen for lunch: rhyming to Fenellan; he had said to her; and that recollection struck the day to blaze; for his friend was a ruined military captain living on a literary quill at the time; and Nataly's tender pleading, 'Could you not help to give him another chance, dear Victor?'—signifying her absolute trust in his ability to do that or more or anything, had actually set him thinking of the Insurance Office; which he started to prosperity, and Fenellan in it, previously an untutored rill of the mountains, if ever was one.

Useless to be dwelling on holiday pictures: Lakelands had hold of him!

Colney or somebody says, that the greater our successes, the greater the slaves we become.—But we must have an aim, my friend, and success must be the aim of any aim!—Yes, and, says Colney, you are to rejoice in the disappointing miss, which saved you from being damned by your bullet on the centre.—You're dead against Nature, old Colney.—That is to carry the flag of Liberty.—By clipping a limb!

Victor overcame the Pessimist in his own royal cranium-Court. He entertained a pronounced dissension with bachelors pretending to independence. It could not be argued publicly, and the more the pity:—for a slight encouragement, he would have done it: his outlook over the waves of bachelors and (by present conditions mostly constrained) spinsters—and another outlook, midnight upon Phlegethon to the thoughts of men, made him deem it urgent. And it helped the plea in his own excuse, as Colney pointed out to the son of Nature. That, he had to admit, was true. He charged it upon Mrs. Burman, for twisting the most unselfish and noblest of his thoughts; and he promised himself it was to cease on the instant when the circumstance, which Nature was remiss in not bringing about to-day or to-morrow, had come to pass. He could see his Nataly's pained endurance beneath her habitual submission. Her effort was a poor one, to conceal her dread of the day of the gathering at Lakelands.

On the Sunday previous to the day, Dr. Themison accompanied the amateurs by rail to Wrensham, to hear 'trial of the acoustics' of the Concert-hall. They were a goodly company; and there was fun in the railway-carriage over Colney's description of Fashionable London's vast octopus Malady-monster, who was letting the doctor fly to the tether of its longest filament for an hour, plying suckers on him the while. He had the look, to general perception, of a man but half-escaped: and as when the notes of things taken by the vision in front are being set down upon tablets in the head behind. Victor observed his look at Nataly. The look was like a door aswing, revealing in concealing. She was not or did not appear struck by it; perhaps, if observant, she took it for a busy professional gentleman's holiday reckoning of the hours before the return train to his harness, and his arrangements for catching it. She was, as she could be on a day of trial, her enchanting majestic self again—defying suspicions. She was his true mate for breasting a world honoured in uplifting her.

Her singing of a duet with Nesta, called forth Dr. Themison's very warm applause. He named the greatest of contraltos. Colney did better service than Fenellan at the luncheon-table: he diverted Nataly and captured Dr. Themison's ear with the narrative of his momentous expedition of European Emissaries, to plead the cause of their several languages at the Court of Japan: a Satiric Serial tale, that hit incidentally the follies of the countries of Europe, and intentionally, one had to think, those of Old England. Nesta set him going. Just when he was about to begin, she made her father laugh by crying out in a rapture, 'Oh! Delphica!' For she was naughtily aware of Dudley Sowerby's distaste for the story and disgust with the damsel Delphica.

Nesta gave Dr. Themison the preliminary sketch of the grand object of the expedition: indeed one of the eminent ones of the world; matter for an Epic; though it is to be feared, that our part in it will not encourage a Cis-Atlantic bard. To America the honours from beginning to end belong.

So, then, Japan has decided to renounce its language, for the adoption of the language it may choose among the foremost famous European tongues. Japan becomes the word for miraculous transformations of a whole people at the stroke of a wand; and let our English enrol it as the most precious of the powerful verbs. An envoy visits the principal Seats of Learning in Europe. He is of a gravity to match that of his unexampled and all but stupefying mission. A fluent linguist, yet an Englishman, the slight American accent contracted during a lengthened residence in the United States is no bar to the patriotism urging him to pay his visit of exposition and invitation from the Japanese Court to the distinguished Doctor of Divinity Dr. Bouthoin. The renown of Dr. Bouthoin among the learned of Japan has caused the special invitation to him; a scholar endowed by an ample knowledge and persuasive eloquence to cite and instance as well as illustrate the superior advantages to Japan and civilization in the filial embrace of mother English. 'For to this it must come predestinated,' says the astonishing applicant. 'We seem to see a fitness in it,' says the cogitative Rev. Doctor. 'And an Island England in those waters, will do wonders for Commerce,' adds the former. 'We think of things more pregnant,' concludes the latter, with a dry gleam of ecclesiastical knowingness. And let the Editor of the

Review upon his recent pamphlet, and let the prelate reprimanding him, and let the newspapers criticizing his pure Saxon, have a care!

Funds, universally the most convincing of credentials, are placed at Dr. Bouthoin's disposal: only it is requested, that for the present the expedition be secret. 'Better so,' says pure Saxon's champion. On a day patented for secresy, and swearing-in the whole American Continent through the cables to keep the secret by declaring the patent, the Rev. Dr. Bouthoin, accompanied by his curate, the Rev. Mancate Semhians, stumbling across portmanteaux crammed with lexicons and dictionaries and other tubes of the voice of Hermes, takes possession of berths in the ship Polypheme, bound, as they mutually conceive, for the biggest adventure ever embarked on by a far-thoughted, high-thoughted, patriotic pair speaking pure Saxon or other.

Colney, with apologies to his hearers, avoided the custom of our period (called the Realistic) to create, when casual opportunity offers, a belief in the narrative by promoting nausea in the audience. He passed under veil the Rev. Doctor's acknowledgement of Neptune's power, and the temporary collapse of Mr. Semhians. Proceeding at once to the comments of these high-class missionaries on the really curious inquisitiveness of certain of the foreign passengers on board, he introduced to them the indisputably learned, the very argumentative, crashing, arrogant, pedantic, dogmatic, philological German gentleman, Dr. Gannius, reeking of the Teutonic Professor, as a library volume of its leather. With him is his fairhaired artless daughter Delphica. An interesting couple for the beguilement of a voyage: she so beautifully moderates his irascible incisiveness! Yet there is a strange tone that they have. What, then, of the polite, the anecdotic Gallic M. Falarique, who studiously engages the young lady in colloquy when Mr. Semhians is agitating outside them to say a word? What of that outpouring, explosive, equally voluble, uncontrolled M. Bobinikine, a Mongol Russian, shaped, featured, hued like the pot-boiled, round and tight young dumpling of our primitive boyhood, which smokes on the dish from the pot? And what of another, hitherto unnoticed, whose nose is of the hooked vulturine, whose name transpires as Pisistratus Mytharete? He hears Dr. Bouthoin declaim some lines of Homer, and beseeches him for the designation of that language. Greek, is it? Greek of the Asiatic ancient days of the beginning of the poetic chants? Dr. Gannius crashes cachinnation. Dr. Bouthoin caps himself with the offended Don. Mr. Semhians opens half an eye and a whole mouth. There must be a mystery, these two exclaim to one another in privacy. Delphica draws Mr. Semhians aside.

Blushing over his white necktie, like the coast of Labrador at the transient wink of its Jack-in-the-box Apollo, Mr. Semhians faintly tells of a conversation he has had with the ingenuous fair one; and she ardent as he for the throning of our incomparable Saxon English in the mouths of the races of mankind. Strange!—she partly suspects the Frenchman, the Russian, the attentive silent Greek, to be all of them bound for the Court of Japan. Concurrents? Can it be? We are absolutely to enter on a contention with rivals? Dr. Bouthoin speaks to Dr. Gannius. He is astonished, he says; he could not have imagined it!

'Have you ever imagined anything?' Dr. Gannius asks him. Entomologist, botanist, palaeontologist, philologist, and at sound of horn a ready regimental corporal, Dr. Gannius wears good manners as a pair of bath-slippers, to rally and kick his old infant of an Englishman; who, in awe of his later renown and manifest might, makes it a point of discretion to be ultra-amiable; for he certainly is not in training, he has no alliances, and he must diplomatize; and the German is a strong one; a relative too; he is the Saxon's cousin, to say the least. This German has the habit of pushing past politeness to carry his argumentative war into the enemy's country: and he presents on all sides a solid rampart of recent great deeds done, and mailed readiness for the doing of more, if we think of assailing him in that way. We are really like the poor beasts which have cast their shells or cases, helpless flesh to his beak. So we are cousinly.

Whether more amused than amazed, we know not, Dr. Gannius hears from 'our simpleton of the pastures,' as he calls the Rev. Doctor to his daughter, that he and Mr. Semhians have absolutely pushed forth upon this most mighty of enterprises naked of any backing from their Government! Babes in the Wood that they are! 'a la grace de dieu' at every turn that cries for astutia, they show no sign or symbol of English arms behind them, to support—and with the grandest of national prizes in view!—the pleading oration before the Court of the elect, erudites, we will call them, of an intelligent, yet half barbarous, people; hesitating, these, between eloquence and rival eloquence, cunning and rival cunning. Why, in such a case, the shadow-nimbus of Force is needed to decide the sinking of the scale. But have these English never read their Shakespeare, that they show so barren an acquaintance with human, to say nothing of semi-barbaric, nature? But it is here that we Germans prove our claim to being the sons of his mind.—Dr. Gannius, in contempt, throws off the mask: he also is a concurrent. And not only is he the chosen by election of the chief Universities of his land, he has behind him, as Athene dilating Achilles, the clenched fist of the Prince of thunder and lightning of his time. German, Japan shall be! he publicly swears before them all. M. Falarique damascenes his sharpest smile; M. Bobinikine double-dimples his puddingest; M. Mytharete rolls a forefinger over his beak; Dr. Bouthoin enlarges his eye on a sunny mote. And such is the masterful effect of a frank diplomacy, that when one party shows his hand, the others find the reverse of concealment in hiding their own.

Dr. Bouthoin and Mr. Semhians are compelled to suspect themselves to be encompassed with rivals, presumptively supported by their Governments. The worthy gentlemen had hoped to tumble into good fortune, as in the blessed old English manner. 'It has even been thus with us: unhelped we do it!' exclaims the Rev. Doctor. He is roused from dejection by hearing Mr. Semhians shyly (he has published verse) tell of the fairtressed Delphica's phosphorial enthusiasm for our galaxy of British Poets. Assisted by Mr. Semhians, he begins to imagine, that he has, in the person of this artless devotee an ally, who will, through her worship of our poets (by treachery to her sire-a small matter) sacrifice her guttural tongue, by enabling him (through the exercise of her arts, charms, intrigues—also a small matter) to obtain the first audience of the Japanese erudites. Delphica, with each of the rivals in turn, is very pretty Comedy. She is aware that M. Falarique is her most redoubtable adversary, by the time that the vast fleet of steamboats (containing newspaper reporters) is beheld from the decks of the Polypheme puffing past Sandy Hook.

There Colney left them, for the next instalment of the serial.

Nesta glanced at Dudley Sowerby. She liked him for his pained frown at the part his countrymen were made to play, but did wish that he would keep from expressing it in a countenance that suggested a worried knot; and mischievously she said: 'Do you take to Delphica?'

He replied, with an evident sincerity, 'I cannot say I do.'

Had Mr. Semhians been modelled on him?

'One bets on the German, of course—with Colney Durance,' Victor said to Dr. Themison, leading him over the grounds of Lakelands.

'In any case, the author teaches us to feel an interest in the rivals. I want to know what comes of it,' said the doctor.

'There's a good opportunity, one sees. But, mark me, it will all end in satire upon poor Old England. According to Colney, we excel in nothing.'

'I do not think there is a country that could offer the entertainment for which I am indebted to you to-day.'

'Ah, my friend, and you like their voices? The contralto?'

'Exquisite.'

Dr. Themison had not spoken the name of Radnor.

'Shall we see you at our next Concert-evening in town?' said Victor; and hearing 'the privilege' mentioned, his sharp bright gaze cleared to limpid. 'You have seen how it stands with us here!' At once he related what indeed Dr. Themison had begun speculatively to think might be the case.

Mrs. Burman Radnor had dropped words touching a husband, and of her desire to communicate with him, in the event of her being given over to the surgeons: she had said, that her husband was a greatly gifted man; setting her head in a compassionate swing. This revelation of the husband soon after, was filling. And this Mr. Radnor's comrade's manner of it, was winning: a not too self-justifying tone; not void of feeling for the elder woman; with a manly eulogy of the younger, who had flung away the world for him and borne him their one dear child. Victor took the blame wholly upon himself. 'It is right that you should know,' he said to the doctor's thoughtful posture; and he stressed the blame; and a flame shot across his eyeballs. He brought home to his hearer the hurricane of a man he was in the passion: indicating the subjection of such a temperament as this Victor Radnor's to trials of the moral restraints beyond his human power.

Dr. Themison said: 'Would you—we postpone that as long as we can: but supposing the poor lady...?'

Victor broke in: 'I see her wish: I will.'

The clash of his answer rang beside Dr. Themison's faltering query.

We are grateful when spared the conclusion of a sentence born to stammer. If for that only, the doctor pressed Victor's hand warmly.

'I may, then, convey some form of assurance, that a request of the kind will be granted?' he said.

'She has but to call me to her,' said Victor, stiffening his back.

CHAPTER XX

THE GREAT ASSEMBLY AT LAKELANDS

Round the neighbourhood of Lakelands it was known that the day of the great gathering there had been authoritatively foretold as fine, by Mr. Victor Radnor; and he delivered his prophecy in the teeth of the South-western gale familiar to our yachting month; and he really inspired belief or a kind of trust; some supposing him to draw from reserves of observation, some choosing to confide in the singularly winged sparkle of his eyes. Lady Rodwell Blachington did; and young Mrs. Blathenoy; and Mrs. Fanning; they were enamoured of it. And when women stand for Hope, and any worshipped man for Promise, nothing less than redoubled confusion of him dissolves the union. Even then they cling to it, under an ejaculation, that it might and should have been otherwise; fancy partly has it otherwise, in her caerulean home above the weeping. So it is good at all points to prophecy with the aspect of the radiant day foretold.

A storm, bearing battle overhead, tore the night to pieces. Nataly's faith in the pleasant prognostic wavered beneath the crashes. She had not much power of heart to desire anything save that which her bosom disavowed. Uproar rather appeased her, calmness agitated. She wished her beloved to be spared from a disappointment, thinking he deserved all successes, because of the rigours inflicted by her present tonelessness of blood and being. Her unresponsive manner with him was not due to lack of fire in the blood or a loss of tenderness. The tender feeling, under privations unwillingly imposed, though willingly shared, now suffused her reflections, owing to a gratitude induced by a novel experience of him; known, as it may chance, and as it does not always chance, to both sexes in wedded intimacy here and there; known to women whose mates are proved quick to compliance with delicate intuitions of their moods of nature. A constant, almost visible, image of the dark thing she desired, and was bound not to desire, and was remorseful for desiring, oppressed her; a perpetual consequent warfare of her spirit and the nature subject to the thousand sensational hypocrisies invoked for concealment of its reviled brutish baseness, held the woman suspended from her emotions. She coldly felt that a caress would have melted her, would have been the temporary rapture. Coldly she had the knowledge that the considerate withholding of it helped her spirit to escape a stain. Less coldly, she thanked at heart her beloved, for being a gentleman in their yoke. It plighted them over flesh.

He talked to her on the pillow, just a few sentences; and, unlike himself, a word of City affairs: 'That fellow Blathenoy, with his increasing multitude of bills at the Bank: must watch him there, sit there regularly. One rather likes his wife. By the way, if you see him near me to-morrow, praise the Spanish climate; don't forget. He heads the subscription list of Lady Blachington's Charity.'

Victor chuckled at Colney's humping of shoulders and mouth, while the tempest seemed echoing a sulphurous pessimist. 'If old Colney had listened to me, when India gave proof of the metal and South Africa began heaving, he'd have been a fairly wealthy man by now... ha! it would have genialized him. A man may be a curmudgeon with money: the rule is for him to cuddle himself and take a side, instead of dashing at his countrymen all round and getting hated. Well, Colney popular, can't be imagined; but entertaining guests would have diluted his acid. He has the six hundred or so a year he started old bachelor on; add his miserable pay for Essays. Literature! Of course, he sours. But don't let me hear of bachelors moralists. There he sits at his Temple Chambers hatching epigrams... pretends to have the office of critic! Honest old fellow, as far as his condition permits. I tell him it will be fine to-morrow.'

'You are generally right, dear,' Nataly said.

Her dropping breath was audible.

Victor smartly commended her to slumber, with heaven's blessing on her and a dose of soft nursery prattle.

He squeezed her hand. He kissed her lips by day. She heard him sigh settling himself into the breast of night for milk of sleep, like one of the world's good children. She could have turned to him, to show him she was in harmony with the holy night and loving world, but for the fear founded on a knowledge of the man he was; it held her frozen to the semblance of a tombstone lady beside her lord, in the aisle where horror kindles pitchy blackness with its legions at one movement. Verily it was the ghost of Mrs. Burman come to the bed, between them.

Meanwhile the sun of Victor Radnor's popularity was already up over the extended circle likely to be drenched by a falsification of his daring augury, though the scud flew swift, and the beeches raved, and the oaks roared and snarled, and pine-trees fell their lengths. Fine tomorrow, to a certainty! he had been heard to say. The doubt weighed for something; the balance inclined with the gentleman who had become so popular: for he had done the trick so suddenly, like a stroke of the wizard; and was a real man, not one of your spangled zodiacs selling for sixpence and hopping to a lucky hit, laughed at nine times out of ten. The reasoning went—and it somewhat affected the mansion as well as the cottage,— that if he had become popular in this astonishing fashion, after making one of the biggest fortunes of modern times, he might, he must, have secret gifts. 'You can't foretell weather!' cried a pothouse sceptic. But the workmen at Lakelands declared that he had foretold it. Sceptics among the common folk were quaintly silenced by other tales of him, being a whiff from the delirium attending any mention of his name.

How had he become suddenly so popular as to rouse in the mind of Mr. Caddis, the sitting Member for the division of the county (said to have the seat in his pocket), a particular inquisitiveness to know the bearing of his politics? Mr. Radnor was rich, true: but these are days when wealthy men, ambitious of notoriety, do not always prove faithful to their class; some of them are cunning to bid for the suffrages of the irresponsible, recklessly enfranchised, corruptible masses. Mr. Caddis, if he had the seat in his pocket, had it from the support of a class trusting him to support its interests: he could count on the landowners, on the clergy, on the retired or retiring or comfortably cushioned merchants resident about Wrensham, on the many obsequious among electoral shopmen; annually he threw open his grounds, and he subscribed, patronized, did what was expected; and he was not popular; he was unpopular. Why? But why was the sun of this 23rd August, shining from its rise royally upon pacified, enrolled and liveried armies of cloud, more agreeable to earth's populations than his pinched appearance of the poor mopped red nose and melancholic rheumy eyelets on a January day! Undoubtedly Victor Radnor risked his repute of prophet. Yet his popularity would have survived the continuance of the storm and deluge. He did this:—and the mystery puzzling the suspicious was nothing wonderful: in addition to a transparent benevolence, he spread a sort of assurance about him, that he thought the better of the people for their thinking well of themselves. It came first from the workmen at his house. 'The right sort, and no humbug: likes you to be men.' Such a report made tropical soil for any new seed.

Now, it is a postulate, to strengthen all poor commoners, that not even in comparison with the highest need we be small unless we yield to think it of ourselves. Do but stretch a hand to the touch of earth in you, and you spring upon combative manhood again, from the basis where all are equal. Humanity's historians, however, tell us, that the exhilaration bringing us consciousness of a stature, is gas which too frequently has to be administered. Certes the cocks among men do not require the process; they get it off the sight of the sun arising or a simple hen submissive: but we have our hibernating bears among men, our yoked oxen, cab horses, beaten dogs; we have on large patches of these Islands, a Saxon population, much wanting assistance, if they are not to feel themselves beaten, driven, caught by the neck, yoked and heavyheaded. Blest, then, is he who gives them a sense of the pride of standing on legs. Beer, ordinarily their solitary helper beneath the iron canopy of wealth, is known to them as a bitter usurer; it knocks them flat in their persons and their fortunes, for the short spell of recreative exaltation. They send up their rough glory round the name of the gentleman—a stranger, but their friend: and never is friend to be thought of as a stranger—who manages to get the holiday for Wrensham and thereabout, that they may hurl away for one jolly day the old hat of a doddered humbleness, and trip to the strains of the internal music he has unwound.

Says he: Is it a Charity Concert? Charity begins at home, says he: and if I welcome you gentry on behalf of the poor of London, why, it follows you grant me the right to make a beginning with the poor of our parts down here. He puts it so, no master nor mistress neither could refuse him. Why, the workmen at his house were nigh pitching the contractors all sprawling on a strike, and Mr. Radnor takes train, harangues 'em and rubs 'em smooth; ten minutes by the clock, they say; and return train to his business in town; by reason of good sense and feeling, it was; poor men don't ask for more. A working man, all the world over, asks but justice and a little relaxation—just a collar of fat to his lean.

Mr. Caddis, M.P., pursuing the riddle of popularity, which irritated and repelled as constantly as it attracted him, would have come nearer to an instructive presentment of it, by listening to these plain fellows, than he was in the line of equipages, at a later hour of the day. The remarks of the comfortably cushioned and wheeled, though they be eulogistic to extravagance, are vapourish when we court them for nourishment; substantially, they are bones to the cynical. He heard enumerations of Mr. Radnor's riches, eclipsing his own past compute. A merchant, a holder of mines, Director of a mighty Bank, projector of running rails, a princely millionaire, and determined to be popular—what was the aim of the man? It is the curse of modern times, that we never can be sure of our Parliamentary seat; not when we have it in our pockets! The Romans have left us golden words with regard to the fickleness of the populace; we have our Horace, our Juvenal, we have our Johnson; and in this vaunted age of reason it is, that we surrender ourselves into the hands of the populace! Panem et circenses! Mr. Caddis repeated it, after his fathers; his fathers and he had not headed them out of that original voracity. There they were, for moneyed legislators to bewail their appetites. And it was an article of his legislation, to keep them there.

Pedestrian purchasers of tickets for the Charity Concert, rather openly, in an envelope of humour, confessed to the bait of the Radnor bread with bit of fun. Savoury rumours were sweeping across Wrensham. Mr. Radnor had borrowed footmen of the principal houses about. Cartloads of provisions had been seen to come. An immediate reward of a deed of benevolence, is a thing sensibly heavenly; and the five-shilling tickets were paid for as if for a packet on the counter. Unacquainted with Mr. Radnor, although the reports of him struck a summons to their gastric juices, resembling in its effect a clamorous cordiality, they were chilled, on their steps along the halfrolled new gravel-roads to the house, by seeing three tables of prodigious length, where very evidently a feast had raged: one to plump the people—perhaps excessively courted by great gentlemen of late; shopkeepers, the villagers, children. These had been at it for two merry hours. They had risen. They were beef and pudding on legs; in some quarters, beer amiably manifest, owing to the flourishes of a military band. Boys, who had shaken room through their magical young corporations for fresh stowage, darted out of a chasing circle to the crumbled cornucopia regretfully forsaken fifteen minutes back, and buried another tart. Plenty still reigned: it was the will of the Master that it should.

We divert our attention, resigned in stoic humour, to the bill of the Concert music, handed us with our tickets at the park-gates: we have no right to expect refreshment; we came for the music, to be charitable. Signora Bianca Luciani: of whom we have read almost to the hearing her; enough to make the mistake at times. The grand violinist Durandarte: forcibly detained on his way to America. Mr. Radnor sent him a blank cheque:—no!—so Mr. Radnor besought him in person: he is irresistible; a great musician himself; it is becoming quite the modern style. We have now English noblemen who play the horn, the fife—the drum, some say! We may yet be Merrie England again, with our nobles taking the lead.

England's nobles as a musical band at the head of a marching and dancing population, pictured happily an old Conservative country, that retained its members of aristocracy in the foremost places while subjecting them to downright uses. Their ancestors, beholding them there, would be satisfied on the point of honour; perhaps enlivened by hearing them at fife and drum.

But middle-class pedestrians, having paid five shillings for a ticket to hear the music they love, and not having full assurance of refreshment, are often, latterly, satirical upon their superiors; and, over this country at least, require the refreshment, that the democratic sprouts in them may be reconciled with aristocracy. Do not listen to them further on the subject. They vote safely enough when the day comes, if there is no praetematurally strong pull the other way.

They perceive the name of the Hon. Dudley Sowerby, fourth down the Concert-bill; marked for a flute-duet with Mr. Victor Radnor, Miss Nesta Victoria Radnor accompanying at the piano. It may mean?... do you want a whisper to suggest to you what it may mean? The father's wealth is enormous; the mother is a beautiful majestic woman in her prime. And see, she sings: a wonderful voice. And lower down, a duet with her daughter: violins and clarionet; how funny; something Hungarian. And in the Second Part, Schubert's Ave Maria—Oh! when we hear that, we dissolve. She was a singer before he married her, they say: a lady by birth one of the first County families. But it was a gift, and she could not be kept from it, and was going, when they met—and it was love! the most perfect duet. For him she abandoned the Stage. You must remember, that in their young days the Stage was many stages beneath the esteem entertained for it now. Domestic Concerts are got up to gratify her: a Miss Fredericks: good old English name. Mr. Radnor calls his daughter, Freddy; so Mr. Taplow, the architect, says. They are for modern music and ancient. Tannhauser, Wagner, you see. Pergolese.

Flute-duet, Mercadante. Here we have him! O—Durandarte: Air Basque, variations—his own. Again, Senor Durandarte, Mendelssohn. Encore him, and he plays you a national piece. A dark little creature a Life-guardsman could hold-up on his outstretched hand for the fifteen minutes of the performance; but he fills the hall and thrills the heart, wafts you to heaven; and does it as though he were conversing with his Andalusian lady-love in easy whispers about their mutual passion for Spanish chocolate all the while: so the musical critic of the Tirra-Lirra says. Express trains every half hour from London; all the big people of the city. Mr. Radnor commands them, like Royalty. Totally different from that old figure of the wealthy City merchant; young, vigorous, elegant, a man of taste, highest culture, speaks the languages of Europe, patron of the Arts, a perfect gentleman. His mother was one of the Montgomerys, Mr. Taplow says.

And it was General Radnor, a most distinguished officer, dying knighted. But Mr. Victor Radnor would not take less than a Barony—and then only with descent of title to his daughter, in her own right.

Mr. Taplow had said as much as Victor Radnor chose that he should say.

Carriages were in flow for an hour: pedestrians formed a wavy coil. Judgeing by numbers, the entertainment was a success; would the hall contain them? Marvels were told of the hall. Every ticket entered and was enfolded; almost all had a seat. Chivalry stood. It is a breeched abstraction, sacrificeing voluntarily and genially to the Fair, for a restoring of the balance between the sexes, that the division of good things be rather in the fair ones' favour, as they are to think: with the warning to them, that the establishment of their claim for equality puts an end to the priceless privileges of petticoats. Women must be mad, to provoke such a warning; and the majority of them submissively show their good sense. They send up an incense of perfumery, all the bouquets of the chemist commingled; most nourishing to the idea of woman in the nose of man. They are a forest foliage—rustle of silks and muslins, magic interweaving, or the mythology, if you prefer it. See, hear, smell, they are Juno, Venus, Hebe, to you. We must have poetry with them; otherwise they are better in the kitchen. Is there—but there is not; there is not present one of the chivalrous breeched who could prefer the shocking emancipated gristly female, which imposes propriety on our sensations and inner dreams, by petrifying in the tender bud of them.

Colonel Corfe is the man to hear on such a theme. He is a colonel of Companies. But those are his diversion, as the British Army has been to the warrior. Puellis idoneus, he is professedly a lady's man, a rose-beetle, and a fine specimen of a common kind: and he has been that thing, that shining delight of the lap of ladies, for a spell of years, necessitating a certain sparkle of the saccharine crystals preserving him, to conceal the muster. He has to be fascinating, or he would look outworn, forlorn. On one side of him is Lady Carmine; on the other, Lady Swanage; dames embedded in the blooming maturity of England's conservatory. Their lords (an Earl, a Baron) are of the lords who go down to the City to sow a title for a repair of their poor incomes, and are to be commended for frankly accepting the new dispensation while they retain the many advantages of the uncancelled ancient. Thus gently does a maternal Old England let them down. Projectors of Companies, Directors, Founders; Railway magnates, actual kings and nobles (though one cannot yet persuade old reverence to do homage with the ancestral spontaneity to the uncrowned, uncoroneted, people of our sphere); holders of Shares in gold mines, Shares in Afric's blue mud of the glittering teeth we draw for English beauty to wear in the ear, on the neck, at the wrist; Bankers and wives of Bankers. Victor passed among them, chatting right and left.

Lady Carmine asked him: 'Is Durandarte counted on?'

He answered: 'I made sure of the Luciani.'

She serenely understood. Artistes are licenced people, with a Bohemian instead of the titular glitter for the bewildering of moralists; as paste will pass for diamonds where the mirror is held up to Nature by bold supernumeraries.

He wished to introduce Nesta. His girl was on the raised orchestral flooring. Nataly held her fast to a music-scroll.

Mr. Peridon, sad for the absence and cause of absence of Louise de Seilles,—summoned in the morning abruptly to Bourges, where her brother lay with his life endangered by an accident at Artillery practise,—Mr. Peridon was generally conductor. Victor was to lead the full force of amateurs in the brisk overture to Zampa. He perceived a movement of Nataly, Nesta, and Peridon. 'They have come,' he said; he jumped on the orchestra boards and hastened to greet the Luciani with Durandarte in the retiring-room.

His departure raised the whisper that he would wield the baton. An opinion was unuttered. His name for the flute-duet with the Hon. Dudley Sowerby had not provoked the reserve opinion; it seemed, on the whole, a pretty thing in him to condescend to do: the sentiment he awakened was not flustered by it. But the act of leading, appeared as an official thing to do. Our soufe of sentiment will be seen subsiding under a breath, without a repressive word to send it down. Sir Rodwell Blachington would have preferred Radnor's not leading or playing either. Colonel Corfe and Mr. Caddis declined to consider such conduct English, in a man of station... notwithstanding Royal Highnesses, who are at least partly English: partly, we say, under our breath, remembering our old ideal of an English gentleman, in opposition to German tastes. It is true, that the whole country is changeing, decomposing!

The colonel fished for Lady Carmine's view. And Lady Swanage too? Both of the distinguished ladies approved of Mr. Radnor's leading—for a leading off. Women are pleased to see their favourite in the place of prominence—as long as Fortune swims him unbuffeted, or one should say, unbattered, up the mounting wave. Besides these ladies had none of the colonel's remainder of juvenile English sense of the manly, his adolescent's intolerance of the eccentric, suspicion and contempt of any supposed affectation, which was not ostentatiously, stalkingly practised to subdue the sex. And you cannot wield a baton without looking affected. And at one of the Colonel's Clubs in town, only five years back, an English musical composer, who had not then made his money—now by the mystery of events knighted!—had been (he makes now fifteen thousand a year) black-balled. 'Fiddler? no; can't admit a Fiddler to associate on equal terms with gentlemen.' Only five years back: and at present we are having the Fiddler everywhere.

A sprinkling of the minor ladies also would have been glad if Mr. Radnor had kept himself somewhat more exclusive. Dr. Schlesien heard remarks, upon which his weighty Teutonic mind sat crushingly. Do these English care one bit for music?—for anything finer than material stuffs?—what that man Durance calls, 'their beef, their beer, and their pew in eternity'? His wrath at their babble and petty brabble doubted that they did.

But they do. Art has a hold of them. They pay for it; and the thing purchased grapples. It will get to their bosoms to breathe from them in time: entirely overcoming the taste for feudalism, which still a little objects to see their born gentleman acting as leader of musicians. A people of slow movement, developing tardily, their country is wanting in the distincter features, from being always in the transitional state, like certain sea-fish rolling head over-you know not head from tail. Without the Welsh, Irish, Scot; in their composition, there would not be much of the yeasty ferment: but it should not be forgotten that Welsh, Irish, Scot, are now largely of their numbers; and the taste for elegance, and for spiritual utterance, for Song, nay, for Ideas, is there among them, though it does not everywhere cover a rocky surface to bewitch the eyes of aliens;—like Louise de Seilles and Dr. Schlesien, for example; aliens having no hostile disposition toward the people they were compelled to criticize; honourably granting, that this people has a great history. Even such has the Lion, with Homer for the transcriber of his deeds. But the gentle aliens would image our emergence from wildness as the unsocial spectacle presented by the drear menagerie Lion, alone or mated; with hardly an animated moment save when the raw red joint is beneath his paw, reminding him of the desert's pasture.

Nevertheless, where Strength is, there is hope:—it may be said more truly than of the breath of Life; which is perhaps but the bucket of breath, muddy with the sediment of the well: whereas we have in Strength a hero, if a malefactor; whose muscles shall haul him up to the light he will prove worthy of, when that divinity has shown him his uncleanness. And when Strength is not exercising, you are sure to see Satirists jump on his back. Dozens, foreign and domestic, are on the back of Old England; a tribute to our quality if at the same time an irritating scourge. The domestic are in excess; and let us own that their view of the potentate, as an apathetic beast of power, who will neither show the power nor woo the graces; pretending all the while to be eminently above the beast, and posturing in an inefficient mimicry of the civilized, excites to satire. Colney Durance had his excuses. He could point to the chief creative minds of the country for generations, as beginning their survey genially, ending venomously, because of an exasperating unreason and scum in the bubble of the scenes, called social, around them. Viola under his chin, he gazed along the crowded hall, which was to him a rich national pudding of the sycophants, the hypocrites, the burlies, the idiots; dregs of the depths and froth of the surface; bowing to one, that they may scorn another; instituting a Charity, for their poorer fawning fellows to relieve their purses and assist them in tricking the world and their Maker: and so forth, a tiresome tirade: and as it was not on his lips, but in the stomach of the painful creature, let him grind that hurdy-gurdy for himself. His friend Victor set it stirring: Victor had here what he aimed at!

How Success derides Ambition! And for this he imperilled the happiness of the worthy woman he loved! Exposed her to our fen-fogs and foul snakes—of whom one or more might be in the assembly now: all because of his insane itch to be the bobbing cork on the wave of the minute! Colney's rapid interjections condensed upon the habitual shrug at human folly, just when Victor, fronting the glassy stare of Colonel Corfe, tapped to start his orchestra through the lively first bars of the overture to Zampa.

We soon perceive that the post Mr. Radnor fills he thoroughly fills, whatever it may be. Zampa takes horse from the opening. We have no amateur conductor riding ahead: violins, 'cellos, piano, wind-stops: Peridon, Catkin, Pempton, Yatt, Cormyn, Colney, Mrs. Cormyn, Dudley Sowerby: they are spirited on, patted, subdued, muted, raised, rushed anew, away, held in hand, in both hands. Not earnestness worn as a cloak, but issuing, we see; not simply a leader of musicians, a leader of men. The halo of the millionaire behind, assures us of a development in the character of England's merchant princes. The homage we pay him flatters us. A delightful overture, masterfully executed; ended too soon; except that the programme forbids the ordinary interpretation of prolonged applause. Mr. Radnor is one of those who do everything consummately. And we have a monition within, that a course of spiritual enjoyment will rouse the call for bodily refreshment. His genial nod and laugh and word of commendation to his troop persuade us oddly, we know not how, of provision to come. At the door of the retiring-room, see, he is congratulated by Luciani and Durandarte. Miss Priscilla Graves is now to sing a Schumann. Down later, it is a duet with the Rev. Septimus Barmby. We have nothing to be ashamed of in her, before an Italian Operatic singer! Ices after the first part is over.

CHAPTER XXI

DARTREY FENELLAN

Had Nataly and Nesta known who was outside helping Skepsey to play ball with the boys, they would not have worked through their share of the performance with so graceful a composure. Even Simeon Fenellan was unaware that his half-brother Dartrey had landed in England. Dartrey went first to Victor's office, where he found Skepsey packing the day's letters and circulars into the bag for the delivery of them at Lakelands. They sprang a chatter, and they missed the last of the express trains which did, not greatly signify, Skepsey said, 'as it was a Concert.' To hear his hero talk, was the music for him; and he richly enjoyed the pacing along the railway-platform.

Arrived on the grounds, they took opposite sides in a game of rounders, at that moment tossing heads or tails for innings. These boys were slovenly players, and were made unhappy by Skepsey's fussy instructions to them in smartness. They had a stupid way of feeding the stick, and they ran sprawling; it concerned Great Britain for them to learn how to use their legs. It was pitiful for the country to see how lumpish her younger children were. Dartrey knew his little man and laughed, after warning him that his English would want many lessons before they stomached the mixture of discipline and pleasure. So it appeared: the pride of the boys in themselves, their confidence, enjoyment of the game, were all gone; and all were speedily out but Skepsey; who ran for the rounder, with his coat off, sharp as a porpoise, and would have got it, he had it in his grasp, when, at the jump, just over the line of the goal, a clever fling, if ever was, caught him a crack on that part of the human frame where sound is best achieved. Then were these young lumps transformed to limber, lither, merry fellows. They rejoiced Skepsey's heart; they did everything better, ran and dodged and threw in a style to win the nod from the future official inspector of Games and Amusements of the common people; a deputy of the Government, proposed by Skepsey to his hero with a deferential eagerness. Dartrey clapped him on the shoulder, softly laughing.

'System—Mr. Durance is right—they must have system, if they are to appreciate a holiday,' Skepsey said; and he sent a wretched gaze around, at the justification of some of the lurid views of Mr. Durance, in signs of the holiday wasted;—impoverishing the country's manhood in a small degree, it may be argued, but we ask, can the country afford it, while foreign nations are drilling their youth, teaching them to be ready to move in squads or masses, like the fist of a pugilist. Skepsey left it to his look to speak his thought. He saw an enemy in tobacco. The drowsiness of beer had stretched various hulks under trees. Ponderous cricket lumbered half-alive. Flabby fun knocked-up a yell. And it was rather vexatious to see girls dancing in good time to the band-music. One had a male-partner, who hopped his loutish burlesque of the thing he could not do.

Apparently, too certainly, none but the girls had a notion of orderly muscular exercise. Of what use are girls! Girls have their one mission on earth; and let them be healthy by all means, for the sake of it; only, they should not seem to prove that old England is better represented on the female side. Skepsey heard, with a nip of spite at his bosom, a small body of them singing in chorus as they walked in step, arm in arm, actually marched: and to the rearward, none of these girls heeding; there were the louts at their burlesque of jigs and fisticuffs! 'Cherry Ripe,' was the song.

'It's delightful to hear them!' said Dartrey.

Skepsey muttered jealously of their having been trained.

The song, which drew Dartrey Fenellan to the quick of an English home, planted him at the same time in Africa to hear it. Dewy on a parched forehead it fell, England the shedding heaven.

He fetched a deep breath, as of gratitude for vital refreshment. He had his thoughts upon the training of our English to be something besides the machinery of capitalists, and upon the country as a blessed mother instead of the most capricious of maudlin step-dames.

He flicked his leg with the stick he carried, said: 'Your master's the man to make a change among them, old friend!' and strolled along to a group surrounding two fellows who shammed a bout at single-stick. Vacuity in the attack on either side, contributed to the joint success of the defense. They paused under inspection; and Dartrey said: 'You're burning to give them a lesson, Skepsey.'

Skepsey had no objection to his hero's doing so, though at his personal cost.

The sticks were handed to them; the crowd increased; their rounders boys had spied them, and came trooping to the scene. Skepsey was directed to hit in earnest. His defensive attitude flashed, and he was at head and right and left leg, and giving point, recovering, thrusting madly, and again at shoulder and thigh, with bravos for reward of a man meaning business; until a topper on his hat, a cut over the right thigh, and the stick in his middlerib, told the spectators of a scientific adversary; and loudly now the gentleman was cheered. An undercurrent of warm feeling ran for the plucky little one at it hot again in spite of the strokes, and when he fetched his master a handsome thud across the shoulder, and the gentleman gave up and complimented him, Skepsey had applause.

He then begged his hero to put the previous couple in position, through a few of the opening movements. They were horribly sheepish at first. Meantime two boys had got hold of sticks, and both had gone to work in Skepsey's gallant style; and soon one was howling. He excused himself, because of the funny-bone, situated, in his case, higher than usual up the arm. And now the pair of men were giving and taking cuts to make a rhinoceros caper.

'Very well; begin that way; try what you can bear,' said Dartrey.

Skepsey watched them, in felicity for love of the fray, pained by the disregard of science.

Comments on the pretty play, indicating a reminiscent acquaintance with it, and the capacity for critical observations, were started. Assaults, wonderful tricks of a slashing Life-Guardsman, one spectator had witnessed at an exhibition in a London hall. Boxing too. You may see displays of boxing still in places. How about a prizefight?—With money on it?—Eh, but you don't expect men to stand up to be knocked into rumpsteaks for nothing?—No, but it's they there bets!—Right, and that's a game gone to ruin along of outsiders.—But it always was and it always will be popular with Englishmen!

Great English names of young days, before the wintry shadow of the Law had blighted them, received their withered laurels. Emulous boys were in the heroic posture. Good! sparring does no hurt: Skepsey seized a likely lad, Dartrey another. Nature created the Ring for them. Now then, arms and head well up, chest hearty, shoulders down, out with the right fist, just below the level of the chin; out with the left fist farther, right out, except for that bit of curve; so, and draw it slightly back for wary-pussy at the spring. Firm you stand, feeling the muscles of both legs, left half a pace ahead, right planted, both stringy. None of your milk-pail looks; show us jaw, you bulldogs. Now then, left from the shoulder, straight at right of head.—Good, and alacrity called on vigour in Skepsey's pupil; Dartrey's had the fist on his mouth before he could parry right arm up. 'Foul blow!' Dartrey cried. Skepsey vowed to the contrary. Dartrey reiterated his charge. Skepsey was a figure of negation, gesticulating and protesting. Dartrey appealed tempestuously to the Ring; Skepsey likewise, in a tone of injury. He addressed a remonstrance to Captain Dartrey.

'Hang your captain, sir! I call you a coward; come on,' said the resolute gentleman, already in ripe form for the attack. His blue eyes were like the springing sunrise over ridges of the seas; and Skepsey jumped to his meaning.

Boys and men were spectators of a real scientific set-to, a lovely show. They were half puzzled, it seemed so deadly. And the little one got in his blows at the gentleman, who had to be hopping. Only, the worse the gentleman caught it, the friendlier his countenance became. That was the wonder, and that gave them the key. But it was deliciously near to the real thing.

Dartrey and Skepsey shook hands.

'And now, you fellows, you're to know, that this is one of the champions; and you take your lesson from him and thank him,' Dartrey said, as he turned on his heel to strike and greet the flow from the house.

'Dartrey come!' Victor, Fenellan, Colney, had him by the hand in turn. Pure sweetness of suddenly awakened joy sat in Nataly's eyes as she swam to welcome him, Nesta moved a step, seemed hesitating, and she tripped forward. 'Dear Captain Dartrey!'

He did not say: 'But what a change in you!'

'It is blue-butterfly, all the same,' Nataly spoke to his look.

Victor hurriedly pronounced the formal introduction between the Hon. Dudley Sowerby and Captain Dartrey Fenellan. The bronze face and the milky bowed to one another ceremoniously; the latter faintly flushing.

'So here you are at last,' Victor said. 'You stay with us.'

'To-morrow or later, if you'll have me. I go down to my people to-night.'

'But you stay in England now?' Nataly's voice wavered on the question.

'There's a chance of my being off to Upper Burmah before the week's ended.'

'Ah, dear, dear!' sighed Fenellan; 'and out of good comes evil!—as grandfather Deucalion exclaimed, when he gallantly handed up his dripping wife from the mud of the Deluge waters. Do you mean to be running and Dewing it on for ever, with only a nod for friends, Dart?'

'Lord, Simmy, what a sound of home there is in your old nonsense!' Dartrey said.

His eyes of strong dark blue colour and the foreign swarthiness of his brows and cheeks and neck mixed the familiar and the strange, in the sight of the women who knew him.

The bill-broker's fair-tressed young wife whispered of curiosity concerning him to Nataly. He dressed like a sailor, he stood like a soldier: and was he married? Yes, he was married.

Mrs. Blathenoy imagined a something in Mrs. Radnor's tone. She could account for it; not by the ordinary reading of the feminine in the feminine, but through a husband who professed to know secrets. She was young in years and experience, ten months wedded, disappointedly awakened, enlivened by the hour, kindled by a novel figure of man, fretful for a dash of imprudence. This Mrs. Radnor should be the one to second her very innocent turn for a galopade; her own position allowed of any little diverting jig or reel, or plunge in a bath—she required it, for the domestic Jacob Blathenoy was a dry chip: proved such, without a day's variation during the whole of the ten wedded months. Nataly gratified her spoken wish. Dartrey Fenellan bowed to the lady, and she withdrew him, seeing composedly that other and greater ladies had the wish ungratified. Their husbands were not so rich as hers, and their complexions would hardly have pleased the handsome brown-faced officer so well.

Banquet, equal to a blast of trumpet, was the detaining word for the multitude. It circulated, one knows not how. Eloquent as the whiffs to the sniffs (and nowhere is eloquence to match it, when the latter are sharpened from within to without), the word was very soon over the field. Mr. Carling may have helped; he had it from Fenellan; and he was among the principal groups, claiming or making acquaintances, as a lawyer should do. The Concert was complimentarily a topic: Durandarte divine!—did not everybody think so? Everybody did, in default of a term for overtopping it. Our language is poor at hyperbole; our voices are stronger. Gestures and heaven-sent eyeballs invoke to display the ineffable. Where was Durandarte now? Gone; already gone; off with the Luciani for evening engagements; he came simply to oblige his dear friend Mr. Radnor. Cheque fifty guineas: hardly more on both sides than an exchange of smiles. Ah, these merchant-princes! What of Mr. Radnor's amateur instrumentalists? Amateurs, they are not to be named: perfect musicians. Mr. Radnor is the perfection of a host. Yes, yes; Mrs. Radnor; Miss Radnor too: delicious voices; but what is it about Mr. Radnor so captivating! He is not quite English, yet he is not at all foreign. Is he very adventurous in business, as they say?

'Soundest head in the City of London,' Mr. Blathenoy remarked.

Sir Rodwell Blachington gave his nod.

The crowd interjected, half-sighing. We ought to be proud of such a man! Perhaps we are a trifle exaggerating, says its heart. But that we are wholly grateful to him, is a distinct conclusion. And he may be one of the great men of his time: he has a quite individual style of dress.

Lady Rodwell Blachington observed to Colney Durance:

'Mr. Radnor bids fair to become the idol of the English people.'

'If he can prove himself to be sufficiently the dupe of the English people,' said Colney.

'Idol—dupe?' interjected Sir Rodwell, and his eyebrows fixed at the perch of Colney's famous 'national interrogation' over vacancy of understanding, as if from the pull of a string. He had his audience with him; and the satirist had nothing but his inner gush of acids at sight of a planted barb.

Colney was asked to explain. He never explained. He performed a series of astonishing leaps, like the branchy baboon above the traveller's head in the tropical forest, and led them into the trap they assisted him to prepare for them. 'No humour, do you say? The English have no humour?' a nephew of Lady Blachington's inquired of him, with polite pugnacity, and was cordially assured, that 'he vindicated them.'

'And Altruistic! another specimen of the modern coinage,' a classical Church dignitary, in grammarian disgust, remarked to a lady, as they passed.

Colney pricked-up his ears. It struck him that he might fish for suggestions in aid of the Grand Argument before the Elders of the Court of Japan. Dr. Wardan, whose recognition he could claim, stated to him, that the lady and he were enumerating words of a doubtfully legitimate quality now being inflicted upon the language.

'The slang from below is perhaps preferable?' said Colney.

'As little-less.'

'But a pirate-tongue, cut-off from its roots, must continue to practise piracy, surely, or else take reinforcements in slang, otherwise it is inexpressive of new ideas.'

'Possibly the new ideas are best expressed in slang.'

'If insular. They will consequently be incommunicable to foreigners. You would, then, have us be trading with tokens instead of a precious currency? Yet I cannot perceive the advantage of letting our ideas be clothed so racy of the obscener soil; considering the pretensions of the English language to become the universal. If we refuse additions from above, they force themselves on us from below.'

Dr. Wardan liked the frame of the observations, disliked the substance.

'One is to understand that the English language has these pretensions?' he said:—he minced in his manner, after the well-known mortar-board and tassel type; the mouthing of a petrifaction: clearly useless to the pleadings of the patriotic Dr. Bouthoin and his curate.

He gave no grip to Colney, who groaned at cheap Donnish sarcasm, and let him go, after dealing him a hard pellet or two in a cracker-covering.

There was Victor all over the field netting his ephemerae! And he who feeds on them, to pay a price for their congratulations and flatteries, he is one of them himself!

Nesta came tripping from the Rev. Septimus Barmby. 'Dear Mr. Durance, where is Captain Dartrey?'

Mrs. Blathenoy had just conducted her husband through a crowd, for an introduction of him to Captain Dartrey. That was perceptible.

Dudley Sowerby followed Nesta closely: he struck across the path of the Rev. Septimus: again he had the hollow of her ear at his disposal.

'Mr. Radnor was excellent. He does everything consummately: really, we are all sensible of it. I am. He must lead us in a symphony. These light "champagne overtures" of French composers, as Mr. Fenellan calls them, do not bring out his whole ability:—Zampa, Le Pre aux clercs, Masaniello, and the like.'

'Your duet together went well.'

'Thanks to you—to you. You kept us together.'

'Papa was the runaway or strain-the-leash, if there was one.'

'He is impetuous, he is so fervent. But, Miss Radnor, I could not be the runaway-with you... with you at the piano. Indeed, I... shall we stroll down? I love the lake.'

'You will hear the bell for your cold dinner very soon.'

'I am not hungry. I would so much rather talk—hear you. But you are hungry? You have been singing twice: three times! Opera singers, they say, eat hot suppers; they drink stout. And I never heard your voice more effective. Yours is a voice that... something of the feeling one has in hearing cathedral voices: carry one up. I remember, in Dresden, once, a Fraulein Kuhnstreich, a prodigy, very young, considering her accomplishments. But it was not the same.'

Nesta wondered at Dartrey Fenellan for staying so long with Mr. and Mrs. Blathenoy.

'Ah, Mr. Sowerby, if I am to have flattery, I cannot take it as a milliner's dumb figure wears the beautiful dress; I must point out my view of some of my merits.'

'Oh! do, I beg, Miss... You have a Christian name and I too: and once ... not Mr. Sowerby: yes, it was Dudley!

'Quite accidentally, and a world of pardons entreated.'

'And Dudley begged Dudley might be Dudley always!'

He was deepening to the Barmby intonation—apparently Cupid's; but a shade more airily Pagan, not so fearfully clerical.

Her father had withdrawn Dartrey Fenellan from Mr. and Mrs. Blathenoy. Dr. Schlesien was bowing with Dartrey.

'And if Durandarte would only—but you are one with Miss Graves to depreciate my Durandarte, in favour of the more classical Jachimo; whom we all admire; but you shall be just,' said she, and she pouted. She had seen her father plant Dartrey Fenellan in the midst of a group of City gentlemen.

Simeon touched among them to pluck at his brother. He had not a chance; he retired, and swam into the salmon-net of seductive Mrs. Blathenoy's broad bright smile.

'It's a matter of mines, and they're hovering in the attitude of the query, like corkscrews over a bottle, profoundly indifferent to blood-relationships,' he said to her.

'Pray, stay and be consoled by me,' said the fair young woman. 'You are to point me out all the distinguished people. Is it true, that your brother has left the army?'

'Dartrey no longer wears the red. Here comes Colonel Corfe, who does. England has her army still!'

'His wife persuaded him?'

'You see he is wearing the black.'

'For her? How very very sad! Tell me—what a funnily dressed woman meeting that gentleman!'

'Hush—a friend of the warrior. Splendid weather, Colonel Corfe.'

'Superb toilettes!' The colonel eyed Mrs. Blathenoy dilatingly, advanced, bowed, and opened the siege.

She decided a calculation upon his age, made a wall of it, smilingly agreed with his encomium of the Concert, and toned her voice to Fenellan's comprehension: 'Did it occur recently?'

'Months; in Africa; I haven't the date.'

'Such numbers of people one would wish to know! Who are those ladies holding a Court, where Mr. Radnor is?'

'Lady Carmine, Lady Swanage—if it is your wish?' interposed the colonel.

She dealt him a forgiving smile. 'And that pleasant-looking old gentleman?'

Colonel Corfe drew-up. Fenellan said: 'Are we veterans at forty or so?'

'Well, it 's the romance, perhaps!' She raised her shoulders.

The colonel's intelligence ran a dog's nose for a lady's interjections. 'The romance?... at forty, fifty? gone? Miss Julinks, the great heiress and a beauty; has chosen him over the heads of all the young men of his time. Cranmer Lotsdale. Most romantic history!'

'She's in love with that, I suppose.'

'Now you direct my attention to him,' said Fenellan, 'the writing of the romantic history has made the texture look a trifle thready. You have a terrible eye.'

It was thrown to where the person stood who had first within a few minutes helped her to form critical estimates of men, more consciously to read them.

'Your brother stays in England?'

'The fear is, that he's off again.'

'Annoying for you. If I had a brother, I would not let him go.'

'How would you detain him?'

'Locks and bolts, clock wrong, hands and arms, kneeling—the fourth act of the Huguenots!'

'He went by way of the window, I think. But that was a lover.'

'Oh! well!' she flushed. She did not hear the 'neglected and astonished colonel speak, and she sought diversion in saying to Fenellan: 'So many people of distinction are assembled here to-day! Tell me, who is that pompous gentleman, who holds his arms up doubled, as he walks?'

'Like flappers of a penguin: and advances in jerks: he is head of the great Firm of Quatley Brothers: Sir Abraham: finances or farms one of the South American Republics: we call him, Pride of Port. He consumes it and he presents it.'

'And who is that little man, who stops everybody?'

'People of distinction indeed! That little man—is your upper lip underrateing him?... When a lady's lip is erratically disdainful, it suggests a misuse of a copious treasury, deserving to be mulcted, punished—how?—who can say?—that little man, now that little man, with a lift of his little finger, could convulse the Bacon Market!'

Mrs. Blathenoy shook. Hearing Colonel Corfe exclaim:

'Bacon Market!' she let fly a peal. Then she turned to a fresh satellite, a round and a ruddy, 'at her service ever,' Mr. Beaves Urmsing, and repeated Fenellan's words. He, in unfeigned wonderment at such unsuspected powers, cried: 'Dear me!' and stared at the little man, making the pretty lady's face a twinkling dew.

He had missed the Concert. Was it first-rate? Ecstasy answered in the female voice.

'Hem'd fool I am to keep appointments!' he muttered.

She reproved him: 'Fie, Mr. Urmsing; it's the making of them, not the keeping!'

'Ah, my dear ma'am, if I'd had Blathenoy's luck when he made a certain appointment. And he was not so much older than me? The old ones get the prizes!'

Mr. Beaves Urmsing prompted Colonel Corfe to laugh in triumph. The colonel's eyebrows were up in fixity over sleepy lids. He brightened to propose the conducting of the pretty woman to the banquet.

'We shall see them going in,' said she. 'Mr. Radnor has a French cook, who does wonders. But I heard him asking for Mr. Beaves Urmsing. I'm sure he expected The Marigolds at his Concert.'

'Anything to oblige the company,' said the rustic ready chorister, clearing his throat.

The lady's feet were bent in the direction of a grassy knoll, where sunflowers, tulips, dahlias, peonies, of the sex eclipsed at a distance its roses and lilies. Fenellan saw Dartrey, still a centre of the merchantmen, strolling thither.

'And do you know, your brother is good enough to dine with us next week, Thursday, down here,' she murmured. 'I could venture to command?—if you are not induced.'

'Whichever word applies to a faithful subject.'

'I do so wish your brother had not left the army!'

'You have one son of Mars.'

Her eyes took the colonel up to cast him down: he was not the antidote. She said to him: 'Luciani's voice wears better than her figure.'

The colonel replied: 'I remember,' and corrected himself, 'at Eton, in jackets: she was not so particularly slim; never knew how to dress. You beat Italians there! She moved one as a youngster.'

'Eton boys are so susceptible!'

'Why, hulloa, don't I remember her coming out!—and do you mean to tell me,' Mr. Beaves Urmsing brutally addressed the colonel, 'that you were at Eton when... why, what age do you give the poor woman, then!' He bellowed, 'Eh?' as it were a bull crowing.

The colonel retreated to one of his defensive corners. 'I am not aware that I meant to tell you anything.'

Mr. Beaves Urmsing turned square-breasted on Fenellan: 'Fellow's a born donkey!'

'And the mother lived?' said Fenellan.

Mr. Beaves Urmsing puffed with wrath at the fellow.

Five minutes later, in the midst of the group surrounding and felicitating Victor, he had sight of Fenellan conversing with fair ones, and it struck a light in him; he went three steps backward, with shouts. 'Dam funny fellow! eh? who is he? I must have that man at my table. Worth fifty Colonel Jackasses! And I 've got a son in the Guards: and as much laugh in him, he 's got, as a bladder. But we'll make a party, eh, Radnor? with that friend o' yours. Dam funny fellow! and precious little of it going on now among the young lot. They're for seeing ghosts and gaping their jaws; all for the quavers instead of the capers.'

He sounded and thrummed his roguish fling-off for the capers. A second glimpse of Fenellan agitated the anecdote, as he called it, seizing Victor's arm, to have him out of earshot of the ladies. Delivery, not without its throes, was accomplished, but imperfectly, owing to sympathetic convulsions, under which Mr. Beaves Urmsing's countenance was crinkled of many colours, as we see the Spring rhubarb-leaf. Unable to repeat the brevity of Fenellan's rejoinder, he expatiated on it to convey it, swearing that it was the kind of thing done in the old days, when men were witty dogs:—'pat! and pat back! as in the pantomime.'

'Repartee!' said Victor. 'He has it. You shall know him. You're the man for him.'

'He for me, that he is!—"Hope the mother's doing well? My card":—eh? Grave as an owl! Look, there goes the donkey, lady to right and left, all ears for him—ha! ha! I must have another turn with your friend. "Mother lived, did she?" Dam funny fellow, all of the olden time! And a dinner, bachelor dinner, six of us, at my place, next week, say Wednesday, half-past six, for a long evening—flowing bowl—eh, shall it be?'

Nesta came looking to find her Captain Dartrey.

Mr. Beaves Urmsing grew courtly of the olden time. He spied Colonel Corfe anew, and 'Donkey!' rose to split the roar at his mouth, and full of his anecdote, he pursued some congenial acquaintances, crying to his host: 'Wednesday, mind! eh? by George, your friend's gizzarded me for the day!'

Plumped with the rich red stream of life, this last of the squires of old England thumped along among the guests, a very tuning-fork to keep them at their pitch of enthusiasm. He encountered Mr. Caddis, and it was an encounter. Mr. Caddis represented his political opinions; but here was this cur of a Caddis whineing his niminy note from his piminy nob, when he was asked for his hearty echo of the praises of this jolly good fellow come to waken the neighbourhood, to be a blessing, a blazing hearth, a fall of manna:—and thank the Lord for him, you desertdog! 'He 's a merchant prince, and he's a prince of a man, if you're for titles. Eh? you "assent to my encomiums." You'll be calling me Mr. Speaker next. Hang me, Caddis, if those Parliamentary benches of yours aren't freezing you from your seat up, and have got to your jaw—my belief!'

Mr. Caddis was left reflecting, that we have, in the dispensations of Providence, when we have a seat, to submit to castigations from butcherly men unaccountably commissioned to solidify the seat. He could have preached a discourse upon Success, to quiet the discontentment of the unseated. And our world of seats oddly gained, quaintly occupied, maliciously beset, insensately envied, needs the discourse. But it was not delivered, else would it have been here written down without mercy, as a medical prescript, one of the grand specifics. He met Victor, and, between his dread of him and the counsels of a position subject to stripes, he was a genial thaw. Victor beamed; for Mr. Caddis had previously stood eminent as an iceberg of the Lakelands' party. Mr. Inchling and Mr. Caddis were introduced. The former in Commerce, the latter in Politics, their sustaining boast was, the being our stable Englishmen; and at once, with cousinly minds, they fell to chatting upon the nothings agreeably and seriously. Colney Durance forsook a set of ladies for fatter prey, and listened to them. What he said, Victor did not hear. The effect was always to be seen, with Inchling under Colney. Fenellan did better service, really good service.

Nataly played the heroine she was at heart. Why think of her as having to act a character! Twice had Carling that afternoon, indirectly and directly, stated Mrs. Burman to be near the end we crape a natural, a defensible, satisfaction to hear of:—not wishing it—poor woman!—but pardonably, before man and all the angels, wishing, praying for the beloved one to enter into her earthly peace by the agency of the other's exit into her heavenly.

Fenellan and Colney came together, and said a word apiece of their friend.

'In his element! The dear old boy has the look of a goldfish, king of his globe.'

'The dear old boy has to me the look of a pot on the fire, with a loose lid.'

I may have the summons from Themison to-morrow, Victor thought. The success of the day, was a wine that rocked the soberest of thoughts. For, strange to confess, ever since the fall on London Bridge, his heart, influenced in some degree by Nataly's depression perhaps, had been shadowed by doubts of his infallible instinct for success. Here, at a stroke, and before entering the house, he had the whole neighbourhood about him: he could feel that he and Nataly stood in the minds of the worthy people variously with the brightness if not with the warmth distinguishable in the bosom of Beaves Urmsing— the idea of whom gave Lakelands an immediate hearth-glow.

Armandine was thirteen minutes, by his watch, behind the time she had named. Small blame to her. He excused her to Lady Carmine, Lady Swanage, Lady Blachington, Mrs. Fanning, Sir Abraham Quatley, Mr. Danny (of Bacon fame) and the rest of the group surrounding Nataly on the mound leftward of the white terraces descending to the lake; where she stood beating her foot fretfully at the word brought by Nesta, that Dartrey Fenellan had departed. It was her sunshine departed. But she went through her task of conversing amiably. Colney, for a wonder, consented to be useful in assisting Fenellan to relate stories of French Cooks; which were, like the Royal Hanoverian oyster, of an age for offering acceptable flavour to English hearers. Nesta drew her mother's attention to Priscilla Graves and Skepsey; the latter bending head and assenting. Nataly spoke of the charm of Priscilla's voice that day, in her duet with the Rev. Septimus. Mr. Pempton looked; he saw that Priscilla was proselytizing. She was perfection to him but for one blotting thing. With grief on his eyelids, he said to Nataly or to himself: 'Meat!'

'Dear friend, don't ride your hobby over us,' she replied.

'But it's with that object they mount it,' said Victor.

The greater ladies of the assembly were quite ready to accuse the sections, down to the individuals, of the social English (reserving our elect) of an itch to be tyrants.

Colney was apologizing for them, with his lash: 'It's merely the sensible effect of a want of polish of the surface when they rub together.'

And he heard Carling exclaim to Victor: 'How comes the fellow here!'

Skepsey had rushed across an open space to intercept a leisurely progressive man, whose hat was of the shape Victor knew; and the man wore the known black gaiters. In appearance, he had the likeness of a fallen parson.

Carling and Victor crossed looks that were questions carrying their answers.

Nataly's eyes followed Victor's. 'Who is the man?' she said; and she got no reply beyond a perky sparkle in his gaze.

Others were noticing the man, who was trying to pass by Skepsey, now on his right side, now on his left.

'There'll be no stopping him,' Carling said, and he slipped to the rear.'

At this juncture, Armandine's mellow bell proclaimed her readiness.

Victor rubbed the back of his head. Nataly asked him: 'Dear, is it that man?'

He nodded scantly: 'Expected, expected. I think we have our summons from Armandine. One moment—poor soul! poor soul! Lady Carmine—Sir Abraham Quatley. Will you lead? Lady Blachington, I secure you. One moment.'

He directed Nataly to pair a few of the guests; he hurried down the slope of sward.

Nataly applied to Colney Durance. 'Do you know the man?—is it that man?'

Colney rejoined: 'The man's name is Jarniman.'

Armandine's bell swung melodiously. The guests had grouped, thickening for the stream to procession. Mrs. Blathenoy claimed Fenellan; she requested him to tell her whether he had known Mrs. Victor Radnor many years. She mused. 'You like her?'

'One likes one's dearest of friends among women, does one not?'

The lady nodded to his response. 'And your brother?'

'Dartrey is devoted to her.'

'I am sure,' said she, 'your brother is a chivalrous gentleman. I like her too.' She came to her sentiment through the sentiment of the chivalrous gentleman. Sinking from it, she remarked that Mr. Radnor was handsome still. Fenellan commended the subject to her, as one to discourse of when she met Dartrey. A smell of a trap-hatch, half-open, afflicted and sharpened him. It was Blathenoy's breath: husbands of young wives do these villanies, for the sake of showing their knowledge. Fenellan forbore to praise Mrs. Victor: he laid his colours on Dartrey. The lady gave ear till she reddened. He meant no harm, meant nothing but good; and he was lighting the most destructive of our lower fires.

Visibly, that man Jarniman was disposed of with ease. As in the street-theatres of crowing Punch, distance enlisted pantomime to do the effective part of the speeches. Jarniman's hat was off, he stood bent, he delivered his message. He was handed over to Skepsey's care for the receiving of meat and drink. Victor returned; he had Lady Blachington's hand on his arm; he was all hers, and in the heart of his company of guests at the same time. Eyes that had read him closely for years, were unable to spell a definite signification on his face, below the overflowing happiness of the hospitable man among contented guests. He had in fact something within to enliven him; and that was the more than suspicion, amounting to an odour of certainty, that Armandine intended one of her grand surprises for her master, and for the hundred and fifty or so to be seated at her tables in the unwarmed house of Lakelands.

CHAPTER XXII

CONCERNS THE INTRUSION OF JARNIMAN

Armandine did her wonders. There is not in the wide range of the Muses a more responsive instrument than man to his marvellous cook; and if his notes were but as flowing as his pedals are zealous, we should be carried on the tale of the enthusiasm she awakened, away from the rutted highroad, where History now thinks of tightening her girdle for an accelerated pace.

The wonders were done: one hundred and seventy guests plenteously fed at tables across the great Concert Hall, down a length of the conservatory-glass, on soups, fish, meats, and the kitchen-garden, under play of creative sauces, all in the persuasive steam of savouriness; every dish, one may say, advancing, curtseying, swimming to be your partner, instead of passively submitting to the eye of appetite, consenting to the teeth, as that rather melancholy procession of the cold, resembling established spinsters thrice-corseted in decorum, will appear to do. Whether Armandine had the thought or that she simply acted in conformity with a Frenchwoman's direct good sense, we do require to smell a sort of animation in the meats we consume. We are still perhaps traceably related to the

Adamite old-youngster just on his legs, who betrayed at every turn his Darwinian beginnings, and relished a palpitating unwillingness in the thing refreshing him; only we young-oldsters cherish the milder taste for willingness, with a throb of the vanquished in it. And a seeming of that we get from the warm roast. The banquet to be fervently remembered, should smoke, should send out a breath to meet us. Victor's crowded saloon-carriage was one voice of eulogy, to raise Armandine high as the finale rockets bursting over Wrensham Station at the start Londonward. How had she managed? We foolishly question the arts of magicians.

Mr. Pempton was an apparent dissentient, as the man must be who is half a century ahead of his fellows in humaneness, and saddened by the display of slaughtered herds and their devourers. He had picked out his vegetable and farinaceous morsels, wherever he could get them uncontaminated; enough for sustenance; and the utmost he could show was, that he did not complain. When mounted and ridden by the satirist, in wrath at him for systematically feasting the pride of the martyr on the maceration of his animal part, he put on his martyr's pride, which assumed a perfect contentment in the critical depreciation of opposing systems: he was drawn to state, as he had often done, that he considered our animal part shamefully and dangerously over nourished, and that much of the immorality of the world was due to the present excessive indulgence in meats. 'Not in drink?' Miss Graves inquired. 'No,' he said boldly; 'not equally; meats are more insidious. I say nothing of taking life—of fattening for that express purpose: diseases of animals: bad blood made: cruelty superinduced: it will be seen to be, it will be looked back on, as a form of, a second stage of, cannibalism. Let that pass. I say, that for excess in drinking, the penalty is paid instantly, or at least on the morrow.'

'Paid by the drunkard's wife, you should say.'

'Whereas intemperance in eating, corrupts constitutionally, more spiritually vitiates, we think: on the whole, gluttony is the least-generous of the vices.'

Colney lured Mr. Pempton through a quagmire of the vices to declare, that it brutalized; and stammeringly to adopt the suggestion, that our breeding of English ladies—those lights of the civilized world—can hardly go with a feeding upon flesh of beasts. Priscilla regretted that champagne should have to be pleaded in excuse of impertinences to her sex. They were both combative, nibbed for epigram, edged to inflict wounds; and they were set to shudder openly at one another's practises; they might have exposed to Colney which of the two maniacal sections of his English had the vaster conceit of superiority in purity; they were baring themselves, as it were with a garment flung-off at each retort. He reproached them for undermineing their countrymen; whose Falstaff panics demanded blood of animals to restore them; and their periods of bragging, that they should brandify their wits to imagine themselves Vikings.

Nataly interposed. She was vexed with him. He let his eyelids drop: but the occasion for showing the prickliness of the bristly social English, could not be resisted. Dr. Peter Yatt was tricked to confess, that small annoyances were, in his experience, powerful on the human frame; and Dr. John Cormyn was very neatly brought round to assure him he was mistaken if he supposed the homoeopathic doctor who smoked was exercising a destructive influence on the efficacy of the infinitesimal doses he prescribed; Dr. Yatt chuckled a laugh at globules; Dr. Cormyn at patients treated as horses; while Mr. Catkin was brought to praise the smoke of tobacco as our sanctuary from the sex; and Mr. Peridon quietly denied, that the taking of it into his nostrils from the puffs of his friend caused him sad silences: Nesta flew to protect the admirer of her beloved Louise. Her subsiding young excitement of the day set her Boating on that moony melancholy in Mr. Peridon.

No one could understand the grounds for Colney's more than usual waspishness. He trotted out the fulgent and tonal Church of the Rev. Septimus; the skeleton of worship, so truly showing the spirit, in that of Dudley Sowerby's family; maliciously admiring both; and he had a spar with Fenellan, ending in a snarl and a shout. Victor said to him: 'Yes, here, as much as you like, old Colney, but I tell you, you've staggered that poor woman Lady Blachington to-day, and her husband too; and I don't know how many besides. What the pleasure of it can be, I can't guess.'

'Nor I,' said Fenellan, 'but I'll own I feel envious; like the girl among a family of boys I knew, who were all of them starved in their infancy by a miserly father, that gave them barely a bit of Graves to eat and not a drop of Pempton to drink; and on the afternoon of his funeral, I found them in the drawing-room, four lank fellows, heels up, walking on their hands, from long practice; and the girl informed me, that her brothers were able so to send the little blood they had in their bodies to their brains, and always felt quite cheerful for it, happy, and empowered to deal with the problems of the universe; as they couldn't on their legs; but she, poor thing, was forbidden to do the same! And I'm like her. I care for decorum too much to get the brain to act on Colney's behaviour; but I see it enraptures him and may be comprehensible to the topsy-turvy.'

Victor rubbed hands. It was he who filled Colney's bag of satiric spite. In addition to the downright lunacy of the courting of country society, by means of the cajolements witnessed this day, a suspicion that Victor was wearing a false face over the signification—of Jarniman's visit and meant to deceive the trustful and too-devoted loving woman he seemed bound to wreck, irritated the best of his nature. He had a resolve to pass an hour with the couple, and speak and insist on hearing plain words before the night had ended. But Fenellan took it out of him. Victor's show of a perfect contentment emulating Pempton's, incited Colney to some of his cunning rapier-thrusts with his dancing adversary; and the heat which is planted in us for the composition: of those cool epigrams, will not allow plain words to follow. Or, handing him over to the police of the Philistines, you may put it, that a habit of assorting spices will render an earnest simplicity distasteful. He was invited by Nataly to come home with them; her wish for his presence, besides personal, was moved by an intuition, that his counsel might specially benefit them. He shrugged; he said he had work at his chambers.

'Work!' Victor ejaculated: he never could reach to a right comprehension of labour, in regard to the very unremunerative occupation of literature. Colney he did not want, and he let him go, as Nataly noticed, without a sign of the reluctance he showed when the others, including Fenellan, excused themselves.

'So! we're alone?' he said, when the door of the hall had closed on them. He kept Nesta talking of the success of the day until she, observing her mother's look, simulated the setting-in of a frenzied yawn. She was kissed, and she tripped to her bed.

'Now we are alone,' Nataly said.

'Well, dear, and the day was, you must own... ' he sought to trifle with her heavy voice; but she recalled him: 'Victor!' and the naked anguish in her cry of his name was like a foreign world threatening the one he filled.

'Ah, yes; that man, that Jarniman. You saw him, I remember. You recollected him?—stouter than he was. In her service ever since. Well, a little drop of bitter, perhaps: no harm, tonic.'

'Victor, is she very ill?'

'My love, don't feel at your side: she is ill, ill, not the extreme case: not yet: old and ill. I told Skepsey to give the man refreshment: he had to do his errand.'

'What? why did he come?'

'Curious; he made acquaintance with Skepsey, and appears to have outwitted poor Skepsey, as far as I see it. But if that woman thinks of intimidating me now—!' His eyes brightened; he had sprung from evasions. 'Living in flagrant sin, she says: you and I! She will not have it; warns me. Heard this day at noon of company at Lakelands. Jarniman off at once. Are to live in obscurity;—you and I! if together! Dictates from her death-bed-I suppose her death-bed.'

'Dearest,' Nataly pressed hand on her left breast, 'may we not think that she may be right?'

'An outrageous tyranny of a decrepit woman naming herself wife when she is only a limpet of vitality, with drugs for blood, hanging-on to blast the healthy and vigorous! I remember old Colney's once, in old days, calling that kind of marriage a sarcophagus. It was to me. There I lay—see myself lying! wasting! Think what you can good of her, by all means! From her bed! despatches that Jarniman to me from her bedside, with the word, that she cannot in her conscience allow—what imposition was it I practised?... flagrant sin?—it would have been an infinitely viler.... She is the cause of suffering enough: I bear no more from her; I've come to the limit. She has heard of Lakelands: she has taken one of her hatreds to the place. She might have written, might have sent me a gentleman, privately. No: it must be done in dramatic style-for effect: her confidential—lawyer?—doctor?—butler! Perhaps to frighten me:—the boy she knew, and—poor soul! I don't mean to abuse her: but such conduct as this is downright brutal. I laugh at it, I snap my fingers. I can afford to despise it. Only I do say it deserves to be called abominable.'

'Victor, has she used a threat?'

'Am I brought to listen to any of her threats!—Funny thing, I 'm certain that woman never can think of me except as the boy she knew. I saw her first when she was first a widow. She would keep talking to me of the seductions of the metropolis—kept informing me I was a young man... shaking her head. I 've told you. She—well, I know we are mixtures, women as well as men. I can, I hope, grant the same—I believe I can—allowances to women as to men; we are poor creatures, all of using one sense: though I won't give Colney his footing; there's a better way of reading us. I hold fast to Nature. No violation of Nature, my good Colney! We can live the lives of noble creatures; and I say that happiness was meant for us:—just as, when you sit down to your dinner, you must do it cheerfully, and you make good blood: otherwise all's wrong. There's the right answer to Colney! But when a woman like that .... and marries a boy: well, twenty-one—not quite that: and an innocent, a positive innocent—it may seem incredible, after a term of school-life: it was a fact: I can hardly understand it myself when I look back. Marries him! And then sets to work to persecute him, because he has blood in his veins, because he worships beauty; because he seeks a real marriage, a real mate. And, I say it! let the world take its own view, the world is wrong! because he preferred a virtuous life to the kind of life she would, she must—why, necessarily!—have driven him to, with a mummy's grain of nature in his body. And I am made of flesh, I admit it.'

'Victor, dearest, her threat concerns only your living at Lakelands.'

'Pray, don't speak excitedly, my love,' he replied to the woman whose tones had been subdued to scarce more than waver. 'You see how I meet it: water off a duck's back, or Indian solar beams on the skin of a Hindoo! I despise it hardly worth contempt;—But, come: our day was a good one. Fenellan worked well. Old Colney was Colney Durance, of course. He did no real mischief.'

'And you will not determine to enter Lakelands—not yet, dear?' said Nataly.

'My own girl, leave it all to me.'

'But, Victor, I must, must know.'

'See the case. You have lots of courage. We can't withdraw. Her intention is mischief. I believe the woman keeps herself alive for it: we've given her another lease!—though it can only be for a very short time; Themison is precise; Carling too. If we hold back—I have great faith in Themison—the woman's breath on us is confirmed. We go down, then; complete the furnishing, quite leisurely; accept—listen—accept one or two invitations: impossible to refuse!—but they are accepted!—and we defy her: a crazy old creature: imagines herself the wife of the ex-Premier, widow of Prince Le Boo, engaged to the Chinese Ambassador, et caetera. Leave the tussle with that woman to me. No, we don't repeat the error of Crayc Farm and Creckholt. And here we have stout friends. Not to speak of Beaver Urmsing: a picture of Old Christmas England! You took to him?—must have taken to Beaver Urmsing! The Marigolds! And Sir Rodwell and Lady Blachington are altogether above the mark of Sir Humphrey and Lady Pottil, and those half and half Mountneys. There's a warm centre of home in Lakelands. But I know my Nataly: she is thinking of our girl. Here is the plan: we stand our ground: my dear soul won't forsake me only there's the thought of Fredi, in the event... improbable enough. I lift Fredi out of the atmosphere awhile; she goes to my cousins the Duvidney ladies.'

Nataly was hit by a shot. 'Can you imagine it, Victor?'

'Regard it as done.'

'They will surely decline!'

'Their feeling for General Radnor is a worship.'

'All the more...?'

'The son inherits it. He goes to them personally. Have you ever known me personally fail? Fredi stays at Moorsedge for a month or two. Dorothea and Virginia Duvidney will give her a taste of a new society; good for the girl. All these little shiftings can be turned to good. Meantime, I say, we stand our ground: but you are not to be worried; for though we have gone too far to recede, we need not and we will not make the entry into Lakelands until—you know: that is, auspiciously, to suit you in every way. Thus I provide to meet contingencies. What one may really fancy is, that the woman did but threaten. There's her point of view to be considered: silly, crazy; but one sees it. We are not sure that she struck a blow at Craye or Creckholt. I wonder she never wrote. She was frightened, when she came to manage her property, of signing her name to anything. Absurd, that sending of Jarniman! However, it's her move; we make a corresponding disposition of our chessmen.'

'And I am to lose my Nesta for a month?' Nataly said, after catching here and there at the fitful gleams of truce or comfort dropped from his words. And simultaneously, the reproach of her mind to her nature for again and so constantly yielding to the domination of his initiative: unable to find the words, even the ideas, to withstand him,—brought big tears. Angry at herself both for the internal feebleness and the exhibition of it, she blinked and begged excuse. There might be nothing that should call her to resist him. She could not do much worse than she had done to-day. The reflection, that to-day she had been actually sustained by the expectation of a death to come, diminished her estimate of to-morrow's burden on her endurance, in making her seem a less criminal woman, who would have no such expectation: which was virtually a stab at a fellow creature's future. Her head was acute to work in the direction of the casuistries and the sensational webs and films. Facing Victor, it was a block.

But the thought came: how could she meet those people about Lakelands, without support of the recent guilty whispers! She said coldly, her heart shaking her: 'You think there has been a recovery?'

'Invalids are up and down. They are—well, no; I should think she dreads the...' he kept 'surgeon' out of hearing. 'Or else she means this for the final stroke: "though I'm lying here, I can still make him feel." That, or—poor woman—she has her notions of right and wrong.'

'Could we not now travel for a few weeks, Victor?'

'Certainly, dear; we will, after we have kept our engagements to dine—I accepted—with the Blathenoys, the Blachingtons, Beaver Urmsing.'

Nataly's vision of the peaceful lost little dairy cottage swelled to brilliance, like the large tear at the fall; darkening under her present effort to comprehend the necessity it was for him to mix and be foremost with the world. Unable to grasp it perfectly in mind, her compassionate love embraced it: she blamed herself, for being the obstruction to him.

'Very well,' she said on a sigh. 'Then we shall not have to let our girl go from us?'

'Just a few weeks. In the middle of dinner, I scribbled a telegram to the Duvidneys, for Skepsey to take.'

'Speaking of Nesta?'

'Of my coming to-morrow. They won't stop me. I dine with them, sleep at the Wells; hotel for a night. We are to be separated for a night.'

She laid her hand in his and gave him a passing view of her face: 'For two, dear. I am... that man's visit— rather shaken: I shall have a better chance of sleeping if I know I am not disturbing you.'

She was firm; and they kissed and parted. Each had an unphrased speculation upon the power of Mrs. Burman to put division between them.

CHAPTER XXIII

The maiden ladies Dorothea and Virginia Duvidney were thin—sweet old-fashioned grey gentlewomen, demurely conscious of their excellence and awake to the temptation in the consciousness, who imposed a certain reflex primness on the lips of the world when addressing them or when alluding to them. For their appearance was picturesque of the ancestral time, and their ideas and scrupulousness of delivery suggested the belated in ripeness; orchard apples under a snow-storm; or any image that will ceremoniously convey the mind's profound appreciation together with the tooth's panic dread of tartness. They were by no means tart; only, as you know, the tooth is apprehensively nervous; an uninviting sign will set it on edge. Even the pen which would sketch them has a spell on it and must don its coat of office, walk the liveried footman behind them.

Their wealth, their deeds of charity, their modesty, their built grey locks, their high repute; a 'Chippendale elegance' in a quaintly formal correctness, that they had, as Colney Durance called it; gave them some queenliness, and allowed them to claim the ear as an oracle and banish rebellious argument. Intuitive knowledge, assisted by the Rev. Stuart Rem and the Rev. Abram Posterley, enabled them to pronounce upon men and things; not without effect; their country owned it; the foreigner beheld it. Nor were they corrupted by the servility of the surrounding ear. They were good women, striving to be humbly good. They might, for all the little errors they nightly unrolled to then perceptions, have stood before the world for a study in the white of our humanity. And this may be but a washed wall, it is true: revolutionary sceptics are measuring the depths of it. But the hue refreshes, the world admires; and we know it an object of aim to the bettermost of the wealthy. If, happily, complacent circumstances have lifted us to the clean paved platform out of grip of puddled clay and bespattering wheeltracks, we get our chance of coming to it.

Possessing, for example, nine thousand pounds per annum in Consols, and not expending the whole of it upon our luxuries, we are, without further privation, near to kindling the world's enthusiasm for whiteness. Yet there, too, we find, that character has its problems to solve; there are shades in salt. We must be charitable, but we should be just; we give to the poor of the land, but we are eminently the friends of our servants; duty to mankind diverts us not from the love we bear to our dog; and with a pathetic sorrow for silt, we discard it from sight and hearing. We hate dirt. Having said so much, having shown it, by sealing the mouth of Mr. Stuart Rem and iceing the veins of Mr. Abram Posterley, in relation to a dreadful public case and a melancholy private, we have a pleased sense of entry into the world's ideal.

At the same time, we protest our unworthiness. Acknowledgeing that they were not purely spotless, these ladies genuinely took the tiny fly-spot for a spur to purification; and they viewed it as a patch to raise in relief their goodness. They gazed on it, saw themselves in it, and veiled it: warned of the cunning of an oft-defeated Tempter.

To do good and sleep well, was their sowing and their reaping. Uneasy consciences could not have slept. The sleeping served for proof of an accurate reckoning and an expungeing of the day's debits. They differed in opinion now and then, as we see companion waves of the river, blown by a gust, roll a shadow between them; and almost equally transient were their differences with a world that they condemned when they could not feel they (as an embodiment of their principles) were leading it. The English world at times betrayed a restiveness in the walled pathway of virtue; for, alas, it closely neighbours the French; only a Channel, often dangerously smooth, to divide: but it is not perverted for long; and the English Funds are always constant and a tower. Would they be suffered to be so, if libertinism were in the ascendant?

Colney Durance was acquainted with the Duvidney ladies. Hearing of the journey to them and the purport of it, he said, with the mask upon glee: 'Then Victor has met his match!' Nataly had sent for him to dine with her in Victor's absence: she was far from grieved, as to the result, by his assurance to her, that Victor had not a chance. Colney thought so. 'Just like him! to be off gaily to try and overcome or come over the greatest power in England.' They were England herself; the squat old woman she has become by reason of her overlapping numbers of the comfortable fund-holder annuitants: a vast body of passives and negatives, living by precept, according to rules of precedent, and supposing themselves to be righteously guided because of their continuing undisturbed. Them he branded, as hypocritical materialists, and the country for pride in her sweetmeat plethora of them:—mixed with an ancient Hebrew fear of offence to an inscrutable Lord, eccentrically appeasable through the dreary iteration of the litany of sinfulness. He was near a truth; and he had the heat of it on him.

Satirists in their fervours might be near it to grasp it, if they could be moved to moral distinctness, mental intention, with a preference of strong plain speech over the crack of their whips. Colney could not or would not praise our modern adventurous, experimental, heroic, tramping active, as opposed to yonder pursy passives and negatives; he had occasions for flicking the fellow sharply: and to speak of the Lord as our friend present with us, palpable to Reason, perceptible to natural piety solely through the reason, which justifies punishment; that would have stopped his mouth upon the theme of God-forsaken creatures. Our satirist is an executioner by profession, a moralist in excuse, or at the tail of it; though he thinks the position reversed, when he moralizes angrily to have his angry use of the scourge condoned. Nevertheless, he fills a serviceable place; and certainly he is not happy in his business. Colney suffered as heavily as he struck. If he had been no more than a mime in the motley of satire, he would have sucked compensation from the acid of his phrases, for the failure to prick and goad, and work amendment.

He dramatized to Nataly some of the scene going on at the Wells: Victor's petition; his fugue in urgency of it; the brief reply of Miss Dorothea and her muted echo Miss Virginia. He was rather their apologist for refusing. But, as when, after himself listening to their 'views,' he had deferentially withdrawn from the ladies of Moorsedge, and had then beheld their strangely-hatted lieutenants and the regiments of the toneless respectable on the pantiles and the mounts, the curse upon the satirist impelled him to generalize. The quiet good ladies were multiplied: they were 'the thousands of their sisters, petticoated or long-coated or buck-skinned; comfortable annuitants under clerical shepherding, close upon outnumbering the labourers they paralyze at home and stultify abroad.' Colney thumped away. The country's annuitants had for type 'the figure with the helmet of the Owl-Goddess and the trident of the Earth-shaker, seated on a wheel, at the back of penny-pieces; in whom you see neither the beauty of nakedness nor the charm of drapery; not the helmet's dignity or the trident's power; but she has patently that which stops the wheel; and poseing for representative of an imperial nation, she helps to pass a penny.' So he passed his epigram, heedless of the understanding or attention of his hearer; who temporarily misjudged him for a man impelled by the vanity of literary point and finish, when indeed it was hot satiric spite, justified of its aim, which crushed a class to extract a drop of scathing acid, in the interests of the country, mankind as well. Nataly wanted a picture painted, colours and details, that she might get a vision of the scene at Moorsedge. She did her best to feel an omen and sound it, in his question 'whether the yearly increasing army of the orderly annuitants and their parasites does not demonstrate the proud old country as a sheath for pith rather than of the vital run of sap.'

Perhaps it was patriotic to inquire; and doubtless she was the weakest of women; she could follow no thought; her heart was beating blindly beside Victor, hopeing for the refusal painful to her through his disappointment.

'You think me foolish,' she made answer to one of Colney's shrugs; 'and it has come to that pitch with me, that I cannot be sensible of a merit except in being one with him—obeying, is the word. And I have never yet known him fail. That terrible Lakelands wears a different look to me, when I think of what he can do; though I would give half my days to escape it.'

She harped on the chord of feverish extravagance; the more hateful to Colney because of his perceiving, that she simulated a blind devotedness to stupefy her natural pride; and he was divided between stamping on her for an imbecile and dashing at Victor for a maniac. But her situation rendered her pitiable. 'You will learn tomorrow what Victor has done,' he said, and thought how the simple words carried the bitterness.

That was uttered within a few minutes of midnight, when the ladies of Moorsedge themselves, after an exhausting resistance to their dearest relative, were at the hall-door of the house with Victor, saying the good-night, to which he responded hurriedly, cordially, dumbly, a baffled man. They clasped hands. Miss Dorothea said:

'You, Victor, always.' Miss Virginia said: 'You will be sure of welcome.' He walked out upon the moonless night; and for lack of any rounded object in the smothering darkness to look at, he could nowhere take moorings to gather himself together and define the man who had undergone so portentous a defeat. He was glad of quarters at an hotel, a solitary bed, absence from his Nataly.

For their parts, the ladies were not less shattered. They had no triumph in their victory: the weight of it bore them down. They closed, locked, shot the bolts and fastened the chain of the door. They had to be reminded by the shaking of their darling dog Tasso's curly silky coat, that he had not taken his evening's trot to notify malefactors of his watchfulness and official wrath at sound of footfall or a fancied one. Without consultation, they unbolted the door, and Tasso went forth, to 'compose his vesper hymn,' as Mr. Posterley once remarked amusingly.

Though not pretending to the Muse's crown so far, the little dog had qualities to entrance the spinster sex. His mistresses talked of him; of his readiness to go forth; of the audible first line of his hymn or sonnet; of his instinct telling him that something was wrong in the establishment. For most of the servants at Moorsedge were prostrated by a fashionable epidemic; a slight attack, the doctor said; but Montague, the butler, had withdrawn for the nursing of his wife; Perrin, the footman, was confined to his chamber; Manton, the favourite maid, had appeared in the morning with a face that caused her banishment to bed; and the cook, Mrs. Bannister, then sighingly agreed to send up cold meat for the ladies' dinner. Hence their melancholy inhospitality to their cousin Victor, who had, in spite of his errors, the right to claim his place at their table, was 'of the blood,' they said. He was recognized as the living prince of it. His every gesture, every word, recalled the General. The trying scene with him had withered them, they did not speak of it; each had to the other the look of a vessel that has come out of a gale. Would they sleep? They scarcely dared ask it of themselves. They had done rightly; silence upon that reflection seemed best. It was the silence of an inward agitation; still they knew the power of good consciences to summon sleep.

Tasso was usually timed for five minutes. They were astonished to discover by the clock, that they had given him ten. He was very quiet: if so, and for whatever he did, he had his reason, they said: he was a dog endowed with reason: endowed—and how they wished that Mr. Stuart Rem would admit it!—with, their love of the little dog believed (and Mr. Posterley acquiesced), a soul. Do but think it of dear animals, and any form of cruelty to them becomes an impossibility, Mr. Stuart Rem! But he would not be convinced: ungenerously indeed he named Mr. Posterley a courtier. The ladies could have retorted, that Mr. Posterley had not a brother who was the celebrated surgeon Sir Nicholas Rem.

Usually Tasso came running in when the hall-door was opened to him. Not a sound of him could be heard. The ladies blew his familiar whistle. He trotted back to a third appeal, and was, unfortunately for them, not caressed; he received reproaches from two forefingers directed straight at his reason. He saw it and felt it. The hug of him was deferred to the tender good-night to him in his basket at the foot of the ladies' beds.

On entering their spacious bed-chamber, they were so fatigued that sleep appeared to their minds the compensating logical deduction. Miss Dorothea suppressed a yawn, and inflicted it upon Miss Virginia, who returned it, with an apology, and immediately had her sister's hand on her shoulder, for, an attempted control of one of the irresistibles; a spectacle imparting bitter shudders and shots to the sympathetic jawbones of an observer. Hand at mouth, for not in privacy would they have been guilty of exposing a grimace, they signified, under an interim smile, their maidenly submission to the ridiculous force of nature: after which, Miss Virginia retired to the dressing-room, absorbed in woeful recollection of the resolute No they had been compelled to reiterate, in response to the most eloquent and, saving for a single instance, admirable man, their cousin, the representative of 'the blood,' supplicating them. A recreant thankfulness coiled within her bosom at the thought, that Dorothea, true to her office of speaker, had tasked herself with the cruel utterance and repetition of the word. Victor's wonderful eyes, his voice, yet more than his urgent pleas; and also, in the midst of his fiery flood of speech, his gentleness, his patience, pathos, and a man's tone through it all; were present to her.

Disrobed, she knocked at the door.

'I have called to you twice,' Dorothea said; and she looked a motive for the call.

'What is it?' said Virginia, with faltering sweetness, with a terrible divination.

The movement of a sigh was made. 'Are you aware of anything, dear?'

Virginia was taken with the contrary movement of a sniff. But the fear informing it prevented it from being venturesome. Doubt of the pure atmosphere of their bed-chamber, appeared to her as too heretic even for the positive essay. In affirming, that she was not aware of anything, her sight fell on Tasso. His eyeballs were those of a little dog that has been awfully questioned.

'It is more than a suspicion,' said Dorothea; and plainly now, while open to the seductions of any pleasing infidel testimony, her nose in repugnance convicted him absolutely.

Virginia's nose was lowered a few inches; it inhaled and stopped midway. 'You must be mistaken, dear. He never... '

'But are you insensible to the...' Dorothea's eyelids fainted.

Virginia dismissed the forlornest of efforts at incredulity. A whiff of Tasso had smitten her. 'Ah!' she exclaimed and fell away. 'Is it Tasso! How was it you noticed nothing before undressing, dear?'

'Thinking of what we have gone through to-night! I forgot him. At last the very strange... The like of it I have not ever!... And upon that thick coat! And, dear, it is late. We are in the morning hours.'

'But, my dear-Oh, dear, what is to be done with him?'

That was the crucial point for discussion. They had no servant to give them aid; Manton, they could not dream of disturbing. And Tasso's character was in the estimate; he hated washing; it balefully depraved his temper; and not only, creature of habit that he was, would he decline to lie down anywhere save in their bedroom, he would lament, plead, insist unremittingly, if excluded; terrifying every poor invalid of the house. Then again, were they at this late hour to dress themselves, and take him downstairs, and light a fire in the kitchen, and boil sufficient water to give him a bath and scrubbing? Cold water would be death to him. Besides, he would ring out his alarum for the house to hear, pour out all his poetry, poor dear, as Mr. Posterley called it, at a touch of cold water. The catastrophe was one to weep over, the dilemma a trial of the strongest intelligences.

In addition to reviews of their solitary alternative-the having of a befouled degraded little dog in their chamber through the night, they were subjected to a conflict of emotions when eyeing him: and there came to them the painful, perhaps irreverent, perhaps uncharitable, thought:—that the sinner who has rolled in the abominable, must cleanse him and do things to polish him and perfume before again embraced even by the mind: if indeed we can ever have our old sentiment for him again! Mr. Stuart Rem might decide it for them. Nay, before even the heart embraces him, he must completely purify himself. That is to say, the ordinary human sinner—save when a relative. Contemplating Tasso, the hearts of the ladies gushed out in pity of an innocent little dog, knowing not evil, dependent on his friends for help to be purified;—necessarily kept at a distance: the very look of him prescribed extreme separation, as far as practicable. But they had proof of a love almost greater than it was previous to the offence, in the tender precautions they took to elude repulsion.

He was rolling on the rug, communicating contagion. Flasks of treble-distilled lavender water, and their favourite, traditional in the family, eau d'Arquebusade, were on the toilet-table. They sprinkled his basket, liberally sprinkled the rug and the little dog. Perfume-pastilles were in one of the sitting-rooms below; and Virginia would have gone down softly to fetch a box, but Dorothea restrained her, in pity for the servants, with the remark: 'It would give us a nightmare of a Roman Catholic Cathedral!' A bit of the window was lifted by Dorothea, cautiously, that prowling outsiders might not be attracted. Tasso was wooed to his basket. He seemed inquisitive; the antidote of his naughtiness excited him; his tail circled after his muzzle several times; then he lay. A silken scarf steeped in eau d'Arquebusade was flung across him.

Their customary devout observances concluded, lights were extinguished, and the ladies kissed, and entered their beds.

Their beds were not homely to them. Dorothea thought that Virginia was long in settling herself. Virginia did not like the sound of Dorothea's double sigh. Both listened anxiously for the doings of Tasso. He rested.

He was uneasy; he was rounding his basket once more; unaware of the exaggeration of his iniquitous conduct, poor innocent, he shook that dreadful coat of his! He had displaced the prophylactic cover of the scarf.

He drove them in a despair to speculate on the contention between the perfume and the stench in junction, with such a doubt of the victory of which of the two, as drags us to fear our worst. It steals into our nostrils, possesses them. As the History of Mankind has informed us, we were led up to our civilization by the nose. But Philosophy warns us on that eminence; to beware of trusting exclusively to our conductor, lest the mind of us at least be plunged back into barbarism. The ladies hated both the cause and the consequence, they had a revulsion from the object, of the above contention. But call it not a contention: there is nobility in that. This was a compromise, a degrading union, with very sickening results. Whether they came of an excess of the sprinkling, could not well be guessed. The drenching at least was righteously intended.

Beneath their shut eyelids, they felt more and more the oppression of a darkness not laden with slumber. They saw it insolidity; themselves as restless billows, driven dashing to the despondent sigh. Sleep was denied them.

Tasso slept. He had sinned unknowingly, and that is not a spiritual sin; the chastisement confers the pardon.

But why was this ineffable blessing denied to them? Was it that they might have a survey of all the day's deeds and examine them under the cruel black beams of Insomnia?

Virginia said: 'You are wakeful.'

'Thoughtful,' was the answer.

A century of the midnight rolled on.

Dorothea said: 'He behaved very beautifully.'

'I looked at the General's portrait while he besought us,' Virginia replied.

'One sees him in Victor, at Victor's age. Try to sleep.'

'I do. I pray that you may.'

Silence courted slumber. Their interchange of speech from the posture of bodies on their backs, had been low and deliberate, in the tone of the vaults. Dead silence recalled the strangeness of it. The night was breathless; their open window a peril bestowing no boon. They were mutually haunted by sound of the gloomy query at the nostrils of each when drawing the vital breath. But for that, they thought they might have slept.

Bed spake to bed:

'The words of Mr. Stuart Rem last Sunday!' 'He said: "Be just." Could one but see direction!'

'In obscurity, feeling is a guide.'

'The heart.'

'It may sometimes be followed.'

'When it concerns the family.'

'He would have the living, who are seeking peace, be just.'

'Not to assume the seat of justice.'

Again they lay as tombstone effigies, that have committed the passage of affairs to another procession of the Ages.

There was a gentle sniff, in hopeless confirmation of the experience of its predecessors. A sister to it ensued.

'Could Victor have spoken so, without assurance in his conscience, that his entreaty was righteously addressed to us? that we...'

'And no others!'

'I think of his language. He loves the child.'

'In heart as in mind, he is eminently gifted; acknowledgeing error.'

'He was very young.'

The huge funereal minutes conducted their sonorous hearse, the hour.

It struck in the bed-room: Three.

No more than three of the clock, it was the voice telling of half the precious restorative night-hours wasted.

Now, as we close our eyelids when we would go to sleep, so must we, in expectation of the peace of mind granting us the sweet oblivion, preliminarily do something which invokes, that we may obtain it.

'Dear,' Dorothea said.

'I know indeed,' said Virginia.

'We may have been!'

'Not designingly.'

'Indeed not. But harsh it may be named, if the one innocent is to be the sufferer.'

'The child can in no sense be adjudged guilty.'

'It is Victor's child.'

'He adores the child.'

Wheels were in mute motion within them; and presently the remark was tossed-up:

'In his coming to us, it is possible to see paternal solicitude'

Thence came fruit of reflection:

'To be instrumental as guides to a tender young life!'

Reflection heated with visions:

'Once our dream!'

They had the happier feeling of composure, though Tasso possessed the room. Not Tasso, but a sublimated offensiveness, issue of the antagonistically combined, dispersed to be the more penetrating; insomuch that it seemed to them they could not ever again make use of eau d'Arquebusade without the vitiating reminder. So true were the words of Mr. Stuart Rem: 'Half measures to purification are the most delusive of our artifices.' Fatigue and its reflections helped to be peacefuller. Their souls were mounting to a serenity above the nauseating degradation, to which the poor little dog had dragged them.

'Victor gave his promise.'

'At least, concession would not imply contact with the guilty.'

Both sighed as they took up the burden of the vaporous Tasso to drop him; with the greater satisfaction in the expelling of their breath.

'It might be said, dear, that concession to his entreaty does not in any way countenance the sin.'

'I can see, dear, how it might be read as a reproof.'

Their exchange of sentences followed meditative pauses; Dorothea leading.

'To one so sensitive as Victor!'

'A month or two of our society for the child!'

'It is not the length of time.'

'The limitation assures against maternal claims.'

'She would not dare.'

'He used the words: "her serious respect" for us. I should not wish to listen to him often.'

'We listen to a higher.'

'It may really be, that the child is like him.'

'Not resembling Mr. Stuart Rem's Clementina!'

'A week of that child gave us our totally sleepless night.' 'One thinks more hopefully of a child of Victor's.'

'He would preponderate.'

'He would.'

They sighed; but it was now with the relief of a lightened oppression.

'If, dear, in truth the father's look is in the child, he has the greater reason to desire for her a taste of our atmosphere.'

'Do not pursue it. Sleep.'

'One prayer!'

'Your mention of our atmosphere, dear, destroys my power to frame one. Do you, for two. But I would cleanse my heart.'

'There is none purer.'

'Hush.'

Virginia spoke a more fervent word of praise of her sister, and had not the hushing response to it. She heard the soft regular breathing. Her own was in downy fellowship with it a moment later.

At the hour of nine, in genial daylight, sitting over the crumbs of his hotel breakfast, Victor received a little note that bore the handwriting of Dorothea Duvidney.

'Dear Victor, we are prepared to receive the child for a month.
In haste, before your train. Our love. D. and V.'

His face flashed out of cloud.

A more precious document had never been handed to him. It chased back to midnight the doubt hovering over his belief in himself;—phrased to say, that he was no longer the Victor Radnor known to the world. And it extinguished a corpse-like recollection of a baleful dream in the night. Here shone radiant witness of his being the very man; save for the spot of his recent confusion in distinguishing his identity or in feeling that he stood whole and solid.—Because of two mature maiden ladies? Yes, because of two maiden ladies, my good fellow. And friend Colney, you know the ladies, and what the getting round them for one's purposes really means.

The sprite of Colney Durance had struck him smartly overnight. Victor's internal crow was over Colney now. And when you have the optimist and pessimist acutely opposed in a mixing group, they direct lively conversations at one another across the gulf of distance, even of time. For a principle is involved, besides the knowledge of the other's triumph or dismay. The couple are scales of a balance; and not before last night had Victor ever consented to think of Colney ascending while he dropped low to graze the pebbles.

He left his hotel for the station, singing the great aria of the fourth Act of the Favorita: neglected since that mighty German with his Rienzi, and Tannhauser, and Tristan and Isolda, had mastered him, to the displacement of his boyhood's beloved sugary -inis and -antes and-zettis; had clearly mastered, not beguiled, him; had wafted him up to a new realm, invigorating if severer. But now his youth would have its voice. He travelled up to town with Sir Abraham Quatley and talked, and took and gave hints upon City and Commercial affairs, while the honeyed Italian of the conventional, gloriously animal, stress and flutter had a revel in his veins, now and then mutedly ebullient at the mouth: honeyed, golden, rich in visions;—having surely much more of Nature's encouragement to her children?

CHAPTER XXIV

NESTA'S ENGAGEMENT

A word in his ear from Fenellan, touching that man Blathenoy, set the wheels of Victor's brain at work upon his defences, for a minute, on the walk Westward. Who knew?—who did not know! He had a torpid consciousness that he cringed to the world, with an entreaty to the great monster to hold off in ignorance; and the next instant, he had caught its miserable spies by the lurcher neck and was towering. He dwelt on his contempt of them, to curtain the power they could stir.

'The little woman, you say, took to Dartrey?'

Fenellan, with the usual apologetic moderation of a second statement, thought 'there was the look of it.'

'Well, we must watch over her. Dartrey!—but Dartrey's an honest fellow with women. But men are men. Very few men spare a woman when the mad fit is on her. A little woman-pretty little woman!— wife to Jacob Blathenoy! She mustn't at her age have any close choosing—under her hand. And Dartrey's just the figure to strike a spark in a tinder-box head.'

'With a husband who'd reduce Minerva's to tinder, after a month of him!'

'He spent his honeymoon at his place at Wrensham; told me so.' Blathenoy had therefore then heard of the building of Lakelands by the Victor Radnor of the City; and had then, we guess—in the usual honeymoon boasting of a windbag with his bride—wheezed the foul gossip, to hide his emptiness and do duty for amusement of the pretty little caged bird. Probably so. But Victor knew that Blathenoy needed him and feared him. Probably the wife had been enjoined to keep silence; for the Blachingtons, Fannings and others were, it could be sworn, blank and unscratched folio sheets on the subject:—as yet; unless Mrs. Burman had dropped venom.

'One pities the little woman, eh, Fenellan?'

'Dartrey won't be back for a week or so; and they're off to Switzerland, after the dinner they give. I heard from him this morning; one of the Clanconans is ill.

'Lucky. But wherever Blathenoy takes her, he must be the same "arid bore," as old Colney says.'

'A domestic simoom,' said Fenellan, booming it: and Victor had a shudder.

'Awful thing, marriage, to some women! We chain them to that domestic round; most of them haven't the means of independence or a chance of winning it; and all that's open to them, if they've made a bad cast for a mate—and good Lord! how are they to know before it's too late!—they haven't a choice except to play tricks or jump to the deuce or sit and "drape in blight," as Colney has it; though his notion of the optional marriages, broken or renewed every seven years!—if he means it. You never know, with him. It sounds like another squirt of savage irony. It's donkey nonsense, eh?'

'The very hee-haw of nonsense,' Fenellan acquiesced.

'Come, come; read your Scriptures; donkeys have shown wisdom,' Victor said, rather leaning to the theme of a fretfulness of women in the legal yoke. 'They're donkeys till we know them for prophets. Who can tell! Colney may be hailed for one fifty years hence.'

Fenellan was not invited to enter the house, although the loneliness of his lodgeings was known, and also, that he played whist at his Club. Victor had grounds for turning to him at the door and squeezing his hand warmly, by way of dismissal. In ascribing them to a weariness at Fenellan's perpetual acquiescence, he put the cover on them, and he stamped it with a repudiation of the charge, that Colney's views upon the great Marriage Question were the 'very hee-haw of nonsense.' They were not the hee-haw; in fact, viewing the host of marriages, they were for discussion; there was no bray about them. He could not feel them to be absurd while Mrs. Burman's tenure of existence barred the ceremony. Anything for a phrase! he murmured of Fenellan's talk; calling him, Dear old boy, to soften the slight.

Nataly had not seen Fenellan or heard from Dartrey; so she continued to be uninformed of her hero's release; and that was in the order of happy accidents. She had hardly to look her interrogation for the news; it radiated. But he stated such matter-of-course briefly. 'The good ladies are ready to receive our girl.'

Her chagrin resolved to a kind of solace of her draggled pride, in the idea, that he who tamed everybody to submission, might well have command of her.

The note, signed D. and V., was shown.

There stood the words. And last night she had been partly of the opinion of Colney Durance. She sank down among the unreasoning abject;—not this time with her perfect love of him, but with a resistance and a dubiety under compression. For she had not quite comprehended why Nesta should go. This readiness of the Duvidney ladies to receive the girl, stopped her mental inquiries.

She begged for a week's delay; 'before the parting'; as her dear old silly mother's pathos whimpered it, of the separation for a month! and he smiled and hummed pleasantly at any small petition, thinking her in error to expect Dartrey's return to town before the close of a week; and then wondering at women, mildly denouncing in his heart the mothers who ran risk of disturbing their daughters' bosoms with regard to particular heroes married or not. Dartrey attracted women: he was one of the men who do it without effort. Victor's provident mind blamed the mother for the indiscreetness of her wish to have him among them. But Dudley had been making way bravely of late; he improved; he began to bloom, like a Spring flower of the garden protected from frosts under glass; and Fredi was the sheltering and nourishing bestower of the lessons. One could see, his questions and other little points revealed, that he had a certain lover's dread of Dartrey Fenellan; a sort of jealousy: Victor understood the feeling. To love a girl, who has her ideal of a man elsewhere in another; though she may know she never can wed the man, and has not the hope of it; is torment to the lover quailing, as we do in this terrible season of the priceless deliciousness, stripped against all the winds that blow; skinless at times. One gets up a sympathy for the poor shy dependent shivering lover. Nevertheless, here was young Dudley waking, visibly becoming bolder. As in the flute-duets, he gained fire from concert. The distance between Cronidge and Moorsedge was two miles and a quarter.

Instead of the delay of a whole week, Victor granted four days, which embraced a musical evening at Mrs. John Cormyn's on the last of the days, when Nesta was engaged to sing with her mother a duet of her own composition, the first public fruit of her lessons in counterpoint from rigid Herr Strauscher, who had said what he had said, in letting it pass: eulogy, coming from him. So Victor heard, and he doated am the surprise to come for him, in a boyish anticipation. The girl's little French ballads under tutelage of Louise de Seilles promised, though they were imitative. If Strauscher let this pass... Victor saw Grand Opera somewhere to follow; England's claim to be a creative musical nation vindicated; and the genius of the fair sex as well.

He heard the duet at Mrs. Cormyn's; and he imagined a hearing of his Fredi's Opera, and her godmother's delight in it; the once famed Sanfredini's consent to be the diva at a rehearsal, and then her compelling her hidalgo duque to consent further: an event not inconceivable. For here was downright genius; the flowering aloe of the many years in formation; and Colney admitted the song to have a streak of genius; though he would pettishly and stupidly say, that our modern newspaper Press is able now to force genius for us twenty or so to the month, excluding Sundays-our short pauses for the incubation of it. Real rare genius was in that song, nothing forced; and exquisite melody; one of those melodies which fling gold chains about us and lead us off, lead us back into Eden. Victor hummed at bars of it on the drive homeward. His darlings had to sing it again in the half-lighted drawing-room. The bubble-happiness of the three was vexed only by tidings heard from Colney during the evening of a renewed instance of Skepsey's misconduct. Priscilla Graves had hurried away to him at the close of Mr. John Cormyn's Concert, in consequence; in grief and in sympathy. Skepsey was to appear before the magistrate next morning, for having administered physical chastisement to his wife during one of her fits of drunkenness. Colney had seen him. His version of the story was given, however, in the objectionable humorous manner: none could gather from it of what might be pleaded for Skepsey. His 'lesson to his wife in the art of pugilism, before granting her Captain's rank among the Defensive Amazons of Old England,' was the customary patent absurdity. But it was odd, that Skepsey always preferred his appeal for help to Colney Durance. Nesta proposed following Priscilla that night. She had hinted her wish, on the way home; she was urgent, beseeching, when her father lifted praises of her:

she had to start with her father by the train at seven in the morning, and she could not hear of poor Skepsey for a number of hours. She begged a day's delay; which would enable her, she said, to join them in dining at the Blachingtons', and seeing dear Lakelands again. 'I was invited, you know.' She spoke in childish style, and under her eyes she beheld her father and mother exchange looks. He had a fear that Nataly might support the girl's petition. Nataly read him to mean, possible dangers among the people at Wrensham. She had seemed hesitating. After meeting Victor's look, her refusal was firm. She tried to make it one of distress for the use of the hard word to her own dear girl. Nesta spied beneath.

But what was it? There was a reason for her going! She had a right to stay, and see and talk with Captain Dartrey, and she was to be deported!

So now she set herself to remember little incidents at Creckholt: particularly a conversation in a very young girl's hearing, upon Sir Humphrey and Lady Pottil's behaviour to the speakers, her parents. She had then, and she now had, an extraordinary feeling, as from a wind striking upon soft summer weather off regions of ice, that she was in her parents' way. How? The feeling was irrational; it could give her no reply, or only the multitudinous which are the question violently repeated. She slept on it.

She and her father breakfasted by the London birds' first twitter. They talked of Skepsey. She spoke of her going as exile. 'No,' said he, 'you're sure to meet friends.'

Her cheeks glowed. It came wholly through the suddenness of the recollection, that the family-seat of one among the friends was near the Wells.

He was allowed to fancy, as it suited him to fancy, that a vivid secret pleasure laid the colour on those ingenuous fair cheeks.

'A solitary flute for me, for a month! I shall miss my sober comrade: got the habit of duetting: and he's gentle, bears with me.'

Tears lined her eyelids. 'Who would not be, dearest dada! But there is nothing to bear except the honour.'

'You like him? You and I always have the same tastes, Fredi.'

Now there was a reddening of the sun at the mount; all the sky aflame. How could he know that it was not the heart in the face! She reddened because she had perused his wishes; had detected a scheme striking off from them, and knew a man to be the object of it; and because she had at the same time the sense of a flattery in her quick divination; and she was responsively emotional, her blood virginal; often it was a tropical lightning.

It looked like the heart doing rich painter's work on maiden features. Victor was naturally as deceived as he wished to be.

From his being naturally so, his remarks on Dudley had an air of embracing him as one of the family. 'His manner to me just hits me.'

'I like to see him with you,' she said.

Her father let his tongue run: 'One of the few young men I feel perfectly at home with! I do like dealing with a gentleman. I can confide in a gentleman: honour, heart, whatever I hold dearest.'

There he stopped, not too soon. The girl was mute, fully agreeing, slightly hardening. She had a painful sense of separation from her dear Louise. And it was now to be from her mother as well: she felt the pain when kissing her mother in bed. But this was moderated by the prospect of a holiday away out of reach of Mr. Barmby's pursuing voice, whom her mother favoured: and her mother was concealing something from her; so she could not make the confidante of her mother. Nataly had no forewarnings. Her simple regrets filled her bosom. All night she had been taking her chastisement, and in the morning it seemed good to her, that she should be denuded, for her girl to learn the felicity of having relatives.

For some reason, over which Nataly mused in the succeeding hours, the girl had not spoken of any visit her mother was to pay to the Duvidney ladies or they to her. Latterly she had not alluded to her mother's family. It might mean, that the beloved and dreaded was laying finger on a dark thing in the dark; reading syllables by touch; keeping silence over the communications to a mind not yet actively speculative, as it is a way with young women. 'With young women educated for the market, to be timorous, consequently secretive, rather snaky,' Colney Durance had said. Her Nesta was not one of the 'framed and glazed' description, cited by him, for an example of the triumph of the product; 'exactly harmonious with the ninny male's ideal of female innocence.' No; but what if the mother had opened her heart to her girl? It had been of late her wish or a dream, shaping hourly to a design, now positively to go through that furnace. Her knowledge of Victor's objection, restrained an impulse that had not won spring enough to act against his counsel or vivify an intelligence grown dull in slavery under him, with regard to the one seeming right course. The adoption of it would have wounded him—therefore her. She had thought of him first; she had also thought of herself, and she blamed herself now. She went so far as to think, that Victor was guilty of the schemer's error of counting human creatures arithmetically, in the sum, without the estimate of distinctive qualities and value here and there. His return to a shivering sensitiveness on the subject of his girl's enlightenment 'just yet,' for which Nataly pitied and loved him, sharing it, with humiliation for doing so, became finally her excuse. We must have some excuse, if we would keep to life.

Skepsey's case appeared in the evening papers. He confessed, 'frankly,' he said, to the magistrate, that, 'acting under temporary exasperation, he had lost for a moment a man's proper self-command.' He was as frank in stating, that he 'occupied the prisoner's place before his Worship a second time, and was a second time indebted to the gentleman, Mr. Colney Durance, who so kindly stood by him.' There was hilarity in the Court at his quaint sententious envelopment of the idiom of the streets, which he delivered with solemnity: 'He could only plead, not in absolute justification—an appeal to human sentiments—the feelings of a man of the humbler orders, returning home in the evening, and his thoughts upon things not without their importance, to find repeatedly the guardian of his household beastly drunk, and destructive.' Colney made the case quite intelligible to the magistrate; who gravely robed a strain of the idiomatic in the officially awful, to keep in tune with his delinquent. No serious harm had been done to the woman. Skepsey was admonished and released. His wife expressed her willingness to forgive him, now he had got his lesson; and she hoped he would understand, that there was no need for a woman to learn pugilism. Skepsey would have explained; but the case was over, he was hustled out.

However, a keen young reporter present smelt fun for copy; he followed the couple; and in a particular evening Journal, laughable matter was printed concerning Skepsey's view of the pugilism to be imparted to women for their physical-protection in extremity, and the distinction of it from the blow conveying the moral lesson to them; his wife having objected to the former, because it annoyed her and he pestered her; and she was never, she said, ready to stand up to him for practice, as he called it, except when she had taken more than he thought wholesome for her: he had no sense. There was a squabble between them, because he chose to scour away to his master's office instead of conducting her home with the honours. Nesta read the young reporter's version, with shrieks. She led the ladies of Moorsedge to discover amusement in it.

At first, as her letter to her mother described them, they were like a pair of pieces of costly China, with the settled smile, and cold. She saw but the outside of them, and she continued reporting the variations, which steadily determined the warmth. On the night of the third day, they kissed her tenderly; they were human figures.

No one could be aware of the trial undergone by the good ladies in receiving her: Victor's child; but, as their phrase would have run, had they dared to give it utterance to one another, a child of sin. How foreign to them, in that character, how strange, when she was looked on as an inhabitant of their house, they hardly dared to estimate; until the timorous estimation, from gradually swelling, suddenly sank; nature invaded them; they could discard the alienating sense of the taint; and not only did they no longer fear the moment when Mr. Stuart Rem or Mr. Posterley might call for evening tea, but they consulted upon inviting the married one of those gentlemen, to 'divert dear Nesta.' Every night she slept well. In all she did, she proved she was 'of the blood.' She had Victor's animated eyes; she might have, they dreaded to think, his eloquence. They put it down to his eloquence entirely, that their resistance to his petition had been overcome, for similarly with the treatment of the private acts of royal personages by lacquey History, there is, in the minds of the ultra-civilized, an insistance, that any event having a consequence in matters personal to them, be at all hazards recorded with the utmost nicety in decency. By such means, they preserve the ceremonial self-respect, which is a necessity of their existence; and so they maintain the regal elevation over the awe-struck subjects of their interiors; who might otherwise revolt, pull down, scatter, dishonour, expose for a shallow fiction the holiest, the most vital to them. A democratic evil spirit is abroad, generated among congregations, often perilously communicating its wanton laughter to the desperate wickedness they know (not solely through the monition of Mr. Stuart Rem) to lurk within. It has to be excluded: on certain points they must not think. The night of Tasso was darkly clouded in the minds of the pure ladies: a rift would have seized their half-slumbering sense of smell, to revive the night, perhaps disorder the stately march of their intelligences.

Victor's eloquence, Victor's influence, Victor's child he carried them as a floodstream, insomuch, that their reception of this young creature of the blot on her birth, was regarded by them in the unmentioned abstract, and the child's presence upon earth seen with the indulgence (without the naughty curiosity) of the loyal moral English for the numerous offspring of the peccadillos of their monarchs. These things pass muster from being 'Britannically cocooned in the purple,' says our irreverent satirist; and the maiden ladies' passion of devotion to 'the blood' helped to blind them; but still more so did the imperious urgency to curtain closely the night of Tasso, throwing all its consequences upon Victor's masterful tongue. Whence it ensued (and here is the danger for illogical individuals as well as vast communities, who continue to batten upon fiction when the convenience of it has taken the place of pleasure), that they had need to exalt his eloquence, for a cloak to their conduct; and doing it, they fell into a habit of yielding to him; they disintegrated under him; rules, principles, morality, were shaken to some confusion. And still proceeding thus, they now and then glanced back, more wonderingly than convicted sinners upon their days of early innocence, at the night when successfully they withstood him. They who had doubted of the rightness of letting Victor's girl come into collision with two clerical gentlemen, one of whom was married, permitted him now to bring the Hon.

Dudley Sowerby to their house, and make appointments to meet Mr. Dudley Sowerby under a roof that sheltered a young lady, evidently the allurement to the scion of aristocracy; of whose family Mr. Stuart Rem had spoken in the very kindling hushed tones, proper to the union of a sacerdotal and an English citizen's veneration.

How would it end? And if some day this excellent Mr. Dudley Sowerby reproached them! He could not have a sweeter bride, one more truly a lady in education and manners; but the birth! the child's name! Their trouble was emitted in a vapour of interjections. Very perplexing was it for the good ladies of strict principles to reflect, as dimly they did, that the concrete presence of dear Nesta silenced and overcame objections to her being upon earth. She seemed, as it were, a draught of redoubtable Nature inebriating morality. But would others be similarly affected? Victor might get his release, to do justice to the mother: it would not cover the child. Prize as they might the quality of the Radnor blood (drawn from the most ancient of original Britain's princes), there was also the Cantor blood for consideration; and it was old, noble, proud. Would it be satisfied in matching itself with great wealth, a radiant health, and the good looks of a young flower? For the sake of the dear girl, the ladies hoped that it would; and they enlarged the outline of their wedding present, while, in their minds, the noble English family which could be satisfied so, was lowered, partaking of the taint they had personally ceased to recognize.

Of one thing they were sure, and it enlisted them: the gentleman loved the girl. Her love of him, had it been prominent to view, would have stirred a feminine sigh; not more, except a feminine lecture to follow. She was quite uninflamed, fresh and cool as a spring. His ardour had no disguise. They measured him by the favourite fiction's heroes of their youth, and found him to gaze, talk, comport himself, according to the prescription; correct grammar, finished sentences, all that is expected of a gentleman enamoured; and ever with the watchful intentness for his lady's faintest first dawn of an inclining to a wish. Mr. Dudley Sowerby's eye upon Nesta was really an apprentice. There is in Love's young season a magnanimity in the male kind. Their superior strength and knowledge are made subservient to the distaff of the weaker and shallower: they crown her queen; her look is their mandate. So was it when Sir Charles and Sir Rupert and the estimable Villiers Davenant touched maidenly hearts to throb: so is it now, with the Hon. Dudley Sowerby.

Very haltingly, the ladies were guilty of a suggestion to Victor. 'Oh! Fredi?' said he; 'admires her, no doubt; and so do I, so we all do; she's one of the nice girls; but as to Cupid's darts, she belongs to the cucumber family, and he shoots without fireing. We shall do the mischief if we put an interdict. Don't you remember the green days when obstacles were the friction to light that match?' Their pretty nod of assent displayed the virgin pride of the remembrance: they dreamed of having once been exceedingly wilful; it refreshed their nipped natures; and dwelling on it, they forgot to press their suggestion. Incidentally, he named the sum his Fredi would convey to her husband; with, as was calculable, the further amount his only child would inherit. A curious effect was produced on them. Though they were not imaginatively mercenary, as the creatures tainted with wealth commonly are, they talked of the sum over and over in the solitude of their chamber. 'Dukes have married for less.' Such an heiress, they said, might buy up a Principality. Victor had supplied them with something of an apology to the gentleman proposing to Nesta in their house.

The chronicle of it is, that Dudley Sowerby did this on the fifteenth day of September; and that it was not known to the damsel's parents before the twenty-third; as they were away on an excursion in South Tyrol:—away, flown, with just a word of the hurried departure to their envious, exiled girl; though they did not tell her of new constructions at the London house partly causing them to fly. Subject to their consent, she wrote, she had given hers. The letter was telegramic on the essential point. She wrote of

Mr. Barmby's having visited Mr. Posterley at the Wells, and she put it just as flatly. Her principal concern, to judge by her writing, was, to know what Mr. Durance had done, during her absence, with the group of emissary-advocates of the various tongues of Europe on board the steam-Liner conducting them the first stage of their journey to the Court of Japan.

Mr. Simeon Fenellan had written his opinion, that all these delegates of the different European nationalities were nothing other than dupes of a New-York Syndicate of American Humorists, not without an eye on the mainchance; and he was sure they would be set to debate publicly, before an audience of high-priced tickets, in the principal North American Cities, previous to the embarcation for Japan at San Francisco. Mr. Fenellan eulogized the immense astuteness of Dr. Gannius in taking his daughter Delphica with him. Dr. Gannius had singled forth poor Dr. Bouthoin for the object of his attacks; but Nesta was chiefly anxious to hear of Delphica's proceedings; she was immensely interested in Delphica, and envied her; and the girl's funny speculations over the play of Delphica's divers arts upon the Greek, and upon the Russian, and upon the English curate Mr. Semhians, and upon M. Falarique—set Gallically pluming and crowing out of an Alsace-Lorraine growl—were clever. Only, in such a letter, they were amazing.

Nataly received it at Campiglio, when about to start for an excursion down the Sarca Valley to Arco. Her letter of reply was delayed. One to Victor from Dudley Sowerby, awaited them, on their return. 'Confirms Fredi,' he said, showing it, and praising it as commendable, properly fervid. She made pretence to read, she saw the words.

Her short beat of wings was over. She had joined herself with Victor's leap for a change, thirsting for the scenery of the white peaks in heaven, to enjoy through his enjoyment, if her own capacity was dead: and she had found it revive, up to some recovery of her old songful readiness for invocations of pleasure. Escape and beauty beckoned ahead; behind were the chains. These two letters of the one fact plucked her back. The chained body bore the fluttering spirit: or it was the spirit in bonds, that dragged the body. Both were abashed before the image of her girl. Out of the riddle of her strange Nesta, one thing was clear: she did not love the man: and Nataly tasted gladness in that, from the cup of poisonous regrets at the thought. Her girl's heart would not be broken. But if he so strongly loved her, as to hold to this engagement?... It might then be worse. She dropped a plumb-line into the young man, sounding him by what she knew of him and judged. She had to revert to Nesta's charm, for the assurance of his anchored attachment.

Her holiday took the burden of her trouble, and amid the beauty of a disenchanted scene, she resumed the London incubus.

'You told him of her being at the Wells? in the neighbourhood, Victor?'

'Didn't you know, my dear, the family-seat is Cronidge, two miles out from the Wells?—and particularly pretty country.'

'I had forgotten, if I ever heard. You will not let him be in ignorance?'

'My dear love, you are pale about it. This is a matter between men. I write, thanking for the honour and so forth; and I appoint an interview; and I show him my tablets. He must be told, necessarily. Incidents of this kind come in their turn. If Dudley does not account himself the luckiest young fellow in the kingdom, he's not worthy of his good fortune. I wish they were both here now, honeymooning among these peaks, seeing the crescent over one, as we did last night!'

'Have you an idea, in reading Nesta's letter?'

'Seems indifferent?—mere trick to hide the blushes. And I, too, I'm interested in Delphica. Delphica and Falarique will be fine stage business. Of course, Dr. Bouthoin and his curate!—we know what Old England has to expect from Colney.'

'At any rate, Mr. Durance hurts no one. You will, in your letter, appoint the day of the interview?'

'Hurts himself! Yes, dearest; appoint for—ten days homeward—eleventh day from to-day. And you to Fredi: a bit of description—as you can, my Nataly! Happy to be a dolomite, to be painted by Nataly's pen.'

The sign is evil, when we have a vexatious ringing in the ear of some small piece of familiar domestic chatter, and subject it to scrutiny, hang on it, worry and magnify it. What will not creatures under sway of the sensational life, catch at to emphasize and strengthen distaste, until distaste shall have a semblance of reason, in the period of the mind's awakening to revolt! Nataly shrank from the name of dolomite, detested the name, though the scenes regained their beauty or something of it beneath her showery vision. Every time Victor spoke of dolomites on the journey homeward, she had at heart an accusation of her cowardice, her duplicity, frailty, treachery to the highest of her worship and sole support of her endurance in the world: not much blaming him: but the degrading view of herself sank them both. On a shifty soil, down goes the idol. For him she could plead still, for herself she could not.

The smell of the Channel brine inspirited her sufficiently to cast off the fit and make it seem, in the main, a bodily depression; owing to causes, of which she was beginning to have an apprehensive knowledge: and they were not so fearful to her as the gloom they displaced.

BOOK IV

CHAPTER XXV

NATALY IN ACTION

A ticket of herald newspapers told the world of Victor's returning to his London. Pretty Mrs. Blathenoy was Nataly's first afternoon visitor, and was graciously received; no sign of inquiry for the cause of the lady's alacrity to greet her being shown. Colney Durance came in, bringing the rumour of an Australian cantatrice to kindle Europe; Mr. Peridon, a seeker of tidings from the city of Bourges; Miss Priscilla Graves, reporting of Skepsey, in a holiday Sunday tone, that his alcoholic partner might at any moment release him; Mr. Septimus Barmby, with a hanged heavy look, suggestive of a wharfside crane swinging the ponderous thing he had to say. 'I have seen Miss Radnor.'

'She was well?' the mother asked, and the grand basso pitched forth an affirmative.

'Dear sweet girl she is!' Mrs. Blathenoy exclaimed to Colney.

He bowed. 'Very sweet. And can let fly on you, like a haggis, for a scratch.'

She laughed, glad of an escape from the conversational formalities imposed on her by this Mrs. Victor Radnor's mighty manner. 'But what girl worth anything!...

We all can do that, I hope, for a scratch!'

Mr. Barmby's Profession dissented.

Mr. Catkin appeared; ten minutes after his Peridon. He had met Victor near the Exchange, and had left him humming the non fu sogno of ERNANI.

'Ah, when Victor takes to Verdi, it's a flat City, and wants a burst of drum and brass,' Colney said; and he hummed a few bars of the march in Attila, and shrugged. He and Victor had once admired that blatancy.

Mr. Pempton appeared, according to anticipation. He sat himself beside Priscilla. Entered Mrs. John Cormyn, voluminous; Mrs. Peter Yatt, effervescent; Nataly's own people were about her and she felt at home.

Mrs. Blathenoy pushed a small thorn into it, by speaking of Captain Fenellan, and aside, as if sharing him with her. Nataly heard that Dartrey had been the guest of these Blathenoys. Even Dartrey was but a man!

Rather lower under her voice, the vain little creature asked: 'You knew her?'

'Her?'

The cool counter-interrogation was disregarded. 'So sad! In the desert! a cup of pure water worth more than barrow-loads of gold! Poor woman!'

'Who?'

'His wife.'

'Wife!'

'They were married?'

Nataly could have cried: Snake! Her play at brevity had certainly been foiled. She nodded gravely. A load of dusky wonders and speculations pressed at her bosom. She disdained to question the mouth which had bitten her.

Mrs. Blathenoy, resolving, that despite the jealousy she excited, she would have her friend in Captain Fenellan, whom she liked—liked, she was sure, quite as innocently as any other woman of his acquaintance did, departed and she hugged her innocence defiantly, with the mournful pride which will sometimes act as a solvent.

A remark or two passed among the company upon her pretty face.

Nataly murmured to Colney: 'Is there anything of Dartrey's wife?'

'Dead,' he answered.

'When?'

'Months back. I had it from Simeon. You didn't hear?'

She shook her head. Her ears buzzed. If he had it from Simeon Fenellan, Victor must have known it.

Her duties of hostess were conducted with the official smile.

As soon as she stood alone, she dropped on a chair, like one who has taken a shot in the heart, and that hideous tumult of wild cries at her ears blankly ceased. Dartrey, Victor, Nesta, were shifting figures of the might-have-been for whom a wretched erring woman, washed clean of her guilt by death, in a far land, had gone to her end: vainly gone: and now another was here, a figure of wood, in man's shape, conjured up by one of the three, to divide the two others; likely to be fatal to her or to them: to her, she hoped, if the choice was to be: and beneath the leaden hope, her heart set to a rapid beating, a fainter, a chill at the core.

She snatched for breath. She shut her eyes, and with open lips, lay waiting; prepared to thank the kindness about to hurry her hence, out of the seas of pain, without pain.

Then came sighs. The sad old servant in her bosom was resuming his labours.

But she had been near it—very near it? A gush of pity for Victor, overwhelmed her hardness of mind.

Unreflectingly, she tried her feet to support her, and tottered to the door, touched along to the stairs, and descended them, thinking strangely upon such a sudden weakness of body, when she would no longer have thought herself the weak woman. Her aim was to reach the library. She sat on the stairs midway, pondering over the length of her journey: and now her head was clearer; for she was travelling to get Railway-guides, and might have had them from the hands of a footman, and imagined that she had considered it prudent to hide her investigation of those books: proofs of an understanding fallen backward to the state of infant and having to begin our drear ascent again.

A slam of the kitchen stair-door restored her. She betrayed no infirmity of footing as she walked past Arlington in the hall; and she was alive to the voice of Skepsey presently on the door-steps. Arlington brought her a note.

Victor had written: 'My love, I dine with Blathenoy in the City, at the Walworth. Business. Skepsey for clothes. Eight of us. Formal. A thousand embraces. Late.'

Skepsey was ushered in. His wife had expired at noon, he said; and he postured decorously the grief he could not feel, knowing that a lady would expect it of him. His wife had fallen down stone steps; she died in hospital. He wished to say, she was no loss to the country; but he was advised within of the prudence of abstaining from comment and trusting to his posture, and he squeezed a drop of conventional sensibility out of it, and felt improved.

Nataly sent a line to Victor: 'Dearest, I go to bed early, am tired. Dine well. Come to me in the morning.'

She reproached herself for coldness to poor Skepsey, when he had gone. The prospect of her being alone until the morning had been so absorbing a relief.

She found a relief also in work at the book of the trains. A walk to the telegraph-station strengthened her. Especially after despatching a telegram to Mr. Dudley Sowerby at Cronidge, and one to Nesta at Moorsedge, did she become stoutly nerved. The former was requested to meet her at Penhurst station at noon. Nesta was to be at the station for the Wells at three o'clock.

From the time of the flying of these telegrams, up to the tap of Victor's knuckle on her bed-room door next morning, she was not more reflectively conscious than a packet travelling to its destination by pneumatic tube. Nor was she acutely impressionable to the features and the voice she loved.

'You know of Skepsey?' she said.

'Ah, poor Skepsey!' Victor frowned and heaved.

'One of us ought to stand beside him at the funeral.'

'Colney or Fenellan?'

'I will ask Mr. Durance.'

'Do, my darling.'

'Victor, you did not tell me of Dartrey's wife.'

'There again! They all get released! Yes, Dartrey! Dartrey has his luck too.'

She closed her eyes, with the desire to be asleep.

'You should have told me, dear.'

'Well, my love! Well—poor Dartrey! I fancy I hadn't a confirmation of the news. I remember a horrible fit of envy on hearing the hint: not much more than a hint: serious illness, was it?—or expected event. Hardly worth while to trouble my dear soul, till certain. Anything about wives, forces me to think of myself—my better self!'

'I had to hear of it first from Mrs. Blathenoy.'

'You've heard of duels in dark rooms:—that was the case between Blathenoy and me last night for an hour.'

She feigned somnolent fatigue over her feverish weariness of heart. He kissed her on the forehead.

Her spell-bound intention to speak of Dudley Sowerby to him, was broken by the sounding of the hall-door, thirty minutes later. She had lain in a trance.

Life surged to her with the thought, that she could decide and take her step. Many were the years back since she had taken a step; less independently then than now; unregretted, if fatal. Her brain was heated for the larger view of things and the swifter summing of them. It could put the man at a remove from her and say, that she had lived with him and suffered intensely. It gathered him to her breast rejoicing in their union: the sharper the scourge, the keener the exultation. But she had one reproach to deafen and beat down. This did not come on her from the world: she and the world were too much foot to foot on the antagonist's line, for her to listen humbly. It came of her quick summary survey of him, which was unnoticed by the woman's present fiery mind as being new or strange in any way: simply it was a fact she now read; and it directed her to reproach herself for an abasement beneath his leadership, a blind subserviency and surrender of her faculties to his greater powers, such as no soul of a breathing body should yield to man: not to the highest, not to the Titan, not to the most Godlike of men. Under cloak, they demand it. They demand their bane.

And Victor!... She had seen into him.

The reproach on her was, that she, in her worship, had been slave, not helper. Scarcely was she irreproachable in the character of slave. If it had been utter slave! she phrased the words, for a further reproach. She remembered having at times murmured, dissented. And it would have been a desperate proud thought to comfort a slave, that never once had she known even a secret opposition to the will of her lord.

But she had: she recalled instances. Up they rose; up rose everything her mind ranged over, subsiding immediately when the service was done. She had not conceived her beloved to be infallible, surest of guides in all earthly-matters. Her intellect had sometimes protested.

What, then, had moved her to swamp it?

Her heart answered. And that heart also was arraigned: and the heart's fleshly habitation acting on it besides: so flagellant of herself was she: covertly, however, and as the chaste among women can consent to let our animal face them. Not grossly, still perceptibly to her penetrative hard eye on herself, she saw the senses of the woman under a charm. She saw, and swam whirling with a pang of revolt from her personal being and this mortal kind.

Her rational intelligence righted her speedily. She could say in truth, by proof, she loved the man: nature's love, heart's love, soul's love. She had given him her life.

It was a happy cross-current recollection, that the very beginning and spring of this wild cast of her life, issued from something he said and did (merest of airy gestures) to signify the blessing of life—how good and fair it is. A drooping mood in her had been struck; he had a look like the winged lyric up in blue heavens: he raised the head of the young flower from its contemplation of grave-mould. That was when he had much to bear: Mrs. Burman present: and when the stranger in their household had begun to pity him and have a dread of her feelings. The lucent splendour of his eyes was memorable, a light above the rolling oceans of Time.

She had given him her life, little aid. She might have closely counselled, wound in and out with his ideas. Sensible of capacity, she confessed to the having been morally subdued, physically as well; swept onward; and she was arrested now by an accident, like a waif of the river-floods by the dip of a branch. Time that it should be! But was not Mr. Durance, inveighing against the favoured system for the education of women, right when he declared them to be unfitted to speak an opinion on any matter external to the household or in a crisis of the household? She had not agreed with him: he presented stinging sentences, which irritated more than they enlightened. Now it seemed to her, that the model women of men make pleasant slaves, not true mates: they lack the worldly training to know themselves or take a grasp of circumstances.

There is an exotic fostering of the senses for women, not the strengthening breath of vital common air. If good fortune is with them, all may go well: the stake of their fates is upon the perpetual smooth flow of good fortune. She had never joined to the cry of the women. Few among them were having it in the breast as loudly.

Hard on herself, too, she perceived how the social rebel had reduced her mind to propitiate a simulacrum, reflected from out, of an enthroned Society within it, by an advocacy of the existing laws and rules and habits. Eminently servile is the tolerated lawbreaker: none so conservative. Not until we are driven back upon an unviolated Nature, do we call to the intellect to think radically: and then we begin to think of our fellows.

Or when we have set ourselves in motion direct for the doing of the right thing: have quitted the carriage at the station, and secured the ticket, and entered the train, counting the passage of time for a simple rapid hour before we have eased heart in doing justice to ourself and to another; then likewise the mind is lighted for radiation. That doing of the right thing, after a term of paralysis, cowardice—any evil name—is one of the mighty reliefs, equal to happiness, of longer duration.

Nataly had it. But her mind was actually radiating, and the comfort to her heart evoked the image of Dartrey Fenellan. She saw a possible reason for her bluntness to the coming scene with Dudley.

At once she said, No! and closed the curtain; knowing what was behind, counting it nought. She repeated almost honestly her positive negative. How we are mixed of the many elements! she thought, as an observer; and self-justifyingly thought on, and with truth, that duty urged her upon this journey; and proudly thought, that she had not a shock of the painful great organ in her breast at the prospect at the end, or any apprehension of its failure to carry her through.

Yet the need of peace or some solace needed to prepare her for her interview turned her imagination burningly on Dartrey. She would not allow herself to meditate over hopes and schemes:—Nesta free: Dartrey free. She vowed to her soul sacredly—and she was one of those in whom the Divinity lives, that they may do so—not to speak a word for the influencing of Dudley save the one fact. Consequently, for a personal indulgence, she mused; she caressed maternally the object of her musing; of necessity, she excluded Nesta; but in tenderness she gave Dartrey a fair one to love him.

The scene was waved away. That one so loving him, partly worthy of him, ready to traverse the world now beside him—who could it be other than she who knew and prized his worth? Foolish! It is one of the hatefuller scourges upon women whenever, a little shaken themselves, they muse upon some man's image, that they cannot put in motion the least bit of drama without letting feminine self play a part; generally to develop into a principal part... The apology makes it a melancholy part.

Dartrey's temper of the caged lion dominated by his tamer, served as keynote for any amount of saddest colouring. He controlled the brute: but he held the contempt of danger, the love of strife, the passion for adventure; he had crossed the desert of human anguish. He of all men required a devoted mate, merited her. Of all men living, he was the hardest to match with a woman—with a woman deserving him.

The train had quitted London. Now for the country, now for free breathing! She who two days back had come from Alps, delighted in the look on flat green fields. It was under the hallucination of her saying in flight adieu to them, and to England; and, that somewhere hidden, to be found in Asia, Africa, America, was the man whose ideal of life was higher than enjoyment. His caged brute of a temper offered opportunities for delicious petting; the sweetest a woman can bestow: it lifts her out of timidity into an adoration still palpitatingly fearful. Ah, but familiarity, knowledge, confirmed assurance of his character, lift her to another stage, above the pleasures. May she not prove to him how really matched with him she is, to disdain the pleasures, cheerfully accept the burdens, meet death, if need be; readily face it as the quietly grey to-morrow: at least, show herself to her hero for a woman—the incredible being to most men—who treads the terrors as well as the pleasures of humanity beneath her feet, and may therefore have some pride in her stature. Ay, but only to feel the pride of standing not so shamefully below his level beside him.

Woods were flying past the carriage-windows. Her solitary companion was of the class of the admiring gentlemen. Presently he spoke. She answered. He spoke again. Her mouth smiled, and her accompanying look of abstract benevolence arrested the tentative allurement to conversation.

New ideas were set revolving in her. Dartrey and Victor grew to a likeness; they became hazily one man, and the mingled phantom complimented her on her preserving a good share of the beauty of her youth. The face perhaps: the figure rather too well suits the years! she replied. To reassure her, this Dartrey-Victor drew her close and kissed her; and she was confused and passed into the breast of Mrs. Burman expecting an operation at the hands of the surgeons. The train had stopped. 'Penhurst?' she said.

'Penhurst is the next station,' said the gentleman. Here was a theme for him! The stately mansion, the noble grounds, and Sidney! He discoursed of them.

The handsome lady appeared interested. She was interested also by his description of a neighbouring village, likely one hundred years hence to be a place of pilgrimage for Americans and for Australians. Age, he said, improves true beauty; and his eyelids indicated a levelling to perform the soft intentness. Mechanically, a ball rose in her throat; the remark was illuminated by a saying of Colney's, with regard to his countrymen at the play of courtship. No laughter came. The gentleman talked on.

All fancies and internal communications left her. Slowness of motion brought her to the plain piece of work she had to do, on a colourless earth, that seemed foggy; but one could see one's way. Resolution is a form of light, our native light in this dubious world.

Dudley Sowerby opened her carriage-door. They greeted.

'You have seen Nesta?' she said.

'Not for two days. You have not heard? The Miss Duvidneys have gone to Brighton.'

'They are rather in advance of the Season.'

She thanked him for meeting her. He was grateful for the summons.

Informing the mother of his betrothed, that he had ridden over from Cronidge, he speculated on the place to select for her luncheon, and he spoke of his horse being led up and down outside the station. Nataly inquired for the hour of the next train to London. He called to one of the porters, obtained and imparted the time; evidently now, as shown by an unevenness of his lifted brows, expecting news of some little weight.

'Your husband is quite well?' he said, in affection for the name of husband.

'Mr. Radnor is well; I have to speak to you; I have more than time.'

'You will lunch at the inn?'

'I shall not eat. We will walk.'

They crossed the road and passed under trees.

'My mother was to have called on the Miss Duvidneys. They left hurriedly; I think it was unanticipated by Nesta. I venture... you pardon the liberty... she allows me to entertain hopes. Mr. Radnor, I am hardly too bold in thinking... I trust, in appealing to you... at least I can promise!

'Mr. Sowerby, you have done my daughter the honour to ask her hand in marriage.'

He said: 'I have,' and had much to say besides, but deferred: a blow was visible. The father had been more encouraging to him than the mother.

'You have not known of any circumstance that might cause hesitation in asking?'

'Miss Radnor?'

'My daughter:—you have to think of your family.'

'Indeed, Mrs. Radnor, I was coming to London tomorrow, with the consent of my family.'

'You address me as Mrs. Radnor. I have not the legal right to the name.'

'Not legal!' said he, with a catch at the word.

He spun round in her sight, though his demeanour was manfully rigid.

'Have I understood, madam...?'

'You would not request me to repeat it. Is that your horse the man is leading?'

'My horse: it must be my horse.'

'Mount and ride back. Leave me: I shall not eat. Reflect, by yourself. You are in a position of one who is not allowed to decide by his feelings. Mr. Radnor you know where to find.'

'But surely, some food? I cannot have misapprehended?'

'I cannot eat. I think you have understood me clearly.'

'You wish me to go?'

'I beg.'

'It pains me, dear madam.'

'It relieves me, if you will. Here is your horse.'

She gave her hand. He touched it and bent. He looked at her. A surge of impossible questions rolled to his mouth and rolled back, with the thought of an incredible thing, that her manner, more than her words, held him from doubting.

'I obey you,' he said.

'You are kind.'

He mounted horse, raised hat, paced on, and again bowing, to one of the wayside trees, cantered. The man was gone; but not from Nataly's vision that face of wet chalk under one of the shades of fire.

CHAPTER XXVI

IN WHICH WE SEE A CONVENTIONAL GENTLEMAN ENDEAVOURING TO EXAMINE A SPECTRE OF HIMSELF

Dudley rode back to Cronidge with his thunderstroke. It filled him, as in those halls of political clamour, where explanatory speech is not accepted, because of a drowning tide of hot blood on both sides. He sought to win attention by submitting a resolution, to the effect, that he would the next morning enter into the presence of Mr. Victor Radnor, bearing his family's feelings, for a discussion upon them. But the brutish tumult, in addition to surcharging, encased him: he could not rightly conceive the nature of feelings: men were driving shoals; he had lost hearing and touch of individual men; had become a house of angrily opposing parties.

He was hurt, he knew; and therefore he supposed himself injured, though there were contrary outcries, and he admitted that he stood free; he had not been inextricably deceived.

The girl was caught away to the thinnest of wisps in a dust-whirl. Reverting to the father and mother, his idea of a positive injury, that was not without its congratulations, sank him down among his disordered deeper sentiments; which were a diver's wreck, where an armoured livid subtermarine, a monstrous puff-ball of man, wandered seriously light in heaviness; trembling his hundredweights to keep him from dancing like a bladder-block of elastic lumber; thinking occasionally, amid the mournful spectacle, of the atmospheric pipe of communication with the world above, whereby he was deafened yet sustained. One tug at it, and he was up on the surface, disengaged from the hideous harness, joyfully no more that burly phantom cleaving green slime, free! and the roaring stopped; the world looked flat, foreign, a place of crusty promise. His wreck, animated by the dim strange fish below, appeared fairer; it winked lurefully when abandoned.

The internal state of a gentleman who detested intangible metaphor as heartily as the vulgarest of our gobblegobbets hate it, metaphor only can describe; and for the reason, that he had in him just something more than is within the compass of the language of the meat-markets. He had—and had it not the less because he fain would not have had—sufficient stuff to furnish forth a soul's epic encounter between Nature and Circumstance: and metaphor, simile, analysis, all the fraternity of old lamps for lighting our abysmal darkness, have to be rubbed, that we may get a glimpse of the fray.

Free, and rejoicing; without the wish to be free; at the same time humbly and sadly acquiescing in the stronger claim of his family to pronounce the decision: such was the second stage of Dudley's perturbation after the blow. A letter of Nesta's writing was in his pocket: he knew her address. He could not reply to her until he had seen her father: and that interview remained necessarily prospective until he had come to his exact resolve, not omitting his critical approval of the sentences giving it shape, stamp, dignity—a noble's crest, as it were.

Nesta wrote briefly. The apostrophe was, 'Dear Mr. Sowerby.' She had engaged to send her address. Her father had just gone. The Miss Duvidneys had left the hotel yesterday for the furnished house facing the sea. According to arrangements, she had a livery-stable hack, and had that morning trotted out to the downs with a riding-master and company, one of whom was 'an agreeable lady.'

He noticed approvingly her avoidance of an allusion to the 'Delphica' of Mr. Durance's incomprehensible serial story, or whatever it was; which, as he had shown her, annoyed him, for its being neither fact nor fun; and she had insisted on the fun; and he had painfully tried to see it or anything of a meaning; and it seemed to him now, that he had been humiliated by the obedience to her lead: she had offended by her harping upon Delphica. However, here it was unmentioned. He held the letter out to seize it in the large, entire.

Her handwriting was good, as good as the writing of the most agreeable lady on earth. Dudley did not blame her for letting the lady be deceived in her—if she knew her position. She might be ignorant of it. And to strangers, to chance acquaintances, even to friends, the position, of the loathsome name, was not materially important. Marriage altered the view. He sided with his family.

He sided, edgeing away, against his family. But a vision of the earldom coming to him, stirred reverential objections, composed of all which his unstained family could protest in religion, to repudiate an alliance with a stained house, and the guilty of a condonation of immorality. Who would have imagined Mr. Radnor a private sinner flaunting for one of the righteous? And she, the mother, a lady—quite a lady; having really a sense of duty, sense of honour! That she must be a lady, Dudley was convinced. He beheld through a porous crape, woven of formal respectfulness, with threads of personal disgust, the scene, striking him drearly like a distant great mansion's conflagration across moorland at midnight, of a lady's breach of bonds and plunge of all for love. How had it been concealed? In Dudley's upper sphere, everything was exposed: Scandal walked naked and unashamed-figurante of the polite world. But still this lady was of the mint and coin, a true lady. Handsome now, she must have been beautiful. And a comprehensible pride (for so would Dudley have borne it) keeps the forsaken man silent up to death:... grandly silent; but the loss of such a woman is enough to kill a man! Not in time, though! Legitimacy evidently, by the mother's confession, cannot protect where it is wanted. Dudley was optically affected by a round spot of the world swinging its shadow over Nesta.

He pitied, and strove to be sensible of her. The effort succeeded so well, that he was presently striving to be insensible. The former state, was the mounting of a wall; the latter, was a sinking through a chasm. There would be family consultations, abhorrent; his father's agonized amazement at the problem presented to a family of scrupulous principles and pecuniary requirements; his mother's blunt mention of the abominable name—mediaevally vindicated in champions of certain princely families indeed, but morally condemned; always under condemnation of the Church: a blot: and handed down: Posterity, and it might be a titled posterity, crying out. A man in the situation of Dudley could not think solely of himself. The nobles of the land are bound in honour to their posterity. There you have one of the prominent permanent distinctions between them and the commonalty.

His mother would again propose her chosen bride for him: Edith Averst, with the dowry of a present one thousand pounds per annum, and prospect of six or so, excluding Sir John's estate, Carping, in Leicestershire; a fair estate, likely to fall to Edith; consumption seized her brothers as they ripened. A fair girl too; only Dudley did not love her; he wanted to love. He was learning the trick from this other one, who had become obscured and diminished, tainted, to the thought of her; yet not extinct. Sight of her was to be dreaded.

Unguiltily tainted, in herself she was innocent. That constituted the unhappy invitation to him to swallow one half of his feelings, which had his world's blessing on it, for the beneficial enlargement and enthronement of the baser unblest half, which he hugged and distrusted. Can innocence issue of the guilty? He asked it, hoping it might be possible: he had been educated in his family to believe, that the laws governing human institutions are divine—until History has altered them. They are altered, to present a fresh bulwark against the infidel. His conservative mind, retiring in good order, occupied the next rearward post of resistance. Secretly behind it, the man was proud of having a heart to beat for the cause of the besiegeing enemy, in the present instance. When this was blabbed to him, and he had owned it, he attributed his weakness to excess of nature, the liking for a fair face.—Oh, but more! spirit was in the sweet eyes. She led him—she did lead him in spiritual things; led him out of common circles of thought, into refreshing new spheres; he had reminiscences of his having relished the juices of the not quite obviously comic, through her indications: and really, in spite of her inferior flimsy girl's education, she could boast her acquirements; she was quick, startlingly; modest, too, in commerce with a slower mind that carried more; though she laughed and was a needle for humour: she taught him at times to put away his contempt of the romantic; she had actually shown him, that his expressed contempt of it disguised a dread: as it did, and he was conscious of the foolishness of it now while pursuing her image, while his intelligence and senses gave her the form and glory of young morning.

Wariness counselled him to think it might be merely the play of her youth; and also the disposition of a man in harness of business, exaggeratingly to prize an imagined finding of the complementary feminine of himself. Venerating purity as he did, the question, whether the very sweetest of pure young women, having such an origin, must not at some time or other show trace of the origin, surged up. If he could only have been sure of her moral exemption from taint, a generous ardour, in reserve behind his anxious dubieties, would have precipitated Dudley to quench disapprobation and brave the world under a buckler of those monetary advantages, which he had but stoutly to plead with the House of Cantor, for the speedy overcoming of a reluctance to receive the nameless girl and prodigious heiress. His family's instruction of him, and his inherited tastes, rendered the aspect of a Nature stripped of the clothing of the laws offensive down to devilish: we grant her certain steps, upon certain conditions accompanied by ceremonies; and when she violates them, she becomes visibly again the revolutionary wicked old beast bent on levelling our sacredest edifices. An alliance with any of her votaries, appeared to Dudley as an act of treason to his house, his class, and his tenets. And nevertheless he was haunted by a cry of criminal happiness for and at the commission of the act.

He would not decide to be 'precipitate,' and the days ran their course, until Lady Grace Halley arrived at Cronidge, a widow. Lady Cantor spoke to her of Dudley's unfathomable gloom. Lady Grace took him aside.

She said, without preface: 'You've heard, have you!'

'You were aware of it?' said he, and his tone was irritable with a rebuke.

'Coming through town, for the first time yesterday. I had it—of all men!—from a Sir Abraham Quatley, to whom I was recommended to go, about my husband's shares in a South American Railway; and we talked, and it came out. He knows; he says, it is not generally known; and he likes, respects Mr. Victor Radnor; we are to keep the secret. Hum? He had heard of your pretensions; and our relationship, etc.: "esteemed" it—you know the City dialect—his duty to mention, etc. That was after I had spied on his forehead the something I wormed out of his mouth. What are you going to do?'

'What can I do!'

'Are you fond of the girl?'

An attachment was indicated, as belonging to the case. She was not a woman to whom the breathing of pastoral passion would be suitable; yet he saw that she despised him for a lover; and still she professed to understand his dilemma. Perplexity at the injustice of fate and persons universally, put a wrinkled mask on his features and the expression of his feelings. They were torn, and the world was torn; and what he wanted, was delay, time for him to define his feelings and behold a recomposed picture of the world. He had already taken six days. He pleaded the shock to his family.

'You won't have such a chance again,' she said. Shrugs had set in.

They agreed as to the behaviour of the girl's mother. It reflected on the father, he thought.

'Difficult thing to proclaim, before an engagement!' Her shoulders were restless.

'When a man's feelings get entangled!'

'Oh! a man's feelings! I'm your British Jury for, a woman's.'

'He has married her?'

She declared to not knowing particulars. She could fib smoothly.

The next day she was on the line to London, armed with the proposal of an appointment for the Hon. Dudley to meet 'the girl's father.'

CONTAINS WHAT IS A SMALL THING OR A GREAT, AS THE SOUL OF THE CHIEF ACTOR MAY DECIDE

Skepsey ushered Lady Grace into his master's private room, and entertained her during his master's absence. He had buried his wife, he said: she feared, seeing his posture of the soaping of hands at one shoulder, that he was about to bewail it; and he did wish to talk of it, to show his modest companionship with her in loss, and how a consolation for our sorrows may be obtained: but he won her approval, by taking the acceptable course between the dues to the subject and those to his hearer, as a model cab should drive considerate equally of horse and fare.

A day of holiday at Hampstead, after the lowering of the poor woman's bones into earth, had been followed by a descent upon London; and at night he had found himself in the immediate neighbourhood of a public house, noted for sparring exhibitions and instructions on the first floor; and he was melancholy, unable quite to disperse 'the ravens' flocking to us on such days: though, if we ask why we have to go out of the world, there is a corresponding inquiry, of what good was our coming into it; and unless we are doing good work for our country, the answer is not satisfactory—except, that we are as well gone. Thinking which, he was accosted by a young woman: perfectly respectable, in every way: who inquired if he had seen a young man enter the door. She described him, and reviled the temptations of those houses; and ultimately, as she insisted upon going in to look for the young man and use her persuasions to withdraw him from 'that snare of Satan,' he had accompanied her, and he had gone upstairs and brought the young man down. But friends, or the acquaintances they call friends, were with him, and they were 'in drink,' and abused the young woman; and she had her hand on the young man's arm, quoting Scripture. Sad to relate of men bearing the name of Englishmen—and it was hardly much better if they pleaded intoxication!—they were not content to tear the young man from her grasp, they hustled her, pushed her out, dragged her in the street.

'It became me to step to her defence: she was meek,' said Skepsey. 'She had a great opinion of the efficacy of quotations from Scripture; she did not recriminate. I was able to release her and the young man she protected, on condition of my going upstairs to give a display of my proficiency. I had assured them, that the poor fellows who stood against me were not a proper match. And of course, they jeered, but they had the evidence, on the pavement. So I went up with them. I was heavily oppressed, I wanted relief, I put on the gloves. He was a bigger man; they laughed at the little one. I told them, it depended upon a knowledge of first principles, and the power to apply them. I will not boast, my lady: my junior by ten years, the man went down; he went down a second time; and the men seemed surprised; I told them, it was nothing but first principles put into action. I mention the incident, for the extreme relief it afforded me at the close of a dark day.'

'So you cured your grief!' said Lady Grace; and Skepsey made way for his master.

Victor's festival-lights were kindled, beholding her; cressets on the window-sill, lamps inside.

'Am I so welcome?' There was a pull of emotion at her smile. 'What with your little factotum and you, we are flattered to perdition when we come here. He has been proposing, by suggestion, like a Court-physician, the putting on of his boxing-gloves, for the consolation of the widowed:—meant most kindly! and it's a thousand pities women haven't their padded gloves.'

'Oh! but our boxing-gloves can do mischief enough. You have something to say, I see.'

'How do you see?'

'Tusk, tush.'

The silly ring of her voice and the pathless tattle changed; she talked to suit her laden look. 'You hit it. I come from Dudley. He knows the facts. I wish to serve you, in every way.'

Victor's head had lifted.

'Who was it?'

'No enemy.'

'Her mother. She did rightly!

'Certainly she did,' said Victor, and he thought that instantaneously of the thing done. 'Oh, then she spoke to him! She has kept it from me. For now nearly a week—six days—I've seen her spying for something she expected, like a face behind a door three inches ajar. She has not been half alive; she refused explanations;—she was expecting to hear from him, of him:—the decision, whatever it's to be!'

'I can't aid you there,' said Lady Grace. 'He's one of the unreadables. He names Tuesday next week.'

'By all means.'

'She?'

'Fredi?—poor Fredi!—ah, my poor girl, yes!—No, she knows nothing. Here is the truth of it.—she, the legitimate, lives: they say she lives. Well, then, she lives against all rules physical or medical, lives by sheer force of will—it's a miracle of the power of a human creature to .... I have it from doctors, friends, attendants, they can't guess what she holds on, to keep her breath. All the happiness in life!—if only it could benefit her. But it 's the cause of death to us. Do you see, dear friend;—you are a friend, proved friend,' he took her hand, and held and pressed it, in great need of a sanguine response to emphasis; and having this warm feminine hand, his ideas ran off with it. 'The friend I need! You have courage. My Nataly, poor dear—she can endure, in her quiet way. A woman of courage would take her place beside me and compel the world to do her homage, help;—a bright ready smile does it! She would never be beaten. Of course, we could have lived under a bushel—stifled next to death! But I am for light, air-battle, if you like. I want a comrade, not a—not that I complain. I respect, pity, love—I do love her, honour: only, we want something else—courage—to face the enemy. Quite right, that she should speak to Dudley Sowerby. He has to know, must know; all who deal closely with us must know. But see a moment: I am waiting to see the impediment dispersed, which puts her at an inequality with the world: and then I speak to all whom it concerns—not before: for her sake. How is it now? Dudley will ask... you understand. And when I am forced to confess, that the mother, the mother of the girl he seeks in marriage, is not yet in that state herself, probably at that very instant the obstacle has crumbled to dust! I say, probably: I have information—doctors, friends, attendants—they all declare it cannot last outside a week. But you are here—true, I could swear! a touch of a hand tells me. A woman's hand? Well, yes: I read by the touch of a woman's hand:—betrays more than her looks or her lips!' He sank his voice. 'I don't talk of condoling: if you are in grief, you know I share it.' He kissed her hand, and laid it on her lap; eyed it, and met her eyes; took a header into her eyes, and lost himself. A nip of his conscience moved his tongue to say: 'As for guilt, if it were known... a couple of ascetics—absolutely!' But this was assumed to be unintelligible; and it was merely the apology to his conscience in communion with the sprite of a petticoated fair one who was being subjected to tender little liberties, necessarily addressed in enigmas. He righted immediately, under a perception of the thoroughbred's contempt for the barriers of wattled sheep; and caught the word 'guilt,' to hide the Philistine citizen's lapse, by relating historically, in abridgement, the honest beauty of the passionate loves of the two whom the world proscribed for honestly loving. There was no guilt. He harped on the word, to erase the recollection of his first use of it.

'Fiddle,' said Lady Grace. 'The thing happened. You have now to carry it through. You require a woman's aid in a social matter. Rely on me, for what I can do. You will see Dudley on Tuesday? I will write. Be plain with him; not forgetting the gilding, I need not remark. Your Nesta has no aversion?'

'Admires, respects, likes; is quite—is willing.'

'Good enough beginning.' She rose, for the atmosphere was heated, rather heavy. 'And if one proves to be of aid, you'll own that a woman has her place in the battle.'

The fair black-clad widow's quick and singular interwreathing of the evanescent pretty pouts and frowns dimpled like the brush of the wind on a sunny pool in a shady place; and her forehead was close below his chin, her lips not far. Her apparel was attractively mourning.

Widows in mourning, when they do not lean over extremely to the Stygian shore, with the complexions of the drugs which expedited the defunct to the ferry, provoke the manly arm within reach of them to pluck their pathetic blooming persons clean away from it. What of the widow who visibly likes the living? Compassion; sympathy, impulse; and gratitude, impulse again, living warmth; and a spring of the blood to wrestle with the King of Terrors for the other poor harper's half-night capped Eurydice; and a thirst, sudden as it is overpowering; and the solicitude, a reflective solicitude, to put the seal on a thing and call it a fact, to the astonishment of history; and a kick of our naughty youth in its coffin; all the insurgencies of Nature, with her colonel of the regiment absent, and her veering trick to drive two vessels at the cross of a track into collision, combine for doing that, which is very much more, and which affects us at times so much less than did the pressure of a soft wedded hand by our own elsewhere pledged one. On the contrary, we triumph, we have the rich flavour of the fruit for our pains; we commission the historian to write in hieroglyphs a round big fact.

The lady passed through the trial submitting, stiffening her shoulders, and at the close, shutting her eyes. She stood cool in her blush, and eyed him, like one gravely awakened. Having been embraced and kissed, she had to consider her taste for the man, and acknowledge a neatness of impetuosity in the deed; and he was neither apologizing culprit nor glorying-bandit when it was done, but something of the lyric God tempering his fervours to a pleased sereneness, not offering a renewal of them. He glowed transparently. He said: 'You are the woman to take a front place in the battle!' With this woman beside him, it was a conquered world.

Comparisons, in the jotting souvenirs of a woman of her class and set, favoured him; for she disliked enterprising libertines and despised stumbling youths; and the genial simple glow of his look assured her, that the vanished fiery moment would not be built on by a dating master. She owned herself. Or did she? Some understanding of how the other woman had been won to the leap with him, was drawing in about her. She would have liked to beg for the story; and she could as little do that as bring her tongue to reproach. If we come to the den! she said to her thought of reproach. Our semi-civilization makes it a den, where a scent in his nostrils will spring the half-tamed animal away to wildness. And she had come unanticipatingly, without design, except perhaps to get a superior being to direct and restrain a gambler's hand perhaps for the fee of a temporary pressure.

'I may be able to help a little—I hope!' she fetched a breath to say, while her eyelids mildly sermonized; and immediately she talked of her inheritance of property in stocks and shares.

Victor commented passingly on the soundness of them, and talked of projects he entertained:— Parliament! 'But I have only to mention it at home, and my poor girl will set in for shrinking.'

He doated on the diverse aspect of the gallant woman of the world.

'You succeed in everything you do,' said she, and she cordially believed it; and that belief set the neighbour memory palpitating. Success folded her waist, was warm upon her lips: she worshipped the figure of Success.

'I can't consent to fail, it's true, when my mind is on a thing,' Victor rejoined.

He looked his mind on Lady Grace. The shiver of a maid went over her. These transparent visages, where the thought which is half design is perceived as a lightning, strike lightning into the physically feebler. Her hand begged, with the open palm, her head shook thrice; and though she did not step back, he bowed to the negation, and then she gave him a grateful shadow of a smile, relieved, with a startled view of how greatly relieved, by that sympathetic deference in the wake of the capturing intrepidity.

'I am to name Tuesday for Dudley?' she suggested.

'At any hour he pleases to appoint.'

'A visit signifies...'

'Whatever it signifies!'

'I'm thinking of the bit of annoyance.'

'To me? Anything appointed, finds me ready the next minute.'

Her smile was flatteringly bright. 'By the way, keep your City people close about you: entertain as much as possible; dine them,' she said.

'At home?'

'Better. Sir Rodwell Blachington, Sir Abraham Quatley: and their wives. There's no drawing back now. And I will meet them.'

She received a compliment. She was on the foot to go.

But she had forgotten the Tiddler mine.

The Tiddler mine was leisurely mounting. Victor stated the figures; he saluted her hand, and Lady Grace passed out, with her heart on the top of them, and a buzz about it of the unexpected having occurred She had her experiences to match new patterns in events; though not very many. Compared with gambling, the game of love was an idle entertainment. Compared with other players, this man was gifted.

Victor went in to Mr. Inchling's room, and kept Inchling from speaking, that he might admire him for he knew not what, or knew not well what. The good fellow was devoted to his wife. Victor in old days had called the wife Mrs. Grundy. She gossiped, she was censorious; she knew—could not but know—the facts; yet never by a shade was she disrespectful. He had a curious recollection of how his knowledge of Inchling and his wife being always in concert, entirely—whatever they might think in private—devoted to him in action, had influenced, if it had not originally sprung, his resolve to cast off the pestilential cloak of obscurity shortening his days, and emerge before a world he could illumine to give him back splendid reflections. Inchling and his wife, it was: because the two were one: and if one, and subservient to him, knowing all the story, why, it foreshadowed a conquered world.

They were the one pulse of the married Grundy beating in his hand. So it had been.

He rattled his views upon Indian business, to hold Inchling silent, and let his mind dwell almost lovingly on the good faithful spouse, who had no phosphorescent writing of a recent throbbing event on the four walls of his room.

Nataly was not so generously encountered in idea.

He felt and regretted this. He greeted her with a doubled affectionateness. Her pitiable deficiency of courage, excusing a man for this and that small matter in the thick of the conflict, made demands on him for gentle treatment.

'You have not seen any one?' she asked.

'City people. And you, my love?'

'Mr. Barmby called. He has gone down to Tunbridge Wells for a week, to some friend there.' She added, in pain of thought: 'I have seen Dartrey. He has brought Lord Clanconan to town, for a consultation, and expects he will have to take him to Brighton.'

'Brighton? What a life for a man like Dartrey, at Brighton!'

Her breast heaved. 'If I cannot see my Nesta there, he will bring her up to me for a day:

'But, my dear, I will bring her up to you, if it is your wish to see her.'

'It is becoming imperative that I should.'

'No hurry, no hurry: wait till the end of next week. And I must see Dartrey, on business, at once!'

She gave the address in a neighbouring square. He had minutes to spare before dinner, and flew. She was not inquisitive.

Colney Durance had told Dartrey that Victor was killing her. She had little animation; her smiles were ready, but faint. After her interview with Dudley, there had been a swoon at home; and her maid, sworn to secrecy, willingly spared a tender-hearted husband—so good a master.

CHAPTER XXVIII

MRS. MARSETT

Little acts of kindness were not beyond the range of Colney Durance, and he ran down to Brighton, to give the exiled Nesta some taste of her friendly London circle. The Duvidney ladies knew that the dreaded gentleman had a regard for the girl. Their own, which was becoming warmer than they liked to think, was impressed by his manner of conversing with her. 'Child though she was,' he paid her the compliment of a sober as well as a satirical review of the day's political matter and recent publications; and the ladies were introduced, in a wonderment, to the damsel Delphica. They listened placidly to a discourse upon her performances, Japanese to their understandings.

At New York, behold, another adventurous representative and advocate of the European tongues has joined the party: Signor Jeridomani: a philologer, of course; a politician in addition; Macchiavelli redivivus, it seems to fair Delphica. The speech he delivers at the Syndicate Delmonico Dinner, is justly applauded by the New York Press as a masterpiece of astuteness. He appears to be the only one of the party who has an eye for the dark. She fancies she may know a more widely awake in the abstract. But now, thanks to jubilant Journals and Homeric laughter over the Continent, the secret is out, in so far as the concurrents are all unmasked and exposed for the edification of the American public. Dr. Bouthoin's eyebrows are up, Mr. Semhians disfigures his name by greatly gaping. Shall they return to their Great Britain indignant? Patriotism, with the sauce of a luxurious expedition at no cost to the private purse, restrains them. Moreover, there is no sign of any one of the others intending to quit the expedition; and Mr. Semhians has done a marvel or two in the cricket-field: Old England looks up where she can. What is painfully extraordinary to our couple, they find in the frigid attitude of the Americans toward their 'common tongue'; together with the rumour of a design to despatch an American rival emissary to Japan.

Nesta listened, inquired, commented, laughed; the ladies could not have a doubt that she was interested and understood. She would have sketches of scenes between Delphica and M. Falarique, with whom the young Germania was cleverly ingenuous indeed—a seminary Celimene; and between Delphica and M. Mytharete, with whom she was archaeological, ravishingly amoebaean of Homer. Dr. Gannius holds a trump card in his artless daughter, conjecturally, for the establishment of the language of the gutturals in the far East. He has now a suspicion, that the inventive M. Falarique, melted down to sobriety by misfortune, may some day startle their camp by the cast of more than a crow into it, and he is bent on establishing alliances; frightens the supple Signor Jeridomani to lingual fixity; eulogizes Football, with Dr. Bouthoin; and retracts, or modifies, his dictum upon the English, that, 'masculine brawn they have in their bodies, but muscle they have not in their feminine minds'; to exalt them, for a signally clean, if a dense, people: 'Amousia, not Alousia, is their enemy:'—How, when we have the noblest crop of poets? 'You have never heartily embraced those aliens among you until you learnt from us, that you might brag of them.'—Have they not endowed us with the richest of languages? 'The words of which are used by you, as old slippers, for puns.' Mr. Semhians has been superciliously and ineffectively punning in foreign presences: he and his chief are inwardly shocked by a new perception; What if, now that we have the populace for paymaster, subservience to the literary tastes of the populace should reduce the nation to its lowest mental level, and render us not only unable to compete with the foreigner, but unintelligible to him, although so proudly paid at home! Is it not thus that nations are seen of the Highest to be devouring themselves?

'For,' says Dr. Gannius, as if divining them, 'this excessive and applauded productiveness, both of your juvenile and your senile, in your modern literature, is it ever a crop? Is it even the restorative perishable stuff of the markets? Is it not rather your street-pavement's patter of raindrops, incessantly in motion, and as fruitful?' Mr. Semhians appeals to Delphica. 'Genius you have,' says she, stiffening his neck-band, 'genius in superabundance':—he throttles to the complexion of the peony:—'perhaps criticism is wanting.' Dr. Gannius adds: 'Perhaps it is the drill-sergeant everywhere wanting for an unrivalled splendid rabble!'

Colney left the whole body of concurrents on the raised flooring of a famous New York Hall, clearly entrapped, and incited to debate before an enormous audience, as to the merits of their respective languages. 'I hear,' says Dr. Bouthoin to Mr. Semhians (whose gape is daily extending), 'that the tickets cost ten dollars!'

There was not enough of Delphicafor Nests.

Colney asked: 'Have you seen any of our band?'

'No,' she said, with good cheer, and became thoughtful, conscious of a funny reason for the wish to hear of the fictitious creature disliked by Dudley. A funny and a naughty reason, was it? Not so very naughty: but it was funny; for it was a spirit of opposition to Dudley, without an inferior feeling at all, such as girls should have.

Colney brought his viola for a duet; they had a pleasant musical evening, as in old days at Creckholt; and Nesta, going upstairs with the ladies to bed, made them share her father's amused view of the lamb of the flock this bitter gentleman became when he had the melodious instrument tucked under his chin. He was a guest for the night. Dressing in the early hour, Nests saw him from her window on the parade, and soon joined him, to hear him at his bitterest, in the flush of the brine. 'These lengths of blank-faced terraces fronting sea!' were the satirist's present black beast. 'So these moneyed English shoulder to the front place; and that is the appearance they offer to their commercial God!' He gazed along the miles of 'English countenance,' drearily laughing. Changeful ocean seemed to laugh at the spectacle. Some Orphic joke inspired his exclamation: 'Capital!'

'Come where the shops are,' said Nesta.

'And how many thousand parsons have you here?'

'Ten, I think,' she answered in his vein, and warmed him; leading him contemplatively to scrutinize her admirers: the Rev. Septimus; Mr. Sowerby.

'News of our friend of the whimpering flute?'

'Here? no. I have to understand you!'

Colney cast a weariful look backward on the 'regiments of Anglo-Chinese' represented to him by the moneyed terraces, and said: 'The face of a stopped watch!—the only meaning it has is past date.'

He had no liking for Dudley Sowerby. But it might have been an allusion to the general view of the houses. But again, 'the meaning of it past date,' stuck in her memory. A certain face close on handsome, had a fatal susceptibility to caricature.

She spoke of her 'exile': wanted Skepsey to come down to her; moaned over the loss of her Louise. The puzzle of the reason for the long separation from her parents, was evident in her mind, and unmentioned.

They turned on to the pier.

Nesta reminded him of certain verses he had written to celebrate her visit to the place when she was a child:

'"And then along the pier we sped,
And there we saw a Whale
He seemed to have a Normous Head,
And not a bit of Tail!"'

'Manifestly a foreigner to our shores, where the exactly inverse condition rules,' Colney said.

'"And then we scampered on the beach,
To chase the foaming wave;
And when we ran beyond its reach
We all became more brave."'

Colney remarked: 'I was a poet—for once.'

A neat-legged Parisianly-booted lady, having the sea, winds very enterprising with her dark wavy, locks and jacket and skirts, gave a cry of pleasure and—a silvery 'You dear!' at sight of Nesta; then at sight of one of us, moderated her tone to a propriety equalling the most conventional. 'We ride to-day?'

'I shall be one,' said Nesta.

'It would not be the commonest pleasure to me, if you were absent.'

'Till eleven, then!'

'After my morning letter to Ned.'

She sprinkled silvery sound on that name or on the adieu, blushed, blinked, frowned, sweetened her lip-lines, bit at the underone, and passed in a discomposure.

'The lady?' Colney asked.

'She is—I meet her in the troop conducted by the riding-master: Mrs. Marsett.'

'And who is Ned?'

'It is her husband, to whom she writes every morning. He is a captain in the army, or was. He is in Norway, fishing.'

'Then the probability is, that the English officer continues his military studies.'

'Do you not think her handsome, Mr. Durance?'

'Ned may boast of his possession, when he has trimmed it and toned it a little!'

'She is different, if you are alone with her.'

'It is not unusual,' said Colney.

At eleven o'clock he was in London, and Nesta rode beside Mrs. Marsett amid the troop.

A South-easterly wind blew the waters to shifty goldleaf prints of brilliance under the sun.

'I took a liberty this morning, I called you "Dear" this morning,' the lady said. 'It's what I feel, only I have no right to blurt out everything I feel, and I was ashamed. I am sure I must have appeared ridiculous. I got quite nervous.'

'You would not be ridiculous to me.'

'I remember I spoke of Ned!

'You have spoken of him before.'

'Oh! I know: to you alone. I should like to pluck out my heart and pitch it on the waves, to see whether it would sink or swim. That's a funny idea, isn't it! I tell you everything that comes up. What shall I do when I lose you! You always make me feel you've a lot of poetry ready-made in you.'

'We will write. And you will have your husband then.'

'When I had finished my letter to Ned, I dropped my head on it and behaved like a fool for several minutes. I can't bear the thought of losing you!'

'But you don't lose me,' said Nesta; 'there is no ground for your supposing that you will. And your wish not to lose me, binds me to you more closely.'

'If you knew!' Mrs. Marsett caught at her slippery tongue, and she carolled: 'If we all knew everything, we should be wiser, and what a naked lot of people we should be!'

They were crossing the passage of a cavalcade of gentlemen, at the end of the East Cliff. One among them, large and dominant, with a playful voice of brass, cried out:

'And how do you do, Mrs. Judith Marsett—ha? Beautiful morning?'

Mrs. Marsett's figure tightened; she rode stonily erect, looked level ahead. Her woman's red mouth was shut fast on a fighting underlip.

'He did not salute you,' Nesta remarked, to justify her for not having responded.

The lady breathed a low thunder: 'Coward!'

'He cannot have intended to insult you,' said Nesta.

'That man knows I will not notice him. He is a beast. He will learn that I carry a horsewhip.'

'Are you not taking a little incident too much to heart?'

The sigh of the heavily laden came from Mrs. Marsett.

'Am I pale? I dare say. I shall go on my knees tonight hating myself that I was born "one of the frail sex." We are, or we should ride at the coward and strike him to the ground. Pray, pray do not look distressed! Now you know my Christian name. That dog of a man barks it out on the roads. It doesn't matter.'

'He has offended you before?'

'You are near me. They can't hurt me, can't touch me, when I think that I 'm talking with you. How I envy those who call you by your Christian name!'

'Nesta,' said smiling Nesta. The smile was forced, that she might show kindness, for the lady was jarring on her.

Mrs. Marsett opened her lips: 'Oh, my God, I shall be crying!—let's gallop. No, wait, I'll tell you. I wish I could! I will tell you of that man. That man is Major Worrell. One of the majors who manage to get to their grade. A retired warrior. He married a handsome woman, above him in rank, with money; a good woman. She was a good woman, or she would have had her vengeance, and there was never a word against her. She must have loved that—Ned calls him, full-blooded ox. He spent her money and he deceived her.—You innocent! Oh, you dear! I'd give the world to have your eyes. I've heard tell of "crystal clear," but eyes like yours have to tell me how deep and clear. Such a world for them to be in! I did pray, and used your name last night on my knees, that you—I said Nesta—might never have to go through other women's miseries. Ah me! I have to tell you he deceived her. You don't quite understand.'

'I do understand,' said Nesta.

'God help you!—I am excited to-day. That man is poison to me. His wife forgave him three times. On three occasions, that unhappy woman forgave him. He is great at his oaths, and a big breaker of them. She walked out one November afternoon and met him riding along with a notorious creature. You know there are bad women. They passed her, laughing. And look there, Nesta, see that groyne; that very one.' Mrs. Marsett pointed her whip hard out. 'The poor lady went down from the height here; she walked into that rough water look!—steadying herself along it, and she plunged; she never came out alive. A week after her burial, Major Worrell—I 've told you enough.'

'We 'll gallop now,' said Nesta.

Mrs. Marsett's talk, her presence hardly less, affected the girl with those intimations of tumult shown upon smooth waters when the great elements are conspiring. She felt that there was a cause why she had to pity, did pity her. It might be, that Captain Marsett wedded one who was of inferior station,' and his wife had to bear blows from cruel people. The supposition seemed probable. The girl accepted it; for beyond it, as the gathering of the gale masked by hills, lay a brewing silence. What? She did not reflect. Her quick physical sensibility curled to some breath of heated atmosphere brought about her by this new acquaintance: not pleasant, if she had thought of pleasure: intensely suggestive of our life at the consuming tragic core, round which the furnace pants. But she was unreflecting, feeling only a beyond and hidden.

Besides, she was an exile. Spelling at dark things in the dark, getting to have the sight which peruses darkness, she touched the door of a mystery that denied her its key, but showed the lock; and her life was beginning to know of hours that fretted her to recklessness. Her friend Louise was absent: she had so few friends—owing to that unsolved reason: she wanted one, of any kind, if only gentle: and this lady seemed to need her: and she flattered; Nesta was in the mood for swallowing and digesting and making sweet blood of flattery.

At one time, she liked Mrs. Marsett best absent: in musing on her, wishing her well, having said the adieu. For it was wearisome to hear praises of 'innocence'; and women can do so little to cure that 'wickedness of men,' among the lady's conversational themes; and 'love' too: it may be a 'plague,' and it may be 'heaven': it is better left unspoken. But there were times when Mrs. Marsett's looks and tones touched compassion to press her hand: an act that had a pledgeing signification in the girl's bosom: and when, by the simple avoidance of ejaculatory fervours, Mrs. Marsett's quieted good looks had a shadow of a tender charm, more pathetic than her outcries were.

These had not always the sanction of polite usage: and her English was guilty of sudden lapses to the Thameswater English of commerce and drainage instead of the upper wells. But there are many uneducated ladies in the land. Many, too, whose tastes in romantic literature betray now and then by peeps a similarity to Nesta's maid Mary's. Mrs. Marsett liked love, blood, and adventure. She had, moreover, a favourite noble poet, and she begged Nesta's pardon for naming him, and she would not name him, and told her she must not read him until she was a married woman, because he did mischief to girls. Thereupon she fell into one of her silences, emerging with a cry of hate of herself for having ever read him. She did not blame the bard. And, ah, poor bard! he fought his battle: he shall not be named for the brand on the name. He has lit a sulphur match for the lover of nature through many a generation; and to be forgiven by sad frail souls who could accuse him of pipeing devil's agent to them at the perilous instant—poor girls too!—is chastisement enough. This it is to be the author of unholy sweets: a Posterity sitting in judgement will grant, that they were part of his honest battle with the hypocrite English Philistine, without being dupe of the plea or at all the thirsty swallower of his sugary brandy. Mrs. Marsett expressed aloud her gladness of escape in never having met a man like him; followed by her regret that 'Ned' was so utterly unlike; except 'perhaps'—and she hummed; she was off on the fraternity in wickedness.

Nesta's ears were fatigued. 'My mother writes of you,' she said, to vary the subject.

Mrs. Marsett looked. She sighed downright: 'I have had my dream of a friend!—It was that gentleman with you on the pier! Your mother objects?'

'She has inquired, nothing more.'

'I am not twenty-three: not as old as I should be, for a guide to you. I know I would never do you harm. That I know. I would walk into that water first, and take Mrs. Worrell's plunge:—the last bath; a thorough cleanser for a woman! Only, she was a good woman and didn't want it, as we—as lots of us do:—to wash off all recollection of having met a man! Your mother would not like me to call you Nesta! I have never begged you to call me Judith. Damnable name!' Mrs. Marsett revelled in the heat of the curse on it, as a relief to torture of the breast, until a sense of the girl's alarmed hearing sent the word reverberating along her nerves and shocked her with such an exposure of our Shaggy wild one on a lady's lips. She murmured: 'Forgive me,' and had the passion to repeat the epithet in shrieks, and scratch up male speech for a hatefuller; but the twitch of Nesta's brows made her say: 'Do pardon me. I did something in Scripture. Judith could again. Since that brute Worrell crossed me riding with you, I loathe my name; I want to do things. I have offended you.'

'We have been taught differently. I do not use those words. Nothing else.'

'They frighten you.'

'They make me shut; that is all.'

'Supposing you were some day to discover... ta-tata, all the things there are in the world.' Mrs. Marsett let fly an artificial chirrup. 'You must have some ideas of me.'

'I think you have had unhappy experiences.'

'Nesta... just now and then! the first time we rode out together, coming back from the downs, I remember, I spoke, without thinking—I was enraged—of a case in the newspapers; and you had seen it, and you were not afraid to talk of it. I remember I thought, Well, for a girl, she's bold! I thought you knew more than a girl ought to know: until—you did—you set my heart going. You spoke of the poor women like an angel of compassion. You said, we were all mixed up with their fate—I forget the words. But no one ever heard in Church anything that touched me so. I worshipped you. You said, you thought of them often, and longed to find out what you could do to help. And I thought, if they could hear you, and only come near you, as I was—ah, my heaven! Unhappy experiences? Yes. But when men get women on the slope to their perdition, they have no mercy, none. They deceive, and they lie; they are false in acts and words; they do as much as murder. They're never hanged for it. They make the Laws! And then they become fathers of families, and point the finger at the "wretched creatures." They have a dozen names against women, for one at themselves.'

'It maddens me at times to think…!' said Nesta, burning with the sting of vile names.

Oh, there are bad women as well as bad men: but men have the power and the lead, and they take advantage of it; and then they turn round and execrate us for not having what they have robbed us of!'

'I blame women—if I may dare, at my age,' said Nesta, and her bosom heaved. 'Women should feel for their sex; they should not allow the names; they should go among their unhappier sisters. At the worst, they are sisters! I am sure, that fallen cannot mean—Christ shows it does not. He changes the tone of Scripture. The women who are made outcasts, must be hopeless and go to utter ruin. We should, if we pretend to be better, step between them and that. There cannot be any goodness unless it is a practiced goodness. Otherwise it is nothing more than paint on canvas. You speak to me of my innocence. What is it worth, if it is only a picture and does no work to help to rescue? I fear I think most of the dreadful names that redden and sicken us.—The Old Testament!—I have a French friend, a Mademoiselle Louise de Seines—you should hear her: she is intensely French, and a Roman Catholic, everything which we are not: but so human, so wise, and so full of the pride of her sex! I love her. It is love. She will never marry until she meets a man who has the respect for women, for all women. We both think we cannot separate ourselves from our sisters. She seems to me to wither men, when she speaks of their injustice, their snares to mislead and their cruelty when they have succeeded. She is right, it is the—brute: there is no other word.'

'And French and good!' Mrs. Marsett ejaculated. 'My Ned reads French novels, and he says, their women…. But your mademoiselle is a real one. If she says all that, I could kneel to her, French or not. Does she talk much about men and women?'

'Not often: we lose our tempers. She wants women to have professions; at present they have not much choice to avoid being penniless. Poverty, and the sight of luxury! It seems as if we produced the situation, to create an envious thirst, and cause the misery. Things are improving for them; but we groan at the slowness of it.'

Mrs. Marsett now declared a belief, that women were nearly quite as bad as men. 'I don't think I could take up with a profession. Unless to be a singer. Ah! Do you sing?'

Nesta smiled: 'Yes, I sing.'

'How I should like to hear you! My Ned's a thorough Englishman—gentleman, you know: he cares only for sport; Shooting, Fishing, Hunting; and Football, Cricket, Rowing, and matches. He's immensely proud of England in those things. And such muscle he has! though he begins to fancy his heart's rather weak. It's digestion, I tell him. But he takes me to the Opera sometimes—Italian Opera; he can't stand German. Down at his place in Leicestershire, he tells me, when there 's company, he has—I'm sure you sing beautifully. When I hear beautiful singing, even from a woman they tell tales of, upon my word, it's true, I feel my sins all melting out of me and I'm new-made: I can't bear Ned to speak. Would you one day, one afternoon, before the end of next week?—it would do me such real good, you can't guess how much; if I could persuade you! I know I'm asking something out of rules. For just half an hour: I judge by your voice in talking. Oh! it would do me good-good-good to hear you sing. There is a tuned piano—a cottage; I don't think it sounds badly. You would not see any great harm in calling on me? once!'

'No,' said Nesta. And it was her nature that projected the word. Her awakened wits were travelling to her from a distance, and she had an intimation of their tidings; and she could not have said what they were; or why, for a moment, she hesitated to promise she would come. Her vision of the reality of things was without written titles, to put the stamp of the world on it. She felt this lady to be one encompassed and in the hug of the elementary forces, which are the terrors to inexperienced pure young women. But she looked at her, and dared trust those lips, those eyes. She saw, through whatever might be the vessel, the spirit of the woman; as the upper nobility of our brood are enabled to do in a crisis mixed of moral aversion and sisterly sympathy, when nature cries to them, and the scales of convention, the mud-spots of accident, even naughtiness, even wickedness, all misfortune's issue, if we but see the one look upward, fall away. Reason is not excluded from these blind throbs of a blood that strikes to right the doings of the Fates. Nesta did not err in her divination of the good and the bad incarnate beside her, though both good and bad were behind a curtain; the latter sparing her delicate senses, appealing to chivalry, to the simply feminine claim on her. Reason, acting in her heart as a tongue of the flames of the forge where we all are wrought, told her surely that the good predominated. She had the heart which is at our primal fires when nature speaks.

She gave the promise to call on Mrs. Marsett and sing to her.

'An afternoon? Oh! what afternoon?' she was asked, and she said: 'This afternoon, if you like.'

So it was agreed: Mrs. Marsett acted violently the thrill of delight she felt in the prospect.

The ladies Dorothea and Virginia, consulted, and pronounced the name of Marsett to be a reputable County name. 'There was a Leicestershire baronet of the name of Marsett.' They arranged to send their button-blazing boy at Nesta's heels. Mrs. Marsett resided in a side-street not very distant from the featureless but washed and orderly terrace of the glassy stare at sea.

CHAPTER XXIX

SHOWS ONE OF THE SHADOWS OF THE WORLD CROSSING A VIRGIN'S MIND

Nasta and her maid were brought back safely through the dusk by their constellation of a boy, to whom the provident ladies had entrusted her. They could not but note how short her syllables were. Her face was only partly seen. They had returned refreshed from their drive on the populous and orderly parade—so fair a pattern of their England!—after discoursing of 'the dear child,' approving her manners, instancing proofs of her intelligence, nay, her possession of 'character.' They did so, notwithstanding that these admissions were worse than their growing love for the girl, to confound established ideas. And now, in thoughtfulness on her behalf, Dorothea said, 'We have considered, Nesta, that you may be lonely; and if it is your wish, we will leave our card on your new acquaintance.' Nesta took her hand and kissed it; she declined, saying, 'No,' without voice.

They had two surprises at the dinner-hour. One was the card of Dartrey Fenellan, naming an early time next day for his visit; and the other was the appearance of the Rev. Stuart Rem, a welcome guest. He had come to meet his Bishop.

He had come also with serious information for the ladies, regarding the Rev. Abram Posterley. No sooner was this out of his mouth than both ladies exclaimed:

'Again!' So serious was it, that there had been a consultation at the Wells; Mr. Posterley's friend, the Rev. Septimus Barmby, and his own friend, the Rev. Groseman Buttermore, had journeyed from London to sit upon the case: and, 'One hoped,' Mr. Stuart Rem said, 'poor Posterley would be restored to the senses he periodically abandoned.' He laid a hand on Tasso's curls, and withdrew it at a menace of teeth. Tasso would submit to rough caresses from Mr. Posterley; he would not allow Mr. Stuart Rem to touch him. Why was that? Perhaps for the reason of Mr. Posterley's being so emotional as perpetually to fall a victim to some bright glance and require the rescue of his friends; the slave of woman had a magnet for animals!

Dorothea and Virginia were drawn to compassionate sentiments, in spite of the provokeing recurrence of Mr. Posterley's malady. He had not an income to support a wife. Always was this unfortunate gentleman entangling himself in a passion for maid or widow of the Wells and it was desperate, a fever. Mr. Stuart Rem charitably remarked on his taking it so severely because of his very scrupulous good conduct. They pardoned a little wound to their delicacy, and asked: 'On this occasion?' Mr. Stuart Rem named a linendraper's establishment near the pantiles, where a fair young woman served. 'And her reputation?' That was an article less presentable through plate-glass, it seemed: Mr. Stuart Rem drew a prolonged breath into his nose.

'It is most melancholy!' they said in unison. 'Nothing positive,' said he. 'But the suspicion of a shadow, Mr. Stuart Rem! You will not permit it?' He stated, that his friend Buttermore might have influence. Dorothea said: 'When I think of Mr. Posterley's addiction to ceremonial observances, and to matrimony, I cannot but think of a sentence that fell from Mr. Durance one day, with reference to that division of our Church: he called it:—you frown! and I would only quote Mr. Durance to you in support of your purer form, as we hold it to be—with the candles, the vestments, Confession, alas! he called it, "Rome and a wife."'

Mr. Stuart Rem nodded an enforced assent: he testily dismissed mention of Mr. Durance, and resumed on Mr. Posterley.

The good ladies now, with some of their curiosity appeased, considerately signified to him, that a young maiden was present.

The young maiden had in heart stuff to render such small gossip a hum of summer midges. She did not imagine the dialogue concerned her in any way. She noticed Mr. Stuart Rem's attentive scrutiny of her from time to time. She had no sensitiveness, hardly a mind for things about her. To-morrow she was to see Captain Dartrey. She dwelt on that prospect, for an escape from the meshes of a painful hour—the most woeful of the hours she had yet known-passed with Judith Marsett: which dragged her soul through a weltering of the deeps, tossed her over and over, still did it with her ideas. It shocked her nevertheless to perceive how much of the world's flayed life and harsh anatomy she had apprehended, and so coldly, previous to Mrs. Marsett's lift of the veil in her story of herself: a skipping revelation, terrible enough to the girl; whose comparison of the previously suspected things with the things now revealed imposed the thought of her having been both a precocious and a callous young woman: a kind of 'Delphica without the erudition,' her mind phrased it airily over her chagrin.—And the silence of Dudley proved him to have discovered his error in choosing such a person—he was wise, and she thanked him. She had an envy of the ignorant-innocents adored by the young man she cordially thanked for quitting her. She admired the white coat of armour they wore, whether bestowed on them by their constitution or by prudence. For while combating mankind now on Judith Marsett's behalf, personally she ran like a hare from the mere breath of an association with the very minor sort of similar charges; ardently she desired the esteem of mankind; she was at moments abject. But had she actually been aware of the facts now known?

Those wits of the virgin young, quickened to shrewdness by their budding senses—and however vividly—require enlightenment of the audible and visible before their sterner feelings can be heated to break them away from a blushful dread and force the mind to know. As much as the wilfully or naturally blunted, the intelligently honest have to learn by touch: only, their understandings cannot meanwhile be so wholly obtuse as our society's matron, acting to please the tastes of the civilized man—a creature that is not clean-washed of the Turk in him—barbarously exacts. The signor aforesaid is puzzled to read the woman, who is after all in his language; but when it comes to reading the maiden, she appears as a phosphorescent hieroglyph to some speculative Egyptologer; and he insists upon distinct lines and characters; no variations, if he is to have sense of surety. Many a young girl is misread by the amount she seems to know of our construction, history, and dealings, when it is not more than her sincere ripeness of nature, that has gathered the facts of life profuse about her, and prompts her through one or other of the instincts, often vanity, to show them to be not entirely strange to her; or haply her filly nature is having a fling at the social harness of hypocrisy. If you (it is usually through the length of ears of your Novelist that the privilege is yours) have overheard queer communications passing between girls, and you must act the traitor eavesdropper or Achilles masquerader to overhear so clearly, these, be assured, are not specially the signs of their corruptness. Even the exceptionally cynical are chiefly to be accused of bad manners. Your Moralist is a myopic preacher, when he stamps infamy, on them, or on our later generation, for the kick they have at grandmother decorum, because you do not or cannot conceal from them the grinning skeleton behind it.

Nesta once had dreams of her being loved: and she was to love in return for a love that excused her for loving double, treble; as not her lover could love, she thought with grateful pride in the treasure she was to pour out at his feet; as only one or two (and they were women) in the world had ever loved. Her notion of the passion was parasitic: man the tree, woman the bine: but the bine was flame to enwind and to soar, serpent to defend, immortal flowers to crown. The choice her parents had made for her in Dudley, behind the mystery she had scent of, nipped her dream, and prepared her to meet, as it were, the fireside of a November day instead of springing up and into the dawn's blue of full summer with swallows on wing. Her station in exile at the Wells of the weariful rich, under the weight of the sullen secret, unenlivened by Dudley's courtship, subdued her to the world's decrees; phrased thus: 'I am not to be a heroine.' The one golden edge to the view was, that she would greatly please her father.

Her dream of a love was put away like a botanist's pressed weed. But after hearing Judith Marsett's wild sobs, it had no place in her cherishing. For, above all, the unhappy woman protested love to have been the cause of her misery. She moaned of 'her Ned'; of his goodness, his deceitfulness, her trustfulness; his pride and the vileness of his friends; her longsuffering and her break down of patience. It was done for the proof of her unworthiness of Nesta's friendship: that she might be renounced, and embraced. She told the pathetic half of her story, to suit the gentle ear, whose critical keenness was lost in compassion. How deep the compassion, mixed with the girl's native respect for the evil-fortuned, may be judged by her inaccessibility to a vulgar tang that she was aware of in the deluge of the torrent, where Innocence and Ned and Love and a proud Family and that beast Worrell rolled together in leaping and shifting involutions.

A darkness of thunder was on the girl. Although she was not one to shrink beneath it like the small bird of the woods, she had to say within herself many times, 'I shall see Captain Dartrey to-morrow,' for a recovery and a nerving. And with her thought of him, her tooth was at her underlip, she struggled abashed, in hesitation over men's views of her sex, and how to bring a frank mind to meet him; to be sure of his not at heart despising; until his character swam defined and bright across her scope. 'He is good to women.' Fragments of conversation, principally her father's, had pictured Captain Dartrey to her most manfully tolerant toward a frivolous wife.

He came early in the morning, instantly after breakfast.

Not two minutes had passed before she was at home with him. His words, his looks, revived her spirit of romance, gave her the very landscapes, and new ones. Yes, he was her hero. But his manner made him also an adored big brother, stamped splendid by the perils of life. He sat square, as if alert to rise, with an elbow on a knee, and the readiest turn of head to speakers, the promptest of answers, eyes that were a brighter accent to the mouth, so vividly did look accompany tone. He rallied her, chatted and laughed; pleased the ladies by laughing at Colney Durance, and inspired her with happiness when he spoke of England:—that 'One has to be in exile awhile, to see the place she takes.'

'Oh, Captain Dartrey, I do like to hear you say so,' she cried; his voice was reassuring also in other directions: it rang of true man.

He volunteered, however, a sad admission, that England had certainly lost something of the great nation's proper conception of Force: the meaning of it, virtue of it, and need for it. 'She bleats for a lesson, and will get her lesson.'

But if we have Captain Dartrey, we shall come through! So said the sparkle of Nesta's eyes.

'She is very like her father,' he said to the ladies.

'We think so,' they remarked.

'There's the mother too,' said he; and Nesta saw that the ladies shadowed.

They retired. Then she begged him to 'tell her of her own dear mother.' The news gave comfort, except for the suspicion, that the dear mother was being worn by her entertaining so largely. 'Papa is to blame,' said Nesta.

'A momentary strain. Your father has an idea of Parliament; one of the London Boroughs.'

'And I, Captain Dartrey, when do I go back to them?'

'Your mother comes down to consult with you. And now, do we ride together?'

'You are free?'

'My uncle, Lord Clan, lets me out.'

'To-day?'

'Why, yes!'

'This morning?'

'In an hour's time.'

'I will be ready.'

Nesta sent a line of excuse to Mrs. Marsett, throwing in a fervent adjective for balm.

That fair person rode out with the troop under conduct of the hallowing squire of the stables, and passed by Nesta on horseback beside Dartrey Fenellan at the steps of a huge hotel; issuing from which, pretty Mrs. Blathenoy was about to mount. Mrs. Marsett looked ahead and coloured, but she could not restrain one look at Nesta, that embraced her cavalier. Nesta waved hand to her, and nodded. Mrs. Marsett withdrew her eyes; her doing so, silent though it was, resembled the drag back to sea of the shingle-wave below her, such a screaming of tattle she heard in the questions discernible through the attitude of the cavalier and of the lady, who paused to stare, before the leap up in the saddle. 'Who is she?—what is she?—how did you know her?—where does she come from?—wears her hat on her brows!—huge gauntlets out of style!—shady! shady! shady!' And as always during her nervous tumults, the name of Worrell made diapason of that execrable uproar. Her hat on her brows had an air of dash, defying a world it could win, as Ned well knew. But she scanned her gauntlets disapprovingly. This town, we are glad to think, has a bright repute for glove-shops. And Mrs. Marsett could applaud herself for sparing Ned's money; she had mended her gloves, if they were in the fashion.—But how does the money come? Hark at that lady and that gentleman questioning Miss Radnor of everything, everything in the world about her! Not a word do they get from Miss Radnor. And it makes them the more inquisitive. Idle rich people, comfortably fenced round, are so inquisitive! And Mrs. Marsett, loving Nesta for the notice of her, maddened by the sting of tongues it was causing, heard the wash of the beach, without consciousness of analogies, but with a body ready to jump out of skin, out of life, in desperation at the sound.

She was all impulse; a shifty piece of unmercenary stratagem occasionally directing it. Arrived at her lodgings, she wrote to Nesta: 'I entreat you not to notice me, if you pass me on the road again. Let me drop, never mind how low I go. I was born to be wretched. A line from you, just a line now and then, only to show me I am not forgotten. I have had a beautiful dream. I am not bad in reality; I love goodness, I know. I cling to the thought of you, as my rescue, I declare. Please, let me hear: if it's not more than "good day" and your initials on a post-card.'

The letter brought Nesta in person to her.

CHAPTER XXX

Could there be confidences on the subject of Mrs. Marsett with Captain Dartrey?—Nesta timidly questioned her heart: she knocked at an iron door shut upon a thing alive. The very asking froze her, almost to stopping her throbs of pity for the woman. With Captain Dartrey, if with any one; but with no one. Not with her mother even. Toward her mother, she felt guilty of knowing. Her mother had a horror of that curtain. Nesta had seen it, and had taken her impressions; she, too, shrank from it; the more when impelled to draw near it. Louise de Seilles would have been another self; Louise was away; when to return, the dear friend could not state. Speaking in her ear, would have been possible; the theme precluded writing.

It was ponderous combustible new knowledge of life for a girl to hold unaided. In the presence of the simple silvery ladies Dorothea and Virginia, she had qualms, as if she were breaking out in spots before them. The ladies fancied, that Mr. Stuart Rem had hinted to them oddly of the girl; and that he might have meant, she appeared a little too cognizant of poor Mr. Abram Posterley's malady—as girls in these terrible days, only too frequently, too brazenly, are. They discoursed to her of the degeneracy of the manners, nay, the morals of young Englishwomen, once patterns! They sketched the young English gentlewoman of their time; indeed a beauty; with round red cheeks, and rounded open eyes, and a demure shut mouth, a puppet's divine ignorance; inoffensive in the highest degree, rightly worshipped. They were earnest, and Nesta struck at herself. She wished to be as they had been, reserving her painful independence.

They were good: they were the ideal women of our country; which demands if it be but the semblance of the sureness of stationary excellence; such as we have in Sevres and Dresden, polished bright and smooth as ever by the morning's flick of a duster; perhaps in danger of accidents—accidents must be kept away; but enviable, admirable, we think, when we are not thinking of seed sown or help given to the generations to follow. Nesta both envied and admired; she revered them; yet her sharp intelligence, larger in the extended boundary of thought coming of strange crimson-lighted new knowledge, discerned in a dimness what blest conditions had fixed them on their beautiful barren eminence. Without challengeing it, she had a rebellious rush of sympathy for our evil-fortuned of the world; the creatures in the battle, the wounded, trodden, mud-stained: and it alarmed her lest she should be at heart one out of the fold.

She had the sympathy, nevertheless, and renewing and increasing with the pulsations of a compassion that she took for her reflective survey. The next time she saw Dartrey Fenellan, she was assured of him, as being the man who might be spoken to; and by a woman: though not by a girl; not spoken to by her. The throb of the impulse precipitating speech subsided to a dumb yearning. He noticed her look: he was unaware of the human sun in the girl's eyes taking an image of him for permanent habitation in her breast. That face of his, so clearly lined, quick, firm, with the blue smile on it like the gleam of a sword coming out of sheath, did not mean hardness, she could have vowed. O that some woman, other than the unhappy woman herself, would speak the words denied to a girl! He was the man who would hearken and help. Essential immediate help was to be given besides the noble benevolence of mind. Novel ideas of manliness and the world's need for it were printed on her understanding. For what could women do in aid of a good cause! She fawned: she deemed herself very despicably her hero's inferior. The thought of him enclosed her. In a prison, the gaoler is a demi-God-hued bright or black, as it may be; and, by the present arrangement between the sexes, she, whom the world allowed not to have an intimation from eye or ear, or from nature's blood-ripeness in commune with them, of certain matters, which it suffers to be notorious, necessarily directed her appeal almost in worship to the man, who was the one man endowed to relieve, and who locked her mouth for shame.

Thus was she, too, being put into her woman's harness of the bit and the blinkers, and taught to know herself for the weak thing, the gentle parasite, which the fiction of our civilization expects her, caressingly and contemptuously, to become in the active, while it is exacted of hero Comedy of Clowns!—that in the passive she be a rockfortress impregnable, not to speak of magically encircled. She must also have her feelings; she must not be an unnatural creature. And she must have a sufficient intelligence; for her stupidity does not flatter the possessing man. It is not an organic growth that he desires in his mate, but a happy composition. You see the world which comes of the pair.

This burning Nesta, Victor's daughter, tempered by Nataly's milder blood, was a girl in whom the hard shocks of the knowledge of life, perforce of the hardness upon pure metal, left a strengthening for generous imagination. She did not sit to brood on her injured senses or set them through speculation touching heat; they were taken up and consumed by the fire of her mind. Nor had she leisure for the abhorrences, in a heart all flowing to give aid, and uplift and restore. Self was as urgent in her as in most of the young; but the gift of humour, which had previously diverted it, was now the quick feeling for her sisterhood, through the one piteous example she knew; and broadening it, through her insurgent abasement on their behalf, which was her scourged pride of sex. She but faintly thought of blaming the men whom her soul besought for justice, for common kindness, to women. There was the danger, that her aroused young ignorance would charge the whole of the misery about and abroad upon the stronger of those two: and another danger, that the vision of the facts below the surface would discolour and disorder her views of existence. But she loved, she sprang to, the lighted world; and she had figures of male friends, to which to cling; and they helped in animating glorious historical figures on the world's library-shelves or under yet palpitating earth. Promise of a steady balance of her nature, too, was shown in the absence of any irritable urgency to be doing, when her bosom bled to help. Beyond the resolve, that she would not abandon the woman who had made confession to her, she formed no conscious resolutions. Far ahead down her journey of the years to come, she did see muffled things she might hope and would strive to do. They were chrysalis shapes. Above all, she flew her blind quickened heart on the wings of an imaginative force; and those of the young who can do that, are in their blood incorruptible by dark knowledge, irradiated under darkness in the mind. Let but the throb be kept for others. That is the one secret, for redemption; if not for preservation.

Victor descended on his marine London to embrace his girl, full of regrets at Fredi's absence from the great whirl 'overhead,' as places of multitudinous assembly, where he shone, always appeared to him. But it was not to last long; she would soon be on the surface again! At the first clasp of her, he chirped some bars of her song. He challenged her to duet before the good ladies, and she kindled, she was caught up by his gaiety, wondering at herself; faintly aware of her not being spontaneous. And she made her father laugh, just in the old way; and looked at herself in his laughter, with the thought, that she could not have become so changed; by which the girl was helped to jump to her humour. Victor turned his full front to Dorothea and Virginia, one sunny beam of delight and although it was Mr. Stuart Rem who was naughty Nesta's victim, and although it seemed a trespass on her part to speak in such a manner of a clerical gentleman, they were seized; they were the opposite partners of a laughing quadrille, lasting till they were tired out.

Victor had asked his girl, if she sang on a Sunday. The ladies remembered, that she had put the question for permission to Mr. Stuart Rem, who was opposed to secular singing.

'And what did he say?' said Victor.

Nesta shook her head: 'It was not what he said, papa; it was his look. His duty compelled him, though he loves music. He had the look of a Patriarch putting his handmaiden away into the desert.'

Dorothea and Virginia, in spite of protests within, laughed to streams. They recollected the look; she had given the portrait of Mr. Stuart Rem in the act of repudiating secular song.

'Victor conjured up a day when this darling Fredi, a child, stood before a famous picture in the Brera, at Milan; when he and her mother noticed the child's very studious graveness; and they had talked of it; he remarking, that she disapproved of the Patriarch; and Nataly, that she was taken with Hagar's face.

He seemed surprised at her not having heard from Dudley.

'How is that?' said he.

'Most probably because he has not written, papa.'

He paused after the cool reply. She had no mournful gaze at all; but in the depths of the clear eyes he knew so well, there was a coil of something animate, whatever it might be. And twice she drew a heavy breath.

He mentioned it in London. Nataly telegraphed at night for her girl to meet her next day at Dartrey's hotel.

Their meeting was incomprehensibly joyless to the hearts of each, though it was desired, and had long been desired, and mother was mother, daughter daughter, without diminution of love between them. They held hands, they kissed and clasped, they showered their tender phrases with full warm truth, and looked into eyes and surely saw one another. But the heart of each was in a battle of its own, taking wounds or crying for supports. Whether to speak to her girl at once, despite the now vehement contrary counsel of Victor, was Nataly's deliberation, under the thought of the young creature's perplexity in not seeing her at the house of the Duvidney ladies: while Nesta conjured in a flash the past impressions of her mother's shrinking distaste from any such hectic themes as this which burdened and absorbed her; and she was almost joining to it, through sympathy with any thought or feeling of one in whom she had such pride; she had the shudder of revulsion. Further, Nataly put on, rather cravenly an air, of distress, or she half designingly permitted her trouble to be seen, by way of affecting her girl's recollection when the confession was to come, that Nesta might then understand her to have been restrained from speaking, not evasive of her duty. The look was interpreted by Nesta as belonging to the social annoyances dating, in her calendar, from Creckholt, apprehensively dreaded at Lakelands. She hinted asking, and her mother nodded; not untruthfully; but she put on a briskness after the nod; and a doubt was driven into Nesta's bosom.

Her dear Skepsey was coming down to her for a holiday, she was glad to hear. Of Dudley, there was no word. Nataly shunned his name, with a superstitious dread lest any mention of him should renew pretensions that she hoped, and now supposed, were quite withdrawn. So she had told poor Mr. Barmby only yesterday, at his humble request to know. He had seen Dudley on the pantiles, walking with a young lady, he said. And 'he feared,' he said; using, a pardonable commonplace of deceit. Her compassion accounted for the 'fear' which was the wish, and caused her not to think it particularly strange, that he should imagine Dudley to have quitted the field. Now that a disengaged Dartrey Fenellan was at hand, poor Mr. Barmby could have no chance.

Dartrey came to her room by appointment. She wanted to see him alone, and he informed her, that Mrs. Blathenoy was in the hotel, and would certainly receive and amuse Nesta for any length of time.

'I will take her up,' said Nataly, and rose, and she sat immediately, and fluttered a hand at her breast. She laughed: 'Perhaps I'm tired!'

Dartrey took Nesta.

He returned, saying: 'There's a lift in the hotel. Do the stairs affect you at all?'

She fenced his sharp look. 'Laziness, I fancy; age is coming on. How is it Mrs. Blathenoy is here?'

'Well! how?' 'Foolish curiosity?' 'I think I have made her of service. I did not bring the lady here.' 'Of service to whom?' 'Why, to Victor!' 'Has Victor commissioned you?' 'You can bear to hear it. Her husband knows the story. He has a grudge... commercial reasons. I fancy it is, that Victor stood against his paper at the table of the Bank. Blathenoy vowed blow for blow. But I think the little woman holds him in. She says she does.' 'Victor prompted you?' 'It occurred as it occurred.' 'She does it for love of us?—Oh! I can't trifle. Dartrey!' 'Tell me.' 'First, you haven't let me know what you think of my Nesta.' 'She's a dear good girl.' 'Not so interesting to you as a flighty little woman!' 'She has a speck of some sort on her mind.' Nataly spied at Dudley's behaviour, and said: 'That will wear away. Is Mr. Blathenoy much here?' 'As often as he can come, I believe.' 'That is...?' 'I have seen him twice.' 'His wife remains?' 'Fixed here for the season.' 'My friend!' 'No harm, no harm!' 'But-to her!' 'You have my word of honour.' 'Yes: and she is doing you a service, at your request; you occasionally reward her with thanks; and she sees you are a man of honour. Do you not know women?'

Dartrey blew his pooh-pooh on feminine suspicions. 'There's very little left of the Don Amoroso in me. Women don't worship stone figures.'

'They do: like the sea-birds. And what do you say to me, Dartrey?—I can confess it: I am one of them: I love you. When last you left England, I kissed your hand. It was because of your manly heart in that stone figure. I kept from crying: you used to scorn us English for the "whimpering fits" you said we enjoy and must have in books, if we can't get them up for ourselves. I could have prayed to have you as brother or son. I love my Victor the better for his love of you. Oh!—poor soul—how he is perverted since that building of Lakelands! He cannot take soundings of the things he does. Formerly he confided in me, in all things: now not one;—I am the chief person to deceive. If only he had waited! We are in a network of intrigues and schemes, every artifice in London—tempting one to hate simple worthy people, who naturally have their views, and see me an impostor, and tolerate me, fascinated by him:— or bribed—it has to be said. There are ways of bribeing. I trust he may not have in the end to pay too heavily for succeeding. He seems a man pushed by Destiny; not irresponsible, but less responsible than most. He is desperately tempted by his never failing. Whatever he does!.. it is true! And it sets me thinking of those who have never had an ailment, up to a certain age, when the killing blow comes. Latterly I have seen into him: I never did before. Had I been stronger, I might have saved, or averted.... But, you will say, the stronger woman would not have occupied my place. I must have been blind too. I did not see, that his nature shrinks from the thing it calls up. He dreads the exposure he courts—or has to combat with all his powers. It has been a revelation to me of him life as well. Nothing stops him. Now it is Parliament—a vacant London Borough. He counts on a death: Ah! terrible! I have it like a snake's bite night and day.'

Nataly concluded: 'There: it has done me some good to speak. I feel so base.' She breathed heavily.

Dartrey took her hand and bent his lips to it. 'Happy the woman who has not more to speak! How long will Nesta stay here?'

'You will watch over her, Dartrey? She stays-her father wishes—up to—ah! We can hardly be in such extreme peril. He has her doctor, her lawyer, and her butler—a favourite servant—to check, and influence, her: She—you know who it is!—does not, I am now convinced, mean persecution. She was never a mean-minded woman. Oh! I could wish she were. They say she is going. Then I am to be made an "honest woman of." Victor wants Nesta, now that she is away, to stay until... You understand. He feels she is safe from any possible kind of harm with those good ladies. And I feel she is the safer for having you near. Otherwise, how I should pray to have you with us! Daily I have to pass through, well, something like the ordeal of the red-hot ploughshares—and without the innocence, dear friend! But it's best that my girl should not have to be doing the same; though she would have the innocence. But she writhes under any shadow of a blot. And for her to learn the things that are in the world, through her mother's history!—and led to know it by the falling away of friends, or say, acquaintances! However ignorant at present, she learns from a mere nothing. I dread!.... In a moment, she is a blaze of light. There have been occurrences. Only Victor could have overcome them! I had to think it better for my girl, that she was absent. We are in such a whirl up there! So I work round again to "how long?" and the picture of myself counting the breaths of a dying woman. The other day I was told I was envied!'

'Battle, battle, battle; for all of us, in every position!' said Dartrey sharply, to clip a softness: 'except when one's attending on an invalid uncle. Then it's peace; rather like extinction. And I can't be crying for the end either. I bite my moustache and tap foot on the floor, out of his hearing; make believe I'm patient. Now I 'll fetch Nesta.'

Mrs. Blathenoy came down with an arm on Nesta's shoulder. She held a telegram, and said to Nataly—

'What can this mean? It's from my husband; he puts "Jacob": my husband's Christian name:—so like my husband, where there's no concealment! There—he says:

"Down to-night else pack ready start to-morrow." Can it signify, affairs are bad with my husband in the city?'

It had that signification to Nataly's understanding. At the same time, the pretty little woman's absurd lisping repetition of 'my husband' did not seem without design to inflict the wound it caused.

In reality, it was not malicious; it came of the bewitchment of a silly tongue by her knowledge of the secret to be controlled: and after contrasting her fortunes with Nataly's, on her way downstairs, she had comforted herself by saying, that at least she had a husband. She was not aware that she dealt a hurt until she had found a small consolation in the indulgence: for Captain Dartrey Fenellan admired this commanding figure of a woman, who could not legally say that which the woman he admired less, if at all, legally could say.

'I must leave you to interpret,' Nataly remarked.

Mrs. Blathenoy resented her unbefitting queenly style. For this reason, she abstained from an intended leading up to mention of the 'singular-looking lady' seen riding with Miss Radnor more than once; and as to whom, Miss Radnor (for one gives her the name) had not just now, when questioned, spoken very clearly. So the mother's alarms were not raised.

And really it was a pity, Mrs. Blathenoy said to Dartrey subsequently; finding him colder than before Mrs. Radnor's visit; it was a pity, because a young woman in Miss Radnor's position should not by any possibility be seen in association with a person of commonly doubtful appearance.

She was denied the petulant satisfaction of rousing the championship bitter to her. Dartrey would not deliver an opinion on Miss Radnor's conduct. He declined, moreover, to assist in elucidating the telegram by 'looking here,' and poring over the lines beside a bloomy cheek. He was petulantly whipped on the arm with her glove, and pouted at. And it was then—and then only or chiefly through Nataly's recent allusion—that the man of honour had his quakings in view of the quagmire, where he was planted on an exceedingly narrow causeway, not of the firmest. For she was a pretty little woman, one of the prize gifts of the present education of women to the men who are for having them quiescent domestic patterns; and her artificial ingenuousness or candid frivolities came to her by nature to kindle the nature of the gentleman on the other bank of the stream, and witch him to the plunge, so greatly mutually regretted after taken: an old duet to the moon.

Dartrey escaped to the Club, where he had a friend. The friend was Colonel Sudley, one of the modern studious officers, not in good esteem with the authorities. He had not forgiven Dartrey for the intemperateness which cut off a brilliant soldier from the service. He was reduced to acknowledge, however, that there was a sparkling defence for him to reply with, in the shape of a fortune gained and where we have a Society forcing us to live up to an expensive level, very trying to a soldier's income, a fortune gained will offer excuses for misconduct short of disloyal or illegal. They talked of the state of the Army: we are moving. True, and at the last Review, the 'march past' was performed before a mounted generalissimo profoundly asleep, head on breast. Our English military 'moving' may now be likened to Somnolency on Horseback. 'Oh, come, no rancour,' said the colonel; 'you know he's a kind old boy at heart; nowhere a more affectionate man alive!'

'So the sycophants are sure of posts!'

'Come, I say! He's devoted to the Service.'

'Invalid him, and he shall have a good epitaph.'

'He's not so responsible as the taxpayer.'

'There you touch home. Mother Goose can't imagine the need for defence until a hand's at her feathers.'

'What about her shrieks now and then?'

'Indigestion of a surfeit?'

They were in a laughing wrangle when two acquaintances of the colonel's came near. One of them recognized Dartrey. He changed a prickly subject to one that is generally as acceptable to the servants of Mars. His companion said: 'Who is the girl out with Judith Marsett?' He flavoured eulogies of the girl's good looks in easy garrison English. She was praised for sitting her horse well. One had met her on the parade, in the afternoon, walking with Mrs. Marsett. Colonel Sudley had seen them on horseback. He remarked to Dartrey:

'And by the way, you're a clean stretch ahead of us. I've seen you go by these windows, with the young lady on one side, and a rather pretty woman on the other too.'

'Nothing is unseen in this town!' Dartrey rejoined.

Strolling to his quarters along the breezy parade at night, he proposed to himself, that he would breathe an immediate caution to Nesta. How had she come to know this Mrs. Marsett? But he was more seriously thinking of what Colney Durance called 'The Mustard Plaster'; the satirist's phrase for warm relations with a married fair one: and Dartrey, clear of any design to have it at his breast, was beginning to take intimations of pricks and burns. They are an almost positive cure of inflammatory internal conditions. They were really hard on him, who had none to be cured.

The hour was nigh midnight. As he entered his hotel, the porter ran off to the desk in his box, and brought him a note, saying, that a lady had left it at half-past nine. Left it?—Then the lady could not be the alarming lady. He was relieved. The words of the letter were cabalistic; these, beneath underlined address:

'I beg you to call on me, if I do not see you this evening. It is urgent; you will excuse me when I explain. Not late to-morrow. I am sure you will not fail to come. I could write what would be certain to bring you. I dare not trust any names to paper.'

The signature was, Judith Marsett.

CHAPTER XXXI

SHOWS HOW THE SQUIRES IN A CONQUEROR'S SERVICE HAVE AT TIMES TO DO KNIGHTLY CONQUEST OF THEMSELVES

By the very earliest of the trains shot away to light and briny air from London's November gloom, which knows the morning through increase of gasjets, little Skepsey was hurried over suburban chimneys, in his friendly third-class carriage; where we have reminders of ancient pastoral times peculiar to our country, as it may chance; but where a man may speak to his neighbour right off without being deemed offensive. That is homely. A social fellow knitting closely to his fellows when he meets them, enjoys it, even at the cost of uncushioned seats he can, if imps are in him, merryandrew as much as he pleases; detested punctilio does not reign there; he can proselytize for the soul's welfare; decry or uphold the national drink; advertize a commercial Firm deriving prosperity from the favour of the multitude; exhort to patriotism. All is accepted. Politeness is the rule, according to Skepsey's experience of the Southern part of the third-class kingdom. And it is as well to mark the divisions, for the better knowledge of our countrymen. The North requires volumes to itself.

The hard-grained old pirate-stock Northward has built the land, and is to the front when we are at our epic work. Meanwhile it gets us a blowzy character, by shouldering roughly among the children of civilization. Skepsey, journeying one late afternoon up a Kentish line, had, in both senses of the word, encountered a long-limbed navvy; an intoxicated, he was compelled by his manly modesty to desire to think; whose loathly talk, forced upon the hearing of a decent old woman opposite him, passed baboonish behaviour; so much so, that Skepsey civilly intervened; subsequently inviting him to leave the carriage and receive a lesson at the station they were nearing. Upon his promising faithfully, that it should be a true and telling lesson, the navvy requested this pygmy spark to flick his cheek, merely to show he meant war in due sincerity; and he as faithfully, all honour, promising not to let it bring about a breakage of the laws of the Company, Skepsey promptly did the deed. So they went forth.

Skepsey alluded to the incident, for an example of the lamentable deficiency in science betrayed by most of our strong men when put to it; and the bitter thought, that he could count well nigh to a certainty on the total absence of science in the long-armed navvy, whose fist on his nose might have been as the magnet of a pin, was chief among his reminiscences after the bout, destroying pleasure for the lover of Old England's might. One blow would have sent Skepsey travelling. He was not seriously struck once. They parted, shaking hands; the navvy confessing himself to have 'drunk a drop'; and that perhaps accounted for his having been 'topped by a dot on him.'

He declined to make oath never to repeat his offence; but said, sending his vanquisher to the deuce, with an amicable push at his shoulder, 'Damned if I ever forget five foot five stretched six foot flat!'

Skepsey counted his feet some small amount higher; but our hearty rovers' sons have their ballad moods when giving or taking a thrashing. One of the third-class passengers, a lad of twenty, became Skepsey's pupil, and turned out clever with the gloves, and was persuaded to enter the militia, and grew soon to be a corporal. Thus there was profit of the affair, though the navvy sank out of sight. Let us hope and pray he will not insult the hearing of females again. If only females knew how necessary it is, for their sakes, to be able to give a lesson now and then! Ladies are positively opposed. And Judges too, who dress so like them. The manhood of our country is kept down, in consequence. Mr. Durance was right, when he said something about the state of war being wanted to weld our races together: and yet we are always praying for the state of peace, which causes cracks and gaps among us! Was that what he meant by illogical? It seemed to Skepsey—oddly, considering his inferior estimate of the value of the fair sex—that a young woman with whom he had recently made acquaintance; and who was in Brighton now, upon missionary work; a member of the 'Army,' an officer of advancing rank, Matilda Pridden, by name; was nearer to the secret of the right course of conduct for individual citizens and the entire country than any gentleman he knew.

Yes, nearer to it than his master was! Thinking of Mr. Victor Radnor, Skepsey fetched a sigh. He had knocked at his master's door at the office one day, and imagining the call to enter, had done so, and had seen a thing he could not expunge. Lady Grace Halley was there. From matters he gathered, Skepsey guessed her to be working for his master among the great folks, as he did with Jarniman, and Mr. Fenellan with Mr. Carling. But is it usual; he asked himself—his natural veneration framing the rebuke to his master thus—to repay the services of a lady so warmly?—We have all of us an ermined owl within us to sit in judgement of our superiors as well as our equals; and the little man, notwithstanding a servant's bounden submissiveness, was forced to hear the judicial pronouncement upon his master's behaviour. His master had, at the same time, been saying most weighty kind words more and more of late: one thing:—that, if he gave all he had to his fellows, and did all he could, he should still be in their debt. And he was a very wealthy gentleman. What are we to think? The ways of our superiors are wonderful. We do them homage: still we feel, we painfully feel, we are beginning to worship elsewhere. It is the pain of a detachment of the very roots of our sea-weed heart from a rock. Mr. Victor Radnor was an honour to his country. Skepsey did not place the name of Matilda Pridden beside it or in any way compare two such entirely different persons. At the same time and most earnestly, while dreading to hear, he desired to have Matilda Pridden's opinion of the case distressing him. He never could hear it, because he could never be allowed to expound the case to her. Skepsey sighed again: he as much as uttered: Oh, if we had a few thousands like her!—But what if we do have them? They won't marry! There they are, all that the country requires in wives and mothers; and like Miss Priscilla Graves, they won't marry!

He looked through sad thoughts across the benches of the compartments to the farther end of the carriage, where sat the Rev. Septimus Barmby, looking at him through a meditation as obscure if not so mournful. Few are the third-class passengers outward at that early hour in the winter season, and Skepsey's gymnastics to get beside the Rev. Septimus were unimpeded; though a tight-packed carriage of us poor journaliers would not have obstructed them with as much as a sneer. Mr. Barmby and Skepsey greeted. The latter said, he had a holiday, to pay a visit to Miss Nesta. The former said, he hoped he should see Miss Nesta. Skepsey then rapidly brought the conversation to a point where Matilda Pridden was comprised. He discoursed of the 'Army' and her position in the Army, giving instances of her bravery, the devotion shown by her to the cause of morality, in all its forms. Mr. Barmby had his fortunes on his hands at the moment, he could not lend an attentive ear; and he disliked this Army, the title it had taken, and the mixing of women and men in its ranks; not to speak of a presumption in its proceedings, and the public marching and singing. Moreover, he enjoyed his one or two permissible glasses: he doubted that the Chiefs of the Army had common benevolence for the inoffensive pipe. But the cause of morality was precious to him; morality and a fit of softness, and the union of the happiest contrast of voices, had set him for a short while, before the dawn of Nesta's day, hankering after Priscilla Graves. Skepsey's narrative of Matilda Pridden's work down at the East of London; was effective; it had the ring to thrill a responsive chord in Mr. Barmby, who mused on London's East, and martyrly service there. His present expectations were of a very different sort; but a beautiful bride, bringing us wealth, is no misleading beam, if we direct the riches rightly. Septimus, a solitary minister in those grisly haunts of the misery breeding vice, must needs accomplish less than a Septimus the husband of one of England's chief heiresses:—only not the most brilliant, owing to circumstances known to the Rev. Groseman Buttermore: strangely, and opportunely, revealed: for her exceeding benefit, it may be hoped. She is no longer the ignorant girl, to reject the protecting hand of one whose cloth is the best of cloaking. A glance at Dudley Sowerby's defection, assures our worldly wisdom too, that now is the time to sue.

Several times while Mr. Barmby made thus his pudding of the desires of the flesh and the spirit, Skepsey's tales of Matilda Pridden's heroism caught his attention. He liked her deeds; he disliked the position in which the young woman placed herself to perform them; and he said so. Women are to be women, he said.

Skepsey agreed: 'If we could get men to do the work, sir!'

Mr. Barmby was launching forth: Plenty of men!—His mouth was blocked by the reflection, that we count the men on our fingers; often are we, as it were, an episcopal thumb surveying scarce that number of followers! He diverged to censure of the marchings and the street-singing: the impediment to traffic, the annoyance to a finely musical ear. He disapproved altogether of Matilda Pridden's military display, pronouncing her to be, 'Doubtless a worthy young person.'

'Her age is twenty-seven,' said Skepsey, spying at the number of his own.

'You have known her long?' Mr. Barmby asked.

'Not long, sir. She has gone through trouble. She believes very strongly in the will:—If I will this, if I will that, and it is the right will, not wickedness, it is done—as good as done; and force is quite superfluous. In her sermons, she exhorts to prayer before action.'

'Preaches?'

'She moves a large assembly, sir.'

'It would seem, that England is becoming Americanized!' exclaimed the Conservative in Mr. Barmby. Almost he groaned; and his gaze was fish-like in vacancy, on hearing the little man speak of the present intrepid forwardness of the sex to be publicly doing. It is for men the most indigestible fact of our century: one that—by contrast throws an overearthly holiness on our decorous dutiful mothers, who contentedly worked below the surface while men unremittingly attended to their interests above.

Skepsey drew forth a paper-covered shilling-book: a translation from the French, under a yelling title of savage hate of Old England and cannibal glee at her doom. Mr. Barmby dropped his eyelashes on it, without comment; nor did he reply to Skepsey's forlorn remark: 'We let them think they could do it!'

Behold the downs. Breakfast is behind them. Miss Radnor likewise: if the poor child has a name. We propose to supply the deficiency. She does not declare war upon tobacco. She has a cultured and a beautiful voice. We abstain from enlargeing on the charms of her person. She has resources, which representatives of a rival creed would plot to secure.

'Skepsey, you have your quarters at the house of Miss Radnor's relatives?' said Mr. Barmby, as they emerged from tunnelled chalk.

'Mention, that I think of calling in the course of the day.'

A biscuit had been their breakfast without a name.

They parted at the station, roused by the smell of salt to bestow a more legitimate title on the day's restorative beginning. Down the hill, along by the shops, and Skepsey, in sight of Miss Nesta's terrace, considered it still an early hour for a visitor; so, to have the sea about him, he paid pier-money, and hurried against the briny wings of a South-wester; green waves, curls of foam, flecks of silver, under low-flying grey-dark cloud-curtains shaken to a rift, where at one shot the sun had a line of Nereids nodding, laughing, sparkling to him. Skepsey enjoyed it, at the back of thoughts military and naval. Visible sea, this girdle of Britain, inspired him to exultations in reverence. He wished Mr. Durance could behold it now and have such a breastful. He was wishing he knew a song of Britain and sea, rather fancying Mr. Durance to be in some way a bar to patriotic poetical recollection, when he saw his Captain Dartrey mounting steps out of an iron anatomy of the pier, and looking like a razor off a strap.

'Why, sir!' cried Skepsey.

'Just a plunge and a dozen strokes,' Dartrey said; 'and you'll come to my hotel and give me ten minutes of the "recreation"; and if you don't come willingly, I shall insult your country.'

'Ah! I wish Mr. Durance were here,' Skepsey rejoined.

'It would upset his bumboat of epigrams. He rises at ten o'clock to a queasy breakfast by candlelight, and proceeds to composition. His picture of the country is a portrait of himself by the artist.'

'But, sir, Captain Dartrey, you don't think as Mr. Durance does of England!'

'There are lots to flatter her, Skepsey! A drilling can't do her harm. You're down to see Miss Nesta. Ladies don't receive quite so early. And have you breakfasted? Come on with me quick.' Dartrey led him on, saying: 'You have an eye at my stick. It was a legacy to me, by word of mouth, from a seaman of a ship I sailed in, who thought I had done him a service; and he died after all. He fell overboard drunk. He perished of the villain stuff. One of his messmates handed me the stick in Cape Town, sworn to deliver it. A good knot to grasp; and it 's flexible and strong; stick or rattan, whichever you please; it gives point or caresses the shoulder; there's no break in it, whack as you may. They call it a Demerara supple-jack. I'll leave it to you.'

Skepsey declared his intention to be the first to depart. He tried the temper of the stick, bent it a bit, and admired the prompt straightening.

'It would give a good blow, sir.'

'Does its business without braining.'

Perhaps for the reason, that it was not a handsome instrument for display on fashionable promenades, Dartrey chose it among his collection by preference; as ugly dogs of a known fidelity are chosen for companions. The Demerara supple-jack surpasses bull-dogs in its fashion of assisting the master; for when once at it, the clownish-looking thing reflects upon him creditably, by developing a refined courtliness of style, while in no way showing a diminution of jolly ardour for the fray. It will deal you the stroke of a bludgeon with the playfulness of a cane. It bears resemblance to those accomplished natural actors, who conversationally present a dramatic situation in two or three spontaneous flourishes, and are themselves again, men of the world, the next minute.

Skepsey handed it back. He spoke of a new French rifle. He mentioned, in the form of query for no answer, the translation of the barking little volume he had shown to Mr. Barmby: he slapped at his breast-pocket, where it was. Not a ship was on the sea-line; and he seemed to deplore that vacancy.

'But it tells both ways,' Dartrey said. 'We don't want to be hectoring in the Channel. All we want, is to be sure of our power, so as not to go hunting and fawning for alliances. Up along that terrace Miss Nesta lives. Brighton would be a choice place for a landing.'

Skepsey temporized, to get his national defences, by pleading the country's love of peace.

'Then you give-up your portion of the gains of war—an awful disgorgement,' said Dartrey. 'If you are really for peace, you toss all your spare bones to the war-dogs. Otherwise, Quakerly preaching is taken for hypocrisy.'

'I 'm afraid we are illogical, sir,' said Skepsey, adopting one of the charges of Mr. Durance, to elude the abominable word.

'In you run, my friend.' Dartrey sped him up the steps of the hotel.

A little note lay on his breakfast-table. His invalid uncle's valet gave the morning's report of the night.

The note was from Mrs. Blathenoy: she begged Captain Dartrey, in double underlinings of her brief words, to mount the stairs. He debated, and he went.

She was excited, and showed a bosom compressed to explode: she had been weeping. 'My husband is off. He bids me follow him. What would you have me do?'

'Go.'

'You don't care what may happen to your friends, the Radnors?'

'Not at the cost of your separation from your husband.'

'You have seen him!'

'Be serious.'

'Oh, you cold creature! You know—you see: I can't conceal. And you tell me to go. "Go!" Gracious heavens! I've no claim on you; I haven't been able to do much; I would have—never mind! believe me or not. And now I'm to go: on the spot, I suppose. You've seen the man I 'm to go to, too. I would bear it, if it were not away from... out of sight of I'm a fool of a woman, I know. There's frankness for you! and I could declare you're saying "impudence" in your heart—or what you have for one. Have you one?'

'My dear soul, it 's a flint. So just think of your duty.' Dartrey played the horrid part of executioner with some skill.

Her bosom sprang to descend into abysses.

'And never a greater fool than when I sent for you to see such a face as I'm showing!' she cried, with lips that twitched and fingers that plucked at her belt. 'But you might feel my hatred of being tied to— dragged about over the Continent by that... perhaps you think a woman is not sensible of vulgarity in her husband! I 'm bothering you? I don't say I have the slightest claim. You never made love to me, never! Never so much as pressed my hand or looked. Others have—as much as I let them. And before I saw you, I had not an idea of another man but that man. So you advise me to go?'

'There's no other course.'

'No other course. I don't see one. What have I been dreaming of! Usually a woman feeling...' she struck at her breast, 'has had a soft word in her ear. "Go!" I don't blame you, Captain Dartrey. At least, you 're not the man to punish a woman for stripping herself, as I 've done. I call myself a fool—I'm a lunatic. Trust me with your hand.'

'There you are.'

She grasped the hand, and shut her eyes to make a long age of the holding on to him. 'Oh, you dear dear fellow!—don't think me unwomanly; I must tell you now: I am naked and can't disguise. I see you are ice—feel: and if you were different, I might be. You won't be hurt by hearing you've made yourself dear to me—without meaning to, I know! It began that day at Lakelands; I fell in love with you the very first minute I set eyes on you! There's a confession for a woman to make! and a married woman! I'm married, and I no more feel allegiance, as they call it, than if there never had been a ceremony and no Jacob Blathenoy was in existence. And why I should go to him! But you shan't be troubled. I did not begin to live, as a woman, before I met you. I can speak all this to you because—we women can't be deceived in that—you are one of the men who can be counted on for a friend.'

'I hope so,' Dartrey said, and his mouth hardened as nature's electricity shot sparks into him from the touch and rocked him.

'No, not yet: I will soon let it drop,' said she, and she was just then thrillingly pretty; she caressed the hand, placing it at her throat and moving her chin on it, as women fondle birds. 'I am positively to go, then?'

'Positively, you are to go; and it's my command.'

'Not in love with any one at all?'

'Not with a soul.'

'Not with a woman?'

'With no woman.'

'Nor maid?'

'No! and no to everything. And an end to the catechism!'

'It is really a flint that beats here?' she said, and with a shyness in adventurousness, she struck the point of her forefinger on the rib. 'Fancy me in love with a flint! And running to be dutiful to a Jacob Blathenoy, at my flint's command. I'm half in love with doing what I hate, because this cold thing here bids me do it. I believe I married for money, and now it looks as if I were to have my bargain with poverty to bless it.'

'There I may help,' said Dartrey, relieved at sight of a loophole, to spring to some initiative out of the paralysis cast on him by a pretty little woman's rending of her veil. A man of honour alone with a woman who has tossed concealment to the winds, is a riddled target indeed: he is tempted to the peril of cajoleing, that he may escape from the torment and the ridicule; he is tempted to sigh for the gallant spirit of his naughty adolescence. 'Come to me—will you?—apply to me, if there's ever any need. I happen to have money. And forgive me for naming it.'

She groaned: 'Don't! I'm, sure, and I thought it from the first, you're one of the good men, and the woman who meets you is lucky, and wretched, and so she ought to be! Only to you should I!... do believe that! I won't speak of what excuses I've got. You've seen.'

'Don't think of them: there'll be danger in it.

'Shall you think of me in danger?'

'Silly, silly! Don't you see you have to do with a flint! I've gone through fire. And if I were in love with you, I should start you off to your husband this blessed day.'

'And you're not the slightest wee wee bit in love with me!'

'Perfectly true; but I like you; and if we're to be hand in hand, in the time to come, you must walk firm at present.'

'I'm to go to-day?'

'You are.'

'Without again.'

The riddled target kicked. Dartrey contrasted Jacob Blathenoy with the fair wife, and commiseratingly exonerated her; he lashed at himself for continuing to be in this absurdest of postures, and not absolutely secure for all that. His head shook. 'Friends, you'll find best.'

'Well!' she sighed, 'I feel I'm doomed to go famished through life. There's never to be such a thing as, love, for me! I can't tell you no woman could: though you'll say I've told enough. I shall burn with shame when I think of it. I could go on my knees to have your arms round me once. I could kill myself for saying it!—I should feel that I had one moment of real life.—I know I ought to admire you. They say a woman hates if she's refused. I can't: I wish I were able to. I could have helped the Radnors better by staying here and threatening never to go to him unless he swore not to do them injury. He's revengeful. Just as you like. You say "Go," and I go. There. I may kiss your hand?'

'Give me yours.'

Dartrey kissed the hand. She kissed the mark of his lips. He got himself away, by promising to see her to the train for Paris. Outside her door, he was met by the reflection, coming as a thing external, that he might veraciously and successfully have pleaded a passionate hunger for breakfast: nay, that he would have done so, if he had been downright in earnest. For she had the prettiness to cast a spell; a certain curve at the lips, a fluttering droop of the eyelids, a corner of the eye, that led long distances away to forests and nests. This little woman had the rosy-peeping June bud's plumpness. What of the man who refused to kiss her once? Cold antecedent immersion had to be thanked; and stringent vacuity; perhaps a spotting ogre-image of her possessor. Some sense of right-doing also, we hope. Dartrey angrily attributed his good conduct to the lowest motives. He went so far as to accuse himself of having forborne to speak of breakfast, from a sort of fascinated respect for the pitch of a situation that he despised and detested. Then again, when beginning to eat, his good conduct drew on him a chorus of the jeers of all the martial comrades he had known. But he owned he would have had less excuse than they, had he taken advantage of a woman's inability, at a weak moment, to protect herself: or rather, if he had not behaved in a manner to protect her from herself. He thought of his buried wife, and the noble in the base of that poor soul; needing constantly a present helper, for the nobler to conquer. Be true man with a woman, she must be viler than the devil has yet made one, if she does not follow a strong right lead:—but be patient, of course. And the word patience here means more than most men contain. Certainly a man like Jacob Blathenoy was a mouthful for any woman: and he had bought his wife, he deserved no pity. Not? Probably not. That view, however, is unwholesome and opens on slides. Pity of his wife, too, gets to be fervidly active with her portrait, fetches her breath about us. As for condemnation of the poor little woman, her case was not unexampled, though the sudden flare of it startled rather. Mrs. Victor could read men and women closely. Yes, and Victor, when he schemed—but Dartrey declined to be throwing blame right or left. More than by his breakfast, and in a preferable direction, he was refreshed by Skepsey's narrative of the deeds of Matilda Pridden.

'The right sort of girl for you to know, Skepsey,' he said. 'The best in life is a good woman.'

Skepsey exhibited his book of the Gallic howl.

'They have their fits now and then, and they're soon over and forgotten,' Dartrey said. 'The worst of it is, that we remember.'

After the morning's visit to his uncle, he peered at half a dozen sticks in the corner of the room, grasped their handles, and selected the Demerara supple-jack, for no particular reason; the curved knot was easy to the grasp. It was in his mind, that this person signing herself Judith Marsett, might have something to say, which intimately concerned Nesta. He fell to brooding on it, until he wondered why he had not been made a trifle anxious by the reading of the note overnight. Skepsey was left at Nesta's house.

Dartrey found himself expected by the servant waiting on Mrs. Marsett.

CHAPTER XXXII

SHOWS HOW TEMPER MAY KINDLE TEMPER AND AN INDIGNANT WOMAN GET HER WEAPON

Judith Marsett stood in her room to receive Nesta's hero. She was flushed, and had thinned her lips for utterance of a desperate thing, after the first severe formalities.

Her aim was to preserve an impressive decorum. She was at the same time burning to speak out furious wrath, in words of savage rawness, if they should come, as a manner of slapping the world's cheek for the state to which it reduces its women; whom one of the superior creatures can insult, and laugh.

Men complaining of the 'peace which is near their extinction,' have but to shuffle with the sex; they will experience as remarkable a change as if they had passed off land on to sea.

Dartrey had some flitting notion of the untamed original elements women can bring about us, in his short observant bow to Mrs. Marsett, following so closely upon the scene with Mrs. Blathenoy.

But this handsome woman's look of the dull red line of a sombre fire, that needed only stir of a breath to shoot the blaze, did not at all alarm him. He felt refreshingly strung by it.

She was discerned at a glance to be an aristocratic member of regions where the senses perpetually simmer when they are not boiling. The talk at the Club recurred to him. How could Nesta have come to know the woman? His questioning of the chapter of marvellous accidents, touched Nesta simply, as a young girl to be protected, without abhorrently involving the woman. He had his ideas of the Spirit of Woman stating her case to the One Judge, for lack of an earthly just one: a story different from that which is proclaimed pestilential by the body of censors under conservatory glass; where flesh is delicately nurtured, highly prized; spirit not so much so; and where the pretty tricking of the flesh is taken for a spiritual ascendancy.

In spite of her turbulent breast's burden to deliver, Mrs. Marsett's feminine acuteness was alive upon Dartrey, confirming here and there Nesta's praises of him. She liked his build and easy carriage of a muscular frame: her Ned was a heavy man. More than Dartrey's figure, as she would have said, though the estimate came second, she liked his manner with her. Not a doubt was there, that he read her position. She could impose upon some: not upon masculine eyes like these. They did not scrutinize, nor ruffle a smooth surface with a snap at petty impressions; and they were not cynically intimate or dominating or tentatively amorous: clear good fellowship was in them. And it was a blessedness (whatever might be her feeling later, when she came to thank him at heart) to be in the presence of a man whose appearance breathed of offering her common ground, whereon to meet and speak together, unburdened by the hunting world, and by the stoneing world. Such common ground seems a kind of celestial to the better order of those excluded from it.

Dartrey relieved her midway in a rigid practice of the formalities: 'I think I may guess that you have something to tell me relating to Miss Radnor?'

'It is.' Mrs. Marsett gathered up for an immediate plunge, and deferred it. 'I met her—we went out with the riding-master. She took to me. I like her—I could say' (the woman's voice dropped dead low, in a tremble), 'I love her. She is young: I could kneel to her. Do you know a Major Worrell?'

'Worrell? no.'

'He is a-calls himself a friend of my—of Captain Marsett's. He met us out one day.'

'He permitted himself to speak to Miss Radnor?'

She rejoiced in Dartrey's look. 'Not then. First let me tell you. I can hardly tell you. But Miss Radnor tells me you are not like other men. You have made your conclusions already. Are you asking what right I had to be knowing her? It is her goodness. Accident began it; I did not deceive her; as soon as ever I could I— I have Captain Marsett's promise to me: at present he's situated, he—but I opened my heart to her: as much as a woman can. It came! Did I do very wrong?'

'I'm not here to decide: continue, pray.'

Mrs. Marsett aimed at formal speech, and was driving upon her natural in anger. 'I swear I did it for the best. She is an innocent girl... young lady: only she has a head; she soon reads things. I saw the kind of cloud in her. I spoke. I felt bound to: she said she would not forsake me.—I was bound to! And it was enough to break my heart, to think of her despising me. No, she forgave, pitied;—she was kind. Those are the angels who cause us to think of changeing. I don't care for sermons, but when I meet charity: I won't bore you!'

'You don't.'

'My... Captain Marsett can't bear—he calls it Psalmody. He thinks things ought always to be as they are, with women and men; and women preachers he does detest. She is not one to preach. You are waiting to hear what I have to tell. That man Major Worrell has tried to rob me of everything I ever had to set a value on:—love, I 'd say;—he laughs at a woman like me loving.'

Dartrey nodded, to signify a known sort of fellow.

'She came here.' Mrs. Marsett's tears had risen. 'I ought not to have let her come. I invited her—for once: I am lonely. None of my sex—none I could respect! I meant it for only once. She promised to sing to me. And, Oh! how she sings! You have heard her. My whole heart came out. I declare I believe girls exist who can hear our way of life—and I'm not so bad except compared with that angel, who heard me, and was and is, I could take oath, no worse for it. Some girls can; she is one. I am all for bringing them up in complete innocence. If I was a great lady, my daughters should never know anything of the world until they were married. But Miss Radnor is a young lady who cannot be hurt. She is above us. Oh! what a treasure for a man!—and my God! for any man born of woman to insult a saint, as she is!—He is a beast!'

'Major Worrell met her here?'

'Blame me as much as you like: I do myself. Half my rage with him is at myself for putting her in the way of such a beast to annoy. Each time she came, I said it was to be the last. I let her see what a mercy from heaven she was to me. She would come. It has not been many times. She wishes me either to... Captain Marsett has promised. And nothing seems hard—to me when my own God's angel is by. She is! I'm not such a bad woman, but I never before I knew her knew the meaning of the word virtue. There is the young lady that man worried with his insulting remarks! though he must have known she was a lady:— because he found her in my rooms.'

'You were present when, as you say, he insulted her?'

'I was. Here it commenced; and he would see her downstairs.'

'You heard?'

'Of course, I never left her.'

'Give me a notion...'

'To get her to make an appointment: to let him conduct her home.'

'She was alone?'

'Her maid was below.'

'And this happened...?'

'Yesterday, after dark. My Ned—Captain Marsett encourages him to be familiar. I should be the lowest of women if I feared the threats of such a reptile of a man. I could tell you more. I can't always refuse his visits, though if Ned knew the cur he is! Captain Marsett is easy-going.'

'I should like to know where he lives.'

She went straight to the mantelpiece, and faced about with a card, handing it, quite aware that it was a charge of powder.

Desperate things to be done excused the desperate said; and especially they seemed a cover to the bald and often spotty language leaping out of her, against her better taste, when her temper was up.

'Somewhere not very distant,' said Dartrey perusing. 'Is he in the town to-day, do you know?'

'I am not sure; he may be. Her name...'

'Have no fear. Ladies' names are safe.'

'I am anxious that she may not be insulted again.'

'Did she show herself conscious of it?'

'She stopped speaking: she looked at the door. She may come again—or never! through that man!'

'You receive him, at his pleasure?'

'Captain Marsett wishes me to. He is on his way home. He calls Major Worrell my pet spite. All I want is; not to hear of the man. I swear he came yesterday on the chance of seeing—for he forced his way up past my servant; he must have seen Miss Radnor's maid below.'

'You don't mean, that he insulted her hearing?'

'Oh! Captain Fenellan, you know the style.'

'Well, I thank you,' Dartrey said. 'The young lady is the daughter of my dearest friends. She's one of the precious—you're quite right. Keep the tears back.'

'I will.' She heaved open-mouthed to get physical control of the tide. 'When you say that of her!—how can I help it? It's I fear, because I fear... and I've no right to expect ever... but if I'm never again to look on that dear face, tell her I shall—I shall pray for her in my grave. Tell her she has done all a woman can, an angel can, to save my soul. I speak truth: my very soul! I could never go to the utter bad after knowing her. I don't—you know the world—I'm a poor helpless woman!—don't swear to give up my Ned if he does break the word he promised once; I can't see how I could. I haven't her courage. I haven't—what it is! You know her: it's in her eyes and her voice. If I had her beside me, then I could starve or go to execution—I could, I am certain. Here I am, going to do what you men hate. Let me sit.'

'Here's a chair,' said Dartrey. 'I've no time to spare; good day, for the present. You will permit me to call.'

'Oh! come'; she cried, out of her sobs, for excuse. They were genuine, or she would better have been able to second her efforts to catch a distinct vision of his retreating figure.

She beheld him, when he was in the street, turn for the district where Major Worrell had his lodgeings. That set her mind moving, and her tears fell no longer.

Major Worrell was not at home. Dartrey was informed that he might be at his Club.

At the Club he heard of the major as having gone to London and being expected down in the afternoon. Colonel Sudley named the train: an early train; the major was engaged to dine at the Club. Dartrey had information supplied to him concerning Major Worrell and Captain Marsett, also Mrs. Marsett. She had a history. Worthy citizens read the description of history with interest when the halo of Royalty is round it. They may, if their reading extends, perceive, that it has been the main turbid stream in old Mammon's train since he threw his bait for flesh. They might ask, too, whether it is likely to cease to flow while he remains potent. The lady's history was brief, and bore recital in a Club; came off quite honourably there. Regarding Major Worrell, the tale of him showed him to have a pass among men. He managed cleverly to get his pleasures out of a small income and a 'fund of anecdote.' His reputation indicated an anecdotist of the table, prevailing in the primitive societies, where the art of conversing does not come by nature, and is exercised in monosyllabic undertones or grunts until the narrator's well-masticated popular anecdote loosens a digestive laughter, and some talk ensues. He was Marsett's friend, and he boasted of not letting Ned Marsett make a fool of himself.

Dartrey was not long in shaping the man's character: Worrell belonged to the male birds of upper air, who mangle what female prey they are forbidden to devour. And he had Miss Radnor's name: he had spoken her name at the Club overnight. He had roused a sensation, because of a man being present, Percy Southweare, who was related to a man as good as engaged to marry her. The major never fell into a quarrel with sons of nobles, if he could help it, or there might have been a pretty one.

So Colonel Sudley said.

Dartrey spoke musing: 'I don't know how he may class me; I have an account to square with him.'

'It won't do in these days, my good friend. Come and cool yourself; and we'll lunch here. I shan't leave you.'

'By all means. We'll lunch, and walk up to the station, and you will point him out to me.'

Dartrey stated Major Worrell's offence. The colonel was not astonished; but evidently he thought less of Worrell's behaviour to Miss Radnor in Mrs. Marsett's presence than of the mention of her name at the Club: and that, he seemed to think, had a shade of excuse against the charge of monstrous. He blamed the young lady who could go twice to visit a Mrs. Marsett; partly exposed a suspicion of her. Dartrey let him talk. They strolled along the parade, and were near the pier.

Suddenly saying: 'There, beside our friend in clerical garb: here she comes; judge if that is the girl for the foulest of curs to worry, no matter where she's found.' Dartrey directed the colonel's attention to Nesta and Mr. Barmby turning off the pier and advancing.

He saluted. She bowed. There was no contraction of her eyelids; and her face was white. The mortal life appeared to be deadened in her cold wide look; as when the storm-wind banks a leaden remoteness, leaving blown space of sky.

The colonel said: 'No, that's not the girl a gentleman would offend.'

'What man!' cried Dartrey. 'If we had a Society for the trial of your gentleman!—but he has only to call himself gentleman to get grant of licence: and your Society protects him. It won't punish, and it won't let you. But you saw her: ask yourself—what man could offend that girl!'

'Still, my friend, she ought to keep clear of the Marsetts.'

'When I meet him, I shall treat him as one out of the law.'

'You lead on to an ultimate argument with the hangman.'

We 'll dare it, to waken the old country. Old England will count none but Worrells in time. As for discreet, if you like!—the young lady might have been more discreet. She's a girl with a big heart. If we were all everlastingly discreet!'

Dartrey may have meant, that the consequence of a prolonged conformity would be the generation of stenches to shock to purgeing tempests the tolerant heavens over such smooth stagnancy. He had his ideas about movement; about the good of women, and the health of his England. The feeling of the hopelessness of pleading Nesta's conduct, for the perfect justification of it to son or daughter of our impressing conventional world—even to a friend, that friend a true man, a really chivalrous man—drove him back in a silence upon his natural brotherhood with souls that dare do. It was a wonder, to think of his finding this kinship in a woman. In a girl?—and the world holding that virgin spirit to be unclean or shadowed because its rays were shed on foul places? He clasped the girl. Her smitten clear face, the face of the second sigh after torture, bent him in devotion to her image.

The clasping and the worshipping were independent of personal ardours: quaintly mixed with semi-paternal recollections of the little 'blue butterfly' of the days at Craye. Farm and Creckholt; and he had heard of Dudley Sowerby's pretensions to; her hand. Nesta's youthfulness cast double age on him from the child's past. He pictured the child; pictured the girl, with her look of solitariness of sight; as in the desolate wide world, where her noble compassion for a woman had unexpectedly, painfully, almost by transubstantiation, rack-screwed her to woman's mind. And above sorrowful, holy were those eyes.

They held sway over Dartrey, and lost it some steps on; his demon temper urgeing him to strike at Major Worrell, as the cause of her dismayed expression. He was not the happier for dropping to his nature; but we proceed more easily, all of us, when the strain which lifts us a foot or two off our native level is relaxed.

CHAPTER XXXIII

That ashen look of the rise out of death from one of our mortal wounds, was caused by deeper convulsions in Nesta's bosom than Dartrey could imagine.

She had gone for the walk with Mr. Barmby, reading the omen of his tones in the request. Dorothea and Virginia would have her go. The clerical gentleman, a friend of the Rev. Abram Posterley; and one who deplored poor Mr. Posterley's infatuation; and one besides who belonged to Nesta's musical choir in London: seemed a safe companion for the child. The grand organ of Mr. Barmby's voice, too, assured them of a devout seriousness in him, that arrested any scrupulous little questions. They could not conceive his uttering the nonsensical empty stuff, compliments to their beauty and what not, which girls hear sometimes from inconsiderate gentlemen, to the having of their heads turned. Moreover, Nesta had rashly promised her father's faithful servant Skepsey to walk, out with him in the afternoon; and the ladies hoped she would find the morning's walk to have been enough; good little man though Skepsey was, they were sure. But there is the incongruous for young women of station on a promenade.

Mr. Barmby headed to the pier. After pacing up and down between the briny gulls and a polka-band, he made his way forethoughtfully to the glass-sheltered seats fronting East: where, as his enthusiasm for the solemnity of the occasion excited him to say, 'We have a view of the terraces and the cliffs'; and where not more than two enwrapped invalid figures were ensconsed. Then it was, that Nesta recalled her anticipation of his possible design; forgotten by her during their talk of her dear people: Priscilla Graves and Mr. Pempton, and the Yatts, and Simeon Fenellan, Peridon and Catkin, and Skepsey likewise; and the very latest news of her mother. She wished she could have run before him, to spare him. He would not notice a sign. Girls must wait and hear.

It was an oratorio. She watched the long wave roll on to the sinking into its fellow; and onward again for the swell and the weariful lapse; and up at last bursting to the sheet of white. The far-heard roar and the near commingled, giving Mr. Barmby a semblance to the powers of ocean.

At the first direct note, the burden of which necessitated a pause, she petitioned him to be her friend, to think of himself as her friend.

But a vessel laden with merchandize, that has crossed wild seas for this particular port, is hardly to be debarred from discharging its goods on the quay by simple intimations of their not being wanted. We are precipitated both by the aim and the tedium of the lengthened voyage to insist that they be seen. We believe perforce in their temptingness; and should allurement fail, we fall back to the belief in our eloquence. An eloquence to expose the qualities they possess, is the testification in the promise of their excellence. She is to be induced by feeling to see it. We are asking a young lady for the precious gift of her hand. We respect her; and because of our continued respect, despite an obstruction, we have come to think we have a claim upon her gratitude; could she but be led to understand how different we are from some other man!—from one hitherto favoured among them, unworthy of this prize, however personally exalted and meritorious.

The wave of wide extension rolled and sank and rose, heaving lifeless variations of the sickly streaks on its dull green back.

Dudley Sowerby's defection was hinted at and accounted for, by the worldly test of worldly considerations.

What were they?—Nesta glanced.

An indistinct comparison was modestly presented, of one unmoved by worldly considerations.

But what were they? She was wakened by a lamp, and her darkness was all inflammable to it.

'Oh! Mr. Barmby, you have done me the honour to speak before; you know my answer,' she said.

'You were then subject to an influence. A false, I may say wicked, sentiment upholding celibacy.'

'My poor Louise? She never thought of influencing me. She has her views, I mine. Our friendship does not depend on a "treaty of reciprocity." We are one at heart, each free to judge and act, as it should be in friendship. I heard from her this morning. Her brother will be able to resume his military duties next month. Then she will return to me.'

'We propose!' rejoined Mr. Barmby.

Beholding the involuntary mercurial rogue-dimple he had started from a twitch at the corner, of her lips, the good gentleman pursued: 'Can we dare write our designs for the month to come? Ah!—I will say—Nesta! give me the hope I beg to have. See the seriousness. You are at liberty. That other has withdrawn his pretensions. We will not blame him. He is in expectation of exalted rank. Where there is any shadow...!' Mr. Barmby paused on his outroll of the word; but immediately, not intending to weigh down his gentle hearer with the significance in it, resumed at a yet more sonorous depth: 'He is under the obligation to his family; an old, a venerable family. In the full blaze of public opinion! His conduct can be palliated by us, too. There is a right and wrong in minor things, independent of the higher rectitude. We pardon, we can partly support, the worldly view.'

'There is a shadow?' said Nesta; and her voice was lurefully encouraging.

He was on the footing where men are precipitated by what is within them to blunder. 'On you—no. On you personally, not at all. No. It could not be deemed so. Not by those knowing, esteeming—not by him who loves you, and would, with his name, would, with his whole strength, envelop, shield ... certainly, certainly not.'

'It is on my parents?' she said.

'But to me nothing, nothing, quite nought! To confound the innocent with the guilty!... and excuses may exist. We know but how little we know!'

'It is on both my parents?' she said; with a simplicity that induced him to reply: 'Before the world. But not, I repeat...'

The band-instruments behind the sheltering glass flourished on their termination of a waltz.

She had not heeded their playing. Now she said:

'The music is over; we must not be late at lunch'; and she stood up and moved.

He sprang to his legs and obediently stepped out:

'I shall have your answer to-day, this evening? Nesta!'

'Mr. Barmby, it will be the same. You will be kind to me in not asking me again.'

He spoke further. She was dumb.

Had he done ill or well for himself and for her when he named the shadow on her parents? He dwelt more on her than on himself: he would not have wounded her to win the blest affirmative. Could she have been entirely ignorant?—and after Dudley Sowerby's defection? For such it was: the Rev. Stuart Rem had declared the union between the almost designated head of the Cantor family and a young person of no name, of worse than no birth, impossible: 'absolutely and totally impossible,' he, had said, in his impressive fashion, speaking from his knowledge of the family, and an acquaintance with Dudley. She must necessarily have learnt why Dudley Sowerby withdrew. No parents of an attractive daughter should allow her to remain unaware of her actual position in the world. It is criminal, a reduplication of the criminality! Yet she had not spoken as one astonished. She was mysterious. Women are so: young women most of all. It is undecided still whether they do of themselves conceive principles, or should submit to an imposition of the same upon them in terrorem. Mysterious truly, but most attractive! As Lady Bountiful of a district, she would have in her maturity the majestic stature to suit a dispensation of earthly good things. And, strangely, here she was, at this moment, rivalling to excelling all others of her sex (he verified it in the crowd of female faces passing), when they, if they but knew the facts, would visit her very appearance beside them on a common footing as an intrusion and a scandal. To us who know, such matters are indeed wonderful!

Moved by reflective compassion, Mr. Barmby resumed the wooer's note, some few steps after he had responded to the salutation of Dartrey Fenellan and Colonel Sudley. She did not speak. She turned her forehead to him; and the absence of the world from her eyes chilled his tongue.

He declined the pleasure of the lunch with the Duvidney ladies. He desired to be alone, to question himself fasting, to sound the deed he had done; for he had struck on a suspicion of selfishness in it: and though Love must needs be an egoism, Love is no warrant for the doing of a hurt to the creature beloved. Thoughts upon Skepsey and the tale of his Matilda Pridden's labours in poor neighbourhoods, to which he had been inattentive during the journey down to the sea, invaded him; they were persistent. He was a worthy man, having within him the spiritual impulse curiously ready to take the place where a material disappointment left vacancy. The vulgar sort embrace the devil at that stage. Before the day had sunk, Mr. Barmby's lowest wish was, to be a light, as the instrument of his Church in her ministrations amid the haunts of sin and slime, to such plain souls as Daniel Skepsey and Matilda Pridden. And he could still be that, if Nesta, in the chapters of the future, changed her mind. She might; for her good she would; he reserved the hope. His light was one to burn beneath an extinguisher.

At the luncheon table of the Duvidney ladies, it was a pain to Dorothea and Virginia to witness how poor the appetite their Nesta brought in from the briny blowy walk. They prophesied against her chances of a good sleep at night, if she did not eat heartily. Virginia timidly remarked on her paleness. Both of them put their simple arts in motion to let her know, that she was dear to them: so dear as to make them dread the hour of parting. They named their dread of it. They had consulted in private and owned to one another, that they did really love the child, and dared not look forward to what they would do without her. The dear child's paleness and want of appetite (they remembered they were observing a weak innocent girl) suggested to them mutually the idea of a young female heart sickening, for the old unhappy maiden reason. But, if only she might return with them to the Wells, the Rev. Stuart Rem would assure her to convince her of her not being quite, quite forsaken. He, or some one having sanction from Victor, might ultimately (the ladies waiting anxiously in the next room, to fold her on the warmth of their bosoms when she had heard) impart to her the knowledge of circumstances, which would, under their further tuition concerning the particular sentiments of great families and the strict duties of the scions of the race, help to account for and excuse the Hon. Dudley Sowerby's behaviour.

They went up to the drawing-room, talking of Skepsey and his tale of Miss Pridden, for Nesta's amusement. Any talk of her Skepsey usually quickened her lips to reminiscent smiles and speech. Now she held on to gazeing; and sadly, it seemed; as if some object were not present.

For a vague encouragement, Dorothea said: 'One week, and we are back home at Moorsedge!'—not so far from Cronidge, was implied, for the administering of some foolish temporary comfort. And it was as when a fish on land springs its hollow sides in alien air for the sustaining element; the girl panted; she clasped Dorothea's hand and looked at Virginia: 'My mother—I must see her!' she said. They were slightly stupefied by the unwonted mention of her mother. They made no reply. They never had done so when there was allusion to her mother. Their silence now struck a gong at the girl's bosom.

Dorothea had it in mind to say, that if she thirsted for any special comfort, the friends about her would offer consolation for confidence.

Before she could speak, Perrin the footman entered, bearing the card of the Hon. Dudley Sowerby.

Mr. Dudley Sowerby begged for an immediate interview with Miss Radnor.

The ladies were somewhat agitated, but no longer perplexed as to their duties. They had quitted Moorsedge to avoid the visit of his family. If he followed, it signified that which they could not withstand:—The 'Tivoli falls!' as they named the fateful tremendous human passion, from the reminiscences of an impressive day on their travels in youth; when the leaping torrent had struck upon a tale of love they were reading. They hurriedly entreated Nesta to command her nerves; peremptorily requested her to stay where she was; showed her spontaneously, by way of histrionic adjuration, the face to be worn by young ladies at greetings on these occasions; kissed her and left her; Virginia whispering: 'He is true!'

Dudley entered the drawing-room, charged with his happy burden of a love that had passed through the furnace. She stood near a window, well in the light; she hardly gave him welcome. His address to her was hurried, rather uncertain, coherent enough between the drop and the catch of articulate syllables. He found himself holding his hat. He placed it on the table, and it rolled foolishly; but soon he was by her side, having two free hands to claim her one.

'You are thinking, you have not heard from me! I have been much occupied,' he said. 'My brother is ill, very ill. I have your pardon?'

'Indeed you have—if it has to be asked.'

'I have it?'

'Have I to grant it?'

'I own to remissness!

'I did not blame you.'

'Nesta...!'

Her coldness was unshaken.

He repeated the call of her name. 'I should have written—I ought to have written!—I could not have expressed... You do forgive? So many things!'

'You come from Cronidge to-day?'

'From my family—to you.'

She seemed resentful. His omissions as a correspondent were explicable in a sentence. It had to be deferred.

Reviewing for a moment the enormous internal conflict undergone by him during the period of the silence between them, he wondered at the vastness of the love which had conquered objections, to him so poignant.

There was at least no seeing of the public blot on her birth when looking on her face. Nor when thinking of the beauty of her character, in absence or in presence, was there any. He had mastered distaste to such a degree, that he forgot the assistance he had received from the heiress for enabling him to appreciate the fair young girl. Money is the imperious requirement of superior station; and more money and more: in these our modern days of the merchant's wealth, and the miner's, and the gigantic American and Australian millionaires, high rank is of necessity vowed, in peril of utter eclipse; to the possession of money. Still it is, when assured, a consideration far to the rear with a gentleman in whose bosom love and the buzzing world have fought their battle out. He could believe it thoroughly fought out, by the prolonged endurance of a contest lasting many days and nights; in the midst of which, at one time, the task of writing to tell her of his withdrawal from the engagement, was the cause of his omission to write.

As to her character, he dwelt on the charm of her recovered features, to repress an indicative dread of some intrepid force behind it, that might be unfeminine, however gentle the external lineaments. Her features, her present aristocratic deficiency of colour, greatly pleased him; her character would submit to moulding. Of all young ladies in the world, she should be the one to shrink from a mental independence and hold to the guidance of the man ennobling her. Did she? Her eyes were reading him. She had her father's limpid eyes, and when they concentrated rays, they shot.

'Have you seen my parents, Mr. Sowerby?'

He answered smilingly, for reassuringly: 'I have seen them.'

'My mother?'

'From your mother first. But am I not to be Dudley?'

'She spoke to you? She told you?'

'And yesterday your father—a second time.'

Some remainder of suspicion in the dealing with members of this family, urged Dudley to say: 'I understood from them, you were not?... that you were quite...?'

'I have heard: I have guessed: it was recently—this morning, as it happened. I wish to go to my mother to-day. I shall go to her to-morrow.'

'I might offer to conduct you-now!'

'You are kind; I have Skepsey.' She relieved the situation of its cold-toned strain in adding: 'He is a host.'

'But I may come?—now! Have I not the right? You do not deny it me?'

'You are very generous.'

'I claim the right, then. Always. And subsequently, soon after, my mother hopes to welcome you at Cronidge. She will be glad to hear of your naming of a day. My father bids me... he and all our family.'

'They are very generous.'

'I may send them word this evening of a day you name?'

'No, Mr. Sowerby.

'Dudley?'

'I cannot say it. I have to see my parents.'

'Between us, surely?'

'My whole heart thanks you for your goodness to me. I am unable to say more.'

He had again observed and he slightly crisped under the speculative look she directed on him: a simple unstrained look, that had an air of reading right in, and was worse to bear with than when the spark leaped upon some thought from her eyes: though he had no imagination of anything he concealed—or exposed, and he would have set it down to her temporary incredulousness of his perfect generosity or power to overcome the world's opinion of certain circumstances. That had been a struggle! The peculiar look was not renewed. She spoke warmly of her gratitude. She stated, that she must of necessity see her parents at once. She submitted to his entreaty to conduct her to them on the morrow. It was in the manner of one who yielded step by step, from inability to contend.

Her attitude continuing unchanged, he became sensible of a monotony in the speech with which he assailed it, and he rose to leave, not dissatisfied. She, at his urgent request, named her train for London in the early morning. He said it was not too early. He would have desired to be warmed; yet he liked her the better for the moral sentiment controlling the physical. He had appointments with relatives or connections in the town, and on that pretext he departed, hoping for the speedy dawn of the morrow as soon as he had turned his back on the house.

No, not he the man to have pity of women underfoot! That was the thought, unrevolved, unphrased, all but unconscious, in Nesta: and while her heart was exalting him for his generosity. Under her present sense of the chilling shadow, she felt the comfort there was in being grateful to him for the golden beams which his generosity cast about her. But she had an intelligence sharp to pierce, virgin though she was; and with the mark in sight, however distant, she struck it, unerring as an Artemis for blood of beasts: those shrewd young wits, on the lookout to find a champion, athirst for help upon a desolate road, were hard as any judicial to pronounce the sentence upon Dudley in that respect. She raised him high; she placed herself low; she had a glimpse of the struggle he had gone through; love of her had helped him, she believed. And she was melted; and not the less did the girl's implacable intuition read with the keenness of eye of a man of the world the blunt division in him, where warm humanity stopped short at the wall of social concrete forming a part of this rightly esteemed young citizen. She, too, was divided: she was at his feet; and she rebuked herself for daring to judge—or rather, it was, for having a reserve in her mind upon a man proving so generous with her. She was pulled this way and that by sensibilities both inspiring to blind gratitude and quickening her penetrative view. The certainty of an unerring perception remained.

Dorothea and Virginia were seated in the room below, waiting for their carriage, when the hall-door spoke of the Hon. Dudley's departure; soon after, Nesta entered to them. She swam up to Dorothea's lap, and dropped her head on it, kneeling.

The ladies feared she might be weeping. Dorothea patted her thick brown twisted locks of hair. Unhappiness following such an interview, struck them as an ill sign.

Virginia bent to the girl's ear, and murmured: 'All well?'

She replied: 'He has been very generous.'

Her speaking of the words renewed an oppression, that had darkened her on the descent of stairs. For sensibilities sharp as Nesta's, are not to be had without their penalties: and she who had gone nigh to summing in a flash the nature of Dudley, sank suddenly under that affliction often besetting the young adventurous mind, crushing to young women:—the fascination exercised upon them by a positive adverse masculine attitude and opinion. Young men know well what it is: and if young women have by chance overcome their timidity, to the taking of any step out of the trim pathway, they shrink, with a sense of forlornest isolation. It becomes a subjugation; inciting to revolt, but a heavy weight to cast off. Soon it assumed its material form for the contention between her and Dudley, in the figure of Mrs. Marsett. The Nesta who had been instructed to know herself to be under a shadow, heard, she almost justified Dudley's reproaches to her, for having made the acquaintance of the unhappy woman, for having visited her, for having been, though but for a minute, at the mercy of a coarse gentleman's pursuit. The recollection was a smart buffet.

Her lighted mind punished her thus through her conjuring of Dudley's words, should news of her relations with Mrs. Marsett reach him:—and she would have to tell him. Would he not say: 'I have borne with the things concerning your family. All the greater reason why I must insist'—he would assuredly say he insisted (her humour caught at the word, as being the very word one could foresee and clearly see him uttering in a fit of vehemence) on her immediate abandonment of 'that woman.'

And with Nesta's present enlightenment by dusky beams, upon her parentage, she listened abjectly to Dudley, or the opinion of the majority. Would he not say or think, that her clinging to Mrs. Marsett put them under a kind of common stamp, or gave the world its option to class them together?

These were among the ideas chasing in a head destined to be a battle-field for the enrichment of a harvest-field of them, while the girl's face was hidden on Dorothea's lap, and her breast heaved and heaved.

She distressed them when she rose, by saying she must instantly see her mother.

They saw the pain their hesitation inflicted, and Dorothea said: 'Yes, dear; any day you like.'

'To-morrow—I must go to her to-morrow!'

A suggestion of her mother's coming down, was faintly spoken by one lady, echoed in a quaver by the other.

Nesta shook her head. To quiet the kind souls, she entreated them to give their promise that they would invite her again.

Imagining the Hon. Dudley to have cast her off, both ladies embraced her: not entirely yielding-up their hearts to her, by reason of the pernicious new ideas now in the world to sap our foundations of morality; which warned them of their duty to uphold mentally his quite justifiable behaviour, even when compassionating the sufferings of the guiltless creature loved by them.

CHAPTER XXXIV

CONTAINS DEEDS UNRELATED AND EXPOSITIONS OF FEELINGS

All through the afternoon and evening Skepsey showed indifference to meals by continuing absent: and he was the one with whom Nesta would have felt at home; more at home than with her parents. He and the cool world he moved in were a transparency of peace to her mind; even to his giving of some portion of it, when she had the dear little man present to her in a vivid image of a fish in a glass globe, wandering round and round, now and then shooting across, just as her Skepsey did: he carried his head semihorizontally at his arrowy pace; plain to read though he was, he appeared, under that image created of him, animated by motives inducing to speculation.

She thought of him till she could have reproached him for not returning and helping her to get away from the fever of other thoughts:—this anguish twisting about her parents, and the dreadful trammels of gratitude to a man afflictingly generous, the frown of congregated people.

The latter was the least of evils; she had her charges to bring against them for injustice: uncited, unstirred charges, they were effective as a muffled force to sustain her: and the young who are of healthy lively blood and clean conscience have either emotion or imagination to fold them defensively from an enemy world; whose power to drive them forth into the wilderness they acknowledge. But in the wilderness their souls are not beaten down by breath of mortals; they burn straight flame there up to the parent Spirit.

She could not fancy herself flying thither;—where to be shorn and naked and shivering is no hardship, for the solitude clothes, and the sole true life in us resolves to that steady flame;—she was restrained by Dudley's generosity, which held her fast to have the forgiveness for her uncommitted sin dashed in her face. He surprised her; the unexpected quality in him seemed suddenly to have snared her fast: and she did not obtain release after seeing behind it;—seeing it, by the light of what she demanded, personal, shallow, a lover's generosity. So her keen intellect saw it; and her young blood (for the youthful are thus divided) thrilled in thinking it must be love! The name of the sacred passion lifted it out of the petty cabin of the individual into a quiring cathedral universal, and subdued her. It subdued her with an unwelcome touch of tenderness when she thought of it as involving tenderness for her mother, some chivalrous respect for her mother. Could he love the daughter without some little, which a more intimate knowledge of her dear mother would enlarge? The girl's heart flew to her mother, clung to her, vindicated her dumbly. It would not inquire, and it refused to hear, hungering the while. She sent forth her flights of stories in elucidation of the hidden; and they were like white bird after bird winging to covert beneath a thundercloud; until her breast ached for the voice of the thunder: harsh facts: sure as she was of her never losing her filial hold of the beloved. She and her mother grew together, they were one. Accepting the shadow, they were the closer one beneath it. She had neither vision nor active thought of her father, in whom her pride was.

At the hour of ten, the ladies retired for the enjoyment of their sweet reward. Manton, their maid, came down to sit with Nesta on the watch for Skepsey. Perrin, the footman, returning, as late as twenty minutes to eleven, from his tobacco promenade along the terrace, reported to Manton 'a row in town'; and he repeated to Nesta the policeman's opinion and his own of the 'Army' fellows, and the way to treat them. Both were for rigour.

'The name of "Army" attracts poor Skepsey so, I am sure he would join it, if they would admit him,' Nesta said.

'He has an immense respect for a young woman, who belongs to his "Army"; and one doesn't know what may have come,' said Manton.

Two or three minutes after eleven, a feeble ring at the bell gained admission for some person: whispering was heard in the passage.

Manton played eavesdropper, and suddenly bursting on Skepsey, arrested him when about to dash upstairs. His young mistress's voice was a sufficient command; he yielded; he pitched a smart sigh and stepped into her presence for his countenance to be seen, or the show of a countenance, that it presented.

'Skepsey wanted to rush to bed without saying good night to me?' said she; leaving unnoticed, except for woefulness of tone, his hurried shuffle of remarks on 'his appearance,' and 'little accidents'; ending with an inclination of his disgraceful person to the doorway, and a petition: 'If I might, Miss Nesta?' The implied pathetic reference to a surgically-treated nose under a cross of strips of plaster, could not obtain dismissal for him. And he had one eye of sinister hue, showing beside its lighted-grey fellow as if a sullen punished dragonwhelp had couched near some quick wood-pigeon. The two eyes blinked rapidly. He was a picture of Guilt in the nude, imploring to be sent into concealment.

The cruelty of detaining him was evident.

'Yes, if you must,' Nesta said. 'But, dear Skepsey, will it be the magistrate again to-morrow?'

He feared it would be; he fancied it would needs be. He concluded by stating, that he was bound to appear before the magistrate in the morning; and he begged assistance to keep it from the knowledge of the Miss Duvidneys, who had been so kind to him.

'Has there been bailing of you again, Skepsey?'

'A good gentleman, a resident,' he replied; 'a military gentleman; indeed, a colonel of the cavalry; but, it may so be, retired; and anxious about our vast possessions; though he thinks a translation of a French attack on England unimportant. He says, the Germans despise us most.'

'Then this gentleman thinks you have a good case?'

'He is a friend of Captain Dartrey's.'

Hearing that name, Nesta said: 'Now, Skepsey, you must tell me everything. You are not to mind your looks. I believe, I do always believe you mean well.'

'Miss Nesta, it depends upon the magistrate's not being prejudiced against the street-processionists!

'But you may expect justice from the magistrate, if your case is good?'

'I would not say no, Miss Nesta. But we find, the opinion of the public has its effect with magistrates—their sentences. They are severe on boxing. They have latterly treated the "Army" with more consideration, owing to the change in the public view. I myself have changed.'

'Have you joined it?'

'I cannot say I am a member of it.'

'You walked in the ranks to-day, and you were maltreated? Your friend was there?'

'I walked with Matilda Pridden; that is, parallel, along the pavement.'

'I hope she came out of it unhurt?'

'It is thanks to Captain Dartrey, Miss Nesta?'

This time Nesta looked her question.

Manton interposed: 'You are to speak, Mr. Skepsey'; and she stopped a flood of narrative, that was knocking in his mind to feel its head and to leap—an uninterrupted half-minute more would have shaped the story for the proper flow.

He began, after attending to the throb of his bruises in a manner to correct them rather than solace; and the beginning was the end: 'Captain Dartrey rescued us, before Matilda Pridden suffered harm, to mention—the chin, slight, teeth unshaken; a beautiful set. She is angry with Captain Dartrey, for having recourse to violence in her defence: it is against her principles. "Then you die," she says; and our principles are to gain more by death. She says, we are alive in them; but worse if we abandon them for the sake of living.—I am a little confused; she is very abstruse.—Because, that is the corruptible life, she says. I have found it quite impossible to argue with her; she has always a complete answer; wonderful. In case of Invasion, we are to lift our voices to the Lord; and the Lord's will shall be manifested. If we are robbed, we ask, How came we by the goods? It is unreasonable; it strikes at rights of property. But I have to go on thinking. When in danger, she sings without excitement. When the blow struck her, she stopped singing only an instant. She says, no one fears, who has real faith. She will not let me call her brave. She cannot admire Captain Dartrey. Her principles are opposed. She said to him, "Sir, you did what seemed to you right." She thinks every blow struck sends us back to the state of the beasts. Her principles...'

'How was it Captain Dartrey happened to be present, Skepsey?'

'She is very firm. You cannot move her.—Captain Dartrey was on his way to the station, to meet a gentleman from London, Miss Nesta. He carried a stick—a remarkable stick—he had shown to me in the morning, and he has given it me now. He says, he has done his last with it. He seems to have some of Matilda Pridden's ideas about fighting, when it's over. He was glad to be rid of the stick, he said.'

'But who attacked you? What were the people?'

'Captain Dartrey says, England may hold up her head while she breeds young women like Matilda Pridden: right or wrong, he says: it is the substance.'

Hereupon Manton, sick of Miss Pridden, shook the little man with a snappish word, to bring him to attention. She got him together sufficiently for him to give a lame version of the story; flat until he came to his heroine's behaviour, when he brightened a moment, and he sank back absorbed in her principles and theories of life. It was understood by Nesta, that the processionists, going at a smart pace, found their way blocked and were assaulted in one of the sidestreets; and that Skepsey rushed to the defence of Matilda Pridden; and that, while they were engaged, Captain Dartrey was passing at the end of the street, and recognized one he knew in the thick of it and getting the worst of it, owing to numbers. 'I will show you the stick he did it with, Miss Nests'; said Skepsey, regardless of narrative; and darted out of the room to bring in the Demerara supple-jack; holding which, he became inspired to relate something of Captain Dartrey's deeds.

They gave no pleasure to his young lady, as he sadly perceived:—thus it is with the fair sex ever, so fond of heroes! She shut her eyes from the sight of the Demerara supple-jack descending right and left upon the skulls of a couple of bully lads. 'That will do—you were rescued. And now go to bed, Skepsey; and be up at seven to breakfast with me,' Nesta said, for his battle-damaged face would be more endurable to behold after an interval, she hoped; and she might in the morning dissociate its evil look from the deeds of Captain Dartrey.

The thought of her hero taking active part in a streetfray, was repulsive to her; it swamped his brilliancy. And this distressed her, by withdrawing the support which the thought of him had been to her since mid-day. She lay for sleepless hours, while nursing a deeper pain, under oppression of repugnance to battle-dealing, bloodshedding men. It was long before she grew mindful of the absurdity of the moan recurring whenever reflection wearied. Translated into speech, it would have run:

'In a street of the town! with a stick!'—The vulgar picture pursued her to humiliation; it robbed her or dimmed her possession of the one bright thing she had remaining to her. So she deemed it during the heavy sighs of night; partly conscious, that in some strange way it was as much as tossing her to the man who never could have condescended to the pugnacious using of a stick in a street. He, on the contrary, was a cover to the shamefaced.

Her heart was weak that night. She hovered above it, but not so detached as to scorn it for fawning to one—any one—who would offer her and her mother a cover from scorn. And now she exalted Dudley's generosity, now clung to a low idea of a haven in her father's wealth; and she was unaware, that the second mood was deduced from the first. She did know herself cowardly: she had, too, a critic in her clear head, to spurn at the creature who could think of purchasing the world's respect. Dudley's generosity sprang up to silence the voice. She could praise him, on a review of it, for delicacy, moreover; and the delicacy laid her under a more positive obligation. Her sense of it was not without a toneless quaint faint savour of the romantic, that her humour little humorously caught at, to paint her a picture of former heroes of fiction, who win their trying lady by their perfection of good conduct on a background of high birth; and who are not seen to be wooden before the volume closes. Her fatigue of sleeplessness plunged her into the period of poke-bonnets and peaky hats to admire him; giving her the kind of sweetness we may imagine ourselves to get in the state of tired horse munching hay. If she had gone to her bed with a noble or simply estimable plain image of one of her friends in her heart, to sustain it, she would not have been thus abject. Skepsey's discoloured eye, and Captain Dartrey's behaviour behind it, threw her upon Dudley's generosity, as being the shield for an outcast. Girls, who see at a time of need their ideal extinguished in its appearing tarnished, are very much at the disposal of the pressing suitor. Nesta rose in the black winter morn, summoning the best she could think of to glorify Dudley, that she might not feel so doomed.

According to an agreement overnight, she went to the bedroom of Dorothea and Virginia, to assure them of her having slept well, and say the good-bye to them and their Tasso. The little dog was the growl of a silken ball in a basket. His mistresses excused him, because of his being unused to the appearance of any person save Manton in their bedroom. Dorothea, kissing her, said: 'Adieu, dear child; and there is home with us always, remember. And, after breakfast, however it may be, you will, for our greater feeling of security, have—she has our orders—Manton—your own maid we consider too young for a guardian—to accompany you. We will not have it on our consciences, that by any possibility harm came to you while you were under our charge. The good innocent girl we received from the hands of your father, we return to him; we are sure of that.'

Nesta said: 'Mr. Sowerby promised he would come.'

'However it may be,' Dorothea repeated her curtaining phrase.

Virginia put in a word of apology for Tasso's temper he enjoyed ordinarily a slumber of half an hour's longer duration. He was, Dorothea feelingly added, regularity itself. Virginia murmured: 'Except once!' and both were appalled by the recollection of that night. It had, nevertheless, caused them to reperuse the Rev. Stuart Rem's published beautiful sermon ON DIRT; the words of which were an antidote to the night of Tasso in the nostrils of Mnemosyne; so that Dorothea could reply to her sister, slightly by way of a reproval, quoting Mr. Stuart Rem at his loftiest: '"Let us not bring into the sacred precincts Dirt from the roads, but have a care to spread it where it is a fructification."' Virginia produced the sequent sentence, likewise weighty. Nesta stood between the thin division of their beds, her right hand given to one, her left to the other. They had the semblance of a haven out of storms.

She reflected, after shutting the door of their room, that the residing with them had been a means of casting her—it was an effort to remember how—upon the world where the tree of knowledge grows. She had eaten; and she might be the worse for it; but she was raised to a height that would not let her look with envy upon peace and comfort. Luxurious quiet people were as ripening glass-house fruits. Her bitter gathering of the knowledge of life had sharpened her intellect; and the intellect, even in the young, is, and not less usefully, hard metal rather than fallow soil. But for the fountain of human warmth at her breast, she might have been snared by the conceit of intellect, to despise the simple and conventional, or shed the pity which is charity's contempt. She had only to think of the kindness of the dear good ladies; her heart jumped to them at once. And when she fancied hearing those innocent souls of women embracing her and reproaching her for the knowledge of life she now bore, her words down deep in her bosom were: It has helped me to bear the shock of other knowledge! How would she have borne it before she knew of the infinitely evil? Saving for the tender compassion weeping over her mother, she had not much acute personal grief.

For this world condemning her birth, was the world tolerant of that infinitely evil! Her intellect fortified her to be combative by day, after the night of imagination; which splendid power is not so serviceable as the logical mind in painful seasons: for night revealed the world snorting Dragon's breath at a girl guilty of knowing its vilest. More than she liked to recall, it had driven her scorched, half withered, to the shelter of Dudley. The daylight, spreading thin at the windows, restored her from that weakness. 'We will quit England,' she said, thinking of her mother and herself, and then of her father's surely following them. She sighed thankfully, half way through the breakfast with Skepsey, at sight of the hour by the clock; she was hurriedly sentient of the puzzle of her feelings, when she guessed at a chance that Dudley would be delayed. She supposed herself as possibly feeling not so well able to keep every thought of her head brooding on her mother in Dudley's company.

Skepsey's face was just sufferable by light of day, if one pitied reflecting on his honest intentions; it ceased to discolour another. He dropped a few particulars of his hero in action; but the heroine eclipsed. He was heavier than ever with his Matilda Pridden. At the hour for departure, Perrin had a conveyance at the door. Nesta sent off Skepsey with a complimentary message to Captain Dartrey. Her maid Mary begged her to finish her breakfast; Manton suggested the waiting a further two or three minutes. 'We must not be late,' Nesta said; and when the minute-hand of the clock marked ample time for the drive to the station, she took her seat and started, keeping her face resolutely set seaward, having at her ears the ring of a cry that was to come from Manton. But Manton was dumb; she spied no one on the pavement who signalled to stop them. And no one was at the station to greet them. They stepped into a carriage where they were alone. Dudley with his dreaded generosity melted out of Nesta's thoughts, like the vanishing steam-wreath on the dip between the line and the downs.

She passed into music, as she always did under motion of carriages and trains, whether in happiness or sadness: and the day being one that had a sky, the scenic of music swung her up to soar. None of her heavy burdens enchained, though she knew the weight of them, with those of other painful souls. The pipeing at her breast gave wings to large and small of the visible; and along the downs went stateliest of flowing dances; a copse lengthened to forest; a pool of cattle-water caught grey for flights through enchantment. Cottage-children, wherever seen in groups, she wreathed above with angels to watch them. Her mind all the while was busy upon earth, embracing her mother, eyeing her father. Imagination and our earthly met midway, and still she flew, until she was brought to the ground by a shot. She struggled to rise, uplifting Judith Marsett: a woman not so very much older than her own teens, in the count of years, and ages older; and the world pulling at her heels to keep her low. That unhappiest had no one but a sisterly girl to help her: and how she clung to the slender help! Who else was there?

The good and the bad in the woman struck separate blows upon the girl's resonant nature. She perceived the good, and took it into her reflections. The bad she divined: it approached like some threat of inflammation. Natures resonant as that which animated this girl, are quick at the wells of understanding: and she had her intimations of the world's wisdom in withholding contagious presences from the very mangy of the young, who may not have an aim, or ideal, or strong human compassion, for a preservative. She was assured of her possessing it. She asked herself in her mother's voice, and answered mutely. She had the certainty: for she rebuked the slavish feverishness of the passion, as betrayed by Mrs. Marsett; and the woman's tone, as of strung wires ringing on a rage of the wind. Then followed her cry for the man who could speak to Captain Marsett of his duty in honour. An image of one, accompanying the faster beats of her heart, beguiled her to think away from the cause. He, the one man known to her, would act the brother's part on behalf of the hapless creature.

Nesta just imagined her having supplicated him, and at once imagination came to dust. She had to thank him she knelt to him. For the first time of her life she found herself seized with her sex's shudder in the blood.

CHAPTER XXXV

IN WHICH AGAIN WE MAKE USE OF THE OLD LAMPS FOR LIGHTING AN ABYSMAL DARKNESS

And if Nesta had looked out of her carriage-window soon after the train began to glide, her eagle of imagination would have reeled from the heights, with very different feelings, earlier, perhaps a captive, at sight of the tardy gentleman rushing along the platform, and bending ear to the footman Perrin, and staring for one lost.

The snaky tail of the train imparted to Dudley an apprehension of the ominous in his having missed her. It wound away, and left regrets, which raised a chorus of harsh congratulations from the opposite party of his internal parliament.

Neither party could express an opinion without rousing the other to an uproar.

He had met his cousin Southweare overnight. He had heard, that there was talk of Miss Radnor. Her name was in the mouth of Major Worrell. It was coupled with the name of Mrs. Marsett. A military captain, in the succession to be Sir Edward Marsett, bestowed on her the shadow of his name.

It could be certified, that Miss Radnor visited the woman at her house. What are we to think of Miss Radnor, save that daughters of depraved parents!... A torture undeserved is the Centaur's shirt for driving us to lay about in all directions. He who had swallowed so much—a thunderbolt: a still undigested discharge from the perplexing heavens jumped frantic under the pressure upon him of more, and worse. A girl getting herself talked of at a Club! And she of all young ladies should have been the last to draw round her that buzz of tongues. On such a subject!—The parents pursuing their career of cynical ostentation in London, threw an evil eye of heredity on their offspring in the egg; making anything credible, pointing at tendencies.

An alliance with her was impossible. So said disgust. Anger came like a stronger beast, and extinguished the safety there was in the thing it consumed, by growing so excessive as to require tempering with drops of compassion; which prepared the way for a formal act of cold forgiveness; and the moment that was conceived, he had a passion to commit the horrible magnanimity, and did it on a grand scale, and dissolved his Heart in the grandeur, and slaved himself again.

Far from expungeing the doubt of her, forgiveness gave it a stamp and an edge. His renewed enslavement set him perusing his tyrant keenly, as nauseated captives do; and he saw, that forgiveness was beside the case. For this Nesta Victoria Radnor would not crave it or accept it. He had mentally played the woman to her superior vivaciousness too long for him to see her taking a culprit's attitude. What she did, she intended to do. The mother would not have encouraged her. The father idolized her; and the father was a frank hedonist, whose blood... speculation on horseback gallops to barren extremes. Eyes like hers—if there had not been the miserable dupes of girls! Conduct is the sole guide to female character. That likewise may be the hypocrite's mask.

Popular artists, intent to gratify the national taste for effects called realistic, have figured in scenes of battle the raying fragments of a man from impact of a cannon-ball on his person. Truly thus it may be when flesh contends. But an image of the stricken and scattered mind of the man should, though deficient in the attraction, have a greater significance, forasmuch as it does not exhibit him entirely liquefied and showered into space; it leaves him his legs for the taking of further steps. Dudley, standing on the platform of Nesta's train, one half minute too late, according to his desire before he put himself in motion, was as wildly torn as the vapour shredded streaming to fingers and threads off the upright columnar shot of the shriek from the boiler. He wished every mad antagonism to his wishes: that he might see her, be blind to her; embrace, discard; heal his wound, and tear it wider. He thanked her for the grossness of an offence precluding excuses. He was aware of a glimmer of advocacy in the very grossness. He conjured-up her features, and they said, her innocence was the sinner; they scoffed at him for the dupe he was willing to be. She had enigma's mouth, with the eyes of morning.

More than most girls, she was the girl-Sphinx to him because of her having ideas—or what he deemed ideas. She struck a toning warmth through his intelligence, not dissimilar to the livelier circulation of the blood in the frame breathing mountain air. She really helped him, incited him to go along with this windy wild modern time more cheerfully, if not quite hopefully. For she had been the book of Romance he despised when it appeared as a printed volume: and which might have educated the young man to read some among our riddles in the book of humanity. The white he was ready to take for silver the black were all black; the spotted had received corruption's label. Her youthful French governess

Mademoiselle de Seilles was also peculiarly enigmatic at the mouth conversant, one might expect, with the disintegrating literature of her country. In public, the two talked of St. Louis. One of them in secret visits a Mrs. Marsett. The Southweare women, the Hennen women, and Lady Evelina Reddish, were artless candid creatures in their early days, not transgressing in a glance. Lady Grace Halley had her fit of the devotional previous to marriage. No girl known to Dudley by report or acquaintance had committed so scandalous an indiscretion as Miss Radnor's: it pertained to the insolently vile.

And on that ground, it started the voluble defence. For certain suspected things will dash suspicion to the rebound, when they are very dark. As soon as the charge against her was moderated, the defence expired. He heard the world delivering its judgement upon her; and he sorrowfully acquiesced. She passed from him.

When she was cut off, she sang him in the distance a remembered saying of hers, with the full melody of her voice. One day, treating of modern pessimism, he had draped a cadaverous view of our mortal being in a quotation of the wisdom of the Philosopher Emperor: 'To set one's love upon the swallow is a futility.' And she, weighing it, nodded, and replied: 'May not the pleasure for us remain if we set our love upon the beauty of the swallow's flight?'

There was, for a girl, a bit of idea, real idea, in that meaning, of course, the picture we are to have of the bird's wings in motion, it has often been admired. Oh! not much of an idea in itself: feminine and vague. But it was pertinent, opportune; in this way she stimulated. And the girl who could think it, and call on a Mrs. Marsett, was of the class of mixtures properly to be handed over to chemical experts for analysis!

She had her aspirations on behalf of her sex: she and Mademoiselle de Seilles discussed them; women were to do this, do that:—necessarily a means of instructing a girl to learn what they did do. If the lower part of her face had been as reassuring to him as the upper, he might have put a reluctant faith in the pure-mindedness of these aspirations, without reverting to her origin, and also to recent rumours of her father and Lady Grace Halley. As it was, he inquired of the cognizant, whether an intellectual precocity, devoted by preference to questions affecting the state of women, did not rather more than suggest the existence of urgent senses likewise. She, a girl under twenty, had an interest in public matters, and she called on a Mrs. Marsett. To plead her simplicity, was to be absolutely ignorant of her.

He neighboured sagacity when he pointed that interrogation relating to Nesta's precociousness of the intelligence. For, as they say in dactylomancy, the 'psychical' of women are not disposed in their sensitive early days to dwell upon the fortunes of their sex: a thought or two turns them facing away, with the repugnant shiver. They worship at a niche in the wall. They cannot avoid imputing some share of foulness to them that are for scouring the chamber; and the civilized male, keeping his own chamber locked, quite shares their pale taper's view. The full-blooded to the finger-tips, on the other hand, are likely to be drawn to the subject, by noble inducement as often as by base: Nature at flood being the cause in either instance. This young Nature of the good and the bad, is the blood which runs to power of heart as well as to thirsts of the flesh. Then have men to sound themselves, to discover how much of Nature their abstract honourable conception or representative eidolon of young women will bear without going to pieces; and it will not be much, unless they shall have taken instruction from the poet's pen: for a view possibly of Nature at work to cast the slough, when they see her writhing as in her ugliest old throes. If they have learnt of Nature's priest to respect her, they will less distrust those rare daughters of hers who are moved by her warmth to lift her out of slime. It is by her own live warmth that it has to be done: cold worship at a niche in the wall will not do it.—Well, there is an index, for the enlargement of your charity.

But facts were Dudley's teachers. Physically, morally, mentally, he read the world through facts; that is to say, through the facts he encountered: and he was in consequence foredoomed to a succession of bumps; all the heavier from his being, unlike the horned kind, not unimpressible by the hazy things outside his experience. Even at his darkest over Nesta, it was his indigestion of the misconduct of her parents, which denied to a certain still small advocate within him the right to raise a voice: that good fellow struck the attitude for pleading, and had to be silent; for he was Instinct; at best a stammering speaker in the Court of the wigged Facts. Instinct of this Nesta Radnor's character would have said a brave word, but for her deeds bearing witness to her inheritance of a lawlessly adventurous temperament.

What to do? He was no nearer to an answer when the wintry dusk had fallen on the promenading crowds. To do nothing, is the wisdom of those who have seen fools perish. Facts had not taught him, that the doing nothing, for a length of days after the first shock he sustained, was the reason of how it came that Nesta knitted closer her acquaintance with the 'agreeable lady' she mentioned in her letter to Cronidge. Those excellent counsellors of a mercantile community gave him no warnings, that the 'masterly inactive' part, so greatly esteemed by him for the conduct of public affairs, might be perilous in dealings with a vivid girl: nor a hint, that when facts continue undigested, it is because the sensations are as violent as hysterical females to block them from the understanding. His Robin Goodfellow instinct tried to be serviceable at a crux of his meditations, where Edith Averst's consumptive brothers waved faded hands at her chances of inheriting largely. Superb for the chances: but what of her offspring? And the other was a girl such as the lusty Dame Dowager of fighting ancestors would have signalled to the heir of the House's honours for the perpetuation of his race. No doubt: and the venerable Dame (beautiful in her old-lace frame, or say foliage) of the Ages backward, temp: Ed: III. inflated him with a thought of her: and his readings in modern books on heredity, pure blood, physical regeneration, pronounced approval of Nesta Radnor: and thereupon instinct opened mouth to speak; and a lockjaw seized it under that scowl of his presiding mistrust of Nature.

He clung to his mistrust the more because of a warning he had from the silenced natural voice: somewhat as we may behold how the Conservatism of a Class, in a world of all the evidences showing that there is no stay to things, comes of the intuitive discernment of its finality. His mistrust was his own; and Nesta was not; not yet; though a step would make her his own. Instinct prompting to the step, was a worthless adviser. It spurred him, nevertheless.

He called at the Club for his cousin Southweare, with whom he was not in sympathy; and had information that, Southweare said, 'made the girl out all right.' Girls in these days do things which the sainted stay-at-homes preceding them would not have dreamed of doing. Something had occurred, relating to Major Worrell: he withdrew Miss Radnor's name, acknowledged himself mistaken or amended his report of her, in some way, not quite intelligible. Dudley was accosted by Simeon Fenellan; subsequently by Dartrey. There was gossip over the latter gentleman's having been up before the magistrate, talk of a queer kind of stick, and Dartrey said, laughing, to Simeon: 'Rather lucky I bled the rascal';—whatever the meaning. She nursed one of her adorations for this man, who had yesterday, apparently, joined in a street-fray; so she partook of the stain of the turbid defacing all these disorderly people.

At his hotel at breakfast the next morning, a newspaper furnished an account of Captain Dartrey Fenellan's participation in the strife, after mention of him as nephew of the Earl of Clanconan, 'now a visitor to our town'; and his deeds were accordant with his birth. Such writing was enough to send Dudley an eager listener to Colney Durance. What a people!

Mr. Dartrey Fenellan's card compelled Dudley presently to receive him.

Dartrey, not debarred by considerations, that an allusion to Miss Radnor could be conveyed only in the most delicately obscure manner, spared him no more than the plain English of his relations with her. Requested to come to the Club, at a certain hour of the afternoon, that he might hear Major Worrell's personal contradiction of scandal involving the young lady's name, together with his apology, etc., Dudley declined: and he was obliged to do it curtly; words were wanting. They are hard to find for wounded sentiments rendered complex by an infusion of policy. His present mood, with the something new to digest, held the going to Major Worrell a wrong step; he behaved as if the speaking to Dartrey Fenellan pledged him hardly less. And besides he had a physical abhorrence, under dictate of moral reprobation, of the broad-shouldered sinewy man, whose look of wiry alertness pictured the previous day's gory gutters.

Dartrey set sharp eyes on him for an instant, bowed; and went.

BOOK V

CHAPTER XXXVI

NESTA AND HER FATHER

The day of Nesta's return was one of a number of late when Victor was robbed of his walk Westward by Lady Grace Halley, who seduced his politeness with her various forms of blandishment to take a seat in her carriage; and she was a practical speaker upon her quarter of the world when she had him there. Perhaps she was right in saying—though she had no right to say—that he and she together might have the world under their feet. It was one of those irritating suggestions which expedite us up to a bald ceiling, only to make us feel the gas-bladder's tight extension upon emptiness: It moved him to examine the poor value of his aim, by tying him to the contemptible means: One estimate involved the other, whichever came first. Somewhere he had an idea, that would lift and cleanse all degradations. But it did seem as if he were not enjoying: things pleasant enough in the passage of them were barren, if not prickly, in the retrospect.

He sprang out at the head of the park, for a tramp round it, in the gloom of the girdle of lights, to recover his deadened relish of the thin phantasmal strife to win an intangible prize. His dulled physical system asked, as with the sensations of a man at the start from sleep in the hurrying grip of steam, what on earth he wanted to get, and what was the substance of his gains: what! if other than a precipitous intimacy, a deep crumbling over deeper, with a little woman amusing him in remarks of a whimsical nudity; hardly more. Nay, not more! he said; and at the end of twenty paces, he saw much more; the campaign gathered a circling suggestive brilliancy, like the lamps about the winter park; the Society, lured with glitter, hooked by greed, composed a ravishing picture; the little woman was esteemed as a serviceable lieutenant; and her hand was a small soft one, agreeable to fondle—and avaunt! But so it is in war: we must pay for our allies. What if it had been, that he and she together, with their united powers...? He dashed the silly vision aside, as vainer than one of the bubble-empires blown by boys; and it broke, showing no heart in it. His heart was Nataly's.

Let Colney hint his worst; Nataly bore the strain, always did bear any strain coming in the round of her duties: and if she would but walk, or if she danced at parties, she would scatter the fits of despondency besetting the phlegmatic, like this day's breeze the morning fog; or as he did with two minutes of the stretch of legs.

Full of the grandeur of that black pit of the benighted London, with its ocean-voice of the heart at beat along the lighted outer ring, Victor entered at his old door of the two houses he had knocked into one: a surprise for Fredi!—and heard that his girl had arrived in the morning.

'And could no more endure her absence from her Mammy O!' The songful satirical line spouted in him, to be flung at his girl, as he ran upstairs to the boudoir off the drawing-room.

He peeped in. It was dark. Sensible of presences, he gradually discerned a thick blot along the couch to the right of the door, and he drew near. Two were lying folded together; mother and daughter. He bent over them. His hand was taken and pressed by Fredi's; she spoke; she said tenderly: 'Father.' Neither of the two made a movement. He heard the shivering rise of a sob, that fell. The dry sob going to the waste breath was Nataly's. His girl did not speak again.

He left them. He had no thought until he stood in his dressing-room, when he said 'Good!' For those two must have been lying folded together during the greater part of the day: and it meant, that the mother's heart had opened; the girl knew. Her tone: 'Father,' sweet, was heavy, too, with the darkness it came out of.

So she knew. Good. He clasped them both in his heart; tempering his pity of those dear ones with the thought, that they were of the sex which finds enjoyment in a day of the mutual tear; and envying them; he strained at a richness appearing in the sobs of their close union.

All of his girl's loving soul flew to her mother; and naturally: She would not be harsh on her father. She would say he loved! And true: he did love, he does love; loves no woman but the dear mother.

He flicked a short wring of the hand having taken pressure from an alien woman's before Fredi pressed it, and absolved himself in the act; thinking, How little does a woman know how true we can be to her when we smell at a flower here and there!—There they are, stationary; women the flowers, we the bee; and we are faithful in our seeming volatility; faithful to the hive!—And if women are to be stationary, the reasoning is not so bad. Funny, however, if they here and there imitatively spread a wing, and treat men in that way? It is a breach of the convention; we pay them our homage, that they may serve as flowers, not to be volatile tempters. Nataly never had been one of the sort: Lady Grace was. No necessity existed for compelling the world to bow to Lady Grace, while on behalf of his Nataly he had to... Victor closed the curtain over a gulf-revealed by an invocation of Nature, and showing the tremendous force he partook of so largely, in her motive elements of the devourer. Horrid to behold, when we need a gracious presentation of the circumstances. She is a splendid power for as long as we confine her between the banks: but she has a passion to discover cracks; and if we give her headway, she will find one, and drive at it, and be through, uproarious in her primitive licentiousness, unless we labour body and soul like Dutchmen at the dam. Here she was, and not desired, almost detested! Nature detested! It had come about through the battle for Nataly; chiefly through Mrs. Burman's tenacious hold of the filmy thread she took for life and was enabled to use as a means for the perversion besides bar to the happiness of creatures really living. We may well marvel at the Fates, and tell them they are not moral agents!

Victor's reflections came across Colney Durance, who tripped and stopped them.

Dressed with his customary celerity, he waited for Nesta, to show her the lighted grand double drawing-room: a further proof of how Fortune favoured him: she was to be told, how he one day expressed a wish for greater space, and was informed on the next, that the neighbour house was being vacated, and the day following he was in treaty for the purchase of it; returning from Tyrol, he found his place habitable.

Nesta came. Her short look at him was fond, her voice not faltering; she laid her hand under his arm and walked round the spacious room, praising the general design, admiring the porcelain, the ferns, friezes, hangings, and the grand piano, the ebony inlaid music-stands, the firegrates and plaques, the ottomans, the tone of neutral colour that, as in sound, muted splendour. He told her it was a reception night, with music: and added: 'I miss my... seen anybody lately?'

'Mr. Sowerby?' said she. 'He was to have escorted me back. He may have overslept himself.'

She spoke it plainly; when speaking of the dear good ladies, she set a gentle humour at play, and comforted him, as she intended, with a souvenir of her lively spirit, wanting only in the manner of gaiety.

He allowed, that she could not be quite gay.

More deeply touched the next minute, he felt in her voice, in her look, in her phrasing of speech, an older, much older daughter than the Fredi whom he had conducted to Moorsedge. 'Kiss me,' he said.

She turned to him full-front, and kissed his right cheek and left, and his forehead, saying: 'My love! my papa! my own dear dada!' all the words of her girlhood in her new sedateness; and smiling: like the moral crepuscular of a sunlighted day down a not totally inanimate Sunday Londen street.

He strained her to his breast. 'Mama soon be here?'

'Soon.'

That was well. And possibly at the present moment applying, with her cunning hand, the cosmetics and powders he could excuse for a concealment of the traces of grief.

Satisfied in being a superficial observer, he did not spy to see more than the world would when Nataly entered the dining-room at the quiet family dinner. She performed her part for his comfort, though not prattling; and he missed his Fredi's delicious warble of the prattle running rill-like over our daily humdrum. Simeon Fenellan would have helped. Then suddenly came enlivenment: a recollection of news in the morning's paper. 'No harm before Fredi, my dear. She's a young woman now. And no harm, so to speak-at least, not against the Sanfredini. She has donned her name again, and a villa on Como, leaving her 'duque';—paragraph from a Milanese musical Journal; no particulars. Now, mark me, we shall have her at Lakelands in the Summer. If only we could have her now!'

'It would be a pleasure,' said Nataly. Her heart had a blow in the thought, that a lady of this kind would create the pleasure by not bringing criticism.

'The godmother?' he glistened upon Nesta.

She gave him low half-notes of the little blue butterfly's imitation of the superb contralto; and her hand and head at turn to hint the theatrical operatic attitude.

'Delicious!' he cried, his eyelids were bedewed at the vision of the three of them planted in the past; and here again, out of the dark wood, where something had required to be said, and had been said; and all was happily over, owing to the goodness and sweetness of the two dear innocents;—whom heaven bless! Jealousy of their naturally closer heart-at-heart, had not a whisper for him; part of their goodness and sweetness was felt to be in the not excluding him.

Nesta engaged to sing one of the 'old duets with her mother. She saw her mother's breast lift in a mechanical effort to try imaginary notes, as if doubtful of her capacity, more at home in the dumb deep sigh they fell to. Her mother's heroism made her a sacred woman to the thoughts of the girl, overcoming wonderment at the extreme submissiveness.

She put a screw on her mind to perceive the rational object there might be for causing her mother to go through tortures in receiving and visiting; and she was arrested by the louder question, whether she could think such a man as her father irrational.

People with resounding names, waves of a steady stream, were announced by Arlington, just as in the days, that seemed remote, before she went to Moorsedge; only they were more numerous, and some of the titles had ascended a stage. There were great lords, there were many great ladies; and Lady Grace Halley shuffling amid them, like a silken shimmer in voluminous robes.

They crowded about their host where he stood. 'He, is their Law!' Colney said, speaking unintelligibly, in the absence of the Simeon Fenellan regretted so loudly by Mr. Beaves Urmsing. They had an air of worshipping, and he of swimming.

There were also City magnates, and Lakelands' neighbours: the gentleman representing Pride of Port, Sir Abraham Quatley; and Colonel Corfe; Sir Rodwell and Lady Blachington; Mrs. Fanning; Mr. Caddis. Few young men and maids were seen. Dr. John Cormyn came without his wife, not mentioning her. Mrs. Peter Yatt touched the notes for voices at the piano. Priscilla Graves was a vacancy, and likewise the Rev. Septimus Barmby. Peridon and Catkin, and Mr. Pempton took their usual places. There was no fluting. A famous Canadian lady was the principal singer. A Galician violinist, zig-zagging extreme extensions and contractions of his corporeal frame in execution, and described by Colney as 'Paganini on wall,' failed to supplant Durandarte in Nesta's memory. She was asked by Lady Grace for the latest of Dudley. Sir Abraham Quatley named him with handsome emphasis. Great dames caressed her; openly approved; shadowed the future place among them.

Victor alluded at night to Mrs. John Cormyn's absence. He said: 'A homoeopathic doctor's wife!' nothing more; and by that little, he prepared Nesta for her mother's explanation. The great London people, ignorant or not, were caught by the strong tide he created, and carried on it. But there was a bruiting of the secret among their set; and the one to fall away from her, Nataly marvellingly named Mrs. John

Cormyn; whose marriage was of her making. She did not disapprove Priscilla's behaviour. Priscilla had come to her and, protesting affection, had openly stated, that she required time and retirement to recover her proper feelings. Nataly smiled a melancholy criticism of an inconsequent or capricious woman, in relating to Nesta certain observations Priscilla had dropped upon poor faithful Mr. Pempton, because of his concealment from her of his knowledge of things for this faithful gentleman had been one of the few not ignorant. The rumour was traceable to the City.

'Mother, we walk on planks,' Nesta said.

Nataly answered: 'You will grow used to it.'

Her mother's habitual serenity in martyrdom was deceiving. Nesta had a transient suspicion, that she had grown, from use, to like the whirl of company, for oblivion in the excitement; and as her remembrance of her own station among the crowding people was a hot flush, the difference of their feelings chilled her.

Nataly said: 'It is to-morrow night again; we do not rest.' She smiled; and at once the girl read woman's armour on the dear face, and asked herself, Could I be so brave? The question following was a speechless wave, that surged at her father. She tried to fathom the scheme he entertained. The attempt obscured her conception of the man he was. She could not grasp him, being too young for knowing, that young heads cannot obtain a critical hold upon one whom they see grandly succeeding it is the sun's brilliance to their eyes.

Mother and daughter slept together that night, and their embrace was their world.

Nesta delighted her father the next day by walking beside him into the City, as far as the end of the Embankment, where the carriage was in waiting with her maid to bring her back; and at his mere ejaculation of a wish, the hardy girl drove down in the afternoon for the walk home with him. Lady Grace Halley was at the office. 'I'm an incorrigible Stock Exchange gambler,' she said.

'Only,' Victor bade her beware, 'Mines are undulating in movement, and their heights are a preparation for their going down.'

She said she 'liked a swing.'

Nesta looked at them in turn.

The day after and the day after, Lady Grace was present. She made play with Dudley's name.

This coming into the City daily of a girl, for the sake of walking back in winter weather with her father, struck her as ambiguous: either a jealous foolish mother's device, or that of a weak man beating about for protection. But the woman of the positive world soon read to the contrary; helped a little by the man, no doubt. She read rather too much to the contrary, and took the pedestrian girl for perfect simplicity in her tastes, when Nesta had so far grown watchful as to feel relieved by the lady's departure. Her mother, without sympathy for the lady, was too great of soul for jealousy. Victor had his Nataly before him at a hint from Lady Grace: and he went somewhat further than the exact degree when affirming, that Nataly could not scheme, and was incapable of suspecting.—Nataly could perceive things with a certain accuracy: she would not stoop to a meanness. 'Plot? Nataly?' said he, and shrugged. In fact, the void of plot, drama, shuffle of excitement, reflected upon Nataly. He might have seen as tragic as ever dripped on Stage, had he looked.

But the walk Westward with his girl, together with pride in a daughter who clove her way through all weathers, won his heart to exultation. He told her: 'Fredi does her dada so much good'; not telling her in what, or opening any passage to the mystery of the man he was. She was trying to be a student of life, with her eyes down upon hard earth, despite of her winged young head; she would have compassed him better had he dilated in sublime fashion; but he baffled her perusal of a man of power by the simpleness of his enjoyment of small things coming in his way;—the lighted shops, the crowd, emergence from the crowd, or the meeting near midwinter of a soft warm wind along the Embankment, and dark Thames magnificently coroneted over his grimy flow. There is no grasping of one who quickens us.

His flattery of his girl, too, restored her broken feeling of personal value; it permeated her nourishingly from the natural breath of him that it was.

At times he touched deep in humaneness; and he set her heart leaping on the flash of a thought to lay it bare, with the secret it held, for his help. That was a dream. She could more easily have uttered the words to Captain Dartrey, after her remembered abashing holy tremour of the vision of doing it and casting herself on noblest man's compassionateness; and her imagined thousand emotions;—a rolling music within her, a wreath of cloudglory in her sky;—which had, as with virgins it may be, plighted her body to him for sheer urgency of soul; drawn her by a single unwitting-to-brain, conscious-in-blood, shy curl outward of the sheathing leaf to the flowering of woman to him; even to the shore of that strange sea, where the maid stands choosing this one man for her destiny, as in a trance. So are these young ones unfolded, shade by shade; and a shade is all the difference with them; they can teach the poet to marvel at the immensity of vitality in 'the shadow of a shade.'

Her father shut the glimpse of a possible speaking to him of Mrs. Marsett, with a renewal of his eulogistic allusions to Dudley Sowerby: the 'perfect gentleman, good citizen'; prospective heir to an earldom besides. She bowed to Dudley's merits; she read off the honorific pedimental letters of a handsome statue, for a sign to herself that she passed it.

She was unjust, as Victor could feel, though he did not know how coldly unjust. For among the exorbitant requisitions upon their fellow-creatures made by the young, is the demand, that they be definite: no mercy is in them for the transitional. And Dudley—and it was under her influence, and painfully, not ignobly—was in process of development: interesting to philosophers, if not to maidens.

Victor accused her of paying too much heed to Colney Durance's epigrams upon their friends. He quite joined with his English world in its opinion, that epigrams are poor squibs when they do not come out of great guns. Epigrams fired at a venerable nation, are surely the poorest of popgun paper pellets. The English kick at the insolence, when they are not in the mood for pelleting themselves, or when the armed Foreigner is overshadowing and braceing. Colney's pretentious and laboured Satiric Prose Epic of 'THE RIVAL TONGUES,' particularly offended him, as being a clever aim at no hitting; and sustained him, inasmuch as it was an acid friend's collapse. How could Colney expect his English to tolerate such a spiteful diatribe! The suicide of Dr. Bouthoin at San Francisco was the finishing stroke to the chances of success of the Serial;—although we are promised splendid evolutions on the part of Mr. Semhians; who, after brilliant achievements with bat and ball, abandons those weapons of Old England's modern renown, for a determined wrestle with our English pronunciation of words, and rescue of the spelling of them from the printer. His headache over the present treatment of the verb 'To bid,' was a quaint beginning for one who had soon to plead before Japanese, and who acknowledged now 'in contrition of spirit,' that in formerly opposing the scheme for an Academy, he helped to the handing of our noble language to the rapid reporter of news for an apathetic public. Further, he discovered in astonishment the subordination of all literary Americans to the decrees of their literary authorities; marking a Transatlantic point of departure, and contrasting ominously with the unruly Islanders 'grunting the higgledy-piggledy of their various ways, in all the porker's gut-gamut at the rush to the trough.' After a week's privation of bat and ball, he is, lighted or not, a gas-jet of satire upon his countrymen. As for the 'pathetic sublimity of the Funeral of Dr. Bouthoin,' Victor inveighed against an impious irony in the over dose of the pathos; and the same might be suspected in Britannia's elegy upon him, a strain of hot eulogy throughout. Mr. Semhians, all but treasonably, calls it, Papboat and Brandy:—'our English literary diet of the day': stimulating and not nourishing. Britannia's mournful anticipation, that 'The shroud enwinding this my son is mine!'—should the modern generation depart from the track of him who proved himself the giant in mainly supporting her glory—was, no doubt, a high pitch of the note of Conservatism. But considering, that Dr. Bouthoin 'committed suicide under a depression of mind produced by a surfeit of unaccustomed dishes, upon a physical system inspired by the traditions of exercise, and no longer relieved by the practice'—to translate from Dr. Gannius: we are again at war with the writer's reverential tone, and we know not what to think: except, that Mr. Durance was a Saturday meat market's butcher in the Satiric Art.

Nesta found it pleasanter to see him than to hear of his work: which, to her present feeling, was inhuman. As little as our native public, had she then any sympathy for the working in the idea: she wanted throbs, visible aims, the Christian incarnate; she would have preferred the tale of slaughter—periodically invading all English classes as a flush from the undrained lower, Vikings all—to frigid sterile Satire. And truly it is not a fruit-bearing rod. Colney had to stand on the defence of it against the damsel's charges. He thought the use of the rod, while expressing profound regret at a difference of opinion between him and those noble heathens, beneficial for boys; but in relation to their seniors, and particularly for old gentlemen, he thought that the sharpest rod to cut the skin was the sole saving of them. Insensibility to Satire, he likened to the hard-mouthed horse; which is doomed to the worser thing in consequence. And consequently upon the lack of it, and of training to appreciate it, he described his country's male venerables as being distinguishable from annuitant spinsters only in presenting themselves forked.

'He is unsuccessful and embittered, Victor said to Nesta. 'Colney will find in the end, that he has lost his game and soured himself by never making concessions. Here's this absurd Serial—it fails, of course; and then he has to say, it's because he won't tickle his English, won't enter into a "frowzy complicity" with their tastes.'

'But—I think of Skepsey honest creatures respect Mr. Durance, and he is always ready to help them,' said Nesta.

'If he can patronize.'

'Does he patronize me, dada?'

'You are one of his exceptions. Marry a title and live in state—and then hear him! I am successful, and the result of it is, that he won't acknowledge wisdom in anything I say or do; he will hardly acknowledge the success. It is "a dirty road to success," he says. So that, if successful, I must have rolled myself in mire. I compelled him to admit he was wrong about your being received at Moorsedge: a bit of a triumph!'

Nesta's walks with her father were no loss of her to Nataly; the girl came back to her bearing so fresh and so full a heart; and her father was ever prouder of her: he presented new features of her in his quotations of her sayings, thoughtful sayings. 'I declare she helps one to think,' he said. 'It 's not precocity; it 's healthy inquiry. She brings me nearer ideas of my own, not yet examined, than any one else does. I say, what a wife for a man!'

'She takes my place beside you, dear, now I am not quite strong,' said Nataly. 'You have not seen...?'

'Dudley Sowerby? He's at Cronidge, I believe. His elder brother's in a bad way. Bad business, this looking to a death.'

Nataly eyes revealed a similar gulf.

Let it be cast on Society, then! A Society opposing Nature forces us to these murderous looks upon impediments. But what of a Society in the dance with Nature? Victor did not approve of that. He began, under the influence of Nesta's companionship, to see the Goddess Nature there is in a chastened nature. And this view shook the curtain covering his lost Idea. He felt sure he should grasp it soon and enter into its daylight: a muffled voice within him said, that he was kept waiting to do so by the inexplicable tardiness of a certain one to rise ascending to her spiritual roost. She was now harmless to strike: Themison, Carling, Jarniman, even the Rev. Groseman Buttermore, had been won to the cause of humanity. Her ascent, considering her inability to do further harm below, was most mysteriously delayed. Owing to it, in a manner almost as mysterious, he was kept crossing a bridge having a slippery bit on it. Thanks to his gallant Fredi, he had found his feet again. But there was a bruise where, to his honour, he felt tenderest. And Fredi away, he might be down again—for no love of a slippery bit, proved slippery, one might guess, by a predecessor or two. Ta-ta-ta-to and mum! Still, in justice to the little woman, she had been serviceable.

She would be still more so, if a member of Parliament now on his back here we are with the murder-eye again!

Nesta's never speaking of Lakelands clouded him a little, as an intimation of her bent of mind.

'And does my girl come to her dada to-day?' he said, on the fifth morning since her return; prepared with a villanous resignation to hear, that this day she abstained, though he had the wish for her coming.

'Why, don't you know,' said she, 'we all meet to have tea in Mr. Durance's chambers; and I walk back with you, and there we are joined by mama; and we are to have a feast of literary celebrities.'

'Colney's selection of them! And Simeon Fenellan, I hope. Perhaps Dartrey. Perhaps... eh?'

She reddened. So Dudley Sowerby's unspoken name could bring the blush to her cheeks. Dudley had his excuses in his brother's condition. His father's health, too, was—but this was Dudley calculating. Where there are coronets, calculations of this sort must needs occur; just as where there are complications. Odd, one fancies it, that we walking along the pavement of civilized life, should be perpetually summoning Orcus to our aid, for the sake of getting a clear course.

'And supposing a fog, my dearie?' he said.

'The daughter in search of her father carries a lamp to light her to him through densest fogs as well as over deserts,' etc. She declaimed a long sentence, to set the ripple running in his features; and when he left the room for a last word with Armandine, she flung arms round her mother's neck, murmuring: 'Mother! mother!' a cry equal to 'I am sure I do right,' and understood so by Nataly approving it; she too on the line of her instinct, without an object in sight.

CHAPTER XXXVII

THE MOTHER-THE DAUGHTER

Taking Nesta's hand, on her entry into his chambers with her father, Colney Durance bowed over it and kissed it. The unusual performance had a meaning; she felt she was praised. It might be because she made herself her father's companion. 'I can't persuade him to put on a great-coat,' she said. 'You would defeat his aim at the particular waistcoat of his ambition,' said Colney, goaded to speak, not anxious to be heard.

He kept her beside him, leading her about for introductions to multiform celebrities of both sexes; among them the gentleman editing the Magazine which gave out serially THE RIVAL TONGUES: and there was talk of a dragon-throated public's queer appetite in Letters. The pained Editor deferentially smiled at her cheerful mention of Delphica. 'In, book form, perhaps!' he remarked, with plaintive' resignation; adding: 'You read it?' And a lady exclaimed: 'We all read it!'

But we are the elect, who see signification and catch flavour; and we are reminded of an insatiable monster how sometimes capricious is his gorge. 'He may happen to be in the humour for a shaking!' Colney's poor consolation it was to say of the prospects of his published book: for the funny monster has been known to like a shaking.

'He takes it kinder tickled,' said Fenellan, joining the group and grasping Nesta's hand with a warmth that thrilled her and set her guessing. 'A taste of his favourite Cayenne lollypop, Colney; it fetches the tear he loves to shed, or it gives him digestive heat in the bag of his literary receptacle-fearfully relaxed and enormous! And no wonder; his is to lie him down on notion of the attitude for reading, his back; and he has in a jiffy the funnel of the Libraries inserted into his mouth, and he feels the publishers pouring their gallons through it unlimitedly; never crying out, which he can't; only swelling, which he's obliged to do, with a non-nutritious inflation; and that's his intellectual enjoyment; bearing a likeness to the horrible old torture of the baillir d'eau; and he's doomed to perish in the worst book-form of dropsy. You, my dear Colney, have offended his police or excise, who stand by the funnel, in touch with his palate, to make sure that nothing above proof is poured in; and there's your misfortune. He's not half a bad fellow, you find when you haven't got to serve him.'

'Superior to his official parasites, one supposes!' Colney murmured.

The celebrities were unaffectedly interested in a literary failure having certain merits; they discussed it, to compliment the crownless author; and the fervider they, the more was he endowed to read the meanness prompting the generosity. Publication of a book, is the philosopher's lantern upon one's fellows.

Colney was caught away from his private manufactory of acids by hearing Simeon Fenellan relate to Victor some of the recent occurrences at Brighton. Simeon's tone was unsatisfying; Colney would have the word; he was like steel on the grindstone for such a theme of our national grotesque-sublime.

'That Demerara Supple-jack, Victor! Don't listen to Simeon; he's a man of lean narrative, fit to chronicle political party wrangles and such like crop of carcase prose: this is epical. In DRINK we have Old England's organic Epic; Greeks and Trojans; Parliamentary Olympus, ennobled brewers, nasal fanatics, all the machinery to hand. Keep a straight eye on the primary motives of man, you'll own the English produce the material for proud verse; they're alive there! Dartrey's Demerara makes a pretty episode of the battle. I haven't seen it—if it's possible to look on it: but I hear it is flexible, of a vulgar appearance in repose, Jove's lightning at one time, the thong of AEacus at another. Observe Dartrey marching off to the Station, for the purpose of laying his miraculous weapon across the shoulders of a son of Mars, who had offended. But we have his name, my dear Victor! His name, Simeon?—Worrell; a Major Worrell: his offence being probably, that he obtained military instruction in the Service, and left it at his convenience, for our poor patch and tatter British Army to take in his place another young student, who'll grow up to do similarly. And Dartrey, we assume, is off to stop that system. You behold Sir Dartrey twirling the weapon in preparatory fashion; because he is determined we shall have an army of trained officers instead of infant amateurs heading heroic louts. Not a thought of Beer in Dartrey!— always unpatriotic, you 'll say. Plato entreats his absent mistress to fix eyes on a star: eyes on Beer for the uniting of you English! I tell you no poetic fiction. Seeing him on his way, thus terribly armed, and knowing his intent, Venus, to shield a former favourite servant of Mars, conjured the most diverting of interventions, in the shape of a young woman in a poke-bonnet, and Skepsey, her squire, marching with a dozen or so, informing bedevilled mankind of the hideousness of our hymnification when it is not under secluding sanction of the Edifice, and challengeing criticism; and that was hard by, and real English, in the form of bludgeons, wielded by a battalion of the national idol Bungay Beervat's boys; and they fell upon the hymners. Here you fill in with pastoral similes. They struck the maid adored by Skepsey. And that was the blow which slew them! Our little man drove into the press with a pair of fists able to do their work. A valiant skiff upon a sea of enemies, he was having it on the nob, and suddenly the Demerara lightened. It flailed to thresh. Enough to say, brains would have come. The Bungays made a show of fight. No lack of blood in them, to stock a raw shilling's worth or gush before Achilles rageing. You perceive the picture, you can almost sing the ballad. We want only a few names of the fallen. It was the carving of a maitre chef, according to Skepsey: right-left-and point, with supreme precision: they fell, accurately sliced from the joint. Having done with them, Dartrey tossed the Demerara to Skepsey, and washed his hands of battle; and he let his major go unscathed. Phlebotomy sufficient for the day!'

Nesta's ears hummed with the name of Major Worrell.

'Skepsey did come back to London with a rather damaged frontispiece,' Victor said. 'He can't have joined those people?'

'They may suit one of your militant peacemakers,' interposed Fenellan. 'The most placable creatures alive, and the surest for getting-up a shindy.'

'Suit him! They're the scandal of our streets.' Victor was pricked with a jealousy of them for beguiling him of his trusty servant.

'Look at your country, see where it shows its vitality,' said Colney. 'You don't see elsewhere any vein in movement-movement,' he harped on the word Victor constantly employed to express the thing he wanted to see. 'Think of that, when the procession sets your teeth on edge. They're honest foes of vice, and they move:—in England! Pulpit-preaching has no effect. For gross maladies, gross remedies. You may judge of what you are by the quality of the cure. Puritanism, I won't attempt to paint—it would barely be decent; but compare it with the spectacle of English frivolity, and you'll admit it to be the best show you make. It may still be the saving of you—on the level of the orderly ox: I 've not observed that it aims at higher. And talking of the pulpit, Barmby is off to the East, has accepted a Shoreditch curacy, Skepsey tells me.'

'So there's the reason for our not seeing him!' Victor turned to Nesta.

'Papa, you won't be angry with Skepsey if he has joined those people,' said Nesta. 'I'm sure he thinks of serving his country, Mr. Durance.'

Colney smiled on her. 'And you too?'

'If women knew how!'

'They're hitting on more ways at present than the men—in England.'

'But, Mr. Durance, it speaks well for England when they're allowed the chance here.'

'Good!' Fenellan exclaimed. 'And that upsets his placement of the modern national genders: Germany masculine, France feminine, Old England what remains.'

Victor ruffled and reddened on his shout of 'Neuter?'

Their circle widened. Nesta knew she was on promotion, by her being led about and introduced to ladies. They were encouraging with her. One of them, a Mrs. Marina Floyer, had recently raised a standard of feminine insurrection. She said: 'I hear your praises from Mr. Durance. He rarely praises. You have shown capacity to meditate on the condition of women, he says.'

Nesta drew a shorter breath, with a hope at heart. She speculated in the dark, as to whether her aim to serve and help was not so friendless. And did Mr. Durance approve? But surely she stood in a glorious England if there were men and women to welcome a girl to their councils. Oh! that is the broad free England where gentlemen and gentlewomen accept of the meanest aid to cleanse the land of its iniquities, and do not suffer shame to smite a young face for touching upon horrors with a pure design.

She cried in her bosom: I feel! She had no other expression for that which is as near as great natures may come to the conceiving of the celestial spirit from an emissary angel; and she trembled, the fire ran through her. It seemed to her, that she would be called to help or that certainly they were nearing to an effacement of the woefullest of evils; and if not helping, it would still be a blessedness for her to kneel thanking heaven.

Society was being attacked and defended. She could but studiously listen. Her father was listening. The assailant was a lady; and she had a hearing, although she treated Society as a discrowned monarch on trial for an offence against a more precious: viz., the individual cramped by brutish laws: the individual with the ideas of our time, righteously claiming expansion out of the clutches of a narrow old-world disciplinarian-that giant hypocrite! She flung the gauntlet at externally venerable Institutions; and she had a hearing, where horrification, execration, the foul Furies of Conservatism would in a shortly antecedent day have been hissing and snakily lashing, hounding her to expulsion. Mrs. Marina Floyer gravely seconded her. Colney did the same. Victor turned sharp on him. 'Yes,' Colney said; 'we unfold the standard of extremes in this country, to get a single step taken: that's how we move: we threaten death to get footway. Now, mark: Society's errors will be admitted.'

A gentleman spoke. He began by admitting Society's errors. Nevertheless, it so distinctly exists for the common good, that we may say of Society in relation to the individual, it is the body to the soul. We may wash, trim, purify, but we must not maim it. The assertion of our individuality in opposition to the Government of Society—this existing Society—is a toss of the cap for the erasure of our civilization, et caetera.

Platitudes can be of intense interest if they approach our case.—But, if you please, we ask permission to wash, trim, purify, and we do not get it.—But you have it! Because we take it at our peril; and you, who are too cowardly to grant or withhold, call-up the revolutionary from the pits by your slackness:—etc. There was a pretty hot debate. Both assailant and defendant, to Victor's thinking, spoke well, and each the right thing and he could have made use of both, but he could answer neither. He beat about for the cause of this deficiency, and discovered it in his position. Mentally, he was on the side of Society. Yet he was annoyed to find the attack was so easily answerable when the defence unfolded. But it was absurd to expect it would not be. And in fact, a position secretly rebellious is equal to water on the brain for stultifying us.

Before the controversy was over, a note in Nataly's handwriting called him home. She wrote: 'Make my excuses. C. D. will give Nesta and some lady dinner. A visitor here. Come alone, and without delay. Quite well, robust. Impatient to consult with you, nothing else.'

Nesta was happy to stay; and Victor set forth.

The visitor? plainly Dudley. Nataly's trusting the girl to the chance of some lady being present, was unlike her. Dudley might be tugging at the cord; and the recent conversation upon Society, rendered one of its gilt pillars particularly estimable.—A person in the debate had declared this modern protest on behalf of individualism to represent Society's Criminal Trial. And it is likely to be a long one. And good for the world, that we see such a Trial!—Well said or not, undoubtedly Society is an old criminal: not much more advanced than the state of spiritual worship where bloody sacrifice was offered to a hungry Lord. But it has a case for pleading. We may liken it, as we have it now, to the bumping lumberer's raft; suitable along torrent waters until we come to smoother. Are we not on waters of a certain smoothness at the reflecting level?—enough to justify demands for a vessel of finer design. If Society is to subsist, it must have the human with the logical argument against the cry of the free-flags, instead of presenting a block's obtuseness. That, you need not hesitate to believe, will be rolled downward and disintegrated, sooner than later. A Society based on the logical concrete of humane considerateness:—a Society prohibiting to Mrs. Burman her wielding of a life-long rod....

The personal element again to confuse inquiry!—And Skepsey and Barmby both of them bent on doing work without inquiry of any sort! They were enviable: they were good fellows. Victor clung to the theme because it hinted of next door to his lost Idea. He rubbed the back of his head, fancying a throb there.

Are civilized creatures incapable of abstract thought when their social position is dubious? For if so, we never can be quit of those we forsake.—Apparently Mrs. Burman's unfathomed power lay in her compelling him to summon the devilish in himself and play upon the impish in Society, that he might overcome her.

Victor's house-door stopped this current.

Nataly took his embrace.

'Nothing wrong?' he said, and saw the something. It was a favourable moment to tell her what she might not at another time regard as a small affair. 'News in the City to-day of that South London borough being vacated. Quatley urges me. A death again! I saw Pempton, too. Will you credit me when I tell you he carries his infatuation so far, that he has been investing in Japanese and Chinese Loans, because they are less meat-eaters than others, and vegetarians are more stable, and outlast us all!—Dudley the visitor?' 'Mr. Sowerby has been here,' she said, in a shaking low voice.

Victor held her hand and felt a squeeze more nervous than affectionate.

'To consult with me,' she added. 'My maid will go at ten to bring Nesta; Mr. Durance I can count on, to see her safe home. Ah!' she wailed.

Victor nodded, saying: 'I guess. And, my love, you will receive Mrs. John Cormyn to-morrow morning. I can't endure gaps. Gaps in our circle must never be. Do I guess?—I spoke to Colney about bringing her home.'

Nataly sighed: 'Ah! make what provision we will! Evil—Mr. Sowerby has had a great deal to bear.'

'A worldling may think so.'

Her breast heaved, and the wave burst: but her restraining of tears froze her speech.

'Victor! Our Nesta! Mr. Sowerby is unable to explain. And how the Miss Duvidneys!... At that Brighton!'—The voice he heard was not his darling's deep rich note, it had dropped to toneless hoarseness: 'She has been permitted to make acquaintance—she has been seen riding with—she has called upon—Oh! it is one of those abandoned women. In her house! Our girl! Our Nesta! She was insulted by a man in the woman's house. She is talked of over Brighton. The mother!—the daughter! And grant me this—that never was girl more carefully... never till she was taken from me. Oh! do not forget. You will defend me? You will say, that her mother did with all her soul strive... It is not a rumour. Mr. Sowerby has had it confirmed.' A sob caught her voice.

Victor's hands caressed to console: 'Dudley does not propose to...?'

'Nesta must promise... but how it happened? How! An acquaintance with—contact with!—Oh! cruel!' Each time she ceased speaking, the wrinkles of a shiver went over her, and the tone was of tears coming, but she locked them in.

'An accident!' said Victor; 'some misunderstanding—there can't be harm. Of course, she promises—hasn't to promise. How could a girl distinguish! He does not cast blame on her?'

'Dear, if you would go down to Dartrey to-morrow. He knows:—it is over the Clubs there; he will tell you, before a word to Nesta. Innocent, yes! Mr. Sowerby has not to be assured of that. Ignorant of the character of the dreadful woman? Ah, if I could ever in anything think her ignorant! She frightens me. Mr. Sowerby is indulgent. He does me justice. My duty to her—I must defend myself—has been my first thought. I said in my prayers—she at least!... We have to see the more than common reasons why she, of all girls, should—he did not hint it, he was delicate: her name must not be public.'

'Yes, yes, Dudley is without parallel as a gentleman,' said Victor. 'It does not suit me to hear the word "indulgent." My dear, if you were down there, you would discover that the talk was the talk of two or three men seeing our girl ride by—and she did ride with a troop: why, we've watched them along the parade, often. Clear as day how it happened! I'll go down early to-morrow.'

He fancied Nataly was appeased. And even out of this annoyance, there was the gain of her being won to favour Dudley's hitherto but tolerated suit.

Nataly also had the fancy, that the calm following on her anguish, was a moderation of it. She was kept strung to confide in her girl by the recent indebtedness to her for words heavenly in the strengthening comfort they gave. But no sooner was she alone than her torturing perplexities and her abasement of the hours previous to Victor's coming returned.

For a girl of Nesta's head could not be deceived; she had come home with a woman's intelligence of the world, hard knowledge of it—a knowledge drawn from foul wells, the unhappy mother imagined: she dreaded to probe to the depth of it. She had in her wounded breast the world's idea, that corruption must come of the contact with impurity.

Nataly renewed her cry of despair: 'The mother!—the daughter!'—her sole revelation of the heart's hollows in her stammered speaking to Victor.

She thanked heaven for the loneliness of her bed, where she could repeat: 'The mother!—the daughter!' hearing the world's words:—the daughter excused, by reason of her having such a mother; the mother unpitied for the bruiting of her brazen daughter's name: but both alike consigned to the corners of the world's dust-heaps. She cried out, that her pride was broken. Her pride, her last support of life, had gone to pieces. The tears she restrained in Victor's presence, were called on to come now, and she had none. It might be, that she had not strength for weeping. She was very weak. Rising from bed to lock her door against Nesta's entry to the room on her return at night, she could hardly stand: a chill and a clouding overcame her. The quitted bed seemed the haven of a drifted wreck to reach.

Victor tried the handle of a locked door in the dark of the early winter morning. 'The mother!—the daughter!' had swung a pendulum for some time during the night in him, too. He would rather have been subjected to the spectacle of tears than have heard that toneless voice, as it were the dry torrent-bed rolling blocks instead of melodious, if afflicting, waters.

He told Nesta not to disturb her mother, and murmured of a headache: 'Though, upon my word, the best cure for mama would be a look into Fredi's eyes!' he said, embracing his girl, quite believing in her, just a little afraid of her.

CHAPTER XXXVIII

NATALY, NESTA, AND DARTREY FENELLAN

Pleasant things, that come to us too late for our savour of the sweetness in them, toll ominously of life on the last walk to its end. Yesterday, before Dudley Sowerby's visit, Nataly would have been stirred where the tears we shed for happiness or repress at a flattery dwell when seeing her friend Mrs. John Cormyn enter her boudoir and hearing her speak repentantly, most tenderly. Mrs. John said: 'You will believe I have suffered, dear; I am half my weight, I do think': and she did not set the smile of responsive humour moving; although these two ladies had a key of laughter between them. Nataly took her kiss; held her hand, and at the parting kissed her. She would rather have seen her friend than not: so far she differed from a corpse; but she was near the likeness to the dead in the insensibility to any change of light shining on one who best loved darkness and silence. She cried to herself wilfully, that her pride was broken: as women do when they spurn at the wounding of a dignity they cannot protect and die to see bleeding; for in it they live.

The cry came of her pride unbroken, sore bruised, and after a certain space for recovery combative. She said:

Any expiation I could offer where I did injury, I would not refuse; I would humble myself and bless heaven for being able to pay my debt—what I can of it. All I contend against is, injustice. And she sank into sensational protests of her anxious care of her daughter, too proud to phrase them.

Her one great affliction, the scourging affliction of her utter loneliness;—an outcast from her family; daily, and she knew not how, more shut away from the man she loved; now shut away from her girl;—seemed under the hand of the angel of God. The abandonment of her by friends, was merely the light to show it.

Midday's post brought her a letter from Priscilla Graves, entreating to be allowed to call on her next day.—We are not so easily cast off! Nataly said, bitterly, in relation to the lady whose offending had not been so great. She wrote: 'Come, if sure that you sincerely wish to.'

Having fasted, she ate at lunch in her dressing-room, with some taste of the food, haunted by an accusation of gluttony because of her eating at all, and a vile confession, that she was enabled to eat, owing to the receipt of Priscilla's empty letter: for her soul's desire was to be doing a deed of expiation, and the macerated flesh seemed her assurance to herself of the courage to make amends.—I must have some strength, she said wearifully, in apology for the morsel consumed.

Nesta's being in the house with her, became an excessive irritation. Doubts of the girl's possible honesty to speak a reptile truth under question; amazement at her boldness to speak it; hatred of, the mouth that could: and loathing of the words, the theme; and abomination of herself for conjuring fictitious images to rouse real emotions; all ran counterthreads, that produced a mad pattern in the mind, affrighting to reason: and then, for its preservation, reason took a superrational leap, and ascribed the terrible injustice of this last cruel stroke to the divine scourge, recognized divine by the selection of the mortal spot for chastisement. She clasped her breast, and said: It is mortal. And that calmed her.

She said, smiling: I never felt my sin until this blow came! Therefore the blow was proved divine. Ought it not to be welcomed?—and she appearing no better than one of those, the leprous of the sex! And brought to acknowledgement of the likeness by her daughter!

Nataly drank the poison distilled from her exclamations and was ice. She had denied herself to Nesta's redoubled petition. Nesta knocking at the door a third time and calling, tore the mother two ways: to have her girl on her breast or snap their union in a word with an edge. She heard the voice of Dartrey Fenellan.

He was admitted. 'No, dear,' she said to Nesta; and Nesta's, 'My own mother,' consentingly said, in tender resignation, as she retired, sprang a stinging tear to the mother's eyelids.

Dartrey looked at the door closing on the girl.

'Is it a very low woman?' Nataly asked him in a Church whisper, with a face abashed.

'It is not,' said he, quick to meet any abruptness.

'She must be cunning.'

'In the ordinary way. We say it of Puss before the hounds.'

'To deceive a girl like Nesta!'

'She has done no harm.'

'Dartrey, you speak to a mother. You have seen the woman? She is?—ah!'

'She is womanly, womanly.'

'Quite one of those...?'

'My dear soul! You can't shake them off in that way. She is one of us. If we have the class, we can't escape from it. They are not to bear all the burden because they exist. We are the bigger debtors. I tell you she is womanly.'

'It sounds like horrid cynicism.'

'Friends of mine would abuse it for the reverse.'

'Do not make me hate your chivalry. This woman is a rod on my back. Provided only she has not dropped venom into Nesta's mind!'

'Don't fear!'

'Can you tell me you think she has done no harm to my girl?'

'To Nesta herself?—not any: not to a girl like your girl.'

'To my girl's name? Speak at once. But I know she has. She induced Nesta to go to her house. My girl was insulted in this woman's house.'

Dartrey's forehead ridged with his old fury and a gust of present contempt. 'I can tell you this, that the fellow who would think harm of it, knowing the facts 's not worthy of touching the tips of the fingers of your girl.'

'She is talked of!'

'A good-looking girl out riding with a handsome woman on a parade of idlers!'

'The woman is notorious.' Nataly said it shivering.

He shook his head. 'Not true.'

'She has an air of a lady?'

'She sits a horse well.'

'Would she to any extent deceive me—impose on me here?'

'No.'

'Ah!' Nataly moaned....

'But what?' said Dartrey. 'There was no pretence. Her style is not worse than that of some we have seen. There was no effort to deceive. The woman's plain for you and me to read, she has few of the arts; one or two tricks, if you like: and these were not needed for use. There are women who have them, and have not been driven or let slip into the wilderness.'

'Yes; I know!—those ideas of yours!' Nataly had once admired him for his knightliness toward the weakest women and the women underfoot. 'You have spoken to this woman? She boasted of acquaintance with Nesta?'

'She thanked God for having met her.'

'Is it one of the hysterical creatures?'

Mrs. Marsett appeared fronting Dartrey.

He laughed to himself. 'A clever question. There is a leaning to excitement of manner at times. It 's not hysteria. Allow for her position.'

Nataly took the unintended blow, and bowed to it; and still more harshly said: 'What rank of life does the woman come from?'

'The class educated for a skittish career by your popular Stage and your Book-stalls. I am not precise?'

'Leave Mr. Durance. Is she in any degree commonly well bred?... behaviour, talk-her English.'

'I trench on Mr. Durance in replying. Her English is passable. You may hear...'

'Everywhere, of course! And this woman of slipshod English and excited manners imposed upon Nesta!'

'It would not be my opinion.'

'Did not impose on her!'

'Not many would impose on Nesta Radnor for long.'

'Think what that says, Dartrey!'

'You have had a detestable version of the story.'

'Because an excited creature thanks God to you for having met her!'

'She may. She's a better woman for having met her. Don't suppose we're for supernatural conversions. The woman makes no show of that. But she has found a good soul among her sex—her better self in youth, as one guesses; and she is grateful—feels farther from exile in consequence. She has found a lady to take her by the hand!—not a common case. She can never go to the utterly bad after knowing Nesta. I forget if she says it; I say it. You have heard the story from one of your conventional gentlemen.'

'A true gentleman. I have reason to thank him. He has not your ideas on these matters, Dartrey. He is very sensitive... on Nesta's behalf.'

'With reference to marriage. I'll own I prefer another kind of gentleman. I 've had my experience of that kind of gentleman. Many of the kind have added their spot to the outcasts abominated for uncleanness—in holy unction. Many?—I won't say all; but men who consent to hear black words pitched at them, and help to set good women facing away from them, are pious dolts or rascal dogs of hypocrites. They, if you'll let me quote Colney Durance to you to-day—and how is it he is not in favour?—they are tempting the Lord to turn the pillars of Society into pillars of salt. Down comes the house. And priests can rest in sight of it!—They ought to be dead against the sanctimony that believes it excommunicates when it curses. The relationship is not dissolved so cheaply, though our Society affects to think it is. Barmby's off to the East End of this London, Victor informs me:—good fellow! And there he'll be groaning over our vicious nature. Nature is not more responsible for vice than she is for inhumanity. Both bad, but the latter's the worse of the two.'

Nataly interposed: 'I see the contrast, and see whom it's to strike.'

Dartrey sent a thought after his meaning. 'Hardly that. Let it stand. He 's only one with the world: but he shares the criminal infamy for crushing hope out of its frailest victims. They're that—no sentiment. What a world, too, look behind it!—brutal because brutish. The world may go hang: we expect more of your gentleman. To hear of Nesta down there, and doubt that she was about good work; and come complaining! He had the privilege of speaking to her, remonstrating, if he wished. There are men who think—men!—the plucking of sinners out of the mire a dirty business. They depute it to certain officials.

And your women—it's the taste of the world to have them educated so, that they can as little take the humane as the enlightened view. Except, by the way, sometimes, in secret;—they have a sisterly breast. In secret, they do occasionally think as they feel. In public, the brass mask of the Idol they call Propriety commands or supplies their feelings and thoughts. I won't repeat my reasons for educating them differently. At present we have but half the woman to go through life with—and thank you.'

Dartrey stopped. 'Don't be disturbed,' he added. 'There's no ground for alarm. Not of any sort.'

Nataly said: 'What name?'

'Her name is Mrs. Marsett.'

'The name is...?'

'Captain Marsett: will be Sir Edward. He came back from the Continent yesterday.'

A fit of shuddering seized Nataly. It grew in violence, and speaking out of it, with a pause of sickly empty chatter of the jaws, she said: 'Always that name?'

'Before the maiden name? May have been or not.'

'Not, you say?'

'I don't accurately know.'

Dartrey sprang to his legs. 'My dear soul! dear friend—one of the best! if we go on fencing in the dark, there'll be wounds. Your way of taking this affair disappointed me. Now I understand. It's the disease of a trouble, to fly at comparisons. No real one exists. I wished to protect the woman from a happier sister's judgement, to save you from alarm concerning Nesta:—quite groundless, if you'll believe me. Come, there's plenty of benevolent writing abroad on these topics now: facts are more looked at, and a good woman may join us in taking them without the horrors and loathings of angels rather too much given to claim distinction from the luckless. A girl who's unprotected may go through adventures before she fixes, and be a creature of honest intentions. Better if protected, we all agree. Better also if the world did not favour the girl's multitude of enemies. Your system of not dealing with facts openly is everyway favourable to them. I am glad to say, Victor recognizes what corruption that spread of wealth is accountable for. And now I must go and have a talk with the—what a change from the blue butterfly! Eaglet, I ought to have said. I dine with you, for Victor may bring news.'

'Would anything down there be news to you, Dartrey?'

'He makes it wherever he steps.'

'He would reproach me for not detaining you. Tell Nesta I have to lie down after talking. She has a child's confidence in you.'

A man of middle age! he said to himself. It is the particular ejaculation which tames the senior whose heart is for a dash of holiday. He resolved, that the mother might trust to the discretion of a man of his age; and he went down to Nesta, grave with the weight his count of years should give him. Seeing her, the light of what he now knew of her was an ennobling equal to celestial. For this fair girl was one of the active souls of the world—his dream to discover in woman's form. She, the little Nesta, the tall pure-eyed girl before him, was, young though she was, already in the fight with evil: a volunteer of the army of the simply Christian. The worse for it? Sowerby would think so. She was not of the order of young women who, in sheer ignorance or in voluntary, consent to the peace with evil, and are kept externally safe from the smirch of evil, and are the ornaments of their country, glory of a country prizing ornaments higher than qualities.

Dartrey could have been momentarily incredulous of things revealed by Mrs. Marsett—not incredulous of the girl's heroism: that capacity he caught and gauged in her shape of head, cut of mouth, and the measurements he was accustomed to make at a glance:—but her beauty, or the form of beauty which was hers, argued against her having set foot of thought in our fens. Here and far there we meet a young saint vowed to service along by those dismal swamps: and saintly she looks; not of this earth. Nesta was of the blooming earth. Where do we meet girl or woman comparable to garden-flowers, who can dare to touch to lift the spotted of her sex? He was puzzled by Nesta's unlikeness in deeds and in aspect. He remembered her eyes, on the day when he and Colonel Sudley beheld her; presently he was at quiet grapple with her mind. His doubts cleared off. Then the question came, How could a girl of heroical character be attached to the man Sowerby? That entirely passed belief.

And was it possible his wishes beguiled his hearing? Her tones were singularly vibrating.

They talked for a while before, drawing a deep breath, she said: 'I fancy I am in disgrace with my mother.'

'You have a suspicion why?' said he.

'I have.'

She would have told him why: the words were at her lips. Previous to her emotion on the journey home, the words would have come out. They were arrested by the thunder of the knowledge, that the nobleness in him drawing her to be able to speak of scarlet matter, was personally worshipped.

He attributed the full rose upon her cheeks to the forbidding subject.

To spare pain, he said: 'No misunderstanding with the dear mother will last the day through. Can I help?'

'Oh, Captain Dartrey!'

'Drop the captain. Dartrey will do.'

'How could I!'

'You're not wanting in courage, Nesta.'

'Hardly for that!'

'By-and-by, then.'

'Though I could not say Mr. Fenellan.'

'You see; Dartrey, it must be.'

'If I could!'

'But the fellow is not a captain: and he is a friend, an old friend, very old friend: he'll be tipped with grey in a year or two.'

'I might be bolder then.'

'Imagine it now. There is no disloyalty in your calling your friends by their names.'

Her nature rang to the implication. 'I am not bound.' Dartrey hung fast, speculating on her visibly: 'I heard you were?'

'No. I must be free.'

'It is not an engagement?'

'Will you laugh?—I have never quite known. My father desired it: and my desire is to please him. I think I am vain enough to think I read through blinds and shutters. The engagement—what there was—has been, to my reading, broken more than once. I have not considered it, to settle my thoughts on it, until lately: and now I may suspect it to be broken. I have given cause—if it is known. There is no blame elsewhere. I am not unhappy, Captain Dartrey.'

'Captain by courtesy. Very well. Tell me how Nesta judges the engagement to be broken?'

She was mentally phrasing before she said: 'Absence.'

'He was here yesterday.'

All that the visit embraced was in her expressive look, as of sight drawing inward, like our breath in a spell of wonderment. 'Then I understand; it enlightens me.

My own mother!—my poor mother! he should have come to me. I was the guilty person, not she; and she is the sufferer. That, if in life were direct retribution! but the very meaning of having a heart, is to suffer through others or for them.'

'You have soon seen that, dear girl,' said Dartrey.

'So, my own mother, and loving me as she does, blames me!' Nesta sighed; she took a sharp breath. 'You? do you blame me too?'

He pressed her hand, enamoured of her instantaneous divination and heavenly candour.

But he was admonished, that to speak high approval would not be honourable advantage taken of the rival condemning; and he said: 'Blame? Some think it is not always the right thing to do the right thing. I've made mistakes, with no bad design. A good mother's view is not often wrong.'

'You pressed my hand,' she murmured.

That certainly had said more.

'Glad to again,' he responded. It was uttered airily and was meant to be as lightly done.

Nesta did not draw back her hand. 'I feel strong when you press it.' Her voice wavered, and as when we hear a flask sing thin at the filling, ceased upon evidence of a heart surcharged. How was he to relax the pressure!—he had to give her the strength she craved: and he vowed it should be but for half a minute, half a minute longer.

Her tears fell; she eyed him steadily; she had the look of sunlight in shower.

'Oldish men are the best friends for you, I suppose,' he said; and her gaze turned elusive phrases to vapour.

He was compelled to see the fiery core of the raincloud lighting it for a revealment, that allowed as little as it retained of a shadow of obscurity.

The sight was keener than touch and the run of blood with blood to quicken slumbering seeds of passion.

But here is the place of broken ground and tangle, which calls to honourable men, not bent on sport, to be wary to guard the gunlock. He stopped the word at his mouth. It was not in him to stop or moderate the force of his eyes. She met them with the slender unbendingness that was her own; a feminine of inspirited manhood. There was no soft expression, only the direct shot of light, on both sides; conveying as much as is borne from sun to earth, from earth to sun. And when such an exchange has come between the two, they are past plighting, they are the wedded one.

Nesta felt it, without asking whether she was loved. She was his. She had not a thought of the word of love or the being beloved. Showers of painful blissfulness went through her, as the tremours of a shocked frame, while she sat quietly, showing scarce a sign; and after he had let her hand go, she had the pressure on it. The quivering intense of the moment of his eyes and grasp was lord of her, lord of the day and of all days coming. That is how Love slays Death. Never did girl so give her soul.

She would have been the last to yield it unreservedly to a man untrusted for the character she worshipped. But she could have given it to Dartrey, despite his love of another, because it was her soul, without any of the cravings, except to bestow.

He perceived, that he had been carried on for the number of steps which are countless miles and do not permit the retreat across the desert behind; and he was in some amazement at himself, remindful of the different nature of our restraining power when we have a couple playing on it. Yet here was this girl, who called him up to the heights of young life again: and a brave girl; and she bled for the weak, had no shrinking from the women underfoot: for the reason, that she was a girl sovereignly pure, angelically tender. Was there a point of honour to hold him back?

Nataly entered the room. She kissed Nesta, and sat silent.

'Mother, will you speak of me to him, if I go out?' Nesta said.

'We have spoken,' her mother replied, vexed by the unmaidenly allusion to that theme.

She would have asked, How did you guess I knew of it?—but that the Why should I speak of you to him? struck the louder note in her bosom: and then, What is there that this girl cannot guess!—filled the mother's heart with apprehensive dread: and an inward cry, What things will she not set going, to have them discussed. And the appalling theme, sitting offensive though draped in their midst, was taken for a proof of the girl's unblushingness. After standing as one woman against the world so long, Nataly was relieved to be on the side of a world now convictedly unjust to her in the confounding of her with the shameless. Her mind had taken the brand of that thought:—And Nesta had brought her to it:—And Dudley Sowerby, a generous representative of the world, had kindly, having the deputed power to do so, sustained her, only partially blaming Nesta, not casting them off; as the world, with which Nataly felt, under a sense of the protection calling up all her gratitude to young Dudley, would have approved his doing.

She was passing through a fit of the cowardice peculiar to the tediously strained, who are being more than commonly tried—persecuted, as they say when they are not supplicating their tyrannical Authority for aid. The world will continue to be indifferent to their view of it and behaviour toward it until it ceases to encourage the growth of hypocrites.

These are moments when the faces we are observing drop their charm, showing us our perversion internal, if we could but reflect, to see it. Very many thousand times above Dudley Sowerby, Nataly ranked Dartrey Fenellan; and still she looked at him, where he sat beside Nesta, ungenially, critical of the very features, jealously in the interests of Dudley; and recollecting, too, that she had once prayed for one exactly resembling Dartrey Fenellan to be her Nesta's husband. But, as she would have said, that was before the indiscretion of her girl had shown her to require for her husband a man whose character and station guaranteed protection instead of inciting to rebellion. And Dartrey, the loved and prized, was often in the rebel ranks; he was dissatisfied with matters as they are; was restless for action, angry with a country denying it to him; he made enemies, he would surely bring down inquiries about Nesta's head, and cause the forgotten or quiescent to be stirred; he would scarcely be the needed hand for such a quiver of the lightnings as Nesta was.

Dartrey read Nataly's brows. This unwonted uncomeliness of hers was an indication to one or other of our dusky pits, not a revealing.

CHAPTER XXXIX

A CHAPTER IN THE SHADOW OF MRS. MARSETT

He read her more closely when Arlington brought in the brown paper envelope of the wires—to which the mate of Victor ought to have become accustomed. She took it; her eyelids closed, and her features were driven to whiteness. 'Only these telegrams,' she said, in apology.

'Lakelands on fire?' Dartrey murmured to Nesta; and she answered: 'I should not be sorry.'

Nataly coldly asked her why she would not be sorry.

Dartrey interposed: 'I'm sure she thinks Lakelands worries her mother.'

'That ranks low among the worries,' Nataly sighed, opening the envelope.

Nesta touched her arm: 'Mother! even before Captain Dartrey, if you will let me!'—she turned to him: 'before...' at the end of her breath she said: 'Dartrey Fenellan. You shall see my whole heart, mother.'

Her mother looked from her at him.

'Victor returns by the last train. He telegraphs, that he dines with—' She handed the paper to Dartrey.

'Marsett,' he read aloud; and she flushed; she was angry with him for not knowing, that the name was a term of opprobrium flung at her.

'It's to tell you he has done what he thought good,' said Dartrey. 'In other words, as I interpret, he has completed his daughter's work. So we won't talk about it till he comes. You have no company this evening?'

'Oh! there is a pause to-night! It's nearly as unceasing as your brother Simeon's old French lady in the ronde with her young bridegroom, till they danced her to pieces. I do get now and then an hour's repose,' Nataly added, with a vision springing up of the person to whom the story had applied.

'My dear, you are a good girl to call me Dartrey,' the owner of the name said to Nesta.

Nataly saw them both alert, in the terrible manner peculiar to both, for the directest of the bare statements. She could have protested, that her love of truth was on an equality with theirs; and certainly, that her regard for decency was livelier. Pass the deficiency in a man. But a girl who could speak, by allusion, of Mrs. Marsett—of the existence of a Mrs. Marsett—in the presence of a man: and he excusing, encouraging: and this girl her own girl;—it seemed to her, that the world reeled; she could hardly acknowledge the girl; save under the penitential admission of her sin's having found her out.

She sent Nesta to her room when they went upstairs to dress, unable to endure her presence after seeing her show a placid satisfaction at Dartrey's nod to the request for him to sleep in the house that night. It was not at all a gleam of pleasure, hardly an expression; it was a manner of saying, One drop more in my cup of good fortune! an absurd and an offensive exhibition of silly optimism of the young, blind that they are!

For were it known, and surely the happening of it would be known, that Dudley Sowerby had shaken off the Nesta of no name, who was the abominable Mrs. Marsett's friend, a whirlwind with a trumpet would sweep them into the wilderness on a blast frightfuller than any ever heard.

Nataly had a fit of weeping for want of the girl's embrace, against whom her door was jealously locked. She hoped those two would talk much, madly if they liked, during dinner, that she might not be sensible, through any short silence, of the ardour animating them: especially glowing in Nesta, ready behind her quiet mask to come brazenly forth. But both of them were mercilessly ardent; and a sickness of the fear, that they might fall on her to capture her and hurry her along with them perforce of the allayed, once fatal, inflammable element in herself, shook the warmth from her limbs: causing her to say to herself aloud in a ragged hoarseness, very strangely: Every thought of mine now has a physical effect on me!

They had not been two minutes together when she descended to them. Yet she saw the girl's heart brimming, either with some word spoken to her or for joy of an unmaidenly confession. During dinner they talked, without distressful pauses. Whatever said, whatever done, was manifestly another drop in Nesta's foolish happy cup. Could it be all because Dartrey Fenellan countenanced her acquaintance with that woman? The mother had lost hold of her. The tortured mother had lost hold of herself.

Dartrey in the course of the evening, begged to hear the contralto; and Nataly, refusing, was astounded by the admission in her blank mind of the truth of man's list of charges against her sex, starting from their capriciousness for she could have sung in a crowded room, and she had now a desire for company, for stolid company or giddy, an ocean of it. This led to her thinking, that the world of serious money-getters, and feasts, and the dance, the luxurious displays, and the reverential Sunday service, will always ultimately prove itself right in opposition to critics and rebels, and to any one vainly trying to stand alone: and the thought annihilated her; for she was past the age of the beginning again, and no footing was left for an outsider not self-justified in being where she stood. She heard Dartrey's praise of Nesta's voice for tearing her mother's bosom with notes of intolerable sweetness; and it was haphazard irony, no doubt; we do not the less bleed for the accident of a shot.

At last, after midnight Victor arrived.

Nesta most impudently expected to be allowed to remain. 'Pray, go, dear,' her mother said. Victor kissed his Fredi. 'Some time to-morrow,' said he; and she forbore to beseech him.

He stared, though mildly, at sight of her taking Dartrey's hand for the good-night and deliberately putting her lips to it.

Was she a girl whose notion of rectifying one wrong thing done, was to do another? Nataly could merely observe. A voice pertaining to no one present, said in her ear:—Mothers have publicly slapped their daughter's faces for less than that!—It was the voice of her incapacity to cope with the girl. She watched Nesta's passage from the room, somewhat affected by the simple bearing for which she was reproaching her.

'And our poor darling has not seen a mountain this year!' Victor exclaimed, to have mentionable grounds for pitying his girl. 'I promised Fredi she should never count a year without Highlands or Alps. You remember, mama?—down in the West Highlands. Fancy the dear bit of bundle, Dartrey!—we had laid her in her bed; she was about seven or eight; and there she lay wide awake. "What 's Fredi thinking of?"—"I'm thinking of the tops of the mountains at night, dada."—She could climb them now; she has the legs.'

Nataly said: 'You have some report to make. You dined with those people?'

'The Marsetts: yes:—well-suited couple enough. It's to happen before Winter ends—at once; before Christmas; positively before next Spring. Fredi's doing! He has to manage, arrange.—She's a good-looking woman, good height, well-rounded; well-behaved, too: she won't make a bad Lady Marsett. Every time that woman spoke of our girl, the tears jumped to her eyelids.'

'Come to me before you go to bed,' Nataly said, rising, her voice foundering; 'Good-night, Dartrey.'

She turned to the door; she could not trust herself to shake hands with composure. Not only was it a nauseous mixture she was forced to gulp from Victor, it burned like a poison.

'Really Fredi's doing—chiefly,' said Victor, as soon as Dartrey and he were alone, comfortably settled in the smoking-room. 'I played the man of pomp with Marsett—good heavy kind of creature: attached to the woman. She's the better horse, as far as brains go. Good enough Lady Marsett. I harped on Major Worrell: my daughter insulted. He knew of it—spoke of you properly. The man offered all apologies; he has told the Major he is no gentleman, not a fit associate for gentlemen:—quite so—and has cut him dead. Will marry her, as I said, make her as worthy as he can of the honour of my daughter's acquaintance. Rather comical grimace, when he vowed he'd fasten the tie. He doesn't like marriage. But, he can't give her up. And she's for patronizing the institution. But she is ready to say good-bye to him "rather than see the truest lady in the world insulted"—her words. And so he swallows his dose for health, and looks a trifle sourish. Antecedents, I suppose: has to stomach them. But if a man's fond of a woman—if he knows he saves her from slipping lower—and it's an awful world, for us to let a woman be under its wheels:—I say, a woman who has a man to lean on, unless she's as downright corrupt as two or three of the men we've known:—upon my word, Dartrey, I come round to some of your ideas on these matters. It's this girl of mine, this wee bit of girl in her little nightshirt with the frill, astonishes me most:—"thinking of the tops of the mountains at night!" She has positively done the whole of this work-main part. I smiled when I left the house, to have to own our little Fredi starting us all on the road. It seems, Marsett had sworn he would; amorous vow, you know; he never came nearer to doing it. I hope it's his better mind now; I do hope the man won't have cause to regret it. He speaks of Nesta—sort of rustic tone of awe. Mrs. Marsett has impressed him. He expects the title soon, will leave the army—the poor plucked British army, as you call it!—and lead the life of a country squire: hunting! Well, it's not only the army, it's over Great Britain, with this infernal wealth of ours!—and all for pleasure—eh?—or Paradise lost for a sugar plum! Eh, Dartrey? Upon my word, it appears to me, Esau's the Englishman, Jacob the German, of these times. I wonder old Colney hasn't said it. If we're not plucked, as your regiments are of the officers who have learnt their work, we're emasculated:—the nation's half made-up of the idle and the servants of the idle.'

'Ay, and your country squires and your manufacturers contrive to give the army a body of consumptive louts fit for nothing else than to take the shilling—and not worth it,' said Dartrey.

'Sounds like old Colney,' Victor remarked to himself. 'But, believe me, I'm ashamed of the number of servants who wait on me. It wouldn't so much matter, as Skepsey says, if they were trained to arms and self-respect. That little fellow Skepsey's closer to the right notion, and the right practice, too, than any of us. With his Matilda Pridden! He has jumped out of himself to the proper idea of women, too. And there's a man who has been up three times before the magistrates, and is considered a disorderly subject—one among the best of English citizens, I declare! I never think of Skepsey without the most extraordinary, witless kind of envy—as if he were putting in action an idea I once had and never quite got hold of again. The match for him is Fredi. She threatens to be just as devoted, just as simple, as he. I positively doubt whether any of us could stop her, if she had set herself to do a thing she thought right.'

'I should not like to think our trying it possible,' said Dartrey.

'All very well, but it's a rock ahead. We shall have to alter our course, my friend. You know, I dined with that couple, after the private twenty minutes with Marsett: he formally propounded the invitation, as we were close on his hour, rather late: and I wanted to make the woman happy, besides putting a seal of cordiality on his good intentions—politic! And subsequently I heard from her, that—you'll think nothing of it!—Fredi promised to stand by her at the altar.'

Dartrey said, shrugging: 'She needn't do that.'

'So we may say. You're dealing with Nesta Victoria. Spare me a contest with that girl, I undertake to manage any man or woman living.'

'When the thing to be done is thought right by her.'

'But can we always trust her judgement, my dear Dartrey?'

'In this case, she would argue, that her resolution to keep her promise would bind or help to bind Marsett to fulfil his engagement.'

'Odd, her mother has turned dead round in favour of that fellow Dudley Sowerby! I don't complain; it suits; but one thinks—eh?—women!'

'Well, yes, one thinks or should think, that if you insist on having women rooted to the bed of the river, they'll veer with the tides, like water-weeds, and no wonder.'

'Your heterodoxy on that subject is a mania, Dartrey. We can't have women independent.'

'Then don't be exclaiming about their vagaries.'

Victor mused: 'It's wonderful: that little girl of mine!—good height now: but what a head she has! Oh, she'll listen to reason: only mark what I say:—with that quiet air of hers, the husband, if a young fellow, will imagine she's the most docile of wives in the world. And as to wife, I'm not of the contrary opinion. But qua individual female, supposing her to have laid fast hold of an idea of duty, it's he who'll have to turn the corner second, if they're to trot in the yoke together. Or it may be an idea of service to a friend—or to her sex! That Mrs. Marsett says she feels for—"bleeds" for her sex. The poor woman didn't show to advantage with me, because she was in a fever to please:—talks in jerks, hot phrases. She holds herself well. At the end of the dinner she behaved better. Odd, you can teach women with hints and a lead. But Marsett 's Marsett to the end. Rather touching!—the poor fellow said: Deuce of a bad look-out for me if Judith doesn't have a child! First-rate sportsman, I hear. He should have thought of his family earlier. You know, Dartrey, the case is to be argued for the family as well. You won't listen. And for Society too! Off you go.'

A battery was opened on that wall of composite.

'Ah, well,' said Victor. 'But I may have to beg your help, as to the so-called promise to stand at the altar. I don't mention it upstairs.'

He went to Nataly's room.

She was considerately treated, and was aware of being dandled, that she might have sleep.

She consented to it, in a loathing of the topic.—Those women invade us—we cannot keep them out! was her inward cry: with a reverberation of the unfailing accompaniment: The world holds you for one of them!

Victor tasked her too much when his perpetual readiness to doat upon his girl for whatever she did, set him exalting Nesta's conduct. She thought: Was Nesta so sympathetic with her mother of late by reason of a moral insensibility to the offence?

This was her torture through the night of a labouring heart, that travelled to one dull shock, again and again repeated:—the apprehended sound, in fact, of Dudley Sowerby's knock at the street door. Or sometimes a footman handed her his letter, courteously phrased to withdraw from the alliance. Or else he came to a scene with Nesta, and her mother was dragged into it, and the intolerable subject steamed about her. The girl was visioned as deadly. She might be indifferent to the protection of Dudley's name. Robust, sanguine, Victor's child, she might—her mother listened to a devil's whisper—but no; Nesta's aim was at the heights; she was pure in mind as in body. No, but the world would bring the accusation; and the world would trace the cause: Heredity, it would say. Would it say falsely? Nataly harped on the interrogation until she felt her existence dissolving to a dark stain of the earth, and she found herself wondering at the breath she drew, doubting that another would follow, speculating on the cruel force which keeps us to the act of breathing.—Though I could draw wild blissful breath if I were galloping across the moors! her worn heart said to her youth: and out of ken of the world, I could regain a portion of my self-esteem. Nature thereat renewed her old sustainment with gentle murmurs, that were supported by Dr. Themison's account of the virtuous married lady who chafed at the yoke on behalf of her sex, and deemed the independent union the ideal. Nataly's brain had a short gallop over moorland. It brought her face to face with Victor's girl, and she dropped once more to her remorse in herself and her reproaches of Nesta. The girl had inherited from her father something of the cataract's force which won its way by catching or by mastering, uprooting, ruining!

In the morning she was heavily asleep. Victor left word with Nesta, that the dear mother was not to be disturbed. Consequently, when Dudley called to see Mrs. Victor Radnor, he was informed that Miss Radnor would receive him.

Their interview lasted an hour.

Dudley came to Victor in the City about luncheon time.

His perplexity of countenance was eloquent. He had, before seeing the young lady, digested an immense deal more, as it seemed to him, than any English gentleman should be asked to consume. She now referred him to her father, who had spent a day in Brighton, and would, she said, explain whatever there was to be explained. But she added, that if she was expected to abandon a friend, she could not. Dudley had argued with her upon the nature of friendship, the measurement of its various dues; he had lectured on the choice of friends, the impossibility for young ladies, necessarily inexperienced, to distinguish the right class of friends, the dangers they ran in selecting friends unwarranted by the stamp of honourable families.

'And what did Fredi say to that?' Victor inquired.

'Miss Radnor said—I may be dense, I cannot comprehend—that the precepts were suitable for seminaries of Pharisees. When it is a question of a young lady associating with a notorious woman!'

'Not notorious. You spoil your case if you "speak extremely," as a friend says. I saw her yesterday. She worships "Miss Radnor."'

Nesta will know when she is older; she will thank me,' said Dudley hurriedly. 'As it is at present, I may reckon, I hope, that the association ceases. Her name: I have to consider my family.'

'Good anchorage! You must fight it out with the girl. And depend upon this—you're not the poorer for being the husband of a girl of character; unless you try to bridle her. She belongs to her time. I don't mind owning to you, she has given me a lead.—Fredi 'll be merry to-night. Here's a letter I have from the Sanfredini, dated Milan, fresh this morning; invitation to bring the god-child to her villa on Como in May; desirous to embrace her. She wrote to the office. Not a word of her duque. She has pitched him to the winds. You may like to carry it off to Fredi and please her.'

'I have business,' Dudley replied.

'Away to it, then!' said Victor. 'You stand by me?—we expect our South London borough to be open in January; early next year, at least; may be February. You have family interest there.'

'Personally, I will do my best,' Dudley said; and he escaped, feeling, with the universal censor's angry spite, that the revolutions of the world had made one of the wealthiest of City men the head of a set of Bohemians. And there are eulogists of the modern time! And the man's daughter was declared to belong to it! A visit in May to the Italian cantatrice separated from her husband, would render the maiden an accomplished flinger of caps over the windmills.

At home Victor discovered, that there was not much more than a truce between Nesta and Nataly. He had a medical hint from Dr. Themison, and he counselled his girl to humour her mother as far as could be: particularly in relation to Dudley, whom Nataly now, womanlike, after opposing, strongly favoured. How are we ever to get a clue to the labyrinthine convolutions and changeful motives of the sex! Dartrey's theories were absurd. Did Nataly think them dangerous for a young woman? The guess hinted at a clue of some sort to the secret of her veering.

'Mr. Sowerby left me with an adieu,' said Nesta.

'Mr. Sowerby! My dear, he is bound, bound in honour, bound at heart. You did not dismiss him?'

'I repeated the word he used. I thought of mother. The blood leaves her cheeks at a disappointment now. She has taken to like him.'

'Why, you like him!'

'I could not vow.'

'Tush.'

'Ah, don't press me, dada. But you will see, he has disengaged himself.'

He had done it, though not in formal speech. Slow digestion of his native antagonism to these Bohemians, to say nothing of his judicial condemnation of them, brought him painfully round to the writing of a letter to Nataly; cunningly addressed to the person on whom his instinct told him he had the strongest hold.

She schooled herself to discuss the detested matter forming Dudley's grievance and her own with Nesta; and it was a woeful half-hour for them. But Nataly was not the weeper.

Another interview ensued between Nesta and her suitor. Dudley bore no resemblance to Mr. Barmby, who refused to take the word no from her, and had taken it, and had gone to do holy work, for which she revered him. Dudley took the word, leaving her to imagine freedom, until once more her mother or her father, inspired by him, came interceding, her mother actually supplicating. So that the reality of Dudley's love rose to conception like a London dawn over Nesta; and how, honourably, decently, positively, to sever herself from it, grew to be an ill-visaged problem. She glanced in soul at Dartrey Fenellan for help; she had her wild thoughts. Having once called him Dartrey, the virginal barrier to thoughts was broken; and but for love of her father, for love and pity of her mother, she would have ventured the step to make the man who had her whole being in charge accept or reject her. Nothing else appeared in prospect. Her father and mother were urgently one to favour Dudley; and the sensitive gentleman presented himself to receive his wound and to depart with it. But always he returned. At last, as if under tuition, he refrained from provoking a wound; he stood there to win her upon any terms; and he was a handsome figure, acknowledged by the damsel to be increasing in good looks as more and more his pretensions became distasteful to her. The slight cast of sourness on his lower features had almost vanished, his nature seemed to have enlarged. He complimented her for her 'generous benevolence,' vaguely, yet with evident sincereness; he admitted, that the modern world is 'attempting difficulties with at least commendable intentions'; and that the position of women demands improvement, consideration for them also. He said feelingly: 'They have to bear extraordinary burdens!' There he stopped.

The sharp intelligence fronting him understood, that this compassionate ejaculation was the point where she, too, must cry halt. He had, however—still under tuition, perhaps—withdrawn his voice from the pursuit of her; and so she in gratitude silenced her critical mind beneath a smooth conceit of her having led him two steps to a broader tolerance. Susceptible as she was, she did not influence him without being affected herself in other things than her vanity: his prudishness affected her. Only when her heart flamed did she disdain that real haven of refuge, with its visionary mount of superiority, offered by Society to its effect, in the habit of ignoring the sins it fosters under cloak;—not less than did the naked barbaric time, and far more to the vitiation of the soul. He fancied he was moulding her; therefore winning her. It followed, that he had the lover's desire for assurance of exclusive possession; and reflecting, that he had greatly pardoned, he grew exacting. He mentioned his objections to some of Mr. Dartrey Fenellan's ideas.

Nesta replied: 'I have this morning had two letters to make me happy.'

A provoking evasion. He would rather have seen antagonism bridle and stiffen her figure. 'Is one of them from that gentleman?'

'One is from my dear friend Louise de Seilles. She comes to me early next month.'

'The other?'

'The other is also from a friend.'

'A dear friend?'

'Not so dear. Her letter gives me happiness.'

'She writes—not from France: from...? you tempt me to guess.'

'She writes to tell me, that Mr. Dartrey Fenellan has helped her in a way to make her eternally thankful.'

'The place she writes from is...?'

The drag of his lips betrayed his enlightenment insisted on doubting. He demanded assurance.

'It matters in no degree,' she said.

Dudley 'thought himself excusable for inquiring.'

She bowed gently.

The stings and scorpions and degrading itches of this nest of wealthy Bohemians enraged him.

'Are you—I beg to ask—are you still:—I can hardly think it—Nesta!—I surely have a claim to advise:—it cannot be with your mother's consent:—in communication, in correspondence with...?'

Again she bowed her head; saying: 'It is true.'

'With that person?'

He could not but look the withering disgust of the modern world in a conservative gentleman who has been lured to go with it a little way, only to be bitten. 'I decline to believe it,' he said with forcible sound.

'She is married,' was the rather shameless, exasperating answer.

'Married or not!' he cried, and murmured: 'I have borne—. These may be Mr. Dartrey Fenellan's ideas; they are not mine. I have—Something at least is due to me: Ask any lady:—there are clergymen, I know, clergymen who are for uplifting—quite right, but not associating:—to call one of them a friend! Ask any lady, any! Your mother...'

'I beg you will not distress my mother,' said Nesta.

'I beg to know whether this correspondence is to continue?' said Dudley.

'All my life, if I do not feel dishonoured by it.'

'You are.' He added hastily: 'Counsels of prudence—there is not a lady living who would tell you otherwise. At all events, in public opinion, if it were known—and it would certainly be known,—a lady, wife or spinster, would suffer—would not escape the—at least shadow of defilement from relationship, any degree of intimacy with... hard words are wholesome in such a case: "touch pitch," yes! My sense is coherent.'

'Quite,' said Nesta.

'And you do not agree with me?'

'I do not.'

'Do you pretend to be as able to judge as I?'

'In this instance, better.'

'Then I retire. I cannot retain my place here. You may depend upon it, the world is not wrong when it forbids young ladies to have cognizance of women leading disorderly lives.'

'Only the women, Mr. Sowerby?'

'Men, too, of course.'

'You do not exclude the men from Society.'

'Oh! one reads that kind of argument in books.'

'Oh! the worthy books, then. I would read them, if I could find them.'

'They are banned by self-respecting readers.'

'It grieves me to think differently.'

Dudley looked on this fair girl, as yet innocent girl; and contrasting her with the foulness of the subject she dared discuss, it seemed to him, that a world which did not puff at her and silence, if not extinguish, was in a state of liquefaction.

Remembering his renewed repentances his absence, he said: 'I do hope you may come to see, that the views shared by your mother and me are not erroneous.'

'But do not distress her,' Nesta implored him. 'She is not well. When she has grown stronger, her kind heart will move her to receive the lady, so that she may not be deprived of the society of good women. I shall hope she will not disapprove of me. I cannot forsake a friend.'

'I beg to say good-bye,' said Dudley.

She had seen a rigidity smite him as she spoke; and so little startling was it, that she might have fancied it expected, save for her knowing herself too serious to have played at wiles to gain her ends.

He 'wished her prudent advisers.'

She thanked him. 'In a few days, Louise de Seilles will be here.'

A Frenchwoman and Papist! was the interjection of his twist of brows.

Surely I must now be free? she thought when he had covered his farewell under a salutation regretful in frostiness.

A week later, she had the embrace of her Louise, and Armandine was made happy with a piece of Parisian riband.

Winter was rapidly in passage: changes were visible everywhere; Earth and House of Commons and the South London borough exhibited them; Mrs. Burman was the sole exception. To the stupefaction of physicians, in a manner to make a sane man ask whether she was not being retained as an instrument for one of the darker purposes of Providence—and where are we standing if we ask such things?—she held on to her thread of life.

February went by. And not a word from Themison; nor from Carling, nor from the Rev. Groseman Buttermore, nor from Jarniman. That is to say, the two former accepted invitations to grand dinners; the two latter acknowledged contributions to funds in which they were interested; but they had apparently grown to consider Mrs. Burman as an establishment, one of our fixtures. On the other hand, there was nothing to be feared from her. Lakelands feared nothing: the entry into Lakelands was decreed for the middle of April. Those good creatures enclosed the poor woman and nourished her on comfortable fiction. So the death of the member for the South London borough (fifteen years younger than the veteran in maladies) was not to be called premature, and could by no possibility lead to an exposure of the private history of the candidate for his vacant seat.

CHAPTER XL

AN EXPIATION

Nataly had fallen to be one of the solitary who have no companionship save with the wound they nurse, to chafe it rather than try at healing. So rational a mind as she had was not long in outliving mistaken impressions; she could distinguish her girl's feeling, and her aim; she could speak on the subject with Dartrey; and still her wound bled on. Louise de Seilles comforted her partly, through an exaltation of Nesta. Mademoiselle, however, by means of a change of tone and look when Dudley Sowerby and Dartrey Fenellan were the themes, showed a too pronounced preference of the more unstable one:—or rather, the man adventurous out of the world's highways, whose image, as husband of such a daughter as hers, smote the wounded mother with a chillness. Mademoiselle's occasional thrill of fervency in an allusion to Dartrey, might have tempted a suspicious woman to indulge suppositions, accounting for the young Frenchwoman's novel tenderness to England, of which Nesta proudly, very happily boasted. The suspicion proposed itself, and was rejected: for not even the fever of an insane body could influence Nataly's generous character, to let her moods divert and command her thoughts of persons.

Her thoughts were at this time singularly lucid upon everything about her; with the one exception of the reason why she had come to favour Dudley, and how it was she had been smitten by that woman at Brighton to see herself in her position altogether with the world's relentless, unexamining hard eyes. Bitterness added, of Mrs. Marsett: She is made an honest woman!—And there was a strain of the lower in Nataly, to reproach the girl for causing the reflection to be cast on the unwedded. Otherwise her mind was open; she was of aid to Victor in his confusion over some lost Idea he had often touched on latterly. And she was the one who sent him ahead at a trot under a light, by saying: 'You would found a new and more stable aristocracy of the contempt of luxury' when he talked of combatting the Jews with a superior weapon. That being, in fact, as Colney Durance had pointed out to him, the weapon of self-conquest used by them 'before they fell away to flesh-pottery.' Was it his Idea? He fancied an aching at the back of his head when he speculated. But his Idea had been surpassingly luminous, alive, a creation; and this came before him with the yellow skin of a Theory, bred, born of books. Though Nataly's mention of the aristocracy of self-denying discipline struck a Lucifer in his darkness.

Nesta likewise helped: but more in what she did than in what she said: she spoke intelligently enough to make him feel a certain increase of alarm, amounting to a cursory secret acknowledgement of it, both at her dealings with Dudley and with himself. She so quietly displaced the lady visiting him at the City offices. His girl's disregard of hostile weather, and her company, her talk, delighted him: still he remonstrated, at her coming daily. She came: nor was there an instigation on the part of her mother, clearly none: her mother asked him once whether he thought she met the dreadful Brighton woman. His Fredi drove constantly to walk back beside him Westward, as he loved to do whenever it was practicable; and exceeding the flattery of his possession of the gallant daughter, her conversation charmed him to forget a disappointment caused by the defeat and entire exclusion of the lady visiting him so complimentarily for his advice on stocks, shares, mines, et caetera. The lady resisted; she was vanquished, as the shades are displaced by simple apparition of daylight.

His Fredi was like the daylight to him; she was the very daylight to his mind, whatsoever their theme of converse for by stimulating that ready but vagrant mind to quit the leash of the powerful senses and be a ethereally excursive, she gave him a new enjoyment; which led to reflections—a sounding of Nature, almost a question to her, on the verge of a doubt. Are we, in fact, harmonious with the Great Mother when we yield to the pressure of our natures for indulgence? Is she, when translated into us, solely the imperious appetite? Here was Fredi, his little Fredi—stately girl that she had grown, and grave, too, for all her fun and her sail on wings—lifting him to pleasures not followed by clamorous, and perfectly satisfactory, yet discomposingly violent, appeals to Nature. They could be vindicated. Or could they, when they would not bear a statement of the case? He could not imagine himself stating it namelessly to his closest friend—not to Simeon Fenellan. As for speaking to Dartrey, the notion took him with shivers:—Young Dudley would have seemed a more possible confidant:—and he represented the Puritan world.—And young Dudley was getting over Fredi's infatuation for the woman she had rescued: he was beginning to fancy he saw a right enthusiasm in it;—in the abstract; if only the fair maid would drop an unseemly acquaintance. He had called at the office to say so. Victor stammered the plea for him.

'Never, dear father,' came the smooth answer: a shocking answer in contrast with the tones. Her English was as lucid as her eyes when she continued up to the shock she dealt: 'Do not encourage a good man to waste his thoughts upon me. I have chosen my mate, and I may never marry him. I do not know whether he would marry me. He has my soul. I have no shame in saying I love him. It is to love goodness, greatness of heart. He is a respecter of women—of all women; not only the fortunate. He is the friend of the weaker everywhere. He has been proved in fire. He does not sentimentalize over poor women, as we know who scorns people for doing:—and that is better than hardness, meaning kindly. He is not one of the unwise advocates. He measures the forces against them. He reads their breasts. He likes me. He is with me in my plans. He has not said, has not shown, he loves me. It is too high a thought for me until I hear it.'

'Has your soul!' was all that Victor could reply, while the whole conception of Lakelands quaked under the crumbling structure.

Remonstrance, argument, a word for Dudley, swelled to his lips and sank in dumbness. Her seeming intuition—if it was not a perception—of the point where submission to the moods of his nature had weakened his character, and required her defence of him, struck Victor with a serious fear of his girl: and it was the more illuminatingly damnatory for being recognized as the sentiment which no father should feel. He tried to think she ought not to be so wise of the things of the world. An effort to imagine a reproof, showed him her spirit through her eyes: in her deeds too: she had already done work on the road:—Colney Durance, Dartrey Fenellan, anything but sentimentalists either of them, strongly backing her, upholding her. Victor could no longer so naturally name her Fredi.

He spoke it hastily, under plea of some humorous tenderness, when he ventured. When Dudley, calling on him in the City to discuss the candidature for the South London borough, named her Fredi, that he might regain a vantage of familiarity by imitating her father, it struck Victor as audacious. It jarred in his recollection, though the heir of the earldom spoke in the tone of a lover, was really at high pitch. He appeared to be appreciating her, to have suffered stings of pain; he offered himself; he made but one stipulation. Victor regretfully assured him, he feared he could do nothing. The thought of his entry into Lakelands, with Nesta Victoria refusing the foundation stone of the place, grew dim.

But he was now canvassing for the Borough, hearty at the new business as the braced swimmer on seas, which instantly he became, with an end in view to be gained.

Late one April night, expecting Nataly to have gone to bed, and Nesta to be waiting for him, he reached home, and found Nataly in her sitting-room alone. 'Nesta was tired,' she said: 'we have had a scene; she refuses Mr. Sowerby; I am sick of pressing it; he is very much in earnest, painfully; she blames him for disturbing me; she will not see the right course:—a mother reads her daughter! If my girl has not guidance!—she means rightly, she is rash.'

Nataly could not utter all that her insaneness of feeling made her think with regard to Victor's daughter—daughter also of the woman whom her hard conscience accused of inflammability. 'Here is a note from Dr. Themison, dear.'

Victor seized it, perused, and drew the big breath.

'From Themison,' he said; he coughed.

'Don't think to deceive me,' said she. 'I have not read the contents, I know them.'

'The invitation at last, for to-morrow, Sunday, four P.M. Odd, that next day at eight of the evening I shall be addressing our meeting in the Theatre. Simeon speaks. Beaves Urmsing insists on coming, Tory though he is. Those Tories are jollier fellows than—well, no wonder! There will be no surgical... the poor woman is very low. A couple of days at the outside. Of course, I go.'

'Hand me the note, dear.'

It had to be given up, out of the pocket.

'But,' said Victor, 'the mention of you is merely formal.'

She needed sleep: she bowed her head.

Nataly was the first at the breakfast-table in the morning, a fair Sunday morning. She was going to Mrs. John Cormyn's Church, and she asked Nesta to come with her.

She returned five minutes before the hour of lunch, having left Nesta with Mrs. John. Louise de Seilles undertook to bring Nesta home at the time she might choose. Fenellan, Mr. Pempton, Peridon and Catkin, lunched and chatted. Nataly chatted. At a quarter to three o'clock Victor's carriage was at the door. He rose: he had to keep an appointment. Nataly said to him publicly: 'I come too.' He stared and nodded. In the carriage, he said: 'I'm driving to the Gardens, for a stroll, to have a look at the beasts. Sort of relief. Poor crazy woman! However, it 's a comfort to her: so...!'

'I like to see them,' said Nataly. 'I shall see her. I have to do it.'

Up to the gate of the Gardens Victor was arguing to dissuade his dear soul from this very foolish, totally unnecessary, step. Alighting, he put the matter aside, for good angels to support his counsel at the final moment.

Bears, lions, tigers, eagles, monkeys: they suggested no more than he would have had from prints; they sprang no reflection, except, that the coming hour was a matter of indifference to them. They were about him, and exercised so far a distraction. He took very kindly to an old mother monkey, relinquishing her society at sight of Nataly's heave of the bosom. Southward, across the park, the dread house rose. He began quoting Colney Durance with relish while sarcastically confuting the cynic, who found much pasture in these Gardens. Over Southward, too, he would be addressing a popular assembly to-morrow evening. Between now and then there was a ditch to jump. He put on the sympathetic face of grief. 'After all, a caged wild beast hasn't so bad a life,' he said.—To be well fed while they live, and welcome death as a release from the maladies they develop in idleness, is the condition of wealthy people:—creatures of prey? horrible thought! yet allied to his Idea, it seemed. Yes, but these good caged beasts here set them an example, in not troubling relatives and friends when they come to the gasp! Mrs. Burman's invitation loomed as monstrous—a final act of her cruelty. His skin pricked with dews. He thought of Nataly beside him, jumping the ditch with him, as a relief—if she insisted on doing it. He hoped she would not, for the sake of her composure.

It was a ditch void of bottom. But it was a mere matter of an hour, less. The state of health of the invalid could bear only a few minutes. In any case, we are sure that the hour will pass. Our own arrive? Certainly.

'Capital place for children,' he exclaimed. And here startlingly before him in the clusters of boys and girls, was the difference between young ones and their elders feeling quite as young: the careless youngsters have not to go and sit in the room with a virulent old woman, and express penitence and what not, and hear words of pardon, after their holiday scamper and stare at the caged beasts.

Attention to the children precipitated him upon acquaintances, hitherto cleverly shunned. He nodded them off, after the brightest of greetings.

Such anodyne as he could squeeze from the incarcerated wild creatures, was exhausted. He fell to work at Nataly's 'aristocracy of the contempt of luxury'; signifying, that we the wealthy will not exist to pamper flesh, but we live for the promotion of brotherhood:—ay, and that our England must make some great moral stand, if she is not to fall to the rear and down. Unuttered, it caught the skirts of the Idea: it evaporated when spoken. Still, this theme was almost an exorcism of Mrs. Burman. He consulted his watch. 'Thirteen minutes to four. I must be punctual,' he said. Nataly stepped faster.

Seated in the carriage, he told her he had never felt the horror of that place before. 'Put me down at the corner of the terrace, dear: I won't drive to the door.'

'I come with you, Victor,' she replied.

After entreaties and reasons intermixed, to melt her resolve, he saw she was firm: and he asked himself, whether he might not be constitutionally better adapted to persuade than to dissuade. The question thumped. Having that house of drugs in view, he breathed more freely for the prospect of feeling his Nataly near him beneath the roof.

'You really insist, dear love?' he appealed to her: and her answer: 'It must be,' left no doubt: though he chose to say: 'Not because of standing by me?' And she said: 'For my peace, Victor.' They stepped to the pavement. The carriage was dismissed.

Seventeen houses of the terrace fronting the park led to the funereal one: and the bell was tolled in the breast of each of the couple advancing with an air of calmness to the inevitable black door.

Jarniman opened it. 'His mistress was prepared to see them.'—Not like one near death.—They were met in the hall by the Rev. Groseman Buttermore. 'You will find a welcome,' was his reassurance to them: gently delivered, on the stoop of a large person. His whispered tones were more agreeably deadening than his words.

Mr. Buttermore ushered them upstairs.

'Can she bear it?' Victor said, and heard: 'Her wish ten minutes.'

'Soon over,' he murmured to Nataly, with a compassionate exclamation for the invalid.

They rounded the open door. They were in the drawing-room. It was furnished as in the old time, gold and white, looking new; all the same as of old, save for a division of silken hangings; and these were pale blue: the colour preferred by Victor for a bedroom. He glanced at the ceiling, to bathe in a blank space out of memory. Here she lived,—here she slept, behind the hangings. There was refreshingly that little difference in the arrangement of the room. The corner Northward was occupied by the grand piano; and

Victor had an inquiry in him:—tuned? He sighed, expecting a sight to come through the hangings. Sensible that Nataly trembled, he perceived the Rev. Groseman Buttermore half across a heap of shawl-swathe on the sofa.

Mrs. Burman was present; seated. People may die seated; she had always disliked the extended posture; except for the night's rest, she used to say; imagining herself to be not inviting the bolt of sudden death, in her attitude when seated by day:—and often at night the poor woman had to sit up for the qualms of her dyspepsia!—But I 'm bound to think humanely, be Christian, be kind, benignant, he thought, and he fetched the spirit required, to behold her face emerge from a pale blue silk veiling; as it were, the inanimate wasted led up from the mould by morning.

Mr. Buttermore signalled to them to draw near.

Wasted though it was, the face of the wide orbits for sunken eyes was distinguishable as the one once known. If the world could see it and hear, that it called itself a man's wife! She looked burnt out.

Two chairs had been sent to front the sofa. Execution there! Victor thought, and he garrotted the unruly mind of a man really feeling devoutness in the presence of the shadow thrown by the dread Shade.

'Ten minutes,' Mr. Buttermore said low, after obligingly placing them on the chairs.

He went. They were alone with Mrs. Burman.

No voice came. They were unsure of being seen by the floating grey of eyes patient to gaze from their vast distance. Big drops fell from Nataly's. Victor heard the French timepiece on the mantel-shelf, where a familiar gilt Cupid swung for the seconds: his own purchase. The time of day on the clock was wrong; the Cupid swung.

Nataly's mouth was taking breath of anguish at moments. More than a minute of the terrible length of the period of torture must have gone: two, if not three.

A quaver sounded. 'You have come.' The voice was articulate, thinner than the telephonic, trans-Atlantic by deep-sea cable.

Victor answered: 'We have.'

Another minute must have gone in the silence. And when we get to five minutes we are on the descent, rapidly counting our way out of the house, into the fresh air, where we were half an hour back, among those happy beasts in the pleasant Gardens!

Mrs. Burman's eyelids shut. 'I said you would come.'

Victor started to the fire-screen. 'Your sight requires protection.'

She dozed. 'And Natalia Dreighton!' she next said.

They were certainly now on the five minutes. Now for the slide downward and outward! Nataly should never have been allowed to come.

'The white waistcoat!' struck his ears.

'Old customs with me, always!' he responded. 'The first of April, always. White is a favourite. Pale blue, too. But I fear—I hope you have not distressing nights? In my family we lay great stress on the nights we pass. My cousins, the Miss Duvidneys, go so far as to judge of the condition of health by the nightly record.'

'Your daughter was in their house.'

She knew everything!

'Very fond of my daughter—the ladies,' he remarked.

'I wish her well.'

'You are very kind.'

Mrs. Burman communed within or slept. 'Victor, Natalia, we will pray,' she said.

Her trembling hands crossed their fingers. Nataly slipped to her knees.

The two women mutely praying, pulled Victor into the devotional hush. It acted on him like the silent spell of service in a Church. He forgot his estimate of the minutes, he formed a prayer, he refused to hear the Cupid swinging, he droned a sound of sentences to deaden his ears. Ideas of eternity rolled in semblance of enormous clouds. Death was a black bird among them. The piano rang to Nataly's young voice and his. The gold and white of the chairs welcomed a youth suddenly enrolled among the wealthy by an enamoured old lady on his arm. Cupid tick-ticked.—Poor soul! poor woman! How little we mean to do harm when we do an injury! An incomprehensible world indeed at the bottom and at the top. We get on fairly at the centre. Yet it is there that we do the mischief making such a riddle of the bottom and the top. What is to be said! Prayer quiets one. Victor peered at Nataly fervently on her knees and Mrs. Burman bowed over her knotted fingers. The earnestness of both enforced an effort at a phrased prayer in him. Plungeing through a wave of the scent of Marechale, that was a tremendous memory to haul him backward and forward, he beheld his prayer dancing across the furniture; a diminutive thin black figure, elvish, irreverent, appallingly unlike his proper emotion; and he brought his hands just to touch, and got to the edge of his chair, with split knees. At once the figure vanished. By merely looking at Nataly, he passed into her prayer. A look at Mrs. Burman made it personal, his own. He heard the cluck of a horrible sob coming from him. After a repetition of his short form of prayer deeply stressed, he thanked himself with the word 'sincere,' and a queer side-thought on our human susceptibility to the influence of posture. We are such creatures.

Nataly resumed her seat. Mrs. Burman had raised her head. She said: 'We are at peace.' She presently said, with effort: 'It cannot last with me. I die in nature's way. I would bear forgiveness with me, that I may have it above. I give it here, to you, to all. My soul is cleansed, I trust. Much was to say. My strength will not. Unto God, you both!'

The Rev. Groseman Buttermore was moving on slippered step to the back of the sofa. Nataly dropped before the unseeing, scarce breathing, lady for an instant. Victor murmured an adieu, grateful for being spared the ceremonial shake of hands. He turned away, then turned back, praying for power to speak, to say that he had found his heart, was grateful, would hold her in memory. He fell on a knee before her, and forgot he had done so when he had risen. They were conducted by the Rev. gentleman to the hall-door: he was not speechless. Jarniman uttered something.

That black door closed behind them.

CHAPTER XLI

THE NIGHT OF THE GREAT UNDELIVERED SPEECH

To a man issuing from a mortuary where a skull had voice, London may be restorative as air of Summer Alps. It is by contrast blooming life. Observe the fellowship of the houses shoulder to shoulder; and that straight ascending smoke of the preparation for dinner; and the good policeman yonder, blessedly idle on an orderly Sabbath evening; and the families of the minor people trotting homeward from the park to tea; here and again an amiable carriage of the superimposed people driving to pay visits; they are so social, friendly, inviting to him; they strip him of the shroud, sing of the sweet old world. He cannot but be moved to the extremity of the charitableness neighbouring on tears.

A stupefaction at the shock of the positive reminder, echo of the fact still shouting in his breast, that he had seen Mrs. Burman, and that the interview was over—the leaf turned and the book shut held Victor in a silence until his gratefulness to London City was borne down by the more human burst of gratitude to the dying woman, who had spared him, as much as she could, a scene of the convulsive pathetic, and had not called on him for any utterance of penitence. That worm-like thread of voice came up to him still from sexton-depths: it sounded a larger forgiveness without the word. He felt the sorrow of it all, as he told Nataly; at the same time bidding her smell 'the marvellous oxygen of the park.' He declared it to be quite equal to Lakelands.

She slightly pressed his arm for answer. Perhaps she did not feel so deeply? She was free of the horrid associations with the scent of Marechale. At any rate, she had comported herself admirably!

Victor fancied he must have shuddered when he passed by Jarniman at the door, who was almost now seeing his mistress's ghost—would have the privilege to-morrow. He called a cab and drove to Mrs. John Cormyn's, at Nataly's request, for Nesta and mademoiselle: enjoying the Londonized odour of the cab. Nataly did not respond to his warm and continued eulogies of Mrs. Burman; she rather disappointed him. He talked of the gold and white furniture, he just alluded to the Cupid: reserving his mental comment, that the time-piece was all astray, the Cupid regular on the swing:—strange, touching, terrible, if really the silly gilt figure symbolized!... And we are a silly figure to be sitting in a cab imagining such things!—When Nesta and mademoiselle were opposite, he had the pleasure to see Nataly take Nesta's hand and hold it until they reached home. Those two talking together in the brief words of their deep feeling, had tones that were singularly alike: the mezzo-soprano filial to the divine maternal contralto. Those two dear ones mounted to Nataly's room.

The two dear ones showed themselves heart in heart together once more; each looked the happier for it. Dartrey was among their dinner-guests, and Nataly took him to her little blue-room before she went to bed. He did not speak of their conversation to Victor, but counselled him to keep her from excitement. 'My dear fellow, if you had seen her with Mrs. Burman!' Victor said, and loudly praised her coolness. She was never below a situation, he affirmed.

He followed his own counsel to humour his Nataly. She began panting at a word about Mr. Barmby's ready services. When, however, she related the state of affairs between Dartrey and Nesta, by the avowal of each of them to her, he said, embracing her: 'Your wisdom shall guide us, my love,' and almost extinguished a vexation by concealing it.

She sighed: 'If one could think, that a girl with Nesta's revolutionary ideas of the duties of women, and their powers, would be safe—or at all rightly guided by a man who is both one of the noblest and the wildest in the ideas he entertains!'

Victor sighed too. He saw the earldom, which was to dazzle the gossips, crack on the sky in a futile rocket-bouquet.

She was distressed; she moaned: 'My girl! my girl: I should wish to leave her with one who is more fixed—the old-fashioned husband. New ideas must come in politics, but in Society!—and for women! And the young having heads, are the most endangered. Nesta vows her life to it! Dartrey supports her!'

'See Colney,' said Victor. 'Odd, Colney does you good; some queer way he has. Though you don't care for his RIVAL TONGUES,—and the last number was funny, with Semhians on the Pacific, impressively addressing a farewell to his cricket-bat, before he whirls it away to Neptune—and the blue hand of his nation's protecting God observed to seize it!—Dead failure with the public, of course! However, he seems to seem wise with you. The poor old fellow gets his trouncing from the critics monthly. See Colney to-morrow, my love. Now go to sleep. We have got over the worst. I speak at my Meeting to-morrow and am a champagne-bottle of notes and points for them.'

His lost Idea drew close to him in sleep: or he thought so, when awaking to the conception of a people solidified, rich and poor, by the common pride of simple manhood. But it was not coloured, not a luminous globe: and the people were in drab, not a shining army on the march to meet the Future. It looked like a paragraph in a newspaper, upon which a Leading Article sits, dutifully arousing the fat worm of sarcastic humour under the ribs of cradled citizens, with an exposure of its excellent folly. He would not have it laughed at; still he could not admit it as more than a skirt of the robe of his Idea. For let none think him a mere City merchant, millionnaire, boon-fellow, or music-loving man of the world. He had ideas to shoot across future Ages;—provide against the shrinkage of our Coal-beds; against, and for, if you like, the thickening, jumbling, threatening excess of population in these Islands, in Europe, America, all over our habitable sphere. Now that Mrs. Burman, on her way to bliss, was no longer the dungeon-cell for the man he would show himself to be, this name for successes, corporate nucleus of the enjoyments, this Victor Montgomery Radnor, intended impressing himself upon the world as a factory of ideas. Colney's insolent charge, that the English have no imagination—a doomed race, if it be true!—would be confuted. For our English require but the lighted leadership to come into cohesion, and step ranked, and chant harmoniously the song of their benevolent aim. And that astral head giving, as a commencement, example of the right use of riches, the nation is one, part of the riddle of the future solved.

Surely he had here the Idea? He had it so warmly, that his bath-water heated. Only the vision was wanted.

On London Bridge he had seen it—a great thing done to the flash of brilliant results. That was after a fall.

There had been a fall also of the scheme of Lakelands.

Come to us with no superstitious whispers of indications and significations in the fall!—But there had certainly been a moral fall, fully to the level of the physical, in the maintaining of that scheme of Lakelands, now ruined by his incomprehensible Nesta—who had saved him from falling further. His bath-water chilled. He jumped out and rubbed furiously with his towels and flesh-brushes, chasing the Idea for simple warmth, to have Something inside him, to feel just that sustainment; with the cry: But no one can say I do not love my Nataly! And he tested it to prove it by his readiness to die for her: which is heroically easier than the devotedly living, and has a weight of evidence in our internal Courts for surpassing the latter tedious performance.

His Nesta had knocked Lakelands to pieces. Except for the making of money, the whole year of an erected Lakelands, notwithstanding uninterrupted successes, was a blank. Or rather we have to wish it were a blank. The scheme departs: payment for the enlisted servants of it is in prospect. A black agent, not willingly enlisted, yet pointing to proofs of service, refuses payment in ordinary coin; and we tell him we owe him nothing, that he is not a man of the world, has no understanding of Nature: and still the fellow thumps and alarums at a midnight door we are astonished to find we have in our daylight house. How is it? Would other men be so sensitive to him? Victor was appeased by the assurance of his possession of an exceptionally scrupulous conscience; and he settled the debate by thinking: 'After all, for a man like me, battling incessantly, a kind of Vesuvius, I must have—can't be starved, must be fed—though, pah! But I'm not to be questioned like other men.—But how about an aristocracy of the contempt of distinctions?—But there is no escaping distinctions! my aristocracy despises indulgence.—And indulges?—Say, an exceptional nature! Supposing a certain beloved woman to pronounce on the case?—She cannot: no woman can be a just judge of it.'—He cried: My love of her is testified by my having Barmby handy to right her to-day, tomorrow, the very instant the clock strikes the hour of my release!

Mention of the clock swung that silly gilt figure. Victor entered into it, condemned to swing, and be a thrall. His intensity of sensation launched him on an eternity of the swinging in ridiculous nakedness to the measure of time gone crazy. He had to correct a reproof of Mrs. Burman, as the cause of the nonsense. He ran down to breakfast, hopeing he might hear of that clock stopped, and that sickening motion with it.

Another letter from the Sanfredini in Milan, warmly inviting to her villa over Como, acted on him at breakfast like the waving of a banner. 'We go,' Victor said to Nataly, and flattered-up a smile about her lips—too much a resurrection smile. There was talk of the Meeting at the theatre: Simeon Fenellan had spoken there in the cause of the deceased Member, was known, and was likely to have a good reception. Fun and enthusiasm might be expected.

'And my darling will hear her husband speak to-night,' he whispered as he was departing; and did a mischief, he had to fear, for a shadowy knot crossed Nataly's forehead, she seemed paler. He sent back Nesta and mademoiselle, in consequence, at the end of the Green Park.

Their dinner-hour was early; Simeon Fenellan, Colney Durance, and Mr. Peridon—pleasing to Nataly for his faithful siege of the French fortress—were the only guests. When they rose, Nataly drew Victor aside. He came dismayed to Nesta. She ran to her mother. 'Not hear papa speak? Oh, mother, mother! Then I stay with her. But can't she come? He is going to unfold ideas to us. There!'

'My naughty girl is not to poke her fun at orators,' Nataly said. 'No, dearest; it would agitate me to go. I'm better here. I shall be at peace when the night is over.'

'But you will be all alone here, dear mother.'

Nataly's eyes wandered to fall on Colney. He proposed to give her his company. She declined it. Nesta ventured another entreaty, either that she might be allowed to stay or have her mother with her at the Meeting.

'My love,' Nataly said, 'the thought of the Meeting—' She clasped at her breast; and she murmured: 'I shall be comforted by your being with him. There is no danger there. But I shall be happy, I shall be at peace when this night is over.'

Colney persuaded her to have him for companion. Mr. Peridon, who was to have driven with Nesta and mademoiselle, won admiration by proposing to stay for an hour and play some of Mrs. Radnor's favourite pieces. Nesta and Victor overbore Nataly's objections to the lover's generosity. So Mr. Peridon was left. Nesta came hurrying back from the step of the carriage to kiss her mother again, saying: 'Just one last kiss, my own! And she's not to look troubled. I shall remember everything to tell my own mother. It will soon be over.'

Her mother nodded; but the embrace was passionate.

Nesta called her father into the passage, bidding him prohibit any delivery to her mother of news at the door. 'She is easily startled now by trifles—you have noticed?'

Victor summoned his recollections and assured her he had noticed, as he believed he had 'The dear heart of her is fretting for the night to be over! And think! seven days, and she is in Lakelands. A fortnight, and we have our first Concert. Durandarte! Oh, the dear heart 'll be at peace when I tell her of a triumphant Meeting. Not a doubt of that, even though Colney turns the shadow of his back on us.'

'One critic the less for you!' said Nesta. Skepsey was to meet her carriage at the theatre.

Ten minutes later, Victor and Simeon Fenellan were proceeding thitherward on foot.

'I have my speech,' said Victor. 'You prepare the way for me, following our influential friend Dubbleson; Colewort winds up; any one else they shout for. We shall have a great evening. I suspect I shall find Themison or Jarniman when I get home. You don't believe in intimations? I've had crapy processions all day before my eyes. No wonder, after yesterday!'

'Dubbleson mustn't drawl it out too long,' said Fenellan.

'We 'll drop a hint. Where's Dartrey?'

'He'll come. He's in one of his black moods: not temper. He's got a notion he killed his wife by dragging her to Africa with him. She was not only ready to go, she was glad to go. She had a bit of the heroine in her and a certainty of tripping to the deuce if she was left to herself.'

'Tell Nataly that,' said Victor. 'And tell her about Dartrey. Harp on it. Once she was all for him and our girl. But it's a woman—though the dearest! I defy any one to hit on the cause of their changes. We must make the best of things, if we're for swimming. The task for me to-night will be, to keep from rolling out all I've got in my head. And I'm not revolutionary, I'm for stability. Only I do see, that the firm stepping-place asks for a long stride to be taken. One can't get the English to take a stride—unless it's for a foot behind them: bother old Colney! Too timid, or too scrupulous, down we go into the mire. There!—But I want to say it! I want to save the existing order. I want, Christianity, instead of the Mammonism we 're threatened with. Great fortunes now are becoming the giants of old to stalk the land: or mediaeval Barons. Dispersion of wealth, is the secret. Nataly's of that mind with me. A decent poverty! She's rather wearying, wants a change. I've a steam-yacht in my eye, for next month on the Mediterranean. All our set. She likes quiet. I believe in my political recipe for it.'

He thumped on a method he had for preserving aristocracy—true aristocracy, amid a positively democratic flood of riches.

'It appears to me, you're on the road of Priscilla Graves and Pempton,' observed Simeon. 'Strike off Priscilla's viands and friend Pempton's couple of glasses, and there's your aristocracy established; but with rather a dispersed recognition of itself.'

'Upon my word, you talk like old Colney, except for a twang of your own,' said Victor. 'Colney sours at every fresh number of that Serial. The last, with Delphica detecting the plot of Falarique, is really not so bad. The four disguised members of the Comedie Francaise on board the vessel from San Francisco, to declaim and prove the superior merits of the Gallic tongue, jumped me to bravo the cleverness. And Bobinikine turning to the complexion of the remainder of cupboard dumplings discovered in an emigrant's house-to-let! And Semhians—I forget what and Mytharete's forefinger over the bridge of his nose, like a pensive vulture on the skull of a desert camel! But, I complain, there's nothing to make the English love the author; and it's wasted, he's basted, and the book 'll have no sale. I hate satire.'

'Rough soap for a thin skin, Victor. Does it hurt our people much?'

'Not a bit; doesn't touch them. But I want my friends to succeed!'

Their coming upon Westminster Bridge changed the theme. Victor wished the Houses of Parliament to catch the beams of sunset. He deferred to the suggestion, that the Hospital's doing so seemed appropriate.

'I'm always pleased to find a decent reason for what is,' he said. Then he queried: 'But what is, if we look at it, and while we look, Simeon? She may be going—or she's gone already, poor woman! I shall have that scene of yesterday everlastingly before my eyes, like a drop-curtain. Only, you know, Simeon, they don't feel the end, as we in health imagine. Colney would say, we have the spasms and they the peace. I 've a mind to send up to Regent's Park with inquiries. It would look respectful. God forgive me!—the poor woman perverts me at every turn. Though I will say, a certain horror of death I had—she whisked me out of it yesterday. I don't feel it any longer. What are you jerking at?'

'Only to remark, that if the thing's done for us, we haven't it so much on our sensations.'

'More, if we're sympathetic. But that compels us to be philosophic—or who could live! Poor woman!'

'Waft her gently, Victor!'

'Tush! Now for the South side of the Bridges; and I tell you, Simeon, what I can't mention to-night: I mean to enliven these poor dear people on their forsaken South of the City. I 've my scheme. Elected or not, I shall hardly be accused of bribery when I put down my first instalment.'

Fenellan went to work with that remark in his brain for the speech he was to deliver. He could not but reflect on the genial man's willingness and capacity to do deeds of benevolence, constantly thwarted by the position into which he had plunged himself.

They were received at the verge of the crowd outside the theatre-doors by Skepsey, who wriggled, tore and clove a way for them, where all were obedient, but the numbers lumped and clogged. When finally they reached the stage, they spied at Nesta's box, during the thunder of the rounds of applause, after shaking hands with Mr. Dubbleson, Sir Abraham Quatley, Dudley Sowerby, and others; and with Beaves Urmsing—a politician 'never of the opposite party to a deuce of a funny fellow!—go anywhere to hear him,' he vowed.

'Miss Radnor and Mademoiselle de Seilles arrived quite safely,' said Dudley, feasting on the box which contained them and no Dartrey Fenellan in it.

Nesta was wondering at Dartrey's absence. Not before Mr. Dubbleson, the chairman, the 'gentleman of local influence,' had animated the drowsed wits and respiratory organs of a packed audience by yielding place to Simeon, did Dartrey appear. Simeon's name was shouted, in proof of the happy explosion of his first anecdote, as Dartrey took seat behind Nesta. 'Half an hour with the dear mother,' he said.

Nesta's eyes thanked him. She pressed the hand of a demure young woman sitting close behind. Louise de Seilles. 'You know Matilda Pridden.'

Dartrey held his hand out. 'Has she forgiven me?'

Matilda bowed gravely, enfolding her affirmative in an outline of the no need for it, with perfect good breeding. Dartrey was moved to think Skepsey's choice of a woman to worship did him honour. He glanced at Louise. Her manner toward Matilda Pridden showed her sisterly with Nesta. He said: 'I left Mr. Peridon playing.—A little anxiety to hear that the great speech of the evening is done; it's nothing else. I'll run to her as soon as it's over.'

'Oh, good of you! And kind of Mr. Peridon!' She turned to Louise, who smiled at the simple art of the exclamation, assenting.

Victor below, on the stage platform, indicated the waving of a hand to them, and his delight at Simeon's ringing points: which were, to Dartrey's mind, vacuously clever and crafty. Dartrey despised effects of oratory, save when soldiers had to be hurled on a mark—or citizens nerved to stand for their country.

Nesta dived into her father's brilliancy of appreciation, a trifle pained by Dartrey's aristocratic air when he surveyed the herd of heads agape and another cheer rang round. He smiled with her, to be with her, at a hit here and there; he would not pretend an approval of this manner of winning electors to consider the country's interests and their own. One fellow in the crowded pit, affecting a familiarity with Simeon, that permitted the taking of liberties with the orator's Christian name, mildly amused him. He had no objection to hear 'Simmy' shouted, as Louise de Seilles observed. She was of his mind, in regard to the rough machinery of Freedom.

Skepsey entered the box.

'We shall soon be serious, Miss Nesta,' he said, after a look at Matilda Pridden.

There was a prolonged roaring—on the cheerful side.

'And another word about security that your candidate will keep his promises,' continued Simeon: 'You have his word, my friends!' And he told the story of the old Governor of Goa, who wanted money and summoned the usurers, and they wanted security; whereupon he laid his Hidalgo hand on a cataract of Kronos-beard across his breast, and pulled forth three white hairs, and presented them: 'And as honourably to the usurious Jews as to the noble gentleman himself, that security was accepted!'

Emerging from hearty clamours, the illustrative orator fell upon the question of political specifics:—Mr. Victor Radnor trusted to English good sense too profoundly to be offering them positive cures, as they would hear the enemy say he did. Yet a bit of a cure may be offered, if we 're not for pushing it too far, in pursuit of the science of specifics, in the style of the foreign physician, probably Spanish, who had no practice, and wished for leisure to let him prosecute his anatomical and other investigations to discover his grand medical nostrum. So to get him fees meanwhile he advertised a cure for dyspepsia—the resource of starving doctors. And sure enough his patient came, showing the grand fat fellow we may be when we carry more of the deciduously mortal than of the scraggy vital upon our persons. Any one at a glance would have prescribed water-cresses to him: water-cresses exclusively to eat for a fortnight. And that the good physician did. Away went his patient, returning at the end of the fortnight, lean, and with the appetite of a Toledo blade for succulent slices. He vowed he was the man. Our estimable doctor eyed him, tapped at him, pinched his tender parts; and making him swear he was really the man, and had eaten nothing whatever but unadulterated water-cresses in the interval, seized on him in an ecstasy by the collar of his coat, pushed him into the surgery, knocked him over, killed him, cut him up, and enjoyed the felicity of exposing to view the very healthiest patient ever seen under dissecting hand, by favour of the fortunate discovery of the specific for him. All to further science!—to which, in spite of the petitions of all the scientific bodies of the civilized world, he fell a martyr on the scaffold, poor gentleman! But we know politics to be no such empirical science.

Simeon ingeniously interwove his analogy. He brought it home to Beaves Urmsing, whose laugh drove any tone of apology out of it. Yet the orator was asked: 'Do you take politics for a joke, Simmy?'

He countered his questioner: 'Just to liberate you from your moribund state, my friend.' And he told the story of the wrecked sailor, found lying on the sands, flung up from the foundered ship of a Salvation captain, and how, that nothing could waken him, and there he lay fit for interment; until presently a something of a voice grew down into his ears; and it was his old chum Polly, whom he had tied to a board to give her a last chance in the surges; and Polly shaking the wet from her feathers, and shouting: 'Polly tho dram dry!'—which struck on the nob of Jack's memory, to revive all the liquorly tricks of the cabin under Salvationism, and he began heaving, and at last he shook in a lazy way, and then from sputter to sputter got his laugh loose; and he sat up, and cried; 'That did it! Now to business!' for he was hungry. 'And when I catch the ring of this world's laugh from you, my friend...!' Simeon's application of the story was drowned.

After the outburst, they heard his friend again interruptingly: 'You keep that tongue of yours from wagging, as it did when you got round the old widow woman for her money, Simmy!'

Victor leaned forward. Simeon towered. He bellowed

'And you keep that tongue of yours from committing incest on a lie!'

It was like a lightning-flash in the theatre. The man went under. Simeon flowed. Conscience reproached him with the little he had done for Victor, and he had now his congenial opportunity.

Up in the box, the powers of the orator were not so cordially esteemed. To Matilda Pridden, his tales were barely decently the flesh and the devil smothering a holy occasion to penetrate and exhort. Dartrey sat rigid, as with the checked impatience for a leap. Nesta looked at Louise when some one was perceived on the stage bending to her father: It was Mr. Peridon; he never once raised his face. Apparently he was not intelligible or audible but the next moment Victor sprang erect. Dartrey quitted the box. Nesta beheld her father uttering hurried words to right and left. He passed from sight, Mr. Peridon with him; and Dartrey did not return.

Nesta felt her father's absence as light gone: his eyes rayed light. Besides she had the anticipation of a speech from him, that would win Matilda Pridden. She fancied Simeon Fenellan to be rather under the spell of the hilarity he roused. A gentleman behind him spoke in his ear; and Simeon, instead of ceasing, resumed his flow. Matilda Pridden's gaze on him and the people was painful to behold: Nesta saw her mind. She set herself to study a popular assembly. It could be serious to the call of better leadership, she believed. Her father had been telling her of late of a faith he had in the English, that they (or so her intelligence translated his remarks) had power to rise to spiritual ascendancy, and be once more the Islanders heading the world of a new epoch abjuring materialism—some such idea; very quickening to her, as it would be to this earnest young woman worshipped by Skepsey. Her father's absence and the continued shouts of laughter, the insatiable thirst for fun, darkened her in her desire to have the soul of the good working sister refreshed. They had talked together; not much: enough for each to see at either's breast the wells from the founts of life.

The box-door opened, Dartrey came in. He took her hand. She stood-up to his look. He said to Matilda Pridden: 'Come with us; she will need you.'

'Speak it,' said Nesta.

He said to the other: 'She has courage.'

'I could trust to her,' Matilda Pridden replied.

Nesta read his eyes. 'Mother?'

His answer was in the pressure.

'Ill?'

'No longer.'

'Oh! Dartrey.' Matilda Pridden caught her fast.

'I can walk, dear,' Nesta said.

Dartrey mentioned her father.

She understood: 'I am thinking of him.'

The words of her mother: 'At peace when the night is over,' rang. Along the gassy passages of the back of the theatre, the sound coming from an applausive audience was as much a thunder as rage would have been. It was as void of human meaning as a sea.

CHAPTER XLII

THE LAST

In the still dark hour of that April morning, the Rev. Septimus Barmby was roused by Mr. Peridon, with a scribbled message from Victor, which he deciphered by candlelight held close to the sheet of paper, between short inquiries and communications, losing more and more the sense of it as his intelligence became aware of what dread blow had befallen the stricken man. He was bidden come to fulfil his promise instantly. He remembered the bearing of the promise. Mr. Peridon's hurried explanatory narrative made the request terrific, out of tragically lamentable. A semblance of obedience had to be put on, and the act of dressing aided it. Mr. Barmby prayed at heart for guidance further.

The two gentlemen drove Westward, speaking little; they had the dry sob in the throat.

'Miss Radnor?' Mr. Barmby asked.

'She is shattered; she holds up; she would not break down.'

'I can conceive her to possess high courage.'

'She has her friend Mademoiselle de Seilles.'

Mr. Barmby remained humbly silent. Affectionate deep regrets moved him to say: 'A loss irreparable. We have but one voice of sorrow. And how sudden! The dear lady had no suffering, I trust.'

'She fell into the arms of Mr. Durance. She died in his arms. She was unconscious, he says. I left her straining for breath. She said "Victor"; she tried to smile:—I understood I was not to alarm him.'

'And he too late!'

'He was too late, by some minutes.'

'At least I may comfort. Miss Radnor must be a blessing to him.'

'They cannot meet. Her presence excites him.'

That radiant home of all hospitality seemed opening on from darker chambers to the deadly dark. The immorality in the moral situation could not be forgotten by one who was professionally a moralist. But an incorruptible beauty in the woman's character claimed to plead for her memory. Even the rigorous in defence of righteous laws are softened by a sinner's death to hear excuses, and may own a relationship, haply perceive the faint nimbus of the saint. Death among us proves us to be still not so far from the Nature saying at every avenue to the mind: 'Earth makes all sweet.'

Mr. Durance had prophesied a wailful end ever to the carol of Optimists! Yet it is not the black view which is the right view. There is one between: the path adopted by Septimus Barmby:—if he could but induce his brethren to enter on it! The dreadful teaching of circumstances might help to the persuading of a fair young woman, under his direction... having her hand disengaged. Mr. Barmby started himself in the dream of his uninterred passion for the maiden: he chased it, seized it, hurled it hence, as a present sacrilege:—constantly, and at the pitch of our highest devotion to serve, are we assailed by the tempter! Is it, that the love of woman is our weakness? For if so, then would a celibate clergy have grant of immunity. But, alas, it is not so with them! We have to deplore the hearing of reports too credible. Again we are pushed to contemplate woman as the mysterious obstruction to the perfect purity of soul. Nor is there a refuge in asceticism. No more devilish nourisher of pride do we find than in pain voluntarily embraced. And strangely, at the time when our hearts are pledged to thoughts upon others, they are led by woman to glance revolving upon ourself, our vile self! Mr. Barmby clutched it by the neck.

Light now, as of a strong memory of day along the street, assisted him to forget himself at the sight of the inanimate houses of this London, all revealed in a quietness not less immobile than tombstones of an unending cemetery, with its last ghost laid. Did men but know it!—The habitual necessity to amass matter for the weekly sermon, set him noting his meditative exclamations, the noble army of platitudes under haloes, of good use to men: justifiably turned over in his mind for their good. He had to think, that this act of the justifying of the act reproached him with a lack of due emotion, in sympathy with agonized friends truly dear. Drawing near the hospitable house, his official and a cordial emotion united, as we see sorrowful crape-wreathed countenances. His heart struck heavily when the house was visible.

Could it be the very house? The look of it belied the tale inside. But that threw a ghostliness on the look.

Some one was pacing up and down. They greeted Dudley Sowerby. His ability to speak was tasked. They gathered, that mademoiselle and 'a Miss Pridden' were sitting with Nesta, and that their services in a crisis had been precious. At such times, one of them reflected, woman has indeed her place: when life's battle waxes red. Her soul must be capable of mounting to the level of the man's, then? It is a lesson!

Dudley said he was waiting for Dr. Themison to come forth. He could not tear himself from sight of the house.

The door opened to Dr. Themison departing, Colney Durance and Simeon Fenellan bare-headed. Colney showed a face with stains of the lashing of tears.

Dr. Themison gave his final counsels. 'Her father must not see her. For him, it may have to be a specialist. We will hope the best. Mr. Dartrey Fenellan stays beside him:—good. As to the ceremony he calls for, a form of it might soothe:—any soothing possible! No music. I will return in a few hours.'

He went on foot.

Mr. Barmby begged advice from Colney and Simeon concerning the message he had received—the ceremony requiring his official presidency. Neither of them replied. They breathed the morning air, they gave out long-drawn sighs of relief, looking on the trees of the park.

A man came along the pavement, working slow legs hurriedly. Simeon ran down to him.

'Humour, as much as you can,' Colney said to Mr. Barmby. 'Let him imagine.'

'Miss Radnor?'

'Not to speak of her.'

'The daughter he so loves?'

Mr. Barmby's tender inquisitiveness was unanswered. Were they inducing him to mollify a madman? But was it possible to associate the idea of madness with Mr. Radnor?

Simeon ran back. 'Jarniman,' he remarked. 'It's over!'

'Now!' Colney's shoulders expressed the comment. 'Well, now, Mr. Barmby, you can do the part desired. Come in. It's morning!' He stared at the sky.

All except Dudley passed in.

Mr. Barmby wanted more advice, his dilemma being acute. It was moderated, though not more than moderated, when he was informed of the death of Mrs. Burman Radnor; an event that occurred, according to Jarniman's report, forty-five minutes after Skepsey had a second time called for information of it at the house in Regent's Park—five hours and a half, as Colney made his calculation, after the death of Nataly. He was urged by some spur of senseless irony to verify the calculation and correct it in the minutes.

Dudley crossed the road. No sign of the awful interior was on any of the windows of the house either to deepen awe or relieve. They were blank as eyeballs of the mindless. He shivered. Death is our common cloak; but Calamity individualizes, to set the unwounded speculating whether indeed a stricken man, who has become the cause of woeful trouble, may not be pointing a moral. Pacing on the Park side of the house, he saw Skepsey drive up and leap out with a gentleman, Mr. Radnor's lawyer. Could it be, that there was no Will written? Could a Will be executed now? The moral was more forcibly suggested. Dudley beheld this Mr. Victor Radnor successful up all the main steps, persuasive, popular, brightest of the elect of Fortune, felled to the ground within an hour, he and all his house! And if at once to pass beneath the ground, the blow would have seemed merciful for him. Or if, instead of chattering a mixture of the rational and the monstrous, he had been heard to rave like the utterly distraught.

Recollection of some of the things he shouted, was an anguish: A notion came into the poor man, that he was the dead one of the two, and he cried out: 'Cremation? No, Colney's right, it robs us of our last laugh. I lie as I fall.' He 'had a confession for his Nataly, for her only, for no one else.' He had 'an Idea.' His begging of Dudley to listen without any punctilio (putting a vulgar oath before it), was the sole piece of unreasonableness in the explanation of the idea: and that was not much wilder than the stuff Dudley had read from reports of Radical speeches. He told Dudley he thought him too young to be 'best man to a widower about to be married,' and that Barmby was 'coming all haste to do the business, because of no time to spare.'

Dudley knew but the half, and he did not envy Dartrey Fenellan his task of watching over the wreck of a splendid intelligence, humouring and restraining. According to the rumours, Mr. Radnor had not shown the symptoms before the appearance of his daughter. For awhile he hung, and then fell, like an icicle. Nesta came with a cry for her father. He rose: Dartrey was by. Hugged fast in iron muscles, the unhappy creature raved of his being a caged lion. These things Dudley had heard in the house.

There are scenes of life proper to the grave-cloth.

Nataly's dead body was her advocate with her family, with friends, with the world. Victor had more need of a covering shroud to keep calamity respected. Earth makes all sweet: and we, when the privilege is granted us, do well to treat the terribly stricken as if they had entered to the bosom of earth.

That night's infinite sadness was concentrated upon Nesta. She had need of her strength of mind and body.

The night went past as a year. The year followed it as a refreshing night. Slowly lifting her from our abysses, it was a good angel to the girl. Permission could not be given for her to see her father. She had a home in the modest home of Louise de Seilles on the borders of Dauphins; and with French hearts at their best in winningness around her, she learned again, as an art, the natural act of breathing calmly; she had by degrees a longing for the snow-heights. When her imagination could perch on them with love and pride, she began to recover the throb for a part in human action. It set her nature flowing to the mate she had chosen, who was her counsellor, her supporter, and her sword. She had awakened to new life, not to sink back upon a breast of love, though thoughts of the lover were as blows upon strung musical chords of her bosom. Her union with Dartrey was for the having an ally and the being an ally, in resolute vision of strife ahead, through the veiled dreams that bear the blush. This was behind a maidenly demureness. Are not young women hypocrites? Who shall fathom their guile! A girl with a pretty smile, a gentle manner, a liking for wild flowers up on the rocks; and graceful with resemblances to the swelling proportions of garden-fruits approved in young women by the connoisseur eye of man; distinctly designed to embrace the state of marriage, that she might (a girl of singularly lucid and receptive eyes) the better give battle to men touching matters which they howl at an eccentric matron for naming. So it was. And the yielding of her hand to Dartrey, would have appeared at that period of her revival, as among the baser compliances of the fleshly, if she had not seen in him, whom she owned for leader, her fellow soldier, warrior friend, hero, of her own heart's mould, but a greater.

She was on Como, at the villa of the Signora Giulia Sanfredini, when Dudley's letter reached her, with the supplicating offer of the share of his earldom. An English home meanwhile was proposed to her at the house of his mother the Countess. He knew that he did not write to a brilliant heiress. The generosity she had always felt that he possessed, he thus proved in figures. They are convincing and not melting. But she was moved to tears by his goodness in visiting her father, as well as by the hopeful news he sent. He wrote delicately, withholding the title of her father's place of abode. There were expectations of her father's perfect recovery; the signs were auspicious; he appeared to be restored to the 'likeness to himself' in the instances Dudley furnished:—his appointment with him for the flute-duet next day; and particularly his enthusiastic satisfaction with the largeness and easy excellent service of the residence 'in which he so happily found himself established.' He held it to be, 'on the whole, superior to Lakelands.' The smile and the tear rolled together in Nesta reading these words. And her father spoke repeatedly of longing to embrace his Fredi, of the joy her last letter had given him, of his intention to send an immediate answer: and he showed Dudley a pile of manuscript ready for the post. He talked of public affairs, was humorous over any extravagance or eccentricity in the views he took; notably when he alluded to his envy of little Skepsey. He said he really did envy; and his daughter believed it and saw fair prospects in it.

Her grateful reply to the young earl conveyed all that was perforce ungentle, in the signature of the name of Nesta Victoria Fenellan:—a name he was to hear cited among the cushioned conservatives, and plead for as he best could under a pressure of disapprobation, and compelled esteem, and regrets.

The day following the report of her father's wish to see her, she and her husband started for England. On that day, Victor breathed his last. Dudley had seen the not hopeful but an ominous illumination of the stricken man; for whom came the peace his Nataly had in earth. Often did Nesta conjure up to vision the palpitating form of the beloved mother with her hand at her mortal wound in secret through long years of the wearing of the mask to keep her mate inspirited. Her gathered knowledge of things and her ruthless penetrativeness made it sometimes hard for her to be tolerant of a world, whose tolerance of the infinitely evil stamped blotches on its face and shrieked in stains across the skin beneath its gallant garb. That was only when she thought of it as the world condemning her mother. She had a husband able and ready, in return for corrections of his demon temper, to trim an ardent young woman's fanatical overflow of the sisterly sentiments; scholarly friends, too, for such restrainings from excess as the mind obtains in a lamp of History exhibiting man's original sprouts to growth and fitful continuation of them. Her first experience of the grief that is in pleasure, for those who have passed a season, was when the old Concert-set assembled round her. When she heard from the mouth of a living woman, that she had saved her from going under the world's waggon-wheels, and taught her to know what is actually meant by the good living of a shapely life, Nesta had the taste of a harvest happiness richer than her recollection of the bride's, though never was bride in fuller flower to her lord than she who brought the dower of an equal valiancy to Dartrey Fenellan. You are aware of the reasons, the many, why a courageous young woman requires of high heaven, far more than the commendably timid, a doughty husband. She had him; otherwise would that puzzled old world, which beheld her step out of the ranks to challenge it, and could not blast her personal reputation, have commissioned a paw to maul her character, perhaps instructing the gossips to murmur of her parentage. Nesta Victoria Fenellan had the husband who would have the world respectful to any brave woman. This one was his wife.

Daniel Skepsey rejoices in service to his new master, owing to the scientific opinion he can at any moment of the day apply for, as to the military defences of the country; instead of our attempting to arrest the enemy by vociferations of persistent prayer:—the sole point of difference between him and his Matilda; and it might have been fatal but that Nesta's intervention was persuasive. The two members of the Army first in the field to enrol and give rank according to the merits of either, to both sexes, were made one. Colney Durance (practically cynical when not fancifully, men said) stood by Skepsey at the altar. His published exercises in Satire produce a flush of the article in the Reviews of his books. Meat and wine in turn fence the Hymen beckoning Priscilla and Mr. Pempton. The forms of Religion more than the Channel's division of races keep Louise de Seilles and Mr. Peridon asunder: and in the uniting of them Colney is interested, because it would have so pleased the woman of the loyal heart no longer beating. He let Victor's end be his expiation and did not phrase blame of him. He considered the shallowness of the abstract Optimist exposed enough in Victor's history. He was reconciled to it when, looking on their child, he discerned, that for a cancelling of the errors chargeable to them, the father and mother had kept faith with Nature.

George Meredith – A Concise Bibliography

Novels
The Shaving of Shagpat (1856)
Farina (1857)
The Ordeal of Richard Feverel (1859)
Evan Harrington (1861)
Emilia in England (1864), republished as Sandra Belloni in 1887
Rhoda Fleming (1865)
Vittoria (1867)
The Adventures of Harry Richmond (1871)
Beauchamp's Career (1875)
The House on the Beach (1877)
The Case of General Ople and Lady Camper (1877)
The Tale of Chloe (1879)
The Egoist (1879)
The Tragic Comedians (1880)
Diana of the Crossways (1885)
One of our Conquerors (1891)
Lord Ormont and his Aminta (1894)
The Amazing Marriage (1895)
Celt and Saxon (1910)

Poetry
Poems (1851)
Modern Love (1862)
The Lark Ascending (1881)
Poems and Lyrics of the Joy of Earth (1883)
The Woods of Westermain (1883)
A Faith on Trial (1885)
Ballads and Poems of Tragic Life (1887)
A Reading of Earth (1888)
The Empty Purse (1892)
Odes in Contribution to the Song of French History (1898)
A Reading of Life (1901)
Selected Poems of George Meredith (1903, author's supervision)
Last Poems (1909)

Essays
Essay on Comedy (1877)